CRITICAL STRIKE

JAMES P. SUMNER

BOTH barrels PUBLISHING

JOIN THE MAILING LIST

Why not sign up for James P. Sumner's spam-free newsletter, and stay up-to-date with the latest news, promotions, and new releases?

In exchange for your support, you will receive a **FREE** copy of the prequel novella, *A Hero of War*, which tells the story of a young Adrian, newly recruited to the U.S. Army at the beginning of the Gulf War.

Previously available on Amazon, this title is now exclusive to the author's website. But you have the opportunity to read it for free!

Interested? Details can be found at the end of this book.

This will be epic.

PROLOGUE

May 9, 2020

Two men stood in the shadows of the Capitol building's entrance. Both wore suits and earpieces, with a firearm concealed inside their jackets. The first, Connors, was leaning casually against one of the thick marble columns, smoking a cigarette and staring blankly at the steps that descended before him.

The other man, Stevens, stood across from him, alert, scanning their surroundings. His attention was pulled to his left as footsteps echoed on the tiled floor. His body tensed as the man and woman emerged from the gloom.

He glanced over his shoulder. "Connors, look alive. They're here."

Connors quickly flicked his half-smoked cigarette to the ground. He twisted it out with his foot, then stood upright.

"They don't look happy," he whispered.

"Can't say I blame them," replied Stevens. "Not after everything that's happened."

Moses Buchanan strode with resigned purpose, brief-case in hand. He looked tired. Crow's feet were etched deep into his ebony skin, aging his features beyond their years. His suit jacket was open and flapped in the wind that whipped around the portico.

Despite the sun's glare, the temperature wasn't reflective of the season.

Beside him, Julie took a deep breath. Her fatigue was more from boredom than exertion, although the last twenty-four hours had been a physical strain on both of them.

She pulled out her hair tie and massaged her temples as her smooth, chestnut hair fell to her shoulders.

"How many more of these hearings do we need to go to?" she asked with a sigh.

Buchanan smiled. "As many as we have to. I had to jump through countless hoops when the government was trying to destroy us. I'm prepared to jump through some more so that they can apologize."

They had just finished the third hearing of the day. After discovering the link between Tristar and Orion in the after-math of the Palugan crisis, Buchanan was summoned to Washington. At the request of the president, the investiga-tions into GlobaTech were formally ended. That meant a short-notice, overnight flight from California. Buchanan asked Julie to accompany him, so she could provide specific mission details, should they be asked for.

Both of them were tired.

They descended the steps, flanked by their two security personnel.

"Any word from Ray?" asked Julie.

Buchanan shook his head. "Nothing yet. He should be in position tomorrow." He paused as they started along the pathway toward First Street, then asked, "How's Jericho doing?"

Julie let slip a knowing smile. "With what? Recovering from single-handedly fighting a war in South America, or coming to terms with having to work with Adrian Hell in two days?"

Buchanan grinned. "Both."

"Physically, he's fine. It's Jericho, y'know. He's probably sore as hell, but he won't ever admit that to either of us. As for Adrian... he'll get over it."

"I'm relying on you to make sure he does, Fisher. We've both dealt with Adrian Hell before. We also both knew Josh Winters better than most, so we've heard the stories. That man's gonna walk into my office and start pushing Jericho's buttons because Jericho won't be able to hide his displeasure. We have enough enemies without fighting each other."

Julie nodded. "He'll behave. Don't worry."

"Good. We need that man's help, and we're not going to get it if Jericho pulls his arms off in my office."

Julie laughed but said nothing.

They walked on. Connors was in front of them; Stevens was behind. The pathway wasn't busy. A couple of people sat on one of the large slabs that doubled as benches, drinking a late afternoon coffee.

Up ahead, a black van stopped between the two security posts guarding the entrance to the Capitol building. A GlobaTech operative stepped out and stood to attention beside the open door. The driver remained inside the vehicle.

"I have a final meeting tomorrow with the U.N. Security Council," said Buchanan. "I don't imagine I'll need you for that, so you can head back to Santa Clarita tonight. I'll follow tomorrow afternoon."

"Works for me," replied Julie, failing to hide her relief.

A constant stream of traffic flowed through the three-way intersection on First Street. As they neared the vehicle, the sound of blaring horns filled the air in all directions. Three white sedans appeared, one from each direction, and slid to a halt in the middle of the intersection. More horns wailed in protest, drowning out the noise of screeching tires. Screaming erupted a moment later, when twelve men emerged from the sedans, dressed in black combat gear and armed with automatic weapons.

Instinct took over.

Buchanan was forced to a knee behind the van, with Julie's commanding hand on his shoulder. Connors passed her a loaded handgun.

A heartbeat later, gunfire rained down upon them. Civilians clambered with panic from their vehicles, running away in any direction they could.

"Stay down!" yelled Julie, then returned fire over the roof of their vehicle.

"Just give me a gun and let me help," growled Buchanan in protest.

Stevens thrust a pistol into his hand. Buchanan shrugged Julie off his shoulder and stood beside her, firing back at the unknown assailants.

The twelve men in black formed a wide semicircle and walked slowly toward the van, firing relentlessly. They moved in unison, with practiced symmetry, like predators stalking a vulnerable prey.

The vehicle was peppered with bullets. The rapid, dull *thunk!* as each round penetrated the chassis matched the volume of the gunfire.

Through the van window, Julie saw their driver flail and die in his seat, showered with glass and bullets. Beside her, the other new arrival fell to the ground, dead from a bullet to the face.

"What the hell is going on?" shouted Julie. "Who are these maniacs?"

"Leave one alive and we'll ask," replied Buchanan.

Behind them, the security guards who occupied the stations on either side of the Capitol pathway yelped as their lives were taken in the crossfire.

Julie popped up and opened fire, emptying her magazine at their attackers. Two of them dropped before she ducked back behind the van.

"I'm out!" she shouted.

She crouched beside Buchanan, took the spare magazine Connors offered, and reloaded her weapon.

"We gotta get out of here," she said. "We're pinned down, and there are too many innocent people around us to protect."

"What do you suggest?" asked Buchanan.

She looked across at Stevens, then nodded at Buchanan. "Get him in the back seat, on the ground, with you on top of him." She then turned to Connors. "Get in after them and keep shooting until we're clear. I'll drive."

The four of them took a collective breath.

"Go!" she screamed.

Everyone moved as instructed. Buchanan crawled into the back seat of the van through the sliding side door, staying low and lying flat on the floor. Stevens followed, kneeling on the seat and leaning over the GlobaTech director.

"Stay down, sir," he barked, returning fire through the shattered window.

Buchanan grunted. "Like I have any choice..."

Connors stepped in and held onto the headrest of the

driver's seat, standing upright in the open doorway and firing at their attackers over the roof.

Julie opened the driver's door and yanked the dead operative from the chair, sending him crashing to the sidewalk. She yanked the sidearm from his thigh holster.

"Sorry," she said as she slid behind the wheel.

She tossed the gun on the seat beside her and gunned the engine. She slammed her foot down on the gas and fishtailed away, heading northeast along First Street, toward Constitution Avenue.

Julie glanced in the rearview to see all three sedans already in pursuit. Connors ducked inside and slid the door closed as they gained speed.

"I got one more on the way out, ma'am," he said. "They lost three in total back there."

"That leaves, what? Nine?" She grunted as she was forced to brake hard in order to navigate around stationary traffic ahead of her. "Where the hell did these assholes come from?"

"I don't know. They just appeared from out of nowhere. They must have been waiting for us."

Julie braked again as she slid sideways across the next intersection at speed, narrowly missing other vehicles. Then she accelerated away along Constitution, heading northwest. She hammered down on the horn and ushered people out of the way with frantic gestures.

In the back, both operatives started shooting. Julie split her focus between the road ahead and the rearview, watching the progress of their escape as she navigated the route.

Buchanan shrugged Stevens off him and pushed himself upright. He shifted to kneel low on the seat between Stevens and Connors, then shot back through the shattered rear window.

"Moses, what the hell are you doing?" shouted Julie.

He gritted his teeth. "Helping keep us alive!"

"Well, that's what you pay me for. You're more important than the three of us, so stop being a hero and get your ass on the floor!"

He ducked back down to reload. "Remind me to fire you when this is over."

Julie rolled her eyes. "Whatever you say, boss."

She drew her own weapon, slammed on the brakes, and yanked the wheel to the right, spinning the van one hundred and eighty degrees. As she lined the vehicle up, she threw it in reverse and stamped on the gas again. Through the broken window next to her, she took aim and started shooting.

"What the hell are *you* doing?" said Buchanan.

"My goddamn job!" she replied.

Julie clipped the front wheel of the nearest sedan to them, causing it to spin out and smash into the parked cars lining the road. Out the opposite window, Stevens managed to shoot the driver of the second car. It collided with the tail end of the first one at speed, flipped trunk-over-hood, and landed on its roof. The sound of twisting metal pierced the air like a child's scream.

Behind Julie, Connors leaned out the window, took aim, and fired until he hit the gas tank of the upturned sedan. His fourth bullet found its mark, and both vehicles disappeared in a sudden rush of fire and thick smoke.

The explosion shook the van. Julie dropped her weapon and used both hands to wrestle them under control. She turned sharply to the left, J-turning them to face forward once more. She shifted into drive and continued to speed away.

"Great work, fellas," she called back.

"It's not over yet..." countered Buchanan.

The remaining sedan had swerved around the flaming wrecks, mounting the sidewalk and sending pedestrians scattering to remain in pursuit. Two shooters leaned out of the vehicle and began firing.

Buchanan and the two operatives ducked low in the back. Julie slid as low as she could in her seat as she swerved to avoid the fresh onslaught of bullets.

But they found their mark regardless.

The loud bang of a rear tire blowing out was unmistakable.

"Shit!" shouted Julie as she fought to control the van.

They were approaching a busy intersection ahead, where Constitution met Pennsylvania. She had no choice but to stop; otherwise, she risked flipping the van. She glanced in the rearview to see the sedan matching her decreasing speed. The men inside were no doubt preparing to finish them off, like they tried to outside the Capitol building.

Stevens went to shoot back, but the hammer slammed down on an empty chamber.

"I'm out," he said.

"Me too," said Connors.

Buchanan checked his magazine. "I have five rounds."

Julie glared ahead, her brow creased with deep frustration. She didn't have any bullets left in her own gun, and she had to assume the men behind them would have plenty.

She looked across at the gun she took from the dead operative. She looked back at the road. They were coming up fast on the intersection, and she was running out of options.

"Screw this," she muttered.

She slammed the brakes on, causing sparks to fly out behind them from the damaged wheel. Behind her, the sedan did the same. She took the handgun and sprang out of the vehicle.

"Fisher, get back here!" Buchanan yelled after her.

But she didn't hear him.

Julie walked toward the sedan, weapon raised. The moment she saw the doors begin to open, she started shooting. The man in the back was the first to drop. A bullet caught him in the head as he scrambled out of the vehicle. His body dropped unceremoniously to the road.

She focused on the driver next, who hadn't made any move to get out. Bullets punched effortlessly through the windshield and into his chest.

The remaining passenger had managed to get out and raise his assault rifle. Julie snapped her aim over to him as his finger was moving to the trigger. For a split second, her eyes popped wide as she realized he had the drop on her. She might get him, but he would definitely get her. She took a breath and held it, ready to—

Three shots rang out amid the screams and chaos around her. The last man in black dropped to the ground. Julie let out a long sigh of relief. She looked over to see Buchanan standing on the far side of the van, gun raised, smoke dancing from the barrel.

He stared back at her, his face etched in a battle with his own adrenaline. He said nothing. Just gave a small nod.

Julie returned the gesture.

The four of them regrouped by the van as the scene

settled. The sounds of the scared public were replaced with the wail of sirens.

"That was insane," said Julie. "What the hell *was* that?"

Buchanan sighed. "That, Miss Fisher, was Orion making a move."

"Are you serious?"

He nodded and pointed to the man he shot. There was a Tristar emblem on the right shoulder of the uniform.

She shook her head. "I can't believe they would do something so brazen. How can they possibly expect to get away with this?"

"Apparently, that's no longer a concern for them," said Buchanan. "It would appear we're out of time. Whatever unanswered questions we have about Orion don't matter now. I don't know what happens next, but we need to be ready."

Julie let out a heavy sigh, laced with frustration and disbelief. "Ready for what?"

Buchanan fixed her with a hard stare. "War."

CRITICAL STRIKE
A THRILLERVERSE EVENT

1

ADRIAN HELL

May 10, 2020

Damn, this coffee's good. The coffee is one of the few things I've really enjoyed about Paris. If I'm honest, there isn't much else. For a start, it's full of French people. But mostly, my disdain for this city stems from the fact that the last time I was here, I spent almost a week being shot at, beaten, and chased through the streets. I only came back because I needed to threaten someone.

Still, the coffee's good.

I take a sip and rest back in my seat. I'm sitting outside a café, looking up at the clear skies, enjoying the peace and quiet while it lasts.

Tomorrow, the work begins all over again.

Beside me, Ruby is doing the same. My God, she's stunning. She's wearing over-sized sunglasses and has her hair held back by a thick headband. Then there's the off-the-shoulder, baggy sweater and the tight jeans tucked into her leather boots. She's a real vision.

"What are you looking at, you perv?" she asks, smiling.

I smile back and shrug. "Nothing special."

She flips me the finger. "We both know you were looking at me, and we both know I'm pretty goddamn special."

"No arguments from me."

She has an iced coffee, which she's sipping through a straw. Those things are a disgrace to caffeine. I can smell the vanilla from here...

"What time's our flight?" she asks.

I check my watch. "It's at three. We have plenty of time."

"So, we land in L.A. when? Tomorrow morning?"

"I think so, yeah. It'll be early."

"What time are we supposed to link up with the others?"

I shrug. "Whenever we get there, I guess."

Ruby shifts in her seat to face me. "Adrian, I'm pretty sure this isn't something you can just rock up to whenever you feel like it."

"Well, *I'm* pretty sure no one's gonna say anything to me if we do."

Her eyebrows flick up as she rolls her eyes behind her glasses. "Oh, I think there will be at least one person there who might say something to you..."

I smile. "If *1984 Schwarzenegger* has anything to say to me, he's welcome to say it. Doesn't mean I have to listen to him. That big bastard wouldn't even be here if it wasn't for me."

Ruby sighs. "While that may be true, his dislike for you is well-documented. You're supposed to be on the same side here, so play nice, okay? For me?"

"Well, seeing as it's for you..."

I lean toward her. She meets me halfway and our lips meet. Kissing her turns a heartbeat into a lifetime.

As we part and resume our relaxed postures, a man

walks by our table. He glares at me with eyes like daggers. His lips are pursed so hard, his mouth is barely visible. I hold his gaze until he leaves my sight.

"Friend of yours?" asks Ruby.

I shake my head. "Don't know him. But I recognize his face. He frequents Fortin's casino."

"Ah." She pauses to sip her drink. "It would seem the news of you officially coming out of retirement has gone down like the Titanic."

"I don't care if it went down like Monica Lewinsky. If Blackstar's going to be around for a while, I'm not going through all the bullshit we just went through each time we have to take down a bad guy."

Ruby takes another patient sip of her coffee. "I'm not saying going to Fortin wasn't a good idea. But did you think it through? I mean, if you're officially a working assassin again, won't you have to... y'know... do assassin stuff?"

She's right. I'll need to stay active in order to keep the reputation alive. As that no-name piece of shit who just walked past me proved, people still know who I am... still respect what I've done. They just have a little less fear than they used to.

I shrug. "Maybe, yeah."

"Also, if word gets out that you're working for the government, that could look bad."

"Oh, please. Do you have any idea how many killers in our world have taken contracts on Uncle Sam's dime?"

Ruby lowers her sunglasses and peers over the large rims at me, narrowing those hypnotic emerald eyes of hers. "Taking a contract and taking a salary aren't the same, and you know it. Stop being pedantic."

"*You're* being pedantic..." I mutter to myself.

She shakes her head. We both know she has a point. As always.

Ruby takes out her phone and begins scrolling on it. I finish my coffee and take in the world around me.

A couple of weeks ago, Ruby and I tore up the streets of this city, desperate to find any information on the man we were tasked with taking out. We did, which led us to Rome, but it wasn't easy. Having to fight off the underworld on our own nearly killed us both. The only solution was to go back to that world myself and become one of them again, so no one could come after me.

When I realized that was my only option, I wasn't sure how I felt about it. I've spent years trying to walk away from that life. But walking away didn't really do much good. It hurt a lot of people, including myself. And it ultimately didn't work because here I am, back at it.

If I'm honest, walking back into Fortin's casino last night, telling him I'm done trying to retire... it felt good. The look on his face proved my reputation still holds weight. Although, I'll admit I'm probably a little farther down the pecking order than I used to be.

I'll soon change that.

If I have to start working contracts again, so be it. I'll just do what I did in Tokyo. Keep it low-key, take the jobs I believe are right to take, and handle my business. I don't need the money, and my priority will still be to—

"Oh, shit!"

I look over at Ruby. Her sunglasses are in her hand. Her eyes are wide and fixed on her phone screen.

"What is it?" I ask.

She holds her phone up to me, so I can read what she's looking at.

The news headline says: *GlobaTech Director Attacked by Mercenaries in Bloody Shootout.*

My eyes grow wide. "What the fuck? When? Where?"

Ruby returns to reading the article.

"Yesterday, outside the Capitol building. No mention of who the attackers were, just that they were dressed in..." She pauses to look up at me. "...all black."

I take a deep breath. "Tristar?"

"I think that's a safe bet, yeah."

"Any casualties?"

She scans the article for details. "Couple of GlobaTech guys died, along with a *lot* of bad guys. A few innocent people were injured in the crossfire."

I finish my coffee and get to my feet. "Okay, fine. Maybe we shouldn't be too late for the meeting tomorrow."

I hail a cab, and we're on our way to the airport within minutes.

I shift in my seat as the driver navigates the crowded roads of Paris, turning to look at Ruby. "Looks like Buchanan's concerns about Tristar were justified."

"Schultz's too," she adds, leaning back and letting her head loll to the side to look at me. "Those two have been saying something like this is coming for a long time."

"They have. I don't think they even knew exactly what they were worried about. But that... an all-out assault on the streets of Washington... that's bold."

"It's stupid."

"Terrifying is what it is. Buchanan said he was worried about rogue mercs from Tristar. He said he was also worried they're still operating in whatever shady capacity they always did, just not publicly. There's little that's more frightening than a brazen, rogue militia whose motives are unknown or unclear."

Ruby looks forward and falls silent. I do the same, lost in thought.

After a minute, she says, "How easy do you think it's going to be to find this assassin everyone's worried about?"

I shrug. "I never thought it was going to be easy, but if Tristar is alive and kicking, and this shooter is a part of it all, I think our job just got a whole lot harder."

Silence falls once more. We're nearing the airport now.

I have a bad feeling about this.

2

ROACH

May 10, 2020

Roach sat in his black Challenger, slumped uncomfortably in the passenger seat, holding binoculars to his face. Beside him, his sister Becky matched his pose, twisting to slide down a little farther behind the wheel.

They had watched the facility for three days, noting the comings and goings of trucks and personnel. It was a square compound bordered on all sides by a large concrete wall, which was topped with coils of barbed wire. A large, rolling iron gate guarded the entrance. A security station just outside housed two GlobaTech operatives. Both were visibly armed.

The large truck they were following had driven through the gates a half-hour ago.

Roach thought GlobaTech was hiding something. His and Becky's investigations revealed that GlobaTech's pharmaceutical division was now their most profitable income stream, surpassing weapons manufacturing, after they had ended their government contracts. Such a drastic increase could be attributed to many things, legal or otherwise. Given GlobaTech's documented history, Roach believed it was a thread worth pulling on.

Becky had used her recently expired journalist credentials to approach certain employees and ask them seemingly innocent questions, which she said were part of a piece she was writing. It had taken a few days and a lot of miles, but they found someone who worked at a distribution center who admitted that all the added security didn't sit right with him.

They decided to follow one of the deliveries to that distribution center in Boston.

Becky watched her brother quietly.

"I can feel you staring at me," said Roach after a few moments. He lowered the binoculars and looked over at her. "What?"

She shook her head. "Nothing."

"What is it, Becky? I can tell when something's bothering you. You have the worst poker face."

"Fine," she huffed. She pointed toward the GlobaTech warehouse across the street. "Don't you think you're getting a little... obsessed?"

"No," he replied flatly. "I'm focused on bringing the enemy to justice. I thought you were too."

"But GlobaTech isn't the enemy!" She shuffled upright in her seat and turned to face him. "How many hours have we spent poring over the information they sent you from Tristar's servers? Is there really any doubt who the real enemy is?"

"We know Orion funded Tristar, but that doesn't mean

GlobaTech's innocent. We don't know what their true motives are here. I don't trust them, and I'm going to find evidence that proves they're just as shady as Orion."

"I don't trust them either," Becky said. "Not completely. They bend the rules to get the job done, but they're on the right side of things when it all goes to shit. I think you're doing this because you don't like them. You're letting your personal feelings get in the way of common sense, and it's wasting our goddamn time."

She fell silent.

Roach watched her for a moment, noting the hard expression and the distant, frustrated gaze.

"You finished?" he asked.

She looked at him but said nothing.

"Someone needs to hold them accountable for what they've done."

"What, help establish worldwide peace after 4/17? Help advance medicine and technology beyond anything anyone else was doing? Provide support to war-torn nations for free, at great expense to themselves? Yeah... those *bastards*."

"That's my point," replied Roach. "People are so focused on the good that they ignore the bad. They ignore the monopolization of almost every profitable industry in the world. They ignore the corporate espionage and the unsanctioned missions they carry out overseas. They ignore the fact that, as Orion proved, no single company should have this much power."

"I never said they were perfect," Becky countered. "But what about you?"

He frowned. "What about me?"

"Well, you talk about their corporate espionage. They hacked Tristar illegally to give the data to you."

"I didn't ask them to."

"No, but you took that data anyway. And then what happened? You killed half an office building in New York! The fact that you're capable of waging a one-man war like that is, honestly, frightening and impressive in equal measure."

"I did that to save you."

"I know, and I'm grateful that you did. But looking at this objectively, who's holding *you* accountable for *your* actions? What makes you so different?"

"I went after really bad people, Becky. It's not the same."

"I'm sure GlobaTech would say the same thing. Look, I'm not trying to defend them, okay? I'm pissed at them too for leaving us on our own back in New York. But I can't help trying to see the bigger picture. That's why we make such a good team. I'm the brains; you're the brawn."

She smiled, trying to lighten the mood.

Roach rolled his eyes and looked away, staring out at the GlobaTech facility across from them. "Okay. So, what's the big picture I'm too stupid to see?"

Becky reached over and placed a hand on his arm. She smiled patiently.

"I'm not saying that, am I?"

He looked back at her and nodded. "I know. Go on."

"The thing that's dominated every news cycle for the past few days isn't that the Palugan president was assassinated. It's that GlobaTech failed to stop it."

"Exactly. If they can't do their job, they shouldn't be allowed to represent the U.N. as peacekeepers. They're reckless and ill-prepared for real warfare, and President Herrera's assassination is proof."

"That's exactly what people will think after the beating they've taken in the news. I'm pretty sure it's the only reason

22

they're even on trial right now. But think about it. Knowing what we do about Orion, do you not think there's even a slim chance they could be manipulating the story to hurt GlobaTech?"

Roach didn't say anything. He sat in silence, processing what his sister had said. It made a lot of sense. Despite his own issues with them, he knew if Orion were going to make a move against GlobaTech, that's probably how they would do it.

"That doesn't change anything," he said eventually. "GlobaTech still needs to answer for the things they've done, no matter the circumstances behind them. The fact that all charges have been dropped in the last couple of days, simply because they did one thing right, just goes to show they have too much power and influence."

Becky sighed. "Yeah, *or*... it shows the charges brought against them were bullshit, and people are finally starting to wise up to Orion's game."

Roach shrugged. "Whichever way you look at it, I think GlobaTech's hiding something, and I'm going to find out what it is. If that leads us to Orion's door, so be it. I'll take those bastards down too."

Sensing their heated discussion was suitably defused, Becky fell silent. Roach returned to looking out through the binoculars.

"See anything?" asked Becky.

"Uh-uh," muttered Roach, staring intently ahead.

"You know, that could literally be a shipment of painkillers..."

"You don't need a security detail for Tylenol, Becks."

She frowned. "What are you talking about? We followed that truck for almost three hundred miles and—"

Roach lowered the binoculars and pointed to an SUV

parked on the opposite side of the street, just past the automatic gates leading into the yard. "So did they. And so did the other one that drove in ahead of the truck. Not to mention the armed operatives overseeing the loading of whatever's being moved here."

Becky was silent for a moment. "Yeah, fair point. But what could it be that's so terrible? It's medical supplies."

Roach shrugged. "So they say. Do you trust them?"

"No... not entirely," she said with a sigh.

"Exactly. The way I see it, we have two options. If that truck doesn't leave, we break in there tonight and take a look around. If it does, we follow it and confront the driver. Even if he doesn't know what he was hauling, he's bound to have paperwork that gives us a clue. Either way, this is one of the best chances we've had so far to find something you can use."

Roach looked back over at the facility, resting his elbow on the door and his chin in the palm of his hand. He was focused but impatient.

There had been no movement in or out of the depot since the delivery had arrived. From where they were parked, they had an obscured view through the gate and couldn't see enough to know what was happening inside.

"Can I ask you something?" said Becky.

Roach didn't take his eyes off the security gate. "Sure."

"Where does all this end?"

He looked over at her. "What do you mean?"

"I mean, what needs to happen for you to feel like you've won and move on with your life?"

He held her gaze as he thought about his answer.

After a few moments, he said, "When Tristar's gone and GlobaTech answer for what they did to us, then I'll stop."

"Which is fine, but if an international media conglomerate like Orion couldn't get the job done against GlobaTech, what do you honestly think we can do? And while we're on the subject, what about Orion? Do you not think they need to be brought to justice for their part in all this?"

Roach shrugged. "Their part is mostly speculation. There's enough evidence to justify asking questions but nothing to prove anything. We know what Tristar has done. We know what GlobaTech has done. That's who we go after. Anyway, you're an incredible reporter. If we find something substantial, surely you could write about it and pitch it to one of the bigger newspapers?"

Becky felt her cheeks fill with color. "Thanks. But no major news outlet is going to take me seriously. First of all, despite what we know, even *you* have to admit this would all sound completely far-fetched to an outsider. And second, I lost my credentials when I left *The Topeka Times* to come with you. I might be able to fool a few warehouse workers on minimum wage, but I have no actual standing or credibility with other newspapers."

"Surely, they would take into account your resume? And the merits of the story?"

She sighed patiently. "Will, do you have any idea how many bloggers and online influencers there are nowadays? I would be shoved into a pile of a thousand others just like me. Nothing I say will make a dent."

"Then we work to find something that will. Simple."

She looked away. "Yeah. *Simple.*"

Roach resumed his unblinking observation of the GlobaTech depot.

"Hey, we got movement," he said after a moment.

He raised the binoculars to his eyes as a large truck appeared.

"Is that ours?" asked Becky.

He watched as it turned right out of the gate. He caught sight of the license plate.

"Yeah, it is." He shuffled upright in his seat. "Come on, let's go."

Becky repositioned herself behind the wheel and started the engine. The deep, untamed growl of the Challenger's three hundred horsepower roared into life. She followed at a safe distance—a skill she had developed a lot over the last couple of weeks.

Roach looked in through the gates as they drove past. It was a large yard. He saw trucks backed into loading bays of various warehouses. He saw numerous GlobaTech personnel patrolling and working. Most of them were armed. He also caught sight of the SUV that led the truck inside earlier.

"No security this time," he said.

"Does that mean we're following an empty truck?" asked Becky.

"Possibly. Like I said, there will be paperwork we can ask to see."

She glanced across at him. "Ask?"

Roach jerked his head dismissively. "Ask... demand... take—whatever."

Becky rolled her eyes as she drove on. Up ahead, the truck was signaling left. The GlobaTech distribution center was in west Boston, on an industrial estate close to I-95. A left here would lead back toward Connecticut.

The truck made the turn as the lights changed to red. The intersection was a standard four-way. They were coming up from the south. Roach leaned forward, watching to his left until the truck disappeared from sight. He sat back and glared up at the lights.

"Come on..." he muttered.

The forty-five seconds it took for the lights to change again felt like a lifetime. The instant they got the green, Becky hit the gas and went to make the turn.

A second later, she slammed on the brakes.

"What the hell!" she shouted as a silver van heading the opposite way turned sharply to block her.

"Move it or lose it, asshole," yelled Roach, gesturing angrily.

But then more silver vans appeared from all directions, seemingly from nowhere. Within seconds, all turns on the intersection were blocked, and Roach and Becky were pinned in.

Men filed out of each van, forming two perimeters with rehearsed precision. One group moved to stand with their backs toward the Challenger, facing the disgruntled lines of traffic and issuing warnings. Another, smaller group made a wide circle around the Challenger. They stood, motionless and detached. They each carried a sidearm, which remained holstered.

Roach and Becky looked at each other. He saw the fear in her eyes. She saw the anger in his. He turned and stared out through the windshield, counting thirty men in total. Their uniforms were distinctive.

They were surrounded by GlobaTech operatives.

"Wait here," he said.

His hand moved to the door. She reached out and grabbed his arm.

"Will, you can't go out there! Are you crazy?"

"Relax. If they wanted to do anything besides talk, they wouldn't be standing there like idiots. Stay here. Keep the engine running."

Roach reached into the glove compartment and took out the handgun he kept there. Holding it low, he checked the magazine and made sure a round was chambered. Then he tucked it into his waistband behind him.

He opened the door and climbed out. No one moved or acknowledged him. He turned a slow circle, scanning the entire intersection. There were eight vans in total, all parked so that they blocked every lane in every direction.

He rested his gaze on one of the operatives nearby.

"I don't take kindly to threats," said Roach matter-of-factly. "Move."

The man didn't respond. He glanced momentarily at him.

Roach sighed. "Fine."

As he began to reach for his gun, a voice called out from behind him.

"This ain't a threat, matey. It's just a precaution."

Roach turned to see a man walking toward him. He noted they were about the same height. The man had dark stubble coating his world-weary face.

"And you are?"

The man smiled. "Ray Collins. Nice to finally meet ya, fella."

He extended a hand, which Roach didn't take.

"Fair enough." Collins nodded, then pointed to the car. "Is that ya sister in there?"

Roach turned his body to face him, planting his feet and squaring his shoulders. "You leave her out of this."

Collins smiled and held his hands up. "I come in peace, I promise. I mean no harm to either of ya. But what I got to say is for both of ya."

Roach held his gaze for a moment, then glanced over his

shoulder and nodded to Becky, who was watching intently through the windshield. The engine cut out and the door opened. She stepped out and moved around the hood to stand beside her brother.

Collins nodded a greeting and extended his hand. "Ya must be Becky. It's a pleasure."

Frowning with confusion, she shook it. "Yeah. Sorry... who are you?"

"I was just saying to ya big bro here, the name's Ray Collins. I'm with GlobaTech."

She looked around, gesturing absently to all the vans. "No shit."

He chuckled. "Right. Well, listen, I apologize for the theatrics, but I'm short on time, and I need ya help."

"No," said Roach flatly.

Collins raised an eyebrow. "Ya don't even know what it is..."

"I don't care. The answer's no. I've spent every second since New York trying to find something to bury you for what you did to me."

"Uh-huh. And what did we do to ya, exactly?"

Roach held his gaze, saying nothing. His fist clenched.

Collins was quick to notice. "I was a little busy when ya decided to go all *Rambo* on Tristar's offices. Julie and Jerry told me ya asked for help, and they couldn't give it to ya. I want ya to know that wasn't personal."

Roach scoffed. "Like hell it wasn't. You set me up. You dragged me into this shit, putting my sister's life in danger in the process, then turned your back on me when I needed you. I'll make sure you burn for that."

"I see ya point, and if that's how ya want to play this, more power to ya. But right now, there's a more pressing concern that, frankly, outweighs ya little grudge against my friends."

"So, why aren't the woman and the juice freak here, asking for my help?"

Collins shrugged. "They figured ya might still be a little... hostile toward them after everything that happened. I'm here because they thought a new face might make all this go a little smoother."

Becky huffed. "And how do you think that's working out for you so far, slick?"

Collins laughed. "Not all that great, love, to be fair. Although, I *can* be a bit of an asshole, in my defense."

"That's not a defense."

"Another good point. The pair of ya are pretty sharp."

"Speaking of points," said Roach, "you should get to yours before I lose my patience."

"Are ya saying *this* has been ya patient side so far?"

"Yes."

"Jesus H. Christ. Okay." Collins paced in front of them for a moment. "I'm here because my boss wants ya help."

Roach and Becky exchanged a quick look.

Collins flicked his eyebrows. "Aye, thought that might interest ya."

"How is he?" asked Becky. "After everything yesterday."

"Alive," replied Collins wearily. "Appreciate ya asking." He looked at Roach. "Julie was with him. She's fine too, in case ya were wondering."

Roach shook his head. "I wasn't."

Becky slapped his arm. "Will!"

He ignored her.

Collins sighed. "Okay, well, we all know Orion and Tristar have been cooking something for a while. We think yesterday was them firing the first shot."

"What does that have to do with us?" asked Roach.

"Look, buddy, whether ya like it or not, we're on the same side here. Both Jules and I have recently had a run-in with ya old pal, Jay the psychopathic assassin."

"Yeah? And how did that go?"

"We got our asses kicked."

Roach nodded slowly. "Well, if it makes you feel any better, she tried to sleep with me before we fought."

Collins chuckled nervously. "Heh. Right. Well, anyway... the attack yesterday, that was tip o' the iceberg stuff. It's all hands on deck now, and ya hands are pretty useful, so..."

"The answer's still no."

His shoulders slumped forward slightly. "Seriously?"

Roach shrugged. "I don't like you, and I don't trust the people you work for as far as I can throw them. I've got my own battles to fight, thanks to your friends. If you and Tristar want to blow the shit out of each other, go right ahead. Makes my life easier."

Collins glanced away, shaking his head. "Huh. Ya know, Jules said ya might be a little reluctant to help. She failed to mention how much of a dick ya can be, though."

Roach stepped toward him. "Choose your next words carefully. They might just be your last."

Collins smiled humorlessly as he squared up to him. "Listen, buddy, I saw what ya did in New York. That was real impressive and whatnot. But look around and do the math, okay? I'm here as a friend."

The two men stood inches apart, eye to eye.

"I don't need any friends," said Roach defiantly.

"And I don't care. Ya think Tristar's gonna stop with us? If all this is Orion starting a war with GlobaTech, how soon do ya think it'll be before one of the big bad guys sees a loose end in the shape of you two?"

A tense silence fell as the two men stared unblinkingly at each other. The wind picked up around them, carrying with it a spring chill that spread goosebumps up their arms. The occasional blare of a horn from disgruntled drivers trapped on the other side of GlobaTech's barricade was the only sound.

Becky stepped between them, placed a hand on each man's chest, and pushed them apart. She turned her back to Collins and looked at her brother.

"Will, listen to me. I'm not saying we should trust him, but... maybe we should hear him out."

Almost reluctantly, Roach broke his stare to look at her.

Becky smiled sympathetically. "He might be a jackass, but he makes a good point."

Collins frowned. "Hey, I'm standing right here..."

Becky spun around to look at him. "Yeah, and *I'm* standing right *here*, and I'm telling you, if you're playing us or trying to set us up again, then my brother's wrath will be the least of your concerns."

Collins grinned and took a respectful step back. "Damn. That badass gene runs deep in ya family, huh?"

"Better believe it."

He nodded. "Fair enough. I promise ya, I'm not here for any other reason than the fact we need ya help."

Roach sighed. "Help with what?"

"I'll tell ya on the way." Collins winked at Becky. "Ya gonna love this next part."

She rolled her eyes as he walked away. Side by side, she and Roach followed Collins toward his van.

Roach took the keys to the Challenger from Becky and tossed them to the nearest GlobaTech operative.

"Look after my car," he said.

The man caught them and nodded without a word.

Roach looked back at his sister and whispered, "This is a bad idea."

Becky shrugged. "Maybe. But it'll make one hell of a story."

BRANDON CROW

May 10, 2020

The rattle of the antiquated air conditioning system provided an almost soothing background noise in the control room, drowning out the muted hustle and murmurings of conversation. The thick metal door to the room stood closed. The walls were jagged, formed from earth and limestone, which added to the damp chill in the air.

A large circle of consoles wrapped around the room. Another bank of computers sat in the center, beside a long, flat table that housed a holographic display screen. A team of men and women, dressed in dark gray military uniforms sporting the Tristar logo, worked feverishly at each station.

Brandon Crow and Jay stood side by side, their backs to everyone else. They stared through thick plexiglass, dirtied from prolonged neglect. His shirt sleeves were rolled halfway up his forearms. Darkened patches of sweat formed around his armpits. His tie was fastened but loose. He hadn't shaved in a few days, either. He looked a far cry from the groomed, confident businessman he had been three weeks earlier.

Jay glanced at him out of the corner of her eye. She had noted how beaten he looked. While she understood he had suffered physically in New York, she knew it wasn't about that. Wounds healed. Scars created a blueprint of your survival. But she saw defeat and humiliation in his eyes, and it worried her.

Sprawling out below them was a hangar, built into the hollowed-out mountain base, long-abandoned by the U.S. Air Force. The ceiling was hundreds of feet high. The floor stretched far enough across to house multiple helicopters, a large fleet of vehicles, and several thousand men.

"It's impressive," observed Jay. She brushed her hair over her shoulder, revealing the butterfly tattoo on her neck.

Crow nodded. "It's taken years to build what we have here."

She looked over at him. "You've done amazing work."

He huffed. "I'm glad *someone* thinks so."

"The last couple of weeks have been rough, sure. But look at what we're doing here. No one expected it to be smooth sailing the whole way."

"Hall sure as hell did," said Crow sharply.

Jay gave a resigned nod and let the conversation fade. She sensed Crow's frustration and impatience. It was understandable, given how close they were now. The end of this incredible journey was almost upon them.

"Let me get back out there," she said eventually. "Give me a team, and I'll hunt down GlobaTech's elite for you. Bringing Hall their heads will go a long way. Besides, I owe them. And I owe Roach."

Crow turned to face her. "I know you do, and you'll have your chance. But for now, I need you to stay with me and stay off the radar. You've had nuclear heat on you since Paluga. Pretty soon, that won't matter, but until then, I won't risk anything happening to you."

He regarded her fondly. Despite their similar ages, he had always thought of her as a surrogate daughter, ever since he had discovered her all those years ago. He knew how dangerous she was. But he also knew her seemingly unquenchable thirst for violence sometimes clouded her judgment. She would have a lot of people looking for her right now. More people than she could handle. While he had no doubt she would happily die in a blaze of glory, he would much rather she didn't. He was going to need her.

Jay clenched her fists and shuddered with impatience.

"Fine," she sighed.

As difficult as it was for her to admit, she knew Crow was right. It had been a little over two weeks since they had escaped New York after Roach's attack on their head offices. It had also been four days since she clashed with Ray Collins and Julie Fisher in Brooklyn. After the attempt on the CEO's life yesterday, every GlobaTech operative in the country would be on high alert.

She just needed to bide her time. She would have her vengeance.

One of the men seated at the center console turned in his seat. "Sir, you have an incoming call."

Crow closed his eyes for a moment. He had been expecting this and wasn't looking forward to it.

He turned and pointed to the man's monitor—a large screen with a built-in webcam at the top of the frame. "Put it through, then move."

The man hastily pressed a button on his keyboard and vacated his seat.

Crow sat down. Jay moved behind him, standing to his

right. He stared at the screen as Quincy Hall's image flickered across it. He could see Orion's main boardroom standing empty behind him.

Crow held Hall's gaze, summoning whatever confidence he could, and cleared his throat. "Mr. Hall, it's good of you to call. I was just—"

"Cut the shit, Brandon," snarled Hall. "I wouldn't be calling at all if you hadn't fucked up so spectacularly yesterday. *Again*."

Crow took a breath. "With all due respect, *Quincy*, Buchanan had a security detail *and* one of his elite operatives with him. All things one of *your* board members led me to believe wouldn't be the case."

Hall leaned forward in his chair, resting on the mahogany desk in front of him as he pointed at the screen. "Don't turn this around on me, you piece of shit. You sent twelve men to do that job. You lost all of them and managed to turn Capitol Hill into the goddamn Alamo in the process! I swear to Christ, Brandon, you'd best be ready for the next phase because I'm running out of reasons why you're useful. Seems to me the only thing you've been good for lately is making excuses!"

Crow's jaw clenched so hard that veins began to show in his forehead. He could feel the judgmental side glances from the workers around him. He looked away from the screen momentarily to compose himself.

"Maybe if I had been given the right information beforehand, the outcome would've been more favorable," he replied through gritted teeth.

Hall sat back in his leather seat and waved a dismissive hand. "I don't have time for hypotheticals. We showed the enemy our hand, and now we have to go all in."

Crow sat straight. He felt Jay tense behind him.

"We're ready here," he said. "One hundred percent. What do you need?"

"For now, nothing. There's still one piece on the board not yet in position, but that's only a matter of time. Be ready, Brandon. The timeframe will be tight. When I give you the order, you will have less than an hour to execute."

Crow nodded. "That won't be a problem."

"Good." Hall leaned forward again, dropping his voice to little more than a whisper. "Because I don't need to tell you what will happen if you fail me again."

The screen faded quickly to black as the call ended.

Crow sat back in the chair. As he looked up from the computer, he saw almost everyone in the room had stopped to stare at him. Their eyes were wide with concern.

He sprang to his feet. "What the hell are you all staring at? Get back to work!"

Everyone exchanged nervous glances but didn't immediately move.

Jay took a breath and stepped forward, squaring her shoulders.

"Hey! Are you deaf?" she shouted.

The room jumped and spun around, burying their heads in their computers, fearful of the well-documented wrath Crow's henchwoman was known for.

She watched the room for a moment, then turned to Crow and nodded curtly. He held her gaze, then moved back to the windows and stared out at the hangar floor below, his hands clasped behind his back. Jay moved to his side.

"Are you okay?" she asked.

"What do you think?" he snapped back.

Jay looked over at him but said nothing.

Crow remained fixated on the activity below. Absently, he picked up a handset built into the console in front of him and pressed a button. Moments later, he saw a man below answer, then look up to the observation window.

"Make sure all the choppers and MPVs are fully fueled and ready to go," ordered Crow. "I want all weapons issued and all teams organized and ready."

There was a heavy breath of static on the line. "S-sir, are you saying..."

"No. I'm saying I want to be ready. The order is coming, and I want everything triple-checked. There is no room for mistakes and no time for complacency. Get it done."

He slammed the receiver down. He watched the man he had just spoken to scurry across the hangar floor, moving with fearful purpose.

Crow took a long breath, steeling his jaw as he focused his mind. He could feel Jay's concerned gaze, but he ignored it. Whatever he felt toward Hall, however he felt about himself... now wasn't the time. He needed to be ready because the next time Hall called him would change the world.

4

MOSES BUCHANAN

May 10, 2020

Buchanan sat perched on the edge of his desk, hands resting patiently on his left thigh as he stared blankly at the carpet in his office.

He hadn't slept since the attack. Police officers had wanted to keep him in Washington for questioning, but he played every diplomatic card he had to get out of there. He knew he was no use to anyone if he wasn't in Santa Clarita.

In front of him, Julie paced back and forth, gesturing wildly with her arms as she spoke.

"We have to do something!" she shouted. "We can't let them get away with this. How in the hell did it even happen in the first place?"

At the back of the room, Jericho leaned against the wall, arms folded across his bulking chest. He watched the woman he loved with a mixture of sympathy and admiration. When he had first heard of the attack on her and Buchanan yesterday, his immediate reaction was the same.

He became too angry to know how to process it. But when he saw Julie, he could see she had the unbridled rage more than covered, so he took a step back to let her deal with things however she needed to. It had been less than two weeks since she buried her father. Between that and the Paluga crisis, everyone was on edge.

Jericho knew the only thing more effective than a focused Julie was an angry Julie. Yesterday pushed her too far, and right now, she was exactly where she needed to be.

"This has been coming for a while, and we both know it," said Buchanan, his words measured and deliberate. "I've already spoken to the FBI. They said they will help any way they can to launch an official investigation into the attack and to apprehend those responsible for it."

Julie stopped and glared at him. "We *know* who's responsible for it! We should be hunting them down, not standing here talking about it."

"And we will. But we have to be smart. Right now, GlobaTech is a wounded animal. If we go looking for a fight, we'll lose."

Julie held his gaze as she took deep breaths to subdue the adrenaline. Her gray tee was still damp from a session in the gym before the meeting. Her hair was tied up, but her bangs were matted to her forehead. After a moment, she closed her eyes and paced away toward the window. She turned to lean against it, relishing the coolness of the glass on her back.

Buchanan moved around his desk and sat heavily in his chair, looking at Jericho and Julie in turn. "Paluga hit us hard. Jericho, it goes without saying that you did an incredible job over there. However, while it was the right call to leave a GlobaTech presence in the region, it leaves us short a few thousand pairs of boots on the ground back home.

Couple that with the number of operatives deployed around the world at any given time, and we're in no shape to go picking a fight with Tristar."

"Are we still running with the theory that Orion's pulling the strings behind Tristar's re-emergence?" asked Jericho.

Buchanan nodded. "We are. We have more than enough evidence to justify it, even if we don't have enough to legally prove it. Plus, we know the assassin from Paluga works for Tristar. This... Jay."

Julie huffed. "I owe that bitch. But you're right—she links Tristar to the shooting, which means she links Orion to it too."

"That's *if* we can find the link between them and Tristar."

"I thought we had grounds to access Tristar's servers now?" asked Jericho. "Won't that help?"

"That's one of the things the FBI is doing for us. I'm going to let them handle that investigation so that it's public. Sticking it to us is one thing, but there's no way Orion can spin a formal FBI inquiry. I'm hoping once that gains momentum, they will be too distracted by it to notice we're going after Tristar."

Julie pushed herself off the window and stepped to the middle of the room. Jericho moved to her side.

"What can we do?" she asked Buchanan.

He leaned back in his chair, bridging his fingers together in front of him as he rested his elbows on the arms. "For now, I want you both working the files we confiscated from Tristar's offices in New York. Find anything you can that might help."

Jericho frowned. "Isn't *that* what the FBI should be doing? It's wasting our time if we're covering the same ground."

"Not if you're looking for different things," replied Buchanan, shaking his head. "The FBI will use that information, as well as the access to the main servers, to find a link between Tristar and Orion. I want *you two* to find something that explains Tristar's weaponry—manufacturing or R and D sites... technical specifications and blueprints... *anything* that gives us the how and the where. You find that crazy-ass bullet in there, even better. But for now, if we find where they make their guns, maybe we can shut down the whole operation and prevent them from shooting at us anymore."

The two of them nodded their understanding and headed for the door. Jericho opened it for Julie, who stopped in the threshold to look back at Buchanan.

"Any news from Ray?" she asked.

Buchanan shrugged. "I've heard nothing yet, but he said he would be here tomorrow with Roach in tow, and I have no reason to doubt him."

Jericho rolled his eyes and let out a heavy sigh. "Yeah, tomorrow's when the party *really* starts..."

Buchanan raised an eyebrow. "You've got the rest of the day to get that shit out of your system, soldier. We need all the help we can get, and you *will* play nice."

Jericho gave a resigned smile and a half-hearted salute. "You're the boss."

"Damn right. Now close the door on your way out."

Jericho followed Julie out into the corridor, pulling the door shut as instructed.

Buchanan watched them go and sat quietly for a moment in the fresh silence. He pinched the bridge of his nose with his thumb and forefinger, screwing his eyes closed as he willed the headache to leave the base of his skull.

He had spent more time in the air than on the ground in

the last few days, and the combination of inhuman stress and little sleep was beginning to take its toll. If he could just get five minutes of peace, he knew he could—

There was a knock on his door.

"Goddammit..." he muttered as his secretary, Kim, stepped inside his office.

She smiled apologetically. "Sorry, but you have the president on line one."

He nodded slowly. "Yeah. Yeah... okay. Put him through."

Kim hesitated. "Are you all right?"

He sat straight in his chair, his hand hovering over the desk phone in anticipation for the call. "I'm fine, thank you."

"I can always keep him on hold if you need a couple of minutes..."

Buchanan smiled. "He's the leader of the free world, Kim. You should probably put him straight through."

She rolled her eyes. "I don't care who he is. You need some goddamn sleep..."

"I need to speak with the president. I could probably do with some coffee too."

"Fine."

She ducked back outside, shutting the door behind her. A moment later, Buchanan's phone rang through.

"Mr. President," he said after one ring. "I was going to call you."

The unmistakable rasping of the Texan president preceded his stern tone.

"Goddammit, Moses, what in Christ's name happened yesterday?" barked Schultz.

"I was shot at, sir."

"In *my* goddamn city! How did this happen?"

Buchanan stopped himself from answering the obviously careless question with a sarcastic remark.

"We don't know, sir. They hit us from out of nowhere and didn't have the courtesy to tell us why before the bullets started flying."

"Moses, this isn't the Wild West. God... *damn it!*" He paused. "What are you doing about it?"

Buchanan took a deep breath. "Well, Jericho and Julie are searching for information on Tristar's weapons program. The FBI are searching for a link between Orion and Tristar now that they have access to all the servers. I would appreciate any pressure you can put on them to get a result."

"I just got off the phone with the director of the FBI. He understands the importance."

"Good. Hopefully, we'll find something soon that will tie Orion up in enough bureaucracy to distract them from trying to destroy my company."

"That isn't enough," snapped Schultz. "If Tristar's getting ballsy enough to pull shit like this, we're getting closer and closer to the exact scenario we've been working to avoid. I can't deploy the military on the streets of this country to fight a domestic enemy. An enemy that we know we're ill-equipped to fight. Meanwhile, you boys are on the ropes, barely keeping your heads above water, and as effective as Blackstar is proving to be, they're only five people. And one of *them's* a walking goddamn liability."

Buchanan smiled but said nothing.

Schultz continued. "Damn it, son, we need a knockout blow, and we need it fast."

"I wholeheartedly agree, sir, and we're working on it. We know Tristar was behind President Herrera's assassination. We also know Orion was behind the media embargo and the subsequent attack on this company."

Schultz sighed tersely. "Do you have any idea why Tristar would attack you in the street?"

The question caught Buchanan off-guard. He had been so focused on the attacks themselves, he hadn't given much thought as to why they were actually happening.

"I'm honestly not sure," he admitted. "Orion and Tristar have had GlobaTech in their crosshairs for the last couple of years. We don't know if it's been a joint effort so far or not, although we obviously have our suspicions. As far as I can tell, Orion don't like us because they like to think of themselves as the biggest dog in the yard. When Tristar crossed our path, we reacted exactly how we would to any other threat. I guess you can't please everyone..."

"Well, you better start finding some goddamn answers soon. Believe it or not, the people of this country still look to me to fix bullshit like this, and I'm running out of ways to tell them not to worry about it."

Buchanan sat back in his chair. "I know that, sir. We're doing everything we can. I appreciate everything you're doing to get the various agencies to coordinate their efforts with us. I've brought in some outside help of our own, which should be here tomorrow. Then we can start formulating a plan to end this ourselves."

"So, Blackstar's coming to visit, huh?"

"They are. Along with Mr. Roachford."

"That's a hell of a lot of ego in one goddamn room, Moses. You better be damn sure you know what you're doing."

"I am, Mr. President. We need all the help we can get."

"And if that crazy sonofabitch steps even a pinky toe out of line, I want him gone. You understand?"

Buchanan smiled to himself, recalling the many moments in which he had encountered Adrian Hell's unique ability to make a lasting impression. "I'm sure it'll be fine, sir."

"It had goddamn better be, son."

The line went dead.

Buchanan stared at the receiver for a moment, then placed it back down on the phone. A second later, Kim walked in without knocking, marched over to his desk, and placed a steaming mug of coffee and a bagel in front of him.

"You're not doing anything else until you drink that and eat that," she said firmly.

Buchanan stared at her momentarily, then decided it was best not to argue with her.

"Yes, ma'am," he said quietly.

She nodded. "Damn right."

She left him alone to eat, drink, and wonder what he would ever do without her.

5

QUINCY HALL

May 10, 2020

Quincy Hall stared absently at the aura of the afternoon sun through the tinted glass of his limousine. He sipped at a single malt, cradling the crystal tumbler in his hand almost lovingly as he relished the air conditioning inside the spacious vehicle.

New York City was usually pleasant without being overbearing this time of year. However, the last decade or so had seen a shift in the dependable routine of New York's temperature, meaning the blistering hell of its summers occasionally began early. Consequently, Hall had no desire to step outside the vehicle in the middle of the afternoon.

That's why the meeting would take place inside it.

He was parked on the tarmac of the signature flight runway at Westchester County airport, approximately nine miles east of the Hudson.

Hall looked relaxed. Almost complacent. He wore beige

trousers and a white turtleneck under a light blue sweater vest, as if he had just stepped off the eighteenth tee at the country club. His thinning hair was slicked back. His skin was browned, and his face looked more youthful than his years justified—the result of some recent time spent with a tanning bed and a Botox needle. He sat with his legs crossed, holding his drink on his knee with one hand and drumming his fingers on a brown envelope beside him with the other.

The intercom in the back of the limo crackled into life, and the voice of the driver sitting on the other side of the frosted glass partition came through.

"Sir, they're making their final approach now," he said.

Hall didn't respond. He simply leaned right slightly, so he could see more of the sky through the door's window.

The private jet was paid for out of his own pocket. This was a business meeting but not one he wanted to put through Orion's books. He sat back and waited, savoring his drink as the jet landed and taxied along the runway beside him.

As the noise of its engines died, he glanced across. He saw the door open out and the steps unfold. A man appeared first, carrying an overnight bag. He wore a fitted suit and sunglasses. He walked quickly down the steps, then stood beside them on the tarmac, waiting.

Then a woman appeared. She wore a long overcoat, hung open. It flapped in the wind, revealing her short skirt and toned legs. Despite the heels she wore, she descended the steps with confidence and grace. She ignored the man with her bag and walked directly toward the limo. Her long, straight hair bounced with each step but always fell in such a way as to cover half her face.

Hall smiled as he watched her approach.

He heard the driver's door open. A moment later, the driver himself moved to the side of the limo and opened the door. The woman ducked and climbed in beside Hall without a word. She shuffled slightly in the seat to adjust her coat.

The door closed behind her.

"Drink?" said Hall, gesturing to his own.

The woman shook her head. "I'm good."

Hall looked her up and down, admiring her body without discretion.

"How was Tokyo?" he asked.

Miley Tevani turned her head to look at him, brushing her hair away from her face. Her dark eyes stood out against her seemingly flawless complexion. Closer inspection revealed heavier makeup in places, concealing the light scarring on her cheeks and forehead.

"It's fine," she replied coldly. "I've managed to reunite what remained of Kazawa's family and make it my own. We're rebuilding."

Hall nodded. "Good. If you need anything, you let me know. Having an ally in Japan will be useful. I'm sure our interests will align at some point in the future."

"Thanks. So, do you want to tell me why I'm here?"

"All in good time." He looked her up and down again. "Are you sure you don't want a drink?"

Miley made no effort to hide her eyeroll. "No, I don't. I want to know what you need me to do and how much you're going to pay me to do it."

Hall smiled, yet the humor had left his expression. He placed a hand on her leg, relishing the smoothness of her warm skin against his palm. "You're a strong young woman. I've always admired that about you, Miley."

He started to rub his hand along her thigh. She shifted uncomfortably in her seat, as if trying to scramble away from him. He then squeezed tightly. His unexpectedly strong grip made her wince.

"But make no mistake. You're an asset, and I own your sweet little ass. I'm more powerful than you can imagine, and you will show me the respect I deserve. Am I clear?"

Miley held his gaze, struggling to mask any fear or anger as she willed herself to relax.

"I apologize, Mr. Hall," she said quietly. "Of course."

"Good. I have a job for you." His hand moved from her leg to the envelope beside him, which he then handed to her. "I believe you know him."

She took the envelope and opened it, sliding out a color photograph. She stared at the image blankly. All emotion left her face, like water disappearing down the drain, leaving her completely detached from her inevitable task. Her icy stare burned through the image.

"When the time is right, I need you to kill him," continued Hall. "Will that be a problem?"

Miley pushed the image back into the envelope and dropped it onto the seat between them.

"Not at all," she replied. "Mind if I ask why now?"

"Does it matter?"

She shrugged. "I've been holed up in Tokyo for six months while he's caused you nothing but problems. You could've asked me to take him out any time. Why wait until now?"

Hall looked away and finished his whiskey with a single gulp. He then leaned forward, rested the empty glass on the table in front of him, and retrieved a cigar and lighter. He placed it between his lips and puffed gently on it as he lit the end. He tossed the lighter back onto the table, then took a long drag and blew a plume of thick smoke toward the roof of the limo.

He turned back to Miley. "We are approaching a critical stage of our plans. I have so far... *allowed* his disruptions because the bigger picture was more important than the small deviation that would be needed to remove him. However, that is no longer the case."

Miley nodded. "Would this have anything to do with the attack on GlobaTech's CEO yesterday?"

Hall raised an eyebrow questioningly.

Miley shrugged. "Doesn't exactly take a rocket scientist to figure *that* out."

Hall took another long drag of his cigar and flashed a crooked smile. "GlobaTech has been working to come after us for a long time. And Buchanan... that interfering piece of shit has been colluding with Schultz to find ways to stop us —despite not even knowing what we're planning to do. Unfortunately, they tend to get lucky every now and then, and all their fumbling around in the dark is becoming a problem. Yesterday didn't go the way I wanted, and it showed our hand. Buchanan is trying to bring together every friend he has. Not that it'll make a damn bit of differ-ence. But when the time's right..." He tapped his finger on the envelope, spilling some ash on top of it. "You remove this piece of shit. And when you do, it will cause his collec-tion of wannabes and reprobates to fucking crumble."

Miley took a deep breath, muffling a cough as she inad-vertently caught a lungful of smoke. "Fine. When do you want it done?"

"Not yet. There are still some things that need to be done beforehand. But I want you to be ready. The timing will be critical, and you'll only have one chance to make the impact this needs to make. Understood?"

She nodded. "I'll be waiting for your call."

She reached for the door handle, but Hall placed a hand on her leg again to stop her from moving. She looked back at him to see a smile that made her flesh crawl.

"Now that business has been concluded, maybe I can show you my penthouse?" said Hall. "You're welcome to stay there until you're needed."

Miley sat back in the seat and took a slow breath to compose herself. She placed her hand on top of his momentarily, stared at it, then removed it from her leg.

"Understand something, Mr. Hall," she began. "I might work for you, but you don't own me. I'm the head of a Yakuza family. *Nobody* owns me. And while I might be young, I have generations of violence coursing through my veins, so believe me when I tell you, if you put your hands on me one more time, I will gut you like a fish."

She opened the door and stepped out of the limo. A wave of heat rushed inside, momentarily suffocating the air conditioning.

As she placed a hand on the door, she leaned forward and looked into Hall's eyes. "Also, for the record, my *sweet little ass* would give you a fucking heart attack."

She slammed the door shut and walked away as confidently as she had arrived.

Hall watched her go, smiling to himself.

"God, what I wouldn't do to that..." he muttered.

He picked up the envelope and held his cigar to the corner, watching as smoke began to whisper and dance from it. Eventually, it caught fire. He stared, mesmerized by the small flame, turning the envelope to ensure it spread as efficiently as possible. He then buzzed his own window down and tossed what remained outside.

"We're done here," he said into the intercom.

Seconds later, the engine started and the limo drove away, leaving behind the image of Miley's target on the tarmac, curling in on itself as it burned away to nothing.

6

ROACH

May 10, 2020

Collins was sitting in the same seat on the private jet that he was in a few days ago, when he and Julie first headed to New York. Roach sat opposite, not taking his eyes off him.

Beside him, Becky was looking around the cabin, an expression of childlike wonder on her face. She had only been on a plane a handful of times in her life, but never anything as fancy as this. She noticed a small console on the wall beside her, with three buttons on it.

"What does this do?" she asked, pressing the middle one.

Collins closed his eyes momentarily and sighed. "That... that calls the stewardess. I kinda wish you hadn't done that."

"Why?"

Just then, the curtain at the back of the cabin was brushed aside, and the stewardess appeared. Collins turned to see Louise walking toward them. He smiled apologetically.

"Hey, sorry about that," he said. "I know ya don't like us wastin' ya time. We just—"

"It... it was my fault," said Becky. "I'm sorry. I've... I've never been in a private jet before. I wondered what the button did."

Louise smiled. "It's fine, hon. Can I get you anything?"

Becky was taken aback by the offer. "Oh, wow. Erm... yeah, can I get a glass of water?"

Louise's grin widened. "Sure you don't want a glass of wine or a cocktail?"

Becky's eyes popped. "Is that an option?"

She shrugged. "Of course. You want a Cosmo?"

"Hell yeah!"

"Coming right up." Louise looked at Roach. "What about you, champ? Sitting there looking at *his* ugly mug, I'm guessing you need a whiskey?"

Collins frowned. "Hey!"

Roach shook his head. "I'm fine. Thank you."

Louise turned to leave, but Collins caught her eye.

"Hey, do I not get a drink?" he asked.

"No."

"Why not?"

She leaned over, smiling. "Because you wasted my time."

"Huh? No, I didn't. The new girl pressed the button, not me."

"You're in charge. So, tough."

She walked away, smiling to herself.

Collins turned in his seat and called after her. "Hey, that's not fair. I want a drink. Louise! Damn it, woman, I know what that button does! Louise!"

She disappeared behind the curtain.

"Ah, shite," he muttered, turning back to face the others.

Becky grinned. "So... how long have you been sleeping with the flight attendant?"

Collins huffed nervously and shifted in his seat. "I, ah... I don't know what ya mean."

She nodded slowly. "Right..."

He glanced over at Roach, who still hadn't taken his eyes off him. His eyes were cold. His expression deadpan. His jaw set.

Collins looked away.

A few moments of awkward silence later, Louise reappeared and handed Becky her Cosmopolitan in a cocktail glass. Then she turned back and handed Collins a bottle of beer.

He took it with a smile. "Ah... never let it be said ya ain't good at what ya do, love."

"We both know that's never been said," she replied with a wink.

As she walked away, Roach sat forward in his seat, resting his arms on his knees.

"Okay, you've had your fun," he said sternly. "Tell us why we're here, or we're leaving."

Collins raised an eyebrow, then leaned right to make a show of glancing out the window.

"I mean... we're about fifteen thousand feet above Missouri right now, buddy," he countered. "Pretty sure ya ain't leaving. Besides, there's about three hours of flight time left. No reason to rush. Sit back and enjoy yaself."

"I was enjoying myself just fine in Boston."

"Aye, must be nice to have a hobby... following our trucks around the country for no reason whatsoever."

Roach clenched his fists. "I had every reason..."

Collins waved a dismissive hand. "Yeah, yeah. Whatever ya need to tell yaself, buddy. Wanna know what I think?"

"Not really."

"I think ya don't wanna admit that ya wrong."

"Excuse me?"

"Look, I know Jules said we couldn't help ya back in New York. Now, I suspect ya little sister is the sharper of the two of ya, but given everything ya know about the bad guys, even *you* must be able to see why we couldn't get involved in that *fustercluck* ya caused."

Roach went to speak but held his tongue. He clenched his jaw so hard, his cheeks turned red. He couldn't find the words he wanted; his concentration was clouded by his anger.

Becky sat forward, cradling her half-empty glass in her hands. "It would've been a PR disaster for you, wouldn't it? And given what happened with Paluga, you would argue you made the right call."

Collins glanced over at her and winked.

"See?" he said to Roach. "Told ya she was the smart one."

Roach sat back in his seat, rested his elbows on the arms, and held his hands in front of him, cracking his knuckles. "Let me be clear. I see you flirt with my sister again, I'm going to hit you so hard, your lungs will fly out of your ass. Are we clear?"

Collins held his gaze. "Crystal. So long as ya understand that A... I wasn't flirtin' with her, and B... I ain't Jules or Jerry. I wasn't involved in what went down before, but if I was, I'd have done the exact same thing they did. Ya know why? Because like it or not, it *was* the right call. Just like ya sister said. Now, I'm all for the *strong, silent type* act, but if ya don't pull ya head outta ya ass soon, I'm gonna recommend we don't bother askin' for ya help at all. And then ya can leave whenever ya want. Parachutes are optional."

Roach didn't respond. He sat quietly, watching Collins as he sat back in his seat and swigged his beer. He noticed the tense body language. The impatience in the eyes. The frustration on his face.

Whether he liked it or not, he believed this guy was legit.

He took a deep breath. "Fine. Tell me everything, and I'll tell you if I want to help."

Collins sipped his beer. "Okay. Now we're getting somewhere. What do you know about what happened in Paluga last week?"

Becky shrugged. "Only what the news reported. The president was assassinated. GlobaTech failed to keep the peace and got caught in the middle of a civil war-slash-military coup, which many people hold them responsible for in the first place."

Collins smiled. "Aye. That's what we heard too."

"So, what really happened?" asked Roach.

"The whole thing was a setup."

"How?" asked Becky.

"The political unrest, the new democracy, the pissed off military... all that was for real. But what no one else knows is that the part of the military trying to overthrow the president was armed by Tristar. And they were armed long before we showed up."

"You got proof Tristar deals in stolen weapons?" asked Roach.

"Actually, yeah, we do. But that's not what this is. The weapons weren't stolen and sold by Tristar. They were *made* by them."

Roach and Becky exchanged a look of surprise and concern.

"I didn't know they manufactured weapons," admitted Roach.

Collins nodded. "Heh. Join the club, buddy. But that don't change the fact it's a fact. Tristar seemingly knew the Palugan government was going to hire us before we did. They got the weapons in before the country was locked down. Then our friend Jay snuck in and took the shot that dropped Herrera and some of our guys."

Roach frowned. "Wait. Jay's the shooter? Are you sure?"

"Without a doubt."

Becky shook her head. "I don't understand. How is any of this possible?"

"The working theory is that this is proof Orion's behind all of it. The political landscape over there was no secret. We think Orion manipulated the situation to make sure Globa-Tech got involved. Then, once we were over there and isolated, the military wiped out a few thousand of our guys using state-of-the-art weaponry, and Orion controlled the narrative in the media to make us look so bad that the government felt they needed to step in and finish us off."

Roach took a deep breath as he processed everything Collins said, trying to separate fact from theory in his head.

"I've seen the information you gave me on that flash drive," he said. "Orion's fingerprints are all over it."

"Correct," said Collins. "But there's nothing incriminating on there. The fact they own Tristar on paper doesn't prove they have anything to do with what they do."

"So, Orion being involved at all is just an assumption?"

"Well, not quite. See, the boss man decided to take the passive-aggressive approach with Orion a couple of days before we were approached about the Paluga gig. Had one of the top dogs into his office. Quincy something. A real prick, by all accounts."

"A risky move, considering..." said Becky. "How did he spin it?"

"He used it as an olive branch. Said we had information about Tristar on the back of the shit *Chuckles* here pulled in New York. Found Orion's name all over it. Assumed it was nothing, but we know how it looks. From one empire to another, thought ya might want to fix it on the quiet... that kinda thing."

"Right," said Roach. "And how did that go?"

Collins shrugged. "About as well as ya might expect. Without giving anything away, the guy threatened us, which was basically him admitting we were onto something without actually saying it. Even got a little racist, which didn't help matters. Way I hear it, Buchanan almost punched the guy into the grave."

"He should've..." huffed Becky.

"Aye. I'm with ya there, love."

Roach absently brushed the back of his hand across the stubble on his cheek. "So, this asshole threatened you and then you just so happened to fall victim to the ultimate smear campaign that almost destroyed your entire company?"

Collins nodded. "Yup. Bit of a co-inky-dink, wouldn't ya say?"

Roach didn't respond. He was unwilling to admit to anyone, including himself, that Collins had a point.

"But it didn't work," said Becky. "Isn't that why your boss was in Washington yesterday?"

Collins nodded again. "That's right. Despite initially losing the U.N. contract, we fixed Paluga and exposed Tristar in the process. The government has been making U-turns on their bullshit anti-monopoly charges ever since."

Roach grunted. "You ask me, they shouldn't have."

Collins frowned. "Buddy, have ya not been listening? That was nothing but us getting screwed over."

"Whatever. I don't think any company should have that much power and influence. Maybe it would've been a good thing if GlobaTech had been dismantled."

"Ya know what?" Collins finished his beer and placed the empty bottle in the cup holder beside him. "I'm inclined to agree with ya. We all know the saying about power and responsibility and whatnot. Maybe one company having so much power *is* a bad thing. But it's all about perspective. It's all about which side of the fence ya sitting on. I know ya beef with us is because ya think we're secretly the bad guys. And I'll hold my hands up and admit to ya both right now, there have been times when GlobaTech has cut some ethical and moral corners to get the job done. Real big picture stuff. But let's look at the options here. We use our resources to help people. Sure, we make weapons. But we also make technology and medicine to help advance health-care. When the world went to shit on 4/17, we were the ones —the *only* ones—who stepped up and gave everything we had to help everyone who struggled after it. Without getting one cent in return.

"Then, ya got Orion. They used a shifty security firm they own to steal and kill for reasons unknown. They essentially orchestrated a coup in another country, then used the control they have over the international media to influence the U.S. government and the United Nations to carry out their dirty work. They dragged us through Senate hearings and made the public hate the one company who's *actually* been helping them... essentially destroying everything we've built because we called them out on all their shady shit. Who would ya rather have around, eh?"

Roach and Becky looked at each other. He shrugged but didn't comment. He still felt so much anger toward Globa-

Tech for everything he and his sister had been through. He wasn't ready to forgive them, let alone side with them. But he couldn't deny that a lot of what Collins had said made sense.

Had he been fooled by Orion's lies, like everyone else? There was no denying Tristar were the enemy. Was he focusing his efforts on the wrong people?

"If you're right, you should go public with it," said Becky. "With everything. Even the circumstantial stuff. You have more than enough to form the basis of a narrative. And what you can't prove makes enough sense that it would still cast doubt in people's minds. It will make others start asking questions. It's only a matter of time, surely? I still know people. I can—"

Collins held a hand up apologetically. "That's a grand idea, love, honestly. Do ya think we haven't thought of that already?"

"Then what's stopping you?"

"First rule of war: know ya enemy. Most of what we know comes from information we obtained illegally to give to ya brother. What we know from firsthand experience, there's no physical proof of besides our word. So, at best, going public now would only lead to a war of words in the papers. We all know Orion controls the media, so that's a fight we can't win."

"So, you're working to find something legal that you *can* use, right?" she asked.

"We are."

Roach got to his feet and paced uneasily around the cabin, adjusting each step against the gentle rocking of the flight.

He leaned back against the wall of the cockpit and

folded his arms across his chest. He looked at Collins. "Okay. Let's say your attempt at the sympathy vote worked. What exactly do you need me to do?"

Collins rested back against the soft leather and crossed his legs. "For now, I need ya to trust me enough to meet with my boss tomorrow. There's a full briefing in the morning. Everyone will have a part to play."

He frowned. "Everyone? Who's everyone?"

"Well, Julie and Jericho, ya already know. They're currently trying to find out who made the bullet that killed Herrera. It's like nothing anyone's ever seen before. Some real sci-fi shit. If we find who made it, maybe we find who they made it for."

"That sounds like a waste of time. You know who the shooter is. Why not just go after Jay?"

"Fair question. You're right—we know she was the shooter. But what we don't know is who asked her to pull the trigger."

"Surely, it was Tristar?" said Becky. "We know she works for them."

"Yeah, she does. But was it Tristar who told her to take the shot, or was it Orion? Until we know that, finding her won't help as much as we'd like. Besides..." He looked back at Roach. "She's a real piece of work, as ya know. She fought ya to a draw twice. Hell, she kicked the crap outta me *and* Jules at the same damn time."

Roach nodded. "She's... a handful, yeah."

"That's why Buchanan is bringing in a team of specialists to track her down. Save us from another ass-kicking so we can focus on more important things."

He raised an eyebrow. "Specialists?"

"Aye, a real *best of the best* bunch." Collins smiled. "You'd like the guy in charge."

Roach walked back over to them and sat down.

"I highly doubt that," he said.

Becky sighed and pushed his shoulder. "You don't like anyone."

"That's because most people in my life have either betrayed me, tried to kill me, or both. It's easier and safer to be alone." He looked at Collins. "I'll listen to what your boss has to say. If there's a war to wage, I'll help because I can. But that doesn't mean I've forgiven GlobaTech for dragging the two of us into this shit in the first place."

Collins nodded and smiled. "Works for me. The enemy of my enemy... an' all that. Now, when we land, I'll show ya to the guest quarters. Then ya can both relax before the morning."

Becky frowned. "Guest quarters?"

"Aye, love. The Santa Clarita compound is basically a small town. We have tons of apartment buildings there. Ya each get ya own room and a line of credit for any food and drink ya might want."

She looked over at Roach, who didn't appear as impressed as she was.

She rolled her eyes. "Oh, for God's sake, Will. At least *try* to make the most of this."

He took a long, impatient breath and rested back in his seat. He folded his arms up behind his head and closed his eyes, thinking about everything Collins had told him.

When he was a kid, his mom would always say, *"Once bitten, twice shy."* He had worked for Tristar, doing a lot of things he didn't fully understand without question. It cost him a month of his life and made him a lot of enemies. He wasn't about to make the same mistake again by trusting an organization claiming to be an ally.

But he couldn't deny that a lot of what he had been told

matched up with what he knew—and suspected—about both Tristar's and Orion's true motives. He wasn't done with GlobaTech, but he meant what he said to Collins. If there was a fight to be had, he'd fight.

He just needed to be sure he was on the right side.

7

JULIE FISHER

May 11, 2020

Small clouds of dust danced around their feet in the warm breeze. The muted crunch of boots on gravel was barely audible over the growing noise of another busy day around them.

Jericho and Julie walked side by side with relaxed purpose, both dressed in desert camos and wearing a distinctive black and red GlobaTech tee—a design that had become one of the most recognized in the world.

The sun had already begun its relentless onslaught of the earth, with early temperatures hitting the mid-seventies and showing no signs of plateauing.

Julie glanced across at Jericho as they navigated the network of roads that traced through the GlobaTech compound. She recognized the look on his face. The set jaw... the creased brow... the focused gaze...

She knew what it meant.

"Hey, you good?" she asked.

"Yeah, why?"

"Because you look like you're about to kill somebody."

His expression softened, and his broad shoulders relaxed. He looked over at her. "What? No, I don't."

Julie smiled. "Not anymore. But you did. Are we going to have a problem here?"

"Not from me."

"Uh-huh. If that's the case, then put your face right, soldier. You're not in Paluga anymore."

He raised an eyebrow. "What do you mean?"

She stopped, prompting him to do the same. She stepped in front of him.

"I mean, sometimes that massive ego of yours gets in the way of your brain. We both know your default setting is *throat grab and right hook*. I need to know you're going to exercise some restraint and diplomacy here."

Jericho sighed. "Fine. I just... it pisses me off that we're asking people who don't want to be here for help. We've got more important things to do than babysit someone who hates us."

"Look, we don't know what he wants yet. When I spoke to Ray last night, he said they talked through a lot of things on the flight over here. Maybe he's changed his opinion."

"Jules, we shouldn't have to convince someone that we're the good guys here. Not after everything that's happened. Not with all we know. If he doesn't believe we're on the right side of this by now, he never will, and I don't want people like that standing beside me."

Julie nodded, listening carefully. There were hints of misplaced venom in his words and flashes of anger in his eyes. She knew him better than most, and she could tell when his judgment was clouded.

"Let me ask you something," she said. "And I want you to be honest with me."

Jericho shrugged his massive shoulders. "Sure."

She made a circular motion with her hand, gesturing to him. "All this... is it really about us going to meet Roachford and his sister, or is it more to do with the fact that Adrian Hell was invited without your knowledge?"

Jericho hesitated for a split-second. When he replied, he chose his words carefully. "I couldn't give a shit about Adrian Hell—or Roach, for that matter. What I care about is trusting the people on my side in a fight. And if you openly say you don't want to be here, or that you don't believe I'm on the right side of this, no way am I going to trust you to have my back. It's that simple." He pointed to the building up ahead. "That man and his sister hate us. They blame us for their shit, and he's been actively working to hurt us. I don't want him here."

"That's a fair point, Jericho, but let's not be naïve or arrogant enough not to admit the guy has a point. We *did* get him into this mess, and we *did* turn our backs on him when he asked for help because it was the right thing to do at the time. But if we go in there having already written him off, it won't end well, and we need him. We need as many people as we can get because Orion and Tristar are no joke."

Julie was breathing heavier. Her body had tensed to the point that it was nearly shaking. Jericho placed a large hand on her shoulder and gave an understanding half-smile, recognizing that her own unaddressed issues were influencing her view of this situation.

"I know, Jules. I know. I wish I had been with you in Washington, and I can't tell you how relieved I was to find out you were okay." He took a breath. "I'll be nice to Roachford, okay?"

She nodded. "And what about Adrian?"

Jericho rolled his eyes. "No promises."

They continued walking until they reached the apartment building at the center of the base. It was L-shaped and stood five stories tall. In the middle, bordered on the north and east side by the building itself, was a small park with trees, benches, and a fishpond. It looked peaceful. A small slice of serenity.

It also looked out of place.

The compound contained residential and commercial districts, so it was sometimes easy to forget that it was a large military base. For every convenience store and restaurant, there was a hangar and an armory. For every apartment block, there was a barracks.

It truly was a unique environment.

The two of them cut through the park, toward the main entrance. As they neared the doors, they were pushed open as Roach and Becky appeared. The four of them stopped as they saw each other. An immediate and tense silence fell, suffocating the noises of the world around them.

Roach looked irritated. His face was contorted with frustration and fatigue. His body had tensed. His shoulders had squared. His eyes were fixed on Jericho.

Julie thought his sister looked the polar opposite. She seemed fresh-faced, rested, and almost excited to be there.

Julie extended a hand to Becky. "We haven't officially met. Julie Fisher."

Becky shook it. "Becky Roachford."

She looked at Roach. "Good to see you again, William."

"Hmm," he grunted, his eyes never leaving Jericho's.

Becky tapped his shoulder. "Will, be nice."

He nodded his head toward Jericho. "Them first."

"How much nicer do you want us to be?" asked Jericho. "We flew you here and put you up for the night, despite knowing you hate us."

Roach shrugged. "Yeah, because you need my help. Not because you want to apologize."

"Apologize for what? Cleaning up the mess you made in New York, you mean?"

"A mess I wouldn't have needed to make if you'd have helped when I asked."

Each man took a step forward, never breaking eye contact. Julie saw Becky hesitate, understandably unsure of how to handle the growing tension.

Julie stepped between them and placed a hand on each of their chests, giving a symbolic push. Both men respected it enough to voluntarily take a step back.

"All right, enough." She looked at Jericho. "I told you to behave, and you said you would. So, do it." She turned around and looked Roach in the eyes. "And you. I'm not going to apologize for making a decision that benefitted thousands of people instead of one. Blame us all you want. The fact of the matter is, if we hadn't brought you into this fight, Tristar would've eventually. And when they did, you'd have been far less prepared for this shit than you are now. So, I'll tell all of you, right here and now, what's done is done. What matters is what comes next, and if we're going to weather the coming storm, we need everyone on the same page. Clear?"

"Crystal," muttered Jericho.

Becky shrugged. "Works for me. I just want to get to the truth and help put the bad guys away."

Julie nodded to her, then turned back to Roach. "Well?"

Roach held her gaze. "I don't fight beside people I don't

trust. You want my help, you gotta convince me you're on the right side."

"We feel the same way. We're here to take you to a meeting with Moses Buchanan and some others who have a vested interest in the fight against Orion. Hear us out. You don't like what you hear, you're both free to leave. Deal?"

"Fine." He pointed to Jericho. "But if *he* says one more word, I'll—"

Julie squared up to him and pressed a finger against his chest. "You aren't going to do shit. He'll keep his peace. He's a soldier. His priority is the fight. I trust him with my life, and like him or not, so should you. Personal shit aside, if you opened your eyes even slightly, you would see that both of you are frightening similar people. But I swear to Christ, one more *but*... one more snide remark about blaming us for the shit *you* put yourself in, and you won't need to worry about Tristar *or* Orion—because *I'll* kick your fuckin' ass all the way back to Boston! We clear?"

Roach glanced over at Jericho, who simply shrugged and smiled.

He looked back at Julie and nodded. "Fair enough."

Without a word, Julie spun around, causing her light brown ponytail to waft into Roach's face as she walked away from the group.

Roach stepped to Jericho's side, who had already turned to watch Julie leave.

"I can see why you two are together," he said.

Jericho looked at him. "Who says we're together?"

Roach simply raised an eyebrow, half-smiled, and walked away, following the path Julie had just stormed.

Jericho set off after him.

Becky hurried to his side, reaching up to tap his shoulder. When he looked around, she said, "So, not many people talk to my brother like that. And the ones who do usually regret it. That Julie's pretty badass, isn't she?"

He smiled. "Lady... you have *no* idea."

8

ADAM RAYNE

May 11, 2020

The Range Rover slowed as it turned into the compound, then eventually stopped at the security barrier. The tires skidded slightly on the gravel. Adam Rayne rested a hand on the top of the wheel as he buzzed the window down. Beside him, Jessie winced as the heat from outside rushed in, overwhelming the air conditioning.

A guard wearing a GlobaTech combat uniform stepped up to the vehicle and ducked down.

"Can I help you?" he asked. His voice was firm and professional without being confrontational.

"Yeah," replied Rayne. "We're here to see Moses Buchanan."

The guard raised his eyebrow. "Got an appointment?"

"Got an invitation."

"Wait here."

The guard disappeared back inside the large hut, spoke briefly with his colleague, then picked up a phone.

Link was sitting in the back, slumped with legs resting wide, bouncing them impatiently. He leaned forward between the gap in the seats.

"Real friendly bunch, aren't they?" he said.

"Maybe they know we're all ex-military and secretly hate us," said Jessie, shrugging. She then pointed out through the windshield to the beginnings of the sprawling expanse of the compound. "Have you ever seen anything like it, though?"

"I guess this is the big leagues," added Rayne. "And here's the thing, guys. Like you say, we're not military anymore. We work for Adrian. We contract exclusively for the president, and being here... we just got offered a seat at the table, y'know? Let's remember why we're here."

Link sat back. "Since when did you become the diplomatic one?"

Rayne smiled. "Since I started paying attention. Have you ever watched Adrian? Like, really watched him. How he deals with things... how he thinks. Once you look past the character, that guy sees the big picture better than anyone."

Jessie nodded. "Yeah, and when he doesn't, Ruby's there to help him. I know what you're saying. Personally, while I do find it hard to switch off my old reservations about these guys, I still can't shake the feeling that we don't belong here. Like we're out of our depth compared to all this."

"Imposter syndrome," said Link, almost dismissively. "I get it."

Rayne and Jessie shifted in their seats to look back at him, both with looks of surprise and confusion on their faces.

Link shrugged. "What? I have layers."

"Since when?" joked Rayne.

"Since kiss my ass, that's when."

The three of them shared a brief laugh together.

The guard reappeared beside the Range Rover. Rayne turned back in his seat to look at him.

"You're clear," announced the guard. "Take a left up ahead. Follow the signs for visitor parking. Someone will meet you at your vehicle."

"Thanks, pal," said Rayne.

He watched the barriers in front of him slowly rise, then eased through and followed the directions he was given.

Both Jessie and Link looked out of their side windows as they drove through.

"This place is bigger than the town where I grew up," Jessie commented.

A helicopter shot past them overhead, then disappeared behind the buildings in the distance.

"Jesus... is that a SAM site?" asked Link, pointing.

"It is," said Jessie. "But... damn, that shit's nothing like any SAM site I've seen before. And trust me, I helped develop some of the most advanced weapons systems currently used by the Air Force. This place is unreal."

Rayne smiled to himself. He felt the same awe his team-mates did, but he also felt something else that he wasn't sure they shared. He felt excitement. He felt like he had made it.

Being a SEAL was always a dream for him, which he had accomplished at an impressive level. Then, when Adrian recruited him, his eyes had been opened to a bigger world—a bigger fight—and he had embraced it completely. He looked up to Adrian. He admired him and tried to learn from him at every opportunity. But he realized Blackstar was still just a stepping stone in a grander scheme. Now that he was here, driving through the streets of GlobaTech City, he had no doubt that this was his first visit to the major leagues.

Rayne nosed the Range Rover into a vacant space and killed the engine. The three of them got out and stretched, each turning slow circles, taking in the impressive view.

After a couple of minutes, they saw a man appear out of a nearby building and start walking toward them. He was wearing a black tee and camo pants. A handgun was holstered to his right thigh. He was smiling.

"I'm guessing the three of ya are Blackstar, right?" said Collins.

Rayne smiled. "How can you tell?"

Collins pointed to each of their faces, his grin widening.

"I've seen the look of newbies too many times." He extended a fist, which Rayne bumped courteously. "Ray Collins."

Rayne nodded. "Adam Rayne. This is Jessie and Link."

Collins gave a casual salute to each of them. "Truth be told, I've seen all of ya before, technically. I was drafted in to consult with Adrian and the president when they were first putting Blackstar together. I read ya files. Damn impressive."

"Thanks."

Collins looked around. "Speaking of Adrian, where's your boss and his crazy-ass girlfriend?"

Jessie failed to suppress a smile. "They're on their way. They flew in from Paris late last night."

"Our boy's an old romantic, isn't he?"

Link shrugged. "Pretty sure they were going back there to threaten somebody."

"Exactly! To those two maniacs, that's like a candlelit dinner and a moonlit stroll. Come on, I'll take ya up. The others have just arrived. Adrian's a big boy. He knows where he's going."

Collins set off walking back toward the main building.

The skyscraper towered over the compound like a beacon, glowing as the sun reflected off its windows.

Rayne caught up to him, with Jessie and Link close behind.

"So, who else is here?" he asked.

"The rest of my team, Jules and Jerry. Plus, a fella named Roach, who doesn't like people calling him that, despite it sounding way cooler than his actual name."

"Why's that?"

"Honestly? Not sure. After sitting with him most of yesterday, he's definitely not what ya might call a people person. My guess is he ain't fond of anyone being too familiar with him."

"Who is he?" asked Jessie.

"The short version is, he used to work for Tristar Security. Guy got screwed over and left for dead. He survived. Tristar went after his family, and he... well... he didn't take it all that well."

"What did he do?" asked Link.

"He grabbed a shotgun and tore up a building in New York."

Rayne's eyes went wide. "You mean that siege a couple of weeks back? That was him?"

Collins smiled. "Aye."

"Damn. We thought that was you."

"We wish. But no, that was all him. And listen, the fella has a few... trust issues, okay? We need his help, so tread carefully around him. And *definitely* don't flirt with his sister."

Jessie huffed sarcastically. "Well, there goes *my* big introduction."

Collins laughed. "The three of ya are gonna fit in just fine."

Rayne frowned. "Wait. Ray Collins. Aren't you the guy who helped Adrian in Tokyo a few months back?"

"That's me."

"Damn. That shit was intense. We saw what happened to him online."

"Aye. A lot of people did. That left him in a bad way. But holy shit, did he make up for it afterwards."

"You two known each other long?" asked Link.

Collins stopped by the steps leading up to the main entrance, prompting the others to do the same. They stood in a tight square.

"I've known Adrian a few years, yeah. Helped him out a couple of times."

"With what, if you don't mind my asking?" asked Rayne, genuinely curious.

Collins let out a heavy sigh. "Well, first time I met him, I helped sneak him into Pripyat to rescue his girlfriend."

Jessie raised her eyebrows. "Ruby?"

"Nah, this was before her time. His lady friend back then had been taken by a terrorist organization who tried and failed to recruit Adrian. He went to get her back."

"So, what... the two of you walked into a deserted, radioactive city and killed a bunch of terrorists?" asked Link.

Collins shook his head. "No. Adrian did. I just drove him there. Man, was he pissed..."

"Jesus."

Rayne smiled. "I'm not the least bit surprised."

"Aye. Now listen, when we get inside there, ya need to understand tensions are running a little high, okay?"

"Makes sense," said Jessie. "Given everything that's going on, we get it."

Collins nodded. "Right. All I'm saying is... well, I guess I'm asking the three of ya to help keep things calm and friendly. The boss man is hanging on by a thread after everything that's happened around here recently. Jules is pissed and out for blood after the attack two days ago. Jerry is... heh... let's just say Jericho isn't a big fan of Adrian's. They have history, those two, and haven't seen each other in a long time. He isn't thrilled about him being involved here, and to say the guy has been known to exhibit staggering anger issues would be an understatement. Roach is... Roach, I guess. He ain't happy *ever*, as best I can tell. My point is, folks, when we get up there, the four of us will be the only ones not strung out and thinking clearly, if ya can believe that. I need ya to help me keep things productive in there, okay?"

Rayne nodded. "You got it, man. We're just here to help. Any way we can."

"Happy to hear it. Now come on. Time's a-wasting."

Collins turned and headed up the steps. Rayne followed quickly behind him.

Jessie and Link glanced at each other and raised matching eyebrows.

"This sounds like it'll be fun," said Link quietly.

Jessie shook her head. "You ask me, this sounds like a disaster waiting to happen."

9

BRANDON CROW

May 11, 2020

The crowded control room was unnervingly quiet, save for the familiar rattle of the air conditioning. Crow stood by the center console, leaning forward with his palms spread on the surface. The 2D holographic display showed a topographical map of the United States. He stared intently at the heavy scattering of large dots as they flashed and moved across it.

The late spring heat penetrated the mountain base with ease, adding to the discomfort in the air. Crow's tie was loose around his neck, with the top button of his sweat-stained shirt unfastened. The sleeves were rolled unevenly up his forearms.

His steady breathing masked the anxiety that was crushing his chest. The ability to hide his emotions came from years of top-level boardroom meetings, having spent most of his adult life climbing the corporate ladder. Rule number one was to never show weakness to your peers. He lived in a world of sharks, and every day he had to make sure they never got the scent of blood.

But today he was struggling.

Fear of letting Hall down, combined with the gravity of what the day would bring, meant he was teetering on the edge of his own sanity. For the first time in his life, he felt genuinely intimidated.

Beside him, Jay stood quietly. Her strong, toned arms were folded across her chest as she watched him. She understood what today meant for him. For all of them. A smile crept across her face.

Today would see the enemy fall.

"How are we looking?" she asked eventually.

Crow took a deep breath. "I think we're ready."

"You think?"

He straightened and turned to her. His accusatory glare immediately softened when he saw the icy gaze looking back at him.

"We're ready," he said, turning back to the table. "Everyone's in place. It's taken weeks, but every unit is where it needs to be."

"And the men here?"

Crow nodded. "Ready to deploy the moment we have the order."

"Good. So, now we wait."

Jay walked away, turning her back on Crow. She moved to look down through the large window at the mountain base below them, teeming with people and bustling with activity and purpose.

Crow knew her thirst for vengeance against GlobaTech and Roach would be eating her up inside. But he also knew he could guarantee her loyalty. Not to the cause. Not to Orion or Tristar. To him.

He moved to her side. "We both know the goal here. We know how Hall envisions this playing out. But I want you to know, come Hell or high water, I'll see to it you have your chance to get even with GlobaTech."

Jay shook her head, curling her lip into a sneer. "I don't want to get even with them, Brandon. I want to fucking destroy them."

Crow nodded. She rarely called him Brandon and almost never did it in front of people. The benefit of working so hard to hide his own emotions was gaining the ability to recognize the same struggle in others.

"And we will," he said. "You have my word."

She turned away, remaining by his side as she faced the room. She discreetly placed a hand on his arm and leaned close. "And I give you mine... whatever happens after today... I won't let anyone, including Hall, come after you."

Jay paced over to the table, scanning the room for anyone who might have been watching their exchange. Everyone appeared busy, distracted by their own tasks.

Crow stared out at the large hangar, absently watching two Tristar operatives loading weapons into the back of an attack helicopter. A beep in his pocket distracted him. He reached inside and took out his phone, staring at the message alert on his screen. He wandered over to Jay and showed it to her. The message read:

The final piece will be in place within the hour. It's time.

Jay looked at him. "So, is this it?"

Crow nodded. "This is it."

He slid the phone back into his pocket and took a deep breath. He reached for a thin microphone that stood in front of a small communications panel on the center console. He held the base in his hand, his thumb hovering over the button that would activate it. He flicked a couple of switches, opening all channels, then moved the microphone to his lips. After one final breath, he pressed the button.

"Attention all Tristar personnel. This is Brandon Crow. I am addressing each and every one of you together for the first and only time. Whether you're with me on base or positioned around the country, listen up.

"Our mission began almost three years ago. In that time, our numbers and influence have grown, and we've been able to achieve the unthinkable as we patiently built to this moment. But our mission has always been part of a much larger one. For longer than many of you will ever know, a small, dedicated group of people has strategized and worked toward a single, extraordinary goal. The culmination of everything everyone has worked for—and sacrificed for—is today.

"You are all part of something bigger than yourself. Every man and woman wearing a Tristar uniform will be remembered. Today is the day this great country of ours changes forever. Today is the day the citizens of the United States get back the country our forefathers promised them. Today... is the day we make history."

He paused as the people in the control room with him began clapping and cheering. Below him, across the busy expanse of the hangar, the roar of personnel doing the same rang out in the air.

Crow looked at Jay and saw the fire in her eyes. A menacing smile spread across her face as she saw the conviction in his.

"Today is the day you have all been waiting for," he continued. "Today you take the fight to the real enemy. To the real threat to our freedom. Today, you fight to take back our country... to protect it from the horrors and the tyranny of the world... to rebuild it and strengthen it, so our republic stands strong for future generations. You are ready. You must stay strong, face the fight head-on, and remember why you're doing this and who you're doing it for."

He paused again as more cheering erupted around him.

He turned to look down at the hangar. The hundreds of men and women had stopped to show their admiration and respect for the man who had orchestrated everything Tristar had done to get to that moment.

Crow held up a hand and watched them settle.

He took a long, patient breath, savoring the moment. He pressed the button on the microphone one last time.

"Go."

The people below him scrambled into action. Squads of men and women dressed in combat gear moved with rehearsed efficiency toward the fleet of vehicles parked around the hangar. Jeeps and choppers revved into life.

Crow was overcome with adrenaline. He had commanded every boardroom he had ever entered... owned every meeting... won every negotiation. But nothing had ever come close to the feeling he had right now, having just ordered half a million dedicated, highly trained operatives and mercenaries to fight for their country.

"You did it," whispered Jay, who had appeared beside him.

"*We* did it," he countered. "Thank you."

She shook her head. "Don't go soft on me now. You have a war to win."

He looked over at her. "And you have people to kill."

They shared a smile. Their relationship had developed over the years to be platonic, almost familial. Jay always respected the fact that he was in charge, but he had never regarded her as a subordinate. To him, she was as close to an equal as he had ever allowed. Crow had nurtured her thirst for violence and turned her into the most feared body-guard his organization had. She would be by his side throughout everything that was to come.

"We should go," she said. "We need to be on the road within the hour."

Crow nodded. "I know. Is everything ready?"

"They're fueling up as we speak."

"Good. It's important that we're mobile when the attack begins."

Crow took one last look at the hangar, which already started to empty, then headed for the door. Jay followed closely behind.

10

MOSES BUCHANAN

May 11, 2020

Buchanan stood behind his desk patiently, looking at the room with a hard frown etched onto his face. His corner office was big—a space befitting a man in his position. But he had never seen it so crowded.

On his left, over by the windows, Julie and Jericho rested against the glass, arms folded, motionless. While Julie appeared relaxed and focused, Jericho looked resentful. He stared down at the plush, maroon carpet with unblinking eyes. His breathing was heavy, visibly moving his massive chest slowly up and down.

In front of him, Collins was standing quietly—a first for him, Buchanan mused. His eyes darted left and right, surveying the palpable tension. Next to him, Roach and his sister stood quietly. He, too, didn't appear thrilled to be there. His eyes never left Buchanan's, and his mouth was pressed into an impatient line. Becky's eyes glowed, alive with excitement and apprehension.

On the right, over by the door, stood Blackstar. Buchanan was glad to have their assistance. He found it interesting to see the obvious dynamic they had formed, and he couldn't help but draw comparisons to his own team. Rayne stood in the middle and a step ahead of the others. He was clearly the unspoken leader of the trio. Jessie was by his right shoulder. He took her for Rayne's number two. She was the voice of reason. At the back, Link matched Jericho's posture, and while his physique wasn't quite the size of Jericho's, it was no less impressive. His dark eyes contrasted against his caramel skin, and the definition on his arms was insane. He was the enforcer.

Buchanan smiled, if only to mask his frustration at the tense silence coming from all sides of his office. This was exactly what he had been afraid would happen. Collins had walked them in moments earlier, and no one had said anything. He had nodded a curt greeting to the room before walking over to Roach, leaving the new arrivals by the door, trying not to appear awkward. They carried themselves well, but Buchanan knew that wouldn't last forever. He needed them all on the same page. Everyone deserved to be there.

Finally, Buchanan cleared his throat, drawing the attention of the room.

"Okay, quick introductions." He gestured to his right. "Adam Rayne, Jessie Vickers, Lincoln March... thank you for coming." He swept a hand counterclockwise. "This is who you will be working with. Ray Collins, you've met. This is Julie Fisher and Jericho Stone, the final two-thirds of my own elite trio."

Casual waves and salutes were extended by Blackstar collectively. Julie returned the gesture. Jericho simply nodded.

Buchanan sighed before continuing. "With Mr. Collins is William Roachford and his sister, Rebecca."

Becky looked over and smiled. "Call me Becky."

Rayne nodded, then pointed behind him with his thumb.

"I'm Adam. This is Jessie and Link. It's a pleasure." He took a step forward into the center of the room and turned to face Roach. "So, you're Roach, huh? Nice to meet you, man."

Roach said nothing but adjusted his gaze slightly to stare at him. Rayne hesitated, confused by the lack of reaction.

Becky leaned forward. "He... ah... he doesn't really like people calling him Roach."

Rayne frowned but kept eye contact with him. "Why? It's a badass nickname. Better than Billy, or whatever."

Roach gave an almost imperceptible shake of his head. "Don't call me Billy, either."

Rayne shrugged. "You got it, chief. So, that was you, back in New York a couple of weeks ago?"

"Yeah."

"Damn. I'm a big fan! Glad you're on our side."

Rayne extended a hand, smiling. Roach didn't move until Becky nudged his arm and glared at him. Then he shook it.

"Happy to be working with you," Rayne continued, then turned to face Jericho and Julie. "And you guys were us before we were, right? I've heard great things about you. Thanks for the invite."

Julie stepped to meet him and extended her hand, which he shook gladly. "Glad you accepted. We need all the help we can get right now, and from what I hear, you guys are a force of your own."

"Ah, we do okay. We had a good teacher."

Julie smiled. Behind her, Jericho grunted.

Rayne looked over at him. "You good over there, big guy?"

Jericho pushed himself away from the window and moved to Julie's side.

Rayne tilted his head slightly to look him in the eye. "Jesus... you're a fucking unit, aren't you? Bet you're handy in a fight."

Jericho raised an eyebrow. "Like you wouldn't believe."

Rayne smiled. "Talk about a dream team! Bad guys don't stand a chance."

"Shame some of the bad guys are on our side..."

The two men held each other's gaze. Silence fell, pulled around them by the statement like a blanket.

"Say what you wanna say, man," said Rayne, frowning. "We're all friends here."

Jericho straightened his shoulders, using every one of the six inches he had over him. "I'm saying I don't think we are, and I don't like your boss. I also don't trust the people who work for him."

Behind his desk, Buchanan closed his eyes, pinching the bridge of his nose between thumb and forefinger.

In a flash, Jessie and Link moved to Rayne's side. Julie squared up beside Jericho.

"Hey, we're here to help, okay?" said Rayne, fighting the urge to raise his voice. "We're all on the same side."

Jericho shrugged. "Are we?"

Rayne stepped up to him. "I don't appreciate—"

Collins pushed his way between them and turned to face Jericho. "Hey, Jerry, what did we talk about? Play nice."

Jericho rolled his eyes and stepped back. Julie moved with him.

Collins turned to face Rayne. "New guy... ya ever see *Star Wars*?"

Rayne shrugged. "Yeah..."

"Ya remember that bit on the Millennium Falcon, when the robot's playing chess with Chewbacca?"

"Yeah."

Collins smiled patiently and placed a hand on Rayne's shoulder. "Let the Wookie win, dude."

Rayne went to reply, but Collins glared at him, silently reminding him that they were supposed to be the calm ones.

Rayne nodded. "Fine. But just so you know..." He looked at Jericho over Collins's shoulder. "You keep acting like that to your friends, the enemy won't even break a sweat. And for the record, next time you get up in my face for no reason... I got a Wookie of my own."

Behind him, Link flicked his head toward Jericho, his face deadpan.

Jericho ignored him.

Collins breathed a heavy sigh of relief. "Okay, well, that was fun, eh?"

Everyone stepped away, moving back to their original positions. As Rayne turned, he smiled at Buchanan and winked. Buchanan smiled back, silently acknowledging the effort he had made to break the ice, despite how badly it turned out.

"This was a mistake," muttered Roach, leaning toward Becky.

Buchanan moved around his desk and perched on the edge, folding his arms across his barrel chest. "Okay, now that you've all got the testosterone out of your system, can we get down to business? You all know why you're here, right?"

There was a murmur of agreement.

"Tristar has been a thorn in all our sides for a while. It's time we put a stop to it. Problem is, we're pretty sure Orion is pulling their strings, which means it isn't going to be that easy. Julie?"

Julie stepped forward. "Jericho and I have been working to find out who manufactured the bullet that was used to kill President Herrera and three of our guys. We know Tristar is manufacturing weapons now, and we know they supplied the Palugan army with the tools to start the coup there last week, but so far, we've got zero solid leads."

"What's so special about this bullet, exactly?" asked Jessie.

"It's tech we've never seen before. Uses some kind of miniaturized propulsion system, which is how one round managed to drill its way through four people from five hundred yards away."

The Blackstar trio exchanged a worried look.

"Surely, it was Tristar?" asked Becky. "If they make weapons, it's not exactly a stretch..."

Julie nodded. "Personally, I think you're right. The problem is, there's no proof. No paper trail. No nothing. Ignoring for a moment the issue of them getting into the weapons manufacturing game without anyone knowing in the first place... making them is one thing, but revolutionary technology like this is something else altogether. Believe me, we know."

"So, how do we know it wasn't you?" said Roach.

The question caught everyone off-guard, and the heartbeat of silence that followed it was claustrophobic.

"Care to explain what you mean by that, Mr. Roachford?" Buchanan asked, narrowing his gaze at him.

Roach shrugged. "I mean, your company is shady as shit,

even if you like playing the good guys for the media. Wasn't it just a few years ago when GlobaTech Industries was making arms deals with terrorists?"

All eyes turned to Buchanan, who ignored the sudden spotlight.

He nodded. "GlobaTech's history hasn't always been something to be proud of it. That's no secret, and I'll happily admit it. But since 4/17—and even before that—we flushed out the cancer that was eating away at the heart of this company. We turned everything around and started working to help people, which we've become extremely good at, Mr. Roachford. While we still manufacture weapons and technology here, we no longer have contracts to sell any of it to other parties. Wherever this bullet came from, it wasn't us. And believe me, I would love for it to be something we developed, but the truth is, our top weapons experts and designers are completely baffled by it. Whoever made it, they're lightyears ahead of what we're capable of. Frankly, that scares the hell out of me."

"Can I see it?" asked Jessie. "I helped develop and test drone technology when I was with the Air Force. Maybe I can help?"

Buchanan nodded. "I'll make arrangements for you to sit with Devon. He's our expert who's been trying to figure that thing out. I'm sure he'll appreciate any insight you can offer. Thank you."

Jessie nodded.

Becky looked at Julie. "And what about Orion? Where do they come into all this?"

Julie screwed her face up with frustration. "That's what we're trying to figure out. We know they own Tristar, and we're almost certain they were behind everything that happened in Paluga... and what happened to us. But again, there's no solid proof. If they *are* pulling all the strings, they're irritatingly good at covering their tracks."

Roach huffed.

"Something to add?" she asked him.

He shook his head. "No. I just find it funny how angry you get at people who do what you guys have been doing for years."

Julie rolled her eyes. "I told you what would happen if you didn't stow that shit, *Roach*. It's time you either got on board or got the hell out of here and stopped wasting our goddamn time."

Roach moved to take a step forward, but Becky placed a hand on his arm, stopping him.

"Don't," she said. "Please."

He backed down, choosing to remain silent.

Rayne looked over at him and raised his hand. "Listen, man, I get that you're pissed at these guys over everything that happened, but I gotta ask... why did you take the fight to Tristar if you hate GlobaTech so much?"

Roach regarded him. "Because wrong is wrong, regardless of who's doing it. I don't like people who go out of their way to do bad shit to others."

"Fair enough." Rayne thought for a moment, then frowned. "Speaking of bad shit... how, *exactly,* are you not in prison after what you did?"

"Because we stepped in and protected his ungrateful ass," said Jericho.

Roach glared over at him, but he ignored it.

"We got there minutes after the NYPD and the FBI did," continued Jericho. "We bullshitted them into believing *whoever did this* was working to help us with an ongoing investigation for the U.N. They bought it long enough for us to get in there and remove the security footage, and for *him* to make his escape."

"Huh." Rayne shrugged. "Well, it seems to me, *William*, you'd be up Shit Creek without a paddle if it weren't for these guys. Like 'em or not, if that ain't proof we're on the same team, I don't know what is."

Roach grunted at him. "Doesn't mean I have to like them."

"I honestly don't care if you do or don't," said Buchanan. "The enemy is at our door, folks. We're short on time and even shorter on options, so here's what's going to happen. My guys are going to keep looking for where that bullet came from, as well as anything that links Orion to all this."

"And we're going after the shooter from Paluga, right?" asked Link.

Buchanan nodded. "You are. We know she is a solid link between Tristar and the assassination. Hopefully, she might shed some light on the bigger picture. Give us something we can tie to Orion."

"Consider it done," said Rayne.

"Watch yourselves with her," offered Roach. "Half this room has fought her to a stalemate at some point. She's a lot to handle. Crazy bitch even tried sleeping with me during a fistfight."

Collins shot Julie a preemptive glare to keep quiet. She smiled at him discreetly but said nothing.

"Really?" said Rayne. He looked at Jessie, laughing. "Hey, if that's how she fights, maybe *you* should go after her."

Jessie rolled her eyes. "Jesus..."

He continued chuckling to himself.

"So, what do you want me to do?" Roach asked Buchanan.

"I want you to find Brandon Crow," he replied. "Maybe

this Jay is with him. Maybe she's not. But she made sure he's alive, which means he's either still running Tristar, or he's the best person to ask who is."

Roach nodded. "Good. I owe that piece of shit too."

Buchanan stood and moved to the middle of the room. He turned a slow semicircle, looking at everyone in turn.

"Look, I understand this fight is personal to everyone, myself included. But I need you to understand that what's happening right now is bigger than any vendettas you might have... both inside this room and beyond." He nodded to Roach. "Young man, your ability to wage a one-man war on just about anybody who pisses you off is impressive, but I need your word that, should you find Crow, you will refrain from tearing his head off. We need him alive."

"Of course," said Roach. "There's plenty I want to ask him myself."

"Good." Buchanan looked over at Blackstar. "The same with you three. Jay is a formidable adversary. A killer without a conscience. I appreciate it'll be difficult to apprehend someone who is going out of their way to kill you, but you need to make sure she's brought in alive."

"We'll get it done," said Rayne.

"Thank you. Now, is your boss going to grace us with his presence at any point? This meeting wasn't optional, and he needs to know what we're doing. Regardless of his opinion on the matter, the rules *do* actually apply to him, as well."

Before Rayne had the chance to reply, there was a sharp knock on the door. Everyone looked around as it opened. Kim Mitchell appeared and stood to the side, holding the door open. She glanced apologetically at Buchanan. Adrian and Ruby stepped past her and moved inside the office. Both took a moment to look around.

Adrian smiled. "So, this is where the party is."

11

ADRIAN HELL

May 11, 2020

Christ, you could cut the tension in here with a knife. Everyone's staring at me. If this were any other room, I would say they were all staring at Ruby because... y'know... it's Ruby. But no, this time, it's all eyes on little old me.

Ruby and I arrived a few minutes ago and made our way up here. Kim, the secretary, greeted us and said there's been a lot of raised voices and posturing in here, from what she could tell. She suggested I open with an apology for being late.

I like Kim. I met her once a few years back, when I came here to see Josh. I got the impression that she was to him what he had always been to me: the unwavering lifeline that helped retain order and sanity in an otherwise hectic existence.

As she knocked on the door, Ruby had leaned close to me and whispered for me to be nice. I don't know why she would think I needed someone to say that to me. I'm always nice...

Then we stepped inside and here we are.

I look around the room. No offense to Moses, but I can't see this as anything other than Josh's office, and it takes me a moment to feel comfortable being here again.

Speaking of Moses, he doesn't look happy to see me.

"Nice of you to join us," he says.

I smile. "Yeah, sorry I'm late. Traffic was a nightmare."

"You know we have a runway for private jets here, right?"

"Well, I didn't want to assume we were ready to take things to that level, Moses..."

He shakes his head and rolls his eyes, then steps to meet me, extending his hand. I shake it gladly.

"Thanks for coming," he says.

I nod. "No problem. I'm happy to help."

"You do everything you needed to in Paris?"

"I hope so."

The team's here. Rayne looks at me apologetically. I dread to think what he's said or done. He's getting more like me than I am. I see Collins in the opposite corner, next to two people I don't know. I'm guessing that's the new guy and his sister.

I look ahead and see the reason why the room is parted like the Red Sea marching toward me. Beside me, I feel Ruby move back a couple of steps. I plant my feet and take a steady breath, keeping eye contact with Jericho Stone as he approaches. He stops a couple of feet in front of me.

The collective intake of breath pulls every last sound from the room, leaving a deafening silence that envelops us.

I forgot how big the guy is. His tattooed arms look like anacondas, with hands like footballs stuck to the end. They're both currently balled up into fists that look like they would punch through a brick wall and make the building cry.

He hasn't blinked since he stepped close to me. I note the different colored eyes. Must be a side effect of GlobaTech's handiwork. Suits him.

I smile at him. "Hey, big guy. Sorry I'm late."

His eyes narrow slightly. "Don't bother apologizing. I'm sorry you're here at all."

"Ooh, *sassy!*" I gesture to my own brow, then nod toward the faint scar stretching across his. "How's the head?"

"Fine. How are you? I see the lethal injection didn't stick. Shame."

"Yeah, being dead isn't really my thing. Too boring. I like to keep busy."

"Well, feel free to keep busy somewhere else. We don't need you here."

I sigh. "All right. While I could happily stand here flirting with you all day, if you got something to say to me, say it. I ain't got the time or patience to start arguing with people I'm supposed to be helping."

"I didn't ask for your help, asshole."

"No, your boss did."

He casts a disapproving glance at Buchanan. "Well, if I had been consulted about it beforehand, I would've made damn sure you weren't a part of this. You or your team."

"And why's that, exactly?"

"Because I don't know you, and I don't trust you. I mean, *Blackstar*... seriously? Sounds a lot like Tristar to me."

I shrug. "We're basically the same, except we listen to more My Chemical Romance."

In the corner, Collins lets slip a small chuckle.

Jericho shakes his head. "You think this is funny? We don't need you here."

"Really? That's not what I heard. I figured GlobaTech has finally realized they need to start compensating for the weak links on their roster."

"Meaning?"

I point at Ray. "Meaning, I know him—he's useful." I point behind him toward Julie. "I've spoken with her before, and she helped." Finally, I point at him. "Then there's you. A seven-foot poster boy my best friend plucked from the scrap heap because you look good in a uniform. Tell me, what are you bringing to the table? Besides steroids..."

"I'm bringing plenty. Go ask the people of Paluga."

I frown. "Who?"

"And *that's* my point. Right there. You have no business being here. You're an uneducated, trigger-happy psychopath, and in case you hadn't noticed, your best friend ain't around anymore to justify you. So, watch yourself."

I take a quick breath to remind myself I'm not allowed to shoot anyone.

I take a small step closer to him, adjusting my gaze to keep eye contact. "If I were you, I'd be real careful about how you speak about Josh in front of me."

Jericho steps toward me, so our chests are almost touching. "And if *I* were *you*, I'd take a few steps back while you still can."

"Or... what?"

"Or I'll make you."

I smile. "Heh. I kinda wanna see you try, *Hercules*."

We both take one step backward, giving ourselves enough room to start swinging.

This is a really bad idea.

Satan... I'll be fine. Right, Josh?

Adrian, that man will rip your spleen out through your ears. Don't do it.

Nah, I'll be fine. I'm going to need to kick him in the balls, though. I know it's a shitty move, but my voices of inner reason are right. If he manages to connect with one of those big-ass fists of his, I'm going to land somewhere in Oklahoma.

Fuck it.

I begin to pull my right shoulder back, but I'm stopped by a sudden flurry of movement in the room. Rayne, Jessie, and Link rush toward me, push me back, and put themselves between Jericho and me. Collins and Julie do the same, struggling to move Jericho away, toward the windows opposite me.

A moment later, Buchanan steps into the middle of the room. "All right, enough! Jesus Christ... we have enough people trying to kill us without you two giving them a helping hand. Knock it off. Now."

I feel the room sizzle back to life. I hold my hands up to my team, signaling I'm calm.

"You good?" asks Rayne.

I nod. "I'm fine."

"Good. Because he looked like he was going to kill you."

I raise my eyebrow to him. "Gee, thanks for the vote of confidence there, Buttercup."

He shrugs. "Just saying..."

I look around to find Ruby. I see her walking over to the far corner, heading for the two new people.

She extends a hand to the woman. "Hey. I'm Ruby."

"Becky," she replies, shaking it. "This is my brother, Will."

Ruby offers her hand to him, which he also shakes.

"Your boyfriend's either real brave or real stupid," he says to her.

She smiles. "Yeah, the jury's been out on that one for a while, if I'm honest."

She walks back toward me, smiling patiently.

"You finished making friends?" I ask.

"Well, you weren't gonna do it, grumpy pants."

"*Grumpy*—" I sigh. "Do you mind?"

She shrugs, grinning. "Not in the least."

"Jesus..."

Buchanan looks back and forth between Jericho and me. "Are we good here, gentlemen?"

Jericho huffs but says nothing.

I nod. "I'm good, but I gotta say—"

Ruby tugs at my arm as I move toward the middle of the room. "Adrian... leave it, please."

I shrug her free and look into Jericho's eyes. "I know you don't like me, Jericho. I know when we first met, we were on opposite sides of a grade-one shitstorm. But even back then, you trusted your own instincts enough to hear me out, despite having me on my knees and holding a gun to my head. Not only was I right then, but I also saved your life. You'd be decomposing on a Colombian runway if it weren't for me and Josh. You might think I'm the bad guy. That I'm the enemy. *Your* enemy. But I'm not, man. I'm no saint. I'll admit that. But I'm not the person you think I am. After four years of us both trying to save the world from evil bastards, maybe it's time you accepted that and moved on."

Another silence falls on the room. Jericho pushes through the barrier Julie and Collins are trying to maintain and steps to meet me. This time, he stays a little farther away. I feel Buchanan tense next to us.

He looks at me. "You're right."

"I... I am?" I frown, confused. "Huh."

I honestly didn't expect that little speech to work.

He shrugs. "Yeah. I *don't* like you."

His mouth twitches at one side. The movement was barely visible to the naked eye and lasted about as long as a hiccup, but I'm pretty sure he just tried to smile.

Heh. Sonofabitch.

I nod once and step back. He does the same.

No one in the room even tries to mask their sighs of relief.

I look at Buchanan. "So, what did I miss?"

He rolls his eyes, then reaches behind him to pick up a photograph, which he hands to me. "This is Jay. She's the shooter from Paluga. She's also Brandon Crow's head of security, *and* she's the one who has survived encounters with half the people in this room... more than once."

I take the photo from him and stare at it. "So, she's Tristar, right?"

"She is."

I turn the photo so Buchanan can see it. "You got a better picture? I can't see most of her face, and what I *can* see is blurry because of the distance between her and the camera."

He shakes his head. "That's the best shot of her we have. Taken from the security footage we confiscated from New York."

"Ah, yeah, the siege that was on the news." I look over at the new guy. "That was you, right?"

He nods but says nothing. I look him up and down, trying to get a read on him. Similar height and build to me. Deadpan expression, like he resents the hell out of being here. Looks like he can handle himself.

I step over to him and extend my fist. "I'm Adrian."

I see him looking me up and down, likely doing exactly

what I just did. After a moment, he bumps my fist with his and curls his lips into a half-smile. "Roach."

I'm guessing the woman next to him is his sister. She's staring at him with her mouth open in obvious surprise. Don't know why.

I turn back to Buchanan. "Let me ask you something. Is this Jay employed by Tristar directly, or is she a contractor they have on their books?"

He shrugs. "I don't know. Does it matter?"

Ruby moves to my side. She looks at me, then lets out a heavy sigh. "Yeah, it kinda does."

"Why?" asks Julie, frowning.

I look over at her. "Because if she's an assassin, that's going to cause a serious problem. People in that world... *my* world... we have a strict code about going after each other. Namely, we don't. Ever."

"Are you serious?" asks Jericho.

I nod. "Deadly. Trust me, I just got through fighting half of Paris because I was looking for an assassin. I wasn't even trying to kill the guy. I just wanted to talk to him. But I still had to get permission from a high-ranking member of the underworld to do it. He's what we call a controller. People like him police the global assassin community. Anyway, the problem was, because I was retired, there was nothing stopping every assassin in the city from coming after me, trying to make a name for themselves."

"What does any of that have to do with this?" asks Buchanan.

I look back at him. "Now that I'm working with Blackstar, I figured that's unlikely to be the only time I'll ever need to talk to an assassin, so I... unretired myself. That's what I was doing in Paris."

He closed his eyes and sighed. "Which means..."

"Which means if this Jay *is* an assassin, as opposed to a Tristar employee, I can't go after her without bringing the entire underworld down on me... and on everyone in this room."

Jericho huffs. "That's your problem. She's *your* target. We've all got our own shit to deal with, which you'd know if you'd bothered to show up on time."

I smile humorlessly at him. "Well, as nice as it is to see you being a team player, that's where you're wrong." My smile fades. "It's a problem for all of us because we're all in this together, and it won't take long for every killer in the world to figure that out. Like me or not, big guy, you know who I am and what I'm capable of. Imagine a thousand of me, all dedicating their every waking moment to hunting you. Every one of us in here would be dead within twelve hours, leaving us no use to anyone."

Ruby turns to Buchanan. "Can we get more intel on her? Maybe find out something more solid before we go after her?"

He shakes his head. "That picture and the firsthand accounts from the people in here are all we have. The woman's a ghost. A deadly, violent ghost. Whether she's an assassin or not, our only option is to send a snake to catch a snake. You're it."

Ruby turns to me and places a hand on my arm. "Adrian, what if... what if you sit this one out?"

My brow creases. "What do you mean?"

"I mean, these past couple of weeks would've played out differently if you had taken a step back and let the team do what we hired them to do. You're overdue some recuperation after Tokyo anyway. You know that. If you're not a part of this... if *we're* not a part of this... it won't matter who this Jay is. The team is more than capable of tracking her and bringing her in, and we won't be jeopardizing the mission with our involvement."

Buchanan appears beside us. "She has a point, Adrian. I saw you in the hospital. Frankly, it's a miracle you're alive. And since then, you've spent five months at full speed working with Blackstar. Maybe you *should* think about sitting this one out."

I feel a hand on my shoulder. I turn to see Jessie smiling at me.

"We've got this, boss," she says softly. "You trained us well, and we have Adam coordinating things in the field. You know we're good."

Link nods. "She's right, Adrian."

I look at Rayne. "And what do you think, *Mini Me*?"

He smiles. "I think you're more use to us when you're a hundred percent. We kicked ass in Rome, but it took it out of all of us. Listen, I'll back you without question every time, but if you're asking my honest opinion, I'm with these guys on this one. You're burned out physically and mentally. Way more than any of us. Especially after Paris. This isn't going to be the only fight. We can manage without you in the first quarter, man. It's the fourth when we'll need you, y'know."

I nod slowly and look around the room, aware of every pair of eyes currently staring at me. Roach and his sister seem impassive. Collins flicks his eyebrow at me, silently telling me that he thinks everyone has a point. Jericho has the worst poker face ever, and he's clearly still arguing with himself about not being mad at me anymore.

Whatever.

Next to him, Julie's staring at me. Her eyes are moving all around, as if trying to get a read on both me and the team. Perhaps trying to understand the dynamic. Perhaps drawing inevitable comparisons to her own unit.

But then my attention is pulled away by a strange sight behind her, outside. Through the window, I see a large helicopter landing in the middle of the compound. I don't recall seeing a helipad out there, but I guess that doesn't really matter, given who's inside the chopper.

"You okay?" asks Ruby.

I realize I've been quiet a little longer than would be expected.

I look at her and nod. "Yeah. Sorry. I was just thinking, whoever's playing GlobaTech Bingo is about to get a full house."

She frowns. "What do you mean?"

I point out the window. Everyone turns just as Marine One disappears out of my line of sight. Murmurs ripple around the room.

It would appear the president has arrived.

I look at Buchanan, raising a quizzical eyebrow.

He stares back at me, pressing his mouth into a frustrated line. "Well, shit…"

12

MOSES BUCHANAN

May 11, 2020

Buchanan moved behind his desk, leaned forward slightly, and rested his palms flat on the surface. He stared blankly at the space between them.

Thank God for my corner office, he thought.

It was about to get even more crowded in here. He refocused and watched the powder keg of ego and ability before him. There was a buzz in the room. He didn't think it was excitement. For the most part, he suspected adrenaline. Schultz coming here made this whole thing real for many of them.

Except Roach's sister.

Buchanan frowned as his gaze rested on her. The color had drained from her face. She had stepped away from her brother and was leaning against the far wall, doubled over and holding her stomach.

"Becky, are you okay?" asked Buchanan.

The room fell silent as everyone turned their collective

attention to her. Roach looked around, then moved to her side and placed a hand on her shoulder.

"Hey, what is it?" he asked.

Her breathing was loud and rapid, resembling hyper-ventilation. She looked up at her brother, ignoring everyone else.

"The... the... p-president?" Her eyes grew wide with each word she managed to form. "The president is... is... here?"

Roach narrowed his eyes, confused. "Yeah, apparently. You okay?"

She stood straight, glared at Roach, then smacked his shoulder as her frustration neutralized her nerves. "Do I look okay? How are you so calm? The president of the United States is going to walk through that door any minute, and I'm standing here in leggings and a hoodie with three holes in it! I haven't brushed my hair in, like, two days, for Christ's sake!"

The room exchanged glances of surprise, trying to hold back well-intentioned smiles.

Ruby nudged Jessie with her elbow, then gestured toward Becky with a subtle nod. Jessie nodded back, under-standing the unspoken request, then looked across the room at Julie, who was already staring at them, clearly thinking the same thing.

The three women walked over and congregated around Becky, who looked up through teary eyes at the warm smiles from a natural sisterhood.

Jessie looked at Roach. "You. Move. We got this."

Roach held his hands up and stepped away, knowing better than to say anything.

Ruby put her arm around Becky and hugged her to her side. "Hey, it'll be all right. Schultz is just a guy. He looks like a short, asthmatic John Goodman vacationed in a donut factory. Nothing to be intimidated by."

Becky giggled, sniffed back the emotion, then nodded eagerly. "Thank you."

Julie smiled at her. "We got you, girl. Don't worry."

The three of them huddled around Becky and began fussing over her hair.

Roach had moved over to the window, standing between Collins and Jericho. They moved closer to Buchanan's desk, giving the women some respectful distance. Adrian, Rayne, and Link did the same on the opposite side.

Collins looked over at Jericho. "Hey, Jerry... how come ya never offer to do my hair?"

Jericho rolled his eyes. "Because you can't polish a turd, Ray."

Rayne laughed, then turned to look at Adrian, raising an eyebrow questioningly.

Adrian shook his head. "You offer to do my nails, I swear to God, I will shoot you right in the face."

Buchanan sighed. "Please don't. I'd rather you didn't get blood on my desk."

"Nah. I only get blood on Schultz's desk," he replied, smiling.

"Christ. Can we all focus, please?" Buchanan looked over at the women. "If you're finished, ladies?"

Ruby, Jessie, and Julie moved away, revealing a transformed Becky. Her hair was straight. The hoodie was tied around her waist, revealing the sleeveless tee she had on underneath. Her face was clean, with no evidence she had ever shed a tear.

Collins arched his brow, unable to hide his surprise. "Damn, girl. Ya look great! Nice work, ladies."

Roach shoved his arm. "Hey. What did I tell you about flirting with my sister?"

"Ya said ya would knock my lungs out my ass," said Collins with resignation. "But I wasn't flirting. I was just saying... she looks great. Women like to be told that kinda stuff."

Julie walked over to them and looked at Roach. "He's right. We do. Besides, Ray's about as subtle as a battering ram. His flirting tends to be more... direct. You'd know it if he was."

Roach rolled his eyes. "Whatever."

Just then, the door to Buchanan's office flew open. Usually, Kim would be the first to appear, showing any visitors in, but given the guest, she had little say in whether or not they walked in.

Two Secret Service agents stormed in, quickly looked around the room, then took up position on either side of the door. Their matching black suits were stretched across their bulky frames. Earpieces sat in place on the side of their heads.

President Schultz entered the room, followed by two more agents. He nodded a curt greeting to Buchanan, who returned the gesture. He then spent a moment eyeballing everyone in the room.

"Oh my God!" shouted Becky through a loud laugh, which she couldn't help and instantly regretted.

The image Ruby had painted for her was fresh in her mind and surprisingly accurate. She clasped both hands over her mouth as all eyes focused on her.

Julie suppressed a small smile.

Becky looked at Schultz. "I am... *so* sorry, Mr. President, sir."

Schultz stared at her impassively. "Right. I don't know

who you are, little lady, and now ain't the time for introductions." He addressed the room. "The rest of you know exactly who I am, so I'm gonna cut right to it. Has Moses here told you what we're up against?"

Buchanan stood straight. "I have, sir."

"Good. Tristar—and by association, Orion—have both been on our radar for a while. Perhaps longer than any of you realize. Those sonsofbitches are up to something, and we're gonna find out what it is and stop it. Whatever it takes. Am I clear?"

Jericho took a breath, stretching to his full height and width. "Crystal, sir."

Schultz looked at him, then walked over and extended a hand. Jericho shook it with honor.

"Incredible work in Paluga, soldier," said Schultz. "It was a goddamn tragedy what happened over there."

"Thank you, sir. We all did what we could."

"Well, the way I hear it, it was your leadership skills that helped put an end to the conflict. You ever get tired of the private sector, I'll personally pin two stars to your shoulders."

Jericho was taken aback by the gesture. "Thank you, sir. That means a lot to me."

Schultz turned and stared at Adrian. "And you... what in the holy hell did you do in Paris, son?"

Adrian held up his hands, feigning innocence. "Me? I didn't do anything!"

"Uh-huh. So, why have I had the president *and* the prime minister crawling all over my answering machine for the last three days?"

Adrian sighed. "Fine. I... *may* have shot a few people and blown parts of it up a little bit. But in my defense, half the city was trying to kill me while I was working to complete *your* mission. Sir."

Schultz shook his head. "Christ on a bike..."

Becky leaned toward Ruby and whispered, "How can he talk to the president like that?"

Ruby smiled. "Those two have a little history. It's his way of showing respect."

Becky continued watching in disbelief.

Schultz moved to Buchanan's side, behind his desk, and addressed the room once more.

"I want evidence of Orion's involvement in every goddamn thing Tristar's ever done. I want to find out how a piece of shit company like Tristar got their hands on tech that puts *this place* to shame. I want the shooter from Paluga, and after their goddamn attack on Moses in *my* city, I want to know what the hell Tristar is going to do next."

"So, you're not asking for much, then?" said Adrian.

His comment was ignored.

Buchanan nodded. "Yes, sir. I've already assigned tasks to everyone here. We'll get it done."

Schultz took a deep breath, prompting a guttural cough. He cleared his throat. "Good. For my part, I've spoken to the directors of every federal agency I have. They all understand that GlobaTech is running point on this."

"They must be thrilled about that," said Collins.

"I don't give a damn what they feel about it," replied Schultz. "They'll do whatever the hell I tell them to. They will provide you all with whatever you need, including the space and freedom to work. Everyone in this room is an incredible asset. The threats we're facing are, frankly, just as incredible. You get it done. You hear me? You have carte blanche... a blank check... call it whatever the hell you want.

You do whatever it takes to squash these bastards before they do some serious damage."

Rayne held up a hand.

Schultz stared at him. "We're not in kindergarten, son. Don't embarrass yourself. What?"

He lowered his hand again. "I was just thinking, sir... Orion and Tristar are two completely different beasts. We can just fight Tristar, right? But Orion... they're the Globa-Tech of international media. They're not an enemy we can shoot at. But as these guys have found out, they can hurt us without leaving their chairs. How are we supposed to go after *them*, exactly?"

There was a murmur around the room, acknowledging the good question.

Schultz nodded. "Fair point, son. You get evidence of their involvement in any of this shit, you hand off everything you have to the FBI. They'll do the rest. You find the shooter, you folks get what you can out of her, then you deliver her to the CIA. You come across any resistance from Tristar operatives, you put them down." He looked directly at Adrian. "Preferably with little-to-no collateral damage."

Adrian frowned. "Why did you look at me when you said that?"

"Because you're a maniac and a walking disaster zone?" offered Ruby, looking over at him.

Adrian held his hands out to the side, shrugging. "Hey, whose side are you on?"

Ruby shrugged back. "Just saying..."

"Whatever." He looked at Schultz and Buchanan in turn. "Look, I don't mean to downplay what we're facing here, but am I the only one who thinks we're maybe overreacting a little bit?"

"I would say you are, yes," said Buchanan, raising his eyebrow in slight disbelief.

"Seriously. I've encountered Tristar before. I think we all have. They're nothing special. What they lack in skill, they make up for in numbers, sure, but they're ultimately a poor man's GlobaTech. And Orion, they're a media conglomerate. You don't like them, delete your social media apps. Even if they're pulling the strings, they own *newspapers*. What do we honestly think they can do that would matter on this kind of scale?"

Jericho took a step forward. "Have you not been paying attention? They orchestrated a coup in another country to set us up, then almost destroyed everything GlobaTech has worked for with a news report."

Adrian nodded. "Okay. Besides that..."

"I think the point Jericho is trying to make," said Buchanan, "is that a company with that much power and resources can, theoretically, do whatever the hell they want. Including send a heavily armed paramilitary unit onto the streets of the nation's capital to try to kill me."

"Yeah. I know. It just blows my mind that even the tabloids are trying their luck at world domination. Do you remember the good ol' days when it was just the terrorists and drug kingpins who did that?"

"Hey, guys..." said Link quietly.

Schultz moved toward Adrian. "You know better than anyone that the world is changing. Hell, that's why you're standing here right now. This is the epitome of modern warfare. Deleting your social media just ain't gonna cut it, son."

"Yeah, I know."

"Um... guys," said Link again.

"So, the FBI and everyone else will back off and let us do

our thing?" asked Jessie, who was still standing with Ruby and Becky.

"That's right," said Schultz, turning to face her. "They will support GlobaTech's wider efforts any way they can, but as far as the people in this room are concerned, you have the keys to the city. This is *that* important."

Jessie nodded. "Damn..."

"Hey, assholes!" yelled Link.

The room fell silent in an instant, and everyone looked to him.

He pointed out the window. "Can someone please tell me what the fuck *that* is."

Everyone turned around and stared out the window. The large compound bustled with activity as it always did. Beyond its borders was a mountain range, standing against the clear sky like jagged teeth. The tops were faded to a light blue by distance.

Silhouetted against them was a line of black dots, stretching the full width of the panoramic view offered by Buchanan's corner office. There were a dozen, maybe more, all getting bigger with each second that passed.

Everyone paced slowly toward the window, mouths open, brows furrowed.

A moment later, alarms began to wail. Sirens all around GlobaTech's town screamed into life.

"Boss... what's going on?" asked Collins absently.

Buchanan was lost for words. "I... I don't know. The sirens have never sounded before. It must be some kind of mistake. They mean..."

"They mean... what?" asked Schultz.

"They mean..."

"Damn it, Moses. Spit it out. What the hell's going on here?"

In the distance, flashes of light appeared beneath each of the black dots, which were now close enough to identify as helicopters.

Roach placed a hand on the glass. His eyes were wide, and his jaw hung loose. He was trying to process what he was looking at, while fighting with himself to prioritize reacting over thinking.

"We're under attack..." he muttered to himself.

He glanced down at the compound to see people running in all directions. Silent muzzle flashes rippled across GlobaTech's world as a sea of figures dressed in black flooded into the compound.

He looked up to see trails of smoke tracing across the sky toward them. Then he spun around to face the room.

"We're under attack!" he shouted. "Everybody... get down!"

13

JERICHO STONE

May 11, 2020

The first missile struck the edge of the tall building a few floors below Buchanan's office. The foundations shook as the deafening explosion consumed the world around them.

More impacts followed, seconds apart.

Jericho took Julie's hand and thrust them both toward President Schultz, reacting even before the Secret Service agents did. Everyone in the room followed suit, throwing themselves to the floor.

Roach crawled toward his sister, who was cowering and screaming in the corner.

"Becky!" he yelled. "Becky, I'm coming!"

He reached her and wrapped his arms around her, willing her to believe that the futile gesture of protection would somehow keep her safe from the attack outside.

Collins crouched low and shuffled to Becky's side, opposite Roach. He, too, offered his arms as a shield. Roach nodded a silent *thank you*.

On the other side of the room, Buchanan sat on the floor behind his desk, one arm held up around his head. He glanced around to see Schultz smothered flat beneath Jericho, Julie, and three Secret Service agents. The fourth knelt beside the pile of bodies, one hand resting on the shoulder of a colleague and the other aiming his handgun around the room, immediately alert.

In the middle of the room, Adrian and Ruby lay on their fronts, his arm over her head. The Blackstar team were down on one knee, ducking instinctively, forming a barrier around them.

"Sound off!" shouted Buchanan. "Is everyone okay?"

One by one, they all responded.

He breathed a sigh of relief and closed his eyes. They snapped open a second later. He pushed himself up to one knee, staying low behind his desk, and stared at the door.

"Kim!" he bellowed. His voice was so loud and guttural, it drowned out the warzone outside.

There was a muted shriek from outside his office.

"Get under your desk and stay there! I'm coming!"

A second volley of missiles pelted the building, shaking the floor like an earthquake. Clouds of fire, brick, and dust darkened the world outside the windows. The noise was soon overshadowed by the creaking of foundations, then again a moment later as the fleet of helicopters whizzed over the building.

Sensing the barrage was over, at least for now, Collins moved into a tentative crouch.

"Someone want to tell me what the fuck is happening right now?" he asked.

Rayne looked over at him. "Well, I think... I *think*... we're under attack."

Collins rolled his eyes. "No shit, Sherlock."

Buchanan got to his feet and moved around his desk. Everyone in the room followed his lead, pushing themselves up and looking around, checking on everyone else.

"Moses!" growled Schultz. "Goddammit, what the hell is going on?"

Adrian gestured to Rayne with his thumb. "Didn't we just cover that?"

"Enough," said Buchanan. "We need to focus. Who here is armed?"

Ruby reached behind Adrian and drew one of his Raptors at the same time he did. They both instinctively checked the mags, chambered a round, then flicked the safety off.

"We are," she said.

Jericho drew his *Negotiator* from his thigh holster.

"Us too," he said, speaking for Julie and Collins also.

"We all have our G47s," announced the Secret Service agent closest to the president.

"I'm not," said Roach.

The members of Blackstar looked at each other dejectedly.

"Great. Everyone except us and the new guy, then?" said Rayne.

Buchanan looked at Jericho and nodded, silently passing him command of the situation.

Jericho turned to Adrian. "You and Ruby take point. The Secret Service will hustle the president out behind you." He turned his attention to Rayne. "You and your team will form a perimeter around Roach, Becky, and Buchanan. Julie, Ray, and I will bring up the rear." He moved to the door and addressed the room. "We take the stairs. Our goal is to reach the armory."

"Where is that, exactly?" asked Link.

"Other side of the compound."

There was a reluctant murmur around the room, but nobody spoke.

Jericho continued. "It ain't perfect, but our only chance is to arm ourselves and fight back. Let's move before those choppers circle back around for another bombing run."

He yanked the door open and stood to the side, allowing everyone to file out into the corridor as per his instruction. Following Adrian and Ruby's lead, they ran down the hall toward the stairwell at the opposite end.

Collins stepped behind Kim's desk and extended his hand. From beneath it, she reached up and took it. He hoisted her to her feet, staring for a moment into her dark eyes, blurred with tears and stained with circles of blotched make-up.

"Ya gonna be okay, love," he said softly. "Come on. I got ya."

Holding hands, they ran to catch up with the others. They descended the stairs quickly. The noise of their collective heavy footsteps filled the stairwell.

"Where's everyone else?" asked Roach. "Don't you have people on other floors?"

"Believe it or not, we do have protocols for this kind of thing," said Julie. "This is a first for all of us, but everyone here is well trained—even the office staff. There are emergency exits and stairwells on each floor. They'll be evacuating via specifically allocated routes, to leave this main stairwell free for people like us."

They continued their descent in silence.

Adrian slowed at the top of the final staircase and looked down into the lobby. It was deserted. The floor was covered in patches of debris and small fires. Beyond that, he had a limited view through the entrance doors. He saw a body land heavily on the ground. A gun flew from its grip.

He stopped and held his fist upright, signaling for the others to stop too.

Jericho pushed his way to the front. Seeing Adrian's expression of concern, he glanced toward the doors and saw the lifeless body. His clenched his jaw, glaring into space as he focused his mind on what needed to happen next. Then he looked over at Adrian.

"I need you to do what I tell you," he said. "No questions. No arguments. Understand?"

Adrian nodded without a second's hesitation. "Hey, full-scale war is your specialty, not mine. Tell me what you need and it's done."

Jericho placed a hand on his shoulder and nodded to him, showing his unspoken gratitude. He then turned to address the group, who were standing patiently in a line that wound back up the last flight of stairs.

He took one deep breath—a single, momentary reminder that whatever chain of command there was thirty minutes ago meant nothing anymore. It was his responsibility to get everyone to safety, and he would. Even if it killed him.

"Okay. Here's the plan," he said. "Adrian and I will take point. We'll do our best to clear you a path to Marine One. Rayne, I want you, Jessie, and Link to help the Secret Service get the president and Buchanan onboard and in the air. Julie and Ray will provide covering fire for you."

Roach stepped out of line and toward Jericho. "I want Becky on there too."

Schultz moved to say something, but Buchanan stepped forward to cut him off.

"Of course," he said to Roach. "And Kim will be with her."

At the back of the line, Collins put a comforting arm around Kim and winked at her. She hugged herself into his body for a moment, then moved down the steps to Becky's side. The two of them shared a quick smile and held hands.

"Once they're in the air, the rest of us will head across to the armory," continued Jericho. "From there, we dig in and get our forces organized. Then we drive these bastards back."

Rayne raised his hand slightly. "Ah, not to rain on your parade or anything, but half of us are unarmed. And the half who are only have handguns. How, *exactly*, are you expecting us to survive the sprint across No Man's Land without being cut to shreds?"

Jericho looked him in the eyes and shrugged. "I don't know what to tell you, soldier. You want a gun? Take one from the first piece of shit you see."

At his side, Adrian let slip a small smile.

Jericho descended the final few stairs.

"Let's go," he called back.

The large group fanned out as they crossed the lobby. On the left, the GlobaTech logo had been damaged. The large globe was split in two, with one half barely hanging onto the wall and the other somewhere on the floor behind the large, semicircular front desk.

Opposite, the three large TV screens were equally damaged, with two being destroyed completely. The remaining one stubbornly displayed the news, despite its cracked screen.

Through the shattered glass doors, they got their first look at the true extent of the attack. Many of the vehicles parked out front were nothing more than burning wrecks.

Smoke and flames billowed from buildings all the way across the compound. Civilians were running and screaming in all directions. A few GlobaTech operatives were behind cover, returning fire at the enemy.

The attackers were dressed in black, walking with patience and purpose around the small town, indiscriminately shooting at anything that moved.

"Oh my God..." whispered Jessie.

"Tristar," said Roach. "There are hundreds of them."

"Maybe more," added Buchanan. "There's a whole lot we can't see from here."

Jericho shook his head. "They've sent one for every man, woman, and child on this base. How could this happen without any warning?"

Adrian stood still, a hand covering his mouth. He turned to look at Ruby, and his brow creased with confusion when he saw she wasn't by his side. He quickly looked around and spotted her behind them, staring up at the one working TV. He pushed through the group and walked over to her.

"Ruby, what is it?" he asked, seeing the look of horror on her face.

She pointed at the screen. The picture was fuzzy and lined with static interference, but the sound still came through clearly. They watched together as a reporter stared into the camera, holding a large microphone close to her face. Her eyes were stained with tears.

"...all over the United States. So far, fifteen major cities, including Washington D.C. and New York, are reporting tens of thousands of military personnel on the streets, dressed in black fatigues. We have confirmation that these men are not soldiers. They are not U.S. military. They are..."

She paused, pressing a finger to her ear and listening intently.

"Yes. They work for Tristar Security. These men are mercenaries. They are heavily armed, and law enforcement is urging people not to engage with them. Many police officers and civilians have already been gunned down in the streets. We have... there is no word from the White House, although it is believed that the president left earlier this morning to fly to California. We do not know at this time if he is safe."

Ruby reached for Adrian's hand and gripped it tightly.

"...word that all major airports and harbors are being locked down. Right now, across the country, we are under attack. Let me say that again. The United States is under attack. Stay indoors. Stay hidden. Do not engage the mercenaries you see on the streets. We don't know what they want, but we are urging people to—"

There was a bright flash on the screen, followed by a roar of gunfire. Someone screamed as the female reporter disappeared out of shot. The camera shook and dropped to the ground, offering nothing but an obscured side view of the street and a vehicle's front wheel. Two pairs of boots stepped into shot. There was more gunfire, then a man's lifeless face dropped into view, dominating the full width of the screen.

Ruby gasped as the man's dead eyes stared out at the world. A second later, the feed disappeared altogether.

Adrian and Ruby looked at each other, pale expressions of shock etched onto their faces. As they turned, they saw everyone standing behind them. They had been so distracted by the broadcast, they hadn't heard them walk over.

"Holy hell..." muttered Schultz.

"It's not just us," said Julie absently.

Jericho shook his head. "No. It's happening everywhere.

All over the country." He turned to face the group. "This isn't just an attack... it's an invasion."

As one, they turned slowly to look outside. They saw the gravity of what was unfolding through a new and frightening perspective.

Jericho couldn't hide the fear on his face. He had never felt anything close to this before, and he didn't know how to process it. Any sense of duty he felt to appear strong for the others had gone. But he wasn't afraid of the enemy. He was afraid that no matter what they did here, it wouldn't matter.

He was afraid they were beaten.

Beside him, he felt Julie slide her hand into his. He held it tightly as he looked to his left and right, along the line of friends and allies. He saw the looks on their faces. Without exception, he saw the same fear. The same uncertainty. The same defeat.

He didn't know how to fix this, and that killed him inside.

He looked down at Julie's hand, interlocked with his own. Her knuckles were pale from squeezing. He ran his thumb over the back of her hand. In that moment, he remembered the one thing he did know how to do.

Julie looked at their hands, then up at him.

"Jericho, what do we do?" she whispered.

He looked her in her eyes, took a breath, and set his jaw. "The only thing we can. We fight."

He stepped forward and spun on his heels to face the others, putting his back to the chaos and pulling their attention onto him.

"Listen up. This doesn't change anything. We need to—"

From his left, Rayne and Link rushed forward, cutting him off.

"Get down!" they shouted in unison.

Jericho frowned, then looked over his shoulder to see the line of attack helicopters once again dominating the skyline. They were closer than before, but their shapes were clouded by the smoke and the glare from the missiles they had just fired.

Jericho's eyes went wide. He hesitated only for a fraction of a second but still cursed himself, knowing that could mean the difference between life and death.

"Not down," he said. "Out. Everybody outside, now!"

Everyone lunged for the doors, throwing them open as the barrage of missiles smashed into the towering office block. Hurricanes of dust surrounded them in seconds. The skies rained down brick and glass and fire.

Then their worlds turned black.

14

ROACH

Roach tasted the bitter, coppery flavor of blood on his lips. He pushed himself up on all fours and began crawling instinctively forward. The rhythmic and procedural thrust of each limb felt arduous and sent burning pain coursing through his body.

He squinted through the dust and gravel engrained in his face. His vision was blurred, and a sharp ringing in his ears drowned out the noise of the world around him. He couldn't tell where he was in relation to the last thing he remembered.

After a few moments, he collapsed again, having moved no more than a few feet. He blinked hard until the world shifted back into focus, like a kaleidoscope working in reverse. He found himself staring into the blank, lifeless eyes of a face he didn't recognize.

"Jesus..." he muttered, rolling over onto his back.

He stared up at a sky blackened by thick smoke. Lifting his head slightly, he looked back at the building he had been inside minutes earlier. He lay his head back down slowly, allowing the motion to dictate his gaze as he followed the building upward.

What was left of it, at least.

The second barrage of missile fire had turned it derelict in a heartbeat. The feeble, metal foundations protruded through cracked brickwork. Large holes peppered the exterior from top to bottom, exposing the interior and allowing the multiple fires to breathe.

As his bearings and faculties returned, Roach heard spurts of distant gunfire and screaming in all directions. Then he noticed frantic movement to his right. He rolled to his side and pushed himself upright, standing uneasily still while the blood rush subsided. He could see Jericho shouting, gesturing wildly at the Secret Service agents. He followed Jericho's movements, turning his attention to Marine One, which was, by some miracle, still in one piece.

Becky...

"Becky!" he shouted. "Becky! Where are you?"

"H-here..."

The weak voice came from behind him. He turned to see his sister limping, standing in between Collins and Kim, an arm resting over each of their shoulders.

Roach dashed over to them. "Are you okay? What happened?"

"We got blown to shit is what happened," said Collins. "She's fine, though. I was next to her. We had a bit of a rough landing, but I took the brunt of it. She'll be okay."

Roach took over supporting her, then looked at Collins.

"Thank you," he said.

Collins nodded. "Thank me by getting your sister and Kim over to the chopper. I'll cover you."

Kim moved to the other side of Becky, and the three of them shuffled across the compound, toward the helicopter. Collins hung back and watched, his weapon aimed low and ready, scanning for any Tristar mercenaries who might be sweeping the area for survivors.

Having sent the agents and the president toward the chopper, Jericho glanced over to see Collins and Roach heading in the same direction. He then moved to meet Julie, who was running toward him.

"Are you okay?" he asked her.

She nodded frantically. "I'm fine. Where's Buchanan?"

"I haven't seen him. What about Adrian and the others?"

She shook her head. "I haven't seen them, either."

There was a sudden burst of activity behind them, over by what remained of the building. A large chunk of loose rubble exploded outward, and the body of a man dressed in all black came flying through the gap. He landed awkwardly on the ground.

They both looked up to see Link stepping through, walking toward the Tristar mercenary. His face was contorted in rage and covered in blood. Behind him, Ruby and Rayne climbed out, followed a moment later by Adrian, then finally by Jessie, who was holding an assault rifle.

The four of them fanned out and watched as Link reached down, wrapped both hands around the man in black's throat, and hoisted him upright with ease. The man, visibly dazed and injured, stared into Link's eyes; his own were wide and laced with fear.

With frightening speed and violent precision, Link moved his hands, cupping the man's chin with one and the base of his skull with the other. With a guttural roar, he twisted his torso and shoulders, snapping the man's neck. The crack was audible and sickening. He let the body drop lifelessly at his feet, then looked around at the others.

"Are you good?" asked Jericho.

Link wiped the blood from his face, then wiped his hand on his leg. "Never better."

"Has anyone seen Buchanan?" asked Julie.

"He wasn't in there with us," said Adrian. He flicked his head toward Marine One. "Is he not over there with Schultz, surrounded by agents?"

"I don't think so, no."

Ruby looked around absently, struggling to process everything that had happened in the last few minutes. When the missiles hit, she was standing with Blackstar, and they weren't as close to the doors as Jericho and the others were. She fell backward, landing on top of Adrian. The ceiling had rained down on them, but the debris was large and easy enough to avoid. She had seen Collins dive forward, tackling Becky around the waist and dragging her with him. Jericho and Julie had pulled Kim with them. Roach had been standing farther away and was caught in the fallout of a blast from a missile's impact. He had flown out before a wall of rubble descended, trapping the rest of them inside. The Secret Service had swarmed the president and pulled him away to the side.

Luckily, the veil of concrete and dust was thin, so it wasn't difficult or unsafe to remove. That's when they noticed a sole Tristar mercenary had appeared behind them. The tense, silent standoff was short-lived. Link had charged him and manhandled him through the debris, clearing their path to the outside.

Ruby frowned. Having replayed the last two minutes of

her life in her head, she realized she hadn't seen Buchanan on either side of the rubble.

The rest of them had gathered into a tight huddle, and Jericho was coordinating their route to the armory. She could see the president and his entourage, along with Roach and the others, were almost at the chopper.

Something wasn't right.

She turned and paced slowly back toward what used to be the entrance. She climbed the couple of steps and stood, scanning the debris. She saw nothing but pieces of brick and metal. A few feet away, something fell and smashed onto the ground. Ruby jumped and looked up, seeing the fragile state of the building. There were exposed beams and cables, with concrete dangling precariously from them overhead.

She took a couple of steps back, eager to avoid anything else that might fall.

That's when she saw it.

A small gap in the wall of rubble, close to the ground. Just inside it, she could make out a foot and lower leg.

"Oh my God..." she whispered.

She took a step toward it and carefully removed a couple of bricks. She could now see more of the leg and a hand. It was pale with dust, but the dark skin beneath was unmistakable.

Buchanan.

"I need some help," said Ruby. When none came, she looked around and shouted, "Somebody help!"

In unison, the group turned and sprinted toward her. They slid to a stop by her side, all staring at the motionless leg and hand in the rubble.

Julie gasped, holding a hand to her mouth.

Rayne and Link stepped forward, but Jericho moved in

front of them, blocking their path. He held a hand up to them both. They locked eyes with him. Their accusatory stares immediately softened as they saw his grave expression. They knew what he was about to say.

"What are you doing?" asked Julie. "We need to help him."

Jericho looked at her and shook her head. "We don't know if he's still alive. I'm sorry, but we have to get to the armory. We have to fight back, or there's a chance none of us make it out of here. The priority is securing the president."

Julie opened her mouth to protest, but Jessie stepped to her side, placing a hand on her shoulder that kept her silent.

Jericho sighed. "This is shitty and unfair, but we both know Buchanan would agree with me if he could."

Julie shrugged Jessie's hand off and walked away. Jericho watched her go, his shoulders slumping in defeat.

Adrian moved to his side. "Ruby and I will get him free. You stick to the plan. My team will back you up."

Jericho looked at him and nodded. "Thanks."

Collins had seen the commotion by the building but couldn't make out what was happening from where he was. He saw everyone except Adrian and Ruby start running for the armory. Jericho and Julie opened fire on a group of Tristar mercenaries that were moving to cut them off.

"Ah, shite..." muttered Collins.

A few steps in front of him, Roach and Kim had stopped while Becky rested her leg. Beyond them, he could see two Secret Service agents had already climbed aboard Marine One.

They were no more than twenty feet away now. The blades were starting to spin. Schultz stopped to look behind him, presumably wondering where everyone else was. The remaining agents were forcefully pushing him, urging him to climb the steps.

Collins was distracted by movement to his right. He looked over to see a group of five Tristar personnel fanned out, their weapons leveled and ready to fire. But the one in the middle drew his attention. He was holding a shoulder-mounted rocket launcher.

His eyes went wide. "Look out!"

He took aim and fired, hitting the man in the arm and sending him spiraling to the ground. But he was too late. There was a flash and a *whoosh* of air, and in a heartbeat, the helicopter became engulfed in a small mushroom cloud of fire and smoke.

The blast sent Schultz and the two agents flying backward several feet. It knocked Collins and the others to the ground.

Roach scrambled back to his feet, staring in disbelief at the burning wreck before him. He turned to see the team of Tristar mercenaries walking slowly toward him. Their faces were masked. The four men stood in a line and aimed their assault rifles at Roach.

They had him dead to rights.

He glanced behind him. Kim and Becky were lying flat, their arms over each other's heads. Next to them, Collins was shaking his head, clearly disoriented.

With a heavy sigh, Roach stepped to his right, putting his body directly between his friends and his enemy. He held his hands out to the side and stared the closest man to him right in the eye.

"You won't get away with this," he said. "If we don't stop you, someone else will."

The man shook his head. "No. They won't."

Behind them, another team of men in black appeared,

rushing to the fallen president. They fired short bursts into the bodies of the agents beside him, then dragged a barely conscious Schultz to his feet and hustled him away to a waiting vehicle, off to the side.

Roach looked on helplessly. The compound had fallen. Countless were dead. The president had been taken. In that moment, the painful realization that they had lost hit him like a freight train.

He screwed his eyes shut.

A second later, a cacophony of gunfire rang out around him.

He opened them again to see GlobaTech and Blackstar running toward him. In front of him, all the Tristar men were dead.

"We need to go," said Jericho. "There's nothing more we can do here. Not now."

Roach nodded and reached for his sister, helping her to her feet. Collins had recovered and was doing the same for Kim.

"Fall back to the main gate," said Jericho.

They turned and ran for the security booth by the entrance. Behind them, a couple of Tristar men gave chase, firing aimlessly around them. Julie spun, dropped to one knee, and fired two rounds. Each struck their intended target in the chest.

She stood and caught up with the others. Away to their right, where the compound opened out into the town, they could see pockets of GlobaTech operatives fighting back, protecting groups of civilians. Over to the left, sweeping through the parking lot and across the roads, a swarm of black moved methodically, killing anything in its way.

Adrian and Ruby appeared, out of breath. Kim immediately ran to them.

"What happened?" she asked. "Where's Moses? Is he..."

Adrian shook his head. "No, he's alive, but... he's in a bad way. We got him free, with the help of some of your guys. They're going to get him out of here and get him some medical attention. I'm sorry, Kim. It doesn't look good, but for now, the man's alive, at least."

She nodded. "Thank you for going back for him."

"Don't mention it. We both know he'd have done the same for any one of us." He looked around them. "Where's the president?"

"Taken," said Roach.

Adrian caught his breath. "Holy shit..."

The group spread out, standing in a line, staring in disbelief and horror as an empire burned before them.

Adrian. Ruby. Collins. Kim. Rayne. Jericho. Julie. Roach. Becky. Jessie. Link.

They all watched as flames billowed from almost every building they could see. The mountain range in the distance was completely masked by thick smoke. The air was dominated by the sound of gunfire and carnage. The world GlobaTech built had been consumed by death.

"How could this even happen?" asked Roach. "GlobaTech knew Tristar and Orion were up to something. How did you not see this coming?"

"I don't think anyone could've seen *this* coming, man," countered Rayne.

The silence that fell upon them muted the chaos, and they paused to share the brief moment of uneasy calm.

"This is insane," said Jessie, to no one in particular.

"This is beyond insane," said Becky. "In less than an hour, Tristar has managed to completely destroy the largest corporate entity in the world, invade the entire United

States, and kidnap the president. What the hell are we supposed to do now?"

All eyes instinctively turned to Jericho, who was staring out at the burning ruins of his home. He holstered his *Negotiator*, relaxed his shoulders, and took a long, deep breath.

"There's only one thing left we *can* do," he said, taking Julie's hand in his. "We run."

15

QUINCY HALL

May 12, 2020

Sunlight beamed through the long windows, casting its rays across the surface of the Resolute desk. Quincy Hall sat behind it, staring out in silent awe at the Oval Office around him. Despite his position and standing, despite the years of planning and sacrifice, nothing had truly prepared him for how it would feel to sit there in that iconic room.

He smiled to himself as he straightened his tie. His five thousand-dollar suit was freshly pressed. His thin hair was styled. His face was clean shaven.

He was ready.

In the room with him were four Tristar guards, all armed and positioned around the curve of the wall opposite. Directly in front of him was a TV camera. A member of Orion's board of directors was issuing instructions to a small team of technicians. Away to the left, the remaining members of the board stood quietly, watching Hall with admiration and pride.

"Is everything ready?" he asked one of the technicians.

The man nodded, clasping a hand over the microphone of the headset he was wearing. "You're live in thirty seconds, sir."

Hall took a deep breath and shuffled for comfort in his seat. He clasped his hands in front of him on the desk and looked ahead. He didn't have a speech to read. He knew what he was going to say. He had been preparing for this moment for so long, he had forgotten what his life was like before it all.

All eyes in the room focused on him. The technician standing beside the camera held up a hand and began counting down on his fingers.

Five. Four. Three.

Hall took a final, deep breath to compose himself, then stared into the large lens.

Two. One.

"My fellow Americans, good morning." He flashed his executive smile for a moment, then let it fade. "That's what whoever sits in this chair is supposed to say, isn't it? *My fellow Americans*. Huh. You want to know the truth? Those words haven't meant anything in decades. *Fellow Americans*. For that to mean something, the man sitting where I am now would have to consider himself one of you. He would have to have *your* best interests in mind. Not some convoluted political agenda to push his own conspiratorial ambitions over the needs of the people who elected him in the first place."

He took a short breath, pausing for effect.

"What this country needs... what it's *always* needed... is someone who will service not just the needs of the American people but also the needs of generations to come.

Someone who will fight to protect our future. And that someone is me.

"Now, as the saying goes: Rome wasn't built in a day. If you believe in something, you must be prepared to fight for it. I believe each and every one of you wants the same thing I do, but you've lived under the guise of freedom and the subtle blanket of tyranny for so long that you've forgotten how to ask for it. There are years of corruption and dilution that need to be undone before we, as a nation, can move forward. So, I've done what so many others couldn't. Or, perhaps, *wouldn't*. I've pulled on the thread that will one day soon unravel the broken essence of what used to be so that one day... we can restore our country to its former glory.

"Some of you may know me as the CEO of Orion International, the largest media conglomerate in the world. You may ask what qualifications that gives me to justify sitting here. I would ask what qualifications you think I need. The office of the presidency has become a joke. In the last hundred years, this seat has been occupied by actors, inherited from fathers, infiltrated by our enemies, and been awarded as a prize. I would argue that few qualifications are needed to sit here. However, I believe I *am* qualified. I understand the global political landscape better than anyone, and thanks to my control of the world's media, I'm in the unique position to influence it more than anyone else ever could. I can protect us from the evils of this world because I understand our enemies. But before I can save you from them, I must first save you from yourselves."

He glanced to the Tristar operative nearest the door on the right and nodded. The guard opened it and stepped outside.

Hall continued his address. "That is why I created Tristar, a private militia whose only job is to protect this country.

They do what the U.S. military isn't allowed to do and what the law enforcement agencies aren't prepared to do. Under my order, they have temporarily taken control of this country from you, so they can eradicate everything that has been destroying us from within. Some of you may find this extreme. Some of you may find this frightening. But I promise you, these drastic actions are long overdue and are not undertaken lightly.

"These actions began yesterday. GlobaTech Industries has long been a cancer on this world. Under the illusion of support, they involved themselves in important matters on your behalf without permission or just cause. As a result, they were single-handedly responsible for the largest atrocity in human history. That is why I am declaring that anyone associated with GlobaTech will be treated as an enemy of this new state. If you are found to be working for them or supporting them in any capacity, you will be arrested on sight and shot if you resist."

The Tristar guard reappeared with another man beside him. His hair was disheveled and damp with sweat. His suit was ruffled and torn. Fear was etched onto every inch of his bruised face. The guard held him by his arm with a firm grip.

Hall looked over and beckoned them toward him.

The guard shoved the man forward and marched him to the desk, then tugged him to a stop behind it. He then stepped back and waited just out of shot. The camera panned back slightly as Hall stood to greet the man. He placed a hand on his shoulder and turned back to the camera.

"President Schultz has been removed from office, effective immediately," he announced. "He is being treated as a prisoner of war and is being held in a secure location until such time as he can be tried for the part he played in Globa-Tech's crimes. I have with me here the vice president, Mr. Roe. As outlined in the constitution, he is next in line to be commander-in-chief, should the president be unable to fulfil his duties."

Hall looked past Vice President Roe and held out his hand. With no instruction needed, the guard drew his sidearm, chambered a round, flicked the safety off, and handed it to him by the barrel.

Hall took it and stepped back. Without hesitation, be placed the gun to Roe's head and pulled the trigger. The sound of the gunshot echoed around the room. A crimson mist burst from the back of his head, splashing down onto the navy blue carpet. The lifeless body slumped to the floor.

Hall's expression never changed. There was no emotion over what he had just done. He knew it was necessary. That was it.

Still standing, he looked down the camera once more. "The old chain of command is finished. Remaining heads of government will continue to serve their purpose without the burden of delegated responsibility. The police, the federal agencies... they all now answer to me. The military will move to a permanent state of non-readiness in preparation for being disbanded completely. They will be replaced by Tristar, who will absorb the best and brightest from all arms of the military, allowing them to better serve this country.

"Understand, Tristar is not your enemy. I am not your enemy. We are doing this to protect you. To help you rebuild and learn a better way of life. And to facilitate that even further, all airports and harbors will be locked down within forty-eight hours. No one will be allowed in or out of this country. This will allow us to rebuild without the distraction and harmful influence of outside nations. Any resistance to this will be met with lethal force."

Hall sat down again, composing himself behind his desk.

"I know this will be... an adjustment for many of you. But I will do whatever I can to ensure there is no unnecessary disruption to your everyday lives. This country will function as it always has. There is economy and infrastructure and industry and society that will all still be here tomorrow and the days that come after that. Nothing needs to change. And while you go about your lives, Orion will be working to improve them. I will be making sure this country starts working for you, not against you. Healthcare, taxes, living costs, insurance... everything you have accepted as normal that is fundamentally wrong will be changed. And with Tristar patrolling the streets all across the country, you will be safer than you have ever been.

"In the last ten years, many have tried to do what I've done. But where they failed... I have succeeded. Cunningham's mistake was wanting to fix the system you had. I want to build a new one. Democracy is redundant. Your republic was antiquated. What I've done for you is the only way to truly ensure the safety and the future of this once-great nation."

Hall leaned forward, moved his arms to the side, and tilted his head toward the camera. He smiled to his nation.

"Welcome... to the first Orion dynasty."

SIX MONTHS LATER

16

RAY COLLINS

November 16, 2020

Collins hunched against the bitter cold. A weak frost teased a future snowfall, supported by the thick, pale clouds that blanketed the sky. The crisp air made each breath he took feel like a knife in his chest. When he exhaled, he blew fleetingly thick steam in front of his face.

He walked briskly and quietly, avoiding the pale fluorescent glare of the streetlights where possible. The collar of his overcoat was turned up, protecting his neck from the icy fingers of the winter wind.

GlobaTech had arrived in Cincinnati a little over two weeks ago. Immediately, they began heading out in small teams for two, sometimes three hours at a time, scouting the city, looking for patrols and any local support they could find.

It was after four in the morning. Collins was tired. He felt as if he had been running on fumes for weeks now. Instinct and adrenaline accounted for much of his movement and decision-making. But he knew the dangers being somewhere new presented. This was only the fourth city they had risked visiting in the last three months. It was big and unfamiliar, and he didn't like it. Unfortunately, desperate times often called for desperate measures.

He walked past the Paul Brown Stadium, along West Mehring Way, keeping his head down and staying close to the fence that lined the sidewalk. As he passed under the first of two bridges ahead, he looked around, checking that there was nothing and no one nearby.

The main squad he was travelling with had taken over an abandoned asphalt plant on the outskirts of the city, which faced the Ohio River. It was secluded, with no refugee camps nearby, which meant it was far less likely to be on a Tristar patrol route.

The street opened out as large gravel pits came into view on either side. Collins let out a heavy sigh, briefly creating an extra-large gust of steam in front of him. He didn't like being so exposed, but he was almost back to base and had little choice.

Halfway past the small mountains of rubble, he heard the low, rumbling murmur of an engine. Maybe two. He stopped in his tracks, looking urgently back and forth along the street. A moment later, the faint glow of headlights shone on the road ahead, from around a right dogleg.

"Shit," Collins hissed to himself.

He dashed to his right, scrambling over the gravel. His calves burned. He climbed until he reached a pile large enough to duck behind.

He was shrouded in near total darkness. He peeked around the corner of his cover and watched. Within moments of him hiding, two vehicles appeared from around the corner, cruising along the street. They passed under the far bridge. They were military Jeeps, armor plated, with a protected hatch in the roof for the mounted fifty cal. He could see a man standing behind it in each vehicle, holding the weapon loosely as the small patrol trundled along.

The vehicles drew level with his position, between the two bridges, and slowed to a stop.

Collins closed his eyes and screwed up his face, silently cursing his bad luck.

The Tristar soldiers idly climbed out of the vehicles. All eight of them grouped together, pacing slowly around in small circles. A couple lit up cigarettes as they began talking and laughing among themselves; their voices were amplified in the empty night.

Collins shook his head and muttered to himself, "Are ya kidding me?"

A couple of minutes passed. He was crouched on one knee, and his back leg was beginning to cramp in the cold. He winced as he shuffled to relieve some of the tension that was growing in his thigh. As he did, a single chunk of shattered brick shifted beneath his front foot. It fell away to the side, out from behind his cover, and tumbled defiantly down the mountain of rubble.

His heart skipped in his chest. He held his breath and stared with wide-eyed horror as the piece of brick bounced down to the street.

A single guard stood with his back to Collins, blowing smoke from his cigarette up into the air, listening to the banter from his colleagues. The brick stopped a few feet from him, causing a small pile to avalanche to the street. The man glanced down at it. His body language remained relaxed, but he still looked back over his shoulder.

Collins was maybe twenty feet away from the patrol and roughly ten feet above them on the slope. In the stillness of the early hours, he could hear their voices as clearly as if he were standing beside them.

"The fuck was that?" asked the guard.

The colleague to his right turned to him. "Looks like dirt to me, Danny."

Danny flipped him the finger and turned his body to face the gravel pit.

"Nah, man. Something must be up there," he said. "Why else would it shift randomly like that?"

His colleague moved to his side. "Dude, it's the middle of the night. We're standing between two shit-tips. You wanna head up there and pop a raccoon or something, go right ahead. But we're due back in twenty minutes, and I'm fucking tired. So, are you coming or not?"

Danny continued to stare up into the darkness, taking the final puffs of his cigarette. In the totality of the night, he had no idea he was staring directly into the eyes of his enemy.

Collins stared back, peering carefully over the top of his cover, watching with his mouth clamped shut, planning on how he could take out an entire patrol by himself if he had to.

Eventually, the guard flicked the butt of his cigarette away and walked back to his vehicle. The patrol piled into them, engines revved, and they pulled away. Collins didn't move an inch until the headlights were completely gone from view. Then he let out a heavy sigh of relief.

"Jesus..."

He scrambled down the gravel to the street, then jogged the rest of the way to the hideout, despite knowing it was unlikely that a second patrol would appear this far out so soon after one just left.

He veered left under the second bridge and headed

toward the grounds of the abandoned factory. He crawled through a gap in the wire mesh fence that blocked the exit, then made his way right, past the towering, skeletal blocks of metal framework that surrounded a transmission tower.

The main building was roughly the size of an aircraft hangar. Collins made his way around the back, to a single side door with a stack of wooden crates beside it. As he gripped the handle, he glanced to his right, staring out at the Ohio River. He couldn't see anything, but the sound of the water flowing gently nearby was soothing.

He knocked three times on the door and waited. A moment later, he heard a lock slide back from inside. He pulled the door open and stepped into the dimly lit corridor. He was greeted by a man dressed in GlobaTech fatigues, who nodded a curt greeting.

"Welcome back, sir," he said.

Collins smiled. "Hey, man. Ya miss me?"

"Always, sir."

"And that's why ya my favorite, Sam."

The man rolled his eyes. "It's Thomas, sir."

"Heh. Yeah, I knew that. Sam's my pet name for ya."

"Whatever you say, sir."

Collins walked along the corridor and through a set of double doors at the end, which led him into the main area of the factory. It used to be wide open but had hurriedly been divided into areas for people to sleep, eat, and train.

Small puddles littered the floor. There was no moon in the sky tonight. Lighting inside was limited to candles, with small groups of people huddled around them. There were enough for him to be able to see where he was going.

He made his way toward a small room in the far corner opposite. What was likely used as a foreman's office in another time was now where GlobaTech's senior command gathered to plan their next move.

Collins knocked once on the door, then entered. Julie and Jericho looked up from the papers they were studying on the table in front of them. The windows in the room had been boarded over long ago. The wood had rotted in places but still provided enough of a shield to allow multiple desk lamps to be on without drawing any attention to them from the outside.

"You're late," said Julie as Collins shut the door behind him.

"Aye. Had to wait for a patrol to pass," he explained. He shrugged off his coat and lay it over the back of a nearby chair. "Had me pinned down on a damn gravel pit."

Jericho frowned. "This was nearby?"

"Aye. Just up the road there."

Julie and Jericho shared a glance of concern.

"Okay," said Julie. "We should think about moving on in the next day or two. How did it go?"

Collins shrugged. "Same story as everywhere else. Closer ya get to the city, the more roadblocks and patrols there are."

"Do we have allies here?"

"We do." He tugged at a Velcro patch on his upper arm, tearing it away to reveal a GlobaTech emblem beneath. "Ya flash this to pretty much any civilian, they will help us. I found an elderly couple who invited me into their home, let me shower, gave me some food. Honestly, the only people who turn us away do so because they're scared, and I honestly can't blame them."

Jericho folded his arms across his chest and sighed. "That's great, but it's not a long-term solution. We need to find a way to fight back, and so far, we ain't got shit. Every patrol we take out... they know nothing of any importance. At least, that's what they claim."

"I know," said Julie. "But we have no other choice. Over eighty percent of GlobaTech's manpower was overseas when the doors closed on the U.S. They can't get in to help us, and we've lost maybe half of what we had on T-Day."

Collins groaned. "Ah, I *hate* that name."

Julie shrugged. "I don't know what to tell you, Ray. It was the day Tristar conquered the country. It's just easier to say."

"Yeah, but can't we just say the date? Like everyone does with 4/17?"

"What, and add 5/11 to the calendar? Sounds too much like the other thing to me."

"Aye, well, whatever ya call it, I'm really starting to fucking hate the spring."

Jericho leaned forward, spreading his giant palms across the surface of the table. He nodded at the map of the city laid out in front of him.

"Tell me you found something we can work with?" he asked.

Collins moved to the desk, standing between the others and forming a tight triangle.

"As a matter of fact, I might've done, aye." He pointed to an intersection two miles to the east. "There's a section of road over by the art museum. Kind of a small circuit leading up to the entrance. I saw one vehicle peel off and do a lap of it. It takes them away from the main streets, and there's no overlap with other patrols. Happens once every three hours or so. If we're going to hit anyone, it should be those guys."

Julie nodded, studying the map with the new information in mind.

"That could work," she said after a moment. "How big is the patrol?"

Collins shrugged. "Standard. Four or five guys. One vehicle."

Julie looked up at Jericho. "What do you think?"

He thought for a moment. "It's risky. That patrol might be isolated, but they'll be out in the open, which means we'll be exposed when we attack. No way to do it quietly. There's also every chance they won't know anything."

"I know, damn it!" Julie slammed her hands on the desk. "But what other choice do we have? We've been here for over two weeks. After Ray's encounter just now, we are probably close to outstaying our welcome. If we're going to make a move, we have to do it now. Somebody's got to know something. *Anything* we can use against these bastards is valuable."

"Ya ain't wrong, Jules," said Collins. "Ya both have a point, but if ya ask me, we're long overdue making a little noise. Ya should see the folks here. They might be living normal lives, but they're scared. Military patrols on every street... it's like living in Baghdad. But I'll tell ya both something: these people... they have hope. Ya can see it in their eyes and hear it in their voices when ya talk to them. Thanks to Roach's sister and that cheeky blog of hers, each time we take out a Tristar patrol, the entire country knows about it within a week. That's why everyone helps us. The uprising was started by them, but they want *us* to lead the rebellion. The military's gone. The Feds and the cops are working under duress with the bad guys. We're the only ones who can."

Julie fell silent. She knew Collins was right. From day one, she had struggled to admit to herself that the three of them were essentially leading a rebellion against a tyrannical oppressor. Seeing events like these in newspapers or in movies, tales from places so far away, they didn't seem real.

But now they were living them, and GlobaTech personnel were the only ones in a position to do anything. She knew they had to keep fighting, keep chipping away at Tristar and Orion, and hope they could make a big enough dent in Hall's dynasty to shake it to the ground.

"Fine," she said eventually. "Jericho, how do you want to do this?"

He stared at the map for a minute as his mind calculated and assessed all the different ways they could attack.

"It doesn't need to be overly complicated," he said finally. "It needs to be fast and brutal. We wait until the early hours. Fatigue will be setting in, and the patrol won't be as focused as they would be during the day. There's a tree line running alongside the road. We have a three-hour window to get in place. We lie in wait, then rush them once they're out of sight of the main streets. We'll have the element of surprise. We kill who we need to kill, then take the leader for questioning."

Julie shrugged. "Sounds good to me. Ray?"

Collins nodded. "Aye. That'll work like a charm."

The three of them stood straight.

"Then it's settled," said Julie. "We'll hit them tomorrow, in the early hours."

Collins reached for his coat. "I'm gonna try and get some shut-eye. I reckon the pair of ya should too."

He left the office.

"He's right," said Jericho. "We've been operating on less than three hours a night. We should rest."

"I'll rest when this is over," replied Julie stubbornly.

She leaned forward again, staring blankly at the map. Jericho watched her for a few minutes, noting her eyes weren't moving.

"What are you thinking?" he asked her.

She looked up and smiled weakly. "Honestly? I'm thinking it truly is a sign that the end is nigh when Ray voluntarily goes within a hundred miles of a museum."

They shared a laugh, a much-needed moment of reprieve from the horrors and stresses of the world.

Jericho closed the door, and the two of them fell to the floor within seconds, keen to expend the last few droplets of energy before turning in for the night.

COOKING WITH REBECCA

RECIPE: WINTER WARMERS

Published: November 16, 2020 by Rebecca R. | 213k comments

Listed: *Uncategorized.* **Tags:** *None.*

Winter has arrived early. The darkness before dawn is lasting longer. The temperature is dropping each day. Yet, for many, winter arrived months ago and brought with it changes that made it seem like the cold would last forever.

To prepare for the challenges ahead, today's *recipe* will look at everything that now stands behind us. After all, to fully appreciate how far we've come, we must always look at where we started.

We must also embrace our history, no matter how recent. The last six months happened. No matter how incomprehensible these events have been, we must not deny their existence. Only by analyzing the past do we stand any chance of avoiding our previous mistakes.

So, let us start at the beginning: May 11, 2020.

T-Day.

Tristar's nationwide invasion was sudden and unexpected. It took less than 72 hours for their forces to lock down the entire country. Airports were closed and barricaded. So were the ports and harbors. Roadblocks were established along the Canadian and Mexican borders, which made crossing them impossible.

In less than three days, the United States became a fortress.

Now Tristar soldiers patrol the streets like packs of wolves. Dressed in black and heavily armed, their intimidating and perpetual presence invokes fear across the country. They are free to do whatever they feel is necessary to maintain order.

High-ranking members of the government and the armed forces either fell in line or were removed from their positions. The military was ordered to stand down, pending its full decommissioning. Serving personnel in all branches were given the option to join Tristar's ranks or lose their jobs without compensation. Many of them refused to join the enemy, which is why almost a third of all refugees are former military personnel and their families.

Federal and local law enforcement agencies continued to function as normal, but Tristar had jurisdiction over everything. They claimed they were simply there to assist. They may as well not have been there at all, but playing along kept the men and women who worked for those agencies safe.

At first, many of us understandably refused to accept what was happening. This country has always been so stubbornly dedicated to its freedom and its constitutional rights; it would have been foolish not to expect some kind of civil resistance.

The first couple of weeks that followed saw rioting and fighting in the streets. Images on news broadcasts resembled those of a war-torn third-world nation—damaged buildings, torched vehicles, streets littered with trash and debris and dead bodies...

But slowly, order was restored.

By the end of the second month, life for many people had returned to normal. Almost all major cities across the country went about their day as if nothing had happened. Industry and commerce resumed. The stock market recovered. Society accepted the changes, and people simply adapted.

Well, most of us.

Smaller communities all over the country were taken over by the Tristar patrols that needed somewhere to stay. These occupying forces numbered close to 300 thousand—a number that is still growing every day. That, along with the tens of thousands of civilian deaths and public destruction caused by the invasion, resulted in millions of Americans losing their homes.

Quincy Hall, as both the director of Orion and self-assumed leader of the United States, used the near-limitless resources at his disposal to establish refugee camps across the U.S. Typically, these utilized sections or remains of small towns, such as motels and apartment buildings. They included accommodation for up to a hundred families, contained basic amenities, and were serviced by Tristar-controlled supply routes, which brought food and supplies once a week.

Nationwide travel was not restricted. However, the near-constant checkpoints and roadblocks deterred a lot of people from straying too far from their homes, which resulted in deserted interstates. This meant that, although there weren't any official travel restrictions, people living in the refugee communities were ultimately kept there.

People were told they could apply for residential status in their nearest town or city, but the process was convoluted and difficult, and it included an assessment of their skills and overall usefulness. Hall justified this by saying it was important to focus on growing the economy, and the best way to do that was to prioritize seeking quality employment. He wanted the best people to have the most important jobs and to use the success of key industries to build a better, more widespread economic boom. Thus, it quickly became evident to many people there was little chance of anyone actually making it out of the camps.

Hall cited the illusion of democracy as the main reason for his seizure of control and desire to "fix" the country, but all he had really done was establish an illusion of his own. Because of the influence he has over the media, his way was simply more palatable to the masses. That didn't make it any less corrupt or damaging than the old way, but an over-whelming majority of the nation chose ignorance, which meant the Orion dynasty soon became the new status quo.

But not everyone accepted it.

The Tristar-run camps filled quickly, leaving many people still without a safe place they could call home. Abandoned by the new regime, these outcasts formed their own communities and shanty towns beside the empty interstates and on the outskirts of civilization, away from the prying eyes of their oppressors. The people who built them became family to each other. These communities grew, established relations with others nearby, and began working together to survive. They scavenged from Tristar supply trucks and even ambushed them in more rural areas, where there were fewer patrols.

Word began to spread of these localized attacks. At first, the people fortunate enough to be living normal lives were outraged. They saw these small acts of rebellion as a threat to the way of life they had begrudgingly accepted. They knew Tristar would retaliate, and they feared that retaliation wouldn't be limited to just the people responsible. They were afraid a larger message would be sent.

But the attacks kept happening, and the more they did, the more people began to realize the attacks weren't acts of malice; they were acts of desperation. They began to see through the veil of half-truths Orion had laid over their new world. They began to see the lives millions of others were being forced to live.

So, people began to help.

Refugees started traveling to the outskirts of the cities and towns and camps, sharing their Tristar allowance with those less fortunate. They offered food, clothing, and basic services to the refugees living in these unofficial communities and shanty towns.

Word of this eventually reached the Oval Office. Hall had no place in his new society for those unlucky enough to be cast beyond its walls during the transition. They were a problem he told himself didn't exist if he couldn't see them.

In the years he spent planning this nationwide coup, he believed he had thought of everything. He had considered every outcome. Every reaction. He had contingences for contingences. But there was one thing he hadn't counted on: kindness. Hall wasn't prepared for the human spirit, and it was beginning to threaten the control he had worked so hard to establish.

His reaction was swift and devastating.

Many of the Tristar camps were closed, forcing people to migrate to the refugee communities farther away. Patrols doubled in both size and frequency. The number of checkpoints in and out of populated cities and towns was increased. The option to apply for residency anywhere was rescinded.

The message was heard loud and clear. People's fears had been realized. The kindness and charity stopped.

It took a few weeks, but Hall's wrath eventually subsided, and the patrols returned to normal. Most people simply watched and waited. Hall had shown his true colors. He had shown *exactly* who he was and how he operated. So, yet again, people adapted. Instead of defying his new system, people took the time to properly understand how it worked. Then, like every society throughout history has done, they figured out a way to cheat it.

People learned the routes of patrols and navigated around them. Although the main camps remained eerily abandoned, the refugee communities slowly began to thrive —not significantly enough to attract attention but well enough to provide a sufficient lifestyle for the people living in them.

Refugees began traveling to some of the smaller towns to buy food and use services and facilities. The residents of these towns helped them as best they could without drawing attention to themselves. Knowing the Tristar patrol routes, stores and restaurants opened through the night in slots of two or three hours.

Again, it wasn't long before Hall took notice. This time, however, there was no real explanation other than that people were just... adapting. They were making the best of what they had, and he knew there was nothing he could justify doing to stop it. So, instead, he helped them. He rerouted the supply trucks from the camps he had closed so that they went to the makeshift campsites and communities on the outskirts of the towns and cities. It won him some of the favor he knew he had lost previously, but many people saw through the gesture.

The handouts from Orion and the kindness of nearby communities were helping many Americans get by when they would otherwise have been struggling. People were surviving, but they weren't living. This wasn't a long-term strategy. People had learned that what Hall *said* and what he actually *did* were often two different things. It could be years before he delivered on his promise of a prosperous new way of life for everyone, if at all. To anyone not fortunate enough to live in New York, Chicago, San Francisco, or Seattle, this was nothing more than a Band-Aid on a broken arm.

Something needed to change.

In the shadows, the remains of GlobaTech Industries watched patiently as the new course of history played out. They moved around, mostly at night using back roads, staying mobile, biding their time until they were strong enough to do something to help.

Every place they visited, disguised as refugees themselves, they heard the whispers of revolution. They saw what the people were doing for each other. They also saw the poor conditions and the poverty many Americans were still living in, despite everyone's best efforts.

Quietly, GlobaTech operatives all over the country gradually reunited into one force, falling willingly under the command of Julie Fisher—a strong, commanding woman. She is a hero and an inspiration to all of us.

She alone leads an underground militia that numbers twenty thousand. Of course, they can't move that many people at once without drawing attention to themselves. She knows they will never be a match for Tristar in a straight-up fight. So, they separated into smaller groups and spread out across the country. Living beneath Tristar's radar and surviving on the same kindness as other refugees, they move covertly across the country, helping the many communities of outcasts and forgotten patriots by taking the fight to our enemy, one patrol at a time.

Once again, word began to spread. Tales told around metal barrel campfires of GlobaTech, the once-great corporate empire and saviors of the modern world, began to inspire people. Whenever a group of them arrived somewhere, they were immediately welcomed into the communities and sheltered from view, should any Tristar patrols come calling. They were given food and drink, fresh supplies, and a place to rest, for as long as they needed.

Julie's orders had been explicit from the beginning: ask for help, but do not take more than you need... and do not stay too long.

For years, GlobaTech had its share of detractors—myself included. Yet they selflessly fought to bring the world back from the brink of collapse following the tragedy of 4/17. It was a thankless responsibility and one they shouldered without question or complaint.

And now, despite being on their knees, they shoulder that burden once again.

People who wear the GlobaTech emblem are considered heroes, lauded as the protectors of those who suffer under the oppressive rule of Orion. They fight back against Tristar when necessary, dealing minimal damage but claiming small victories that inspire hope to all who hear of them.

The refugees' defiance has become GlobaTech's rebellion, and millions of Americans quietly unite behind their fight against Quincy Hall, Orion, and his Tristar army. They believe that one day soon, things will once again change.

And they're not alone. Their cause inspires others every day, including me.

Not many people know that my brother and I were there on May 11, 2020, the day GlobaTech fell. I stood alongside Julie Fisher and watched as the famous Santa Clarita compound crumbled to dust. We all wanted to fight, but we knew we couldn't. It wasn't the time. Tristar had GlobaTech beat. That day, they had all of us beat.

So, we ran.

But my brother and I had a different idea about how to deal with this new world order. I'm a journalist. I know the power of a news story, and I knew the second the bombs started dropping on Santa Clarita that the only way through whatever followed was together.

I started this blog to document the journey from T-Day to... whenever this is over. I did this for me, as a cathartic outlet to make life on the road more bearable. But I soon realized the media was controlled by Orion, which meant no one would ever get the full story again. So, each camp we visit, each town, each city, I tell whoever will listen what is really going on. I tell people what I saw. I tell them all what we are doing for each other and what GlobaTech is doing for us. I want to give people hope.

We shouldn't trust social media. We shouldn't trust the news. That's why I write the blog the way I do. It's not tagged. Its metadata is empty. It's written under the guise of a cooking blog in case any wandering Tristar eyes stumble across it online. But really, the only way you can find it is if you already know where to look. And that happens because people all over the country talk to each other. I recently hit two million subscribers, and I cannot thank you enough for supporting it and spreading the tales of hope and inspiration I risk my life to bring to you.

I hope you enjoy this recipe. May it keep you warm and bring you comfort during the cold, unforgiving months ahead. Please share this with your friends and loved ones. Ask them to do the same. The more people see this, the wider and faster hope will spread.

And finally, if you subscribe to any faith or religious belief, please say a prayer for the brave men and women of GlobaTech. They would never ask you to put yourselves at risk to help them, but if you feel safe doing so, please support them any way you can.

17

ROACH

November 16, 2020

Roach jolted awake, tugged from a dreamless sleep by foreign noises. Instinctively, he reached for the gun beneath his pillow, wrapping his hand around it as he listened carefully to the world around him.

The sounds that had stirred his subconscious began to fade into familiarity. After a few moments, he remembered where he was. He sighed with quiet relief as his surroundings took shape in the morning gloom from outside.

He let go of his gun and rolled over on his back, wincing at the unforgiving ground on which he lay. It felt like ice; the cold penetrated the layers he had wrapped himself in with frightening ease.

The downside of traveling in winter.

Roach pushed himself up, stooping while he straightened his clothes and dusted himself down. The tent he had slept in was wide and spacious but not quite high enough for him to stand fully upright inside.

He pulled the zipper, guiding it along its counterclockwise arc to reveal the entrance, then stepped out. The bitter chill in the air took his breath away. He stood straight, stretching out the cramps and the tightness in his body.

He and Becky had arrived at the refugee camp yesterday evening. Huntersville was a small town roughly ten miles north of Charlotte, North Carolina. It was largely abandoned now, save for a settlement of Tristar patrols to the east. The camp was to the north, spread across the intersection of the road leading to the nuclear plant on the banks of Lake Norman. Abandoned vehicles had been positioned to form secure borders for the sixty or so families that stayed here.

"Hey, buddy, you okay?"

The voice dragged Roach from his vacant gaze. He turned and focused on the man standing just beside his tent. He was fussing over a makeshift barbecue made from a grill plate resting over a charred metal barrel with a fire burning inside it. Roach had been introduced to him when they arrived the previous night.

"Did you say something?" asked Roach.

The man smiled. "Yeah, I asked if you wanted a hot dog. You were lost in that thousand-yard stare of yours."

Roach smiled back, friendly and apologetic. "Sorry about that. Early mornings don't agree with me."

"Here." He handed Roach a fresh hot dog. "This will wake you up."

Roach took it gratefully. "Thank you. Hey, it's Henry, right?"

"That's me."

"Mind if I grab one for my sister too?"

"Sure thing."

He passed another one to him.

"I don't suppose you've seen her this morning, have you?" asked Roach.

Henry turned and gestured to the opposite side of the camp with his cooking tongs. "The little lady is over there, telling a story to the kids."

Roach rolled his eyes. "Of course, she is. Thanks for the food. I appreciate it."

"It's my pleasure," he said. "After everything you've been doing, it's the least we can do."

Roach walked away without acknowledging the gratitude. He didn't want to show his discomfort in receiving it.

Becky recounted the exploits of GlobaTech's rebellion everywhere they went, to anyone who would listen. She kept in touch with Julie, speaking once every couple of weeks to keep each other updated. Roach knew this and didn't begrudge her doing it, but he didn't get involved himself. As far as he was concerned, their business was their own. He was content with his own journey. But Becky used these updates to spread hope to the refugees they encountered. It was why they risked visiting larger towns and, on occasion, big cities, once every couple of weeks—so she could upload her blog at an internet café.

There was no denying she was a huge part of why GlobaTech had as much support as they did.

But she also told stories of her brother. She presented their own journey as having been inspired by GlobaTech wanting to take a stand, to take back the country from its new oppressors. His personal crusade to kill the man behind all this garnered even more support. Becky said it was because people saw his journey as more relatable. They wished they had the strength to do it themselves.

Roach didn't like it, but he knew there was no stopping

his sister once she had a hold of a story. It was one of the many things he admired and loved about her.

He walked through the camp in search of her. Groups of tents formed circles around fire pits. He saw a few people huddled together for warmth, wrapped up in thick coats and blankets, but the camp was still quiet. The sun had begun its climb, tinting the morning sky with colorful streaks of dawn. But it was early. The moon was faintly visible in among the light clouds. The wind was gentle, yet it carried with it an icy chill that whipped around the camp.

Roach finally reached the far side, where his sister was squatting by a small fire, talking to a group of children. Their small mouths hung open, engrossed in whatever tale Becky was telling, hanging on her every word.

He stopped a respectful distance away and listened.

"...the more they tried, the more he fought back. He wasn't going to let them past. He wasn't going to let them hurt the people who had been so kind to him."

A tiny hand shot up at the back of the group. Becky looked over and smiled, inviting the question.

"Did he... did he stop the bad men?" asked a young girl, probably no older than eight. Her face was slightly squished beneath the thick hood of a winter coat.

Becky nodded. "He sure did. He stood up for the people who couldn't stand up for themselves. He put himself between the nice people in the camp and the bad people who wanted to hurt them. He protected them, like a true hero."

A chorus of gasps rose from the congregation, then the clapping began.

Becky looked over and saw Roach watching. She smiled. He nodded back and gestured to the hot dog.

She looked back at the children. "So, remember—no

matter how bad things might seem sometimes, there will always be people who look out for you and fight for you. Now make sure you tell your friends all about our hero, okay?"

Each child nodded enthusiastically.

"And... who do we *never* tell these stories to?"

In unison, the kids shouted, "The bad men in black!"

Becky smiled. "That's right. Now go on back to your mommies and daddies, okay? Get yourselves something to eat."

Everyone scrambled to their feet and ran past Roach. He watched them go, then turned back to see Becky walking toward him. He held out the hot dog.

"Good job I never made the leap and went vegan, isn't it?" she said, taking it from him and having a welcome bite.

He shrugged. "I'm not convinced I know what's in it. But food's food. We get it where we can."

They began walking back toward Roach's tent.

"How did you sleep?" she asked him.

"Like I was lying on an intersection in November. You?"

She chuckled. "Yeah, about the same."

"How long were you telling your stories?"

"Ah, not too long. Maybe forty minutes. I was awake. So were the kids. Figured I'd give the parents a little break."

"You're a natural with them."

"Thanks, Will."

He pressed his lips together, forming a hard line. "You shouldn't be filling their heads with that fiction, though. It doesn't do anyone any good."

Becky sighed. "Oh, don't start with this again."

"What?"

"You know what. I'm trying to give these people hope. Help them keep their spirits up."

"That's not your responsibility."

"Then whose is it, hmm?"

"Their own. They need to find their own way to deal with all this, same as us."

She took an extra step and moved in front of him, blocking his path. "Yes, but unlike us, not everyone has the strength to do that. Hearing about everything Julie and GlobaTech are trying to do helps them. They use other people's strength to fuel their own. That's how hope works."

Roach shook his head. "Hope is dangerous. The best thing these people and all the other refugees can do is accept what's happening and adapt to it. That's how they will survive. I'm not saying it isn't shitty losing everything and having to start over, but it is what it is. In the long run, sure... maybe things will change. But until then, people should be focused on staying alive and staying off Tristar's radar. Not listening to stories that, ultimately, will likely lead to disappointment."

Becky rolled her eyes, tired of replaying this same conversation in every camp they visited. "Right. And what about this crusade of yours we're both on, hmm? Walking cross-country to Washington, to the belly of the beast, picking fights with Tristar at every opportunity. And don't try to tell me you're not, Will, because I'm here. Nine times out of ten, we can avoid every patrol you end up killing. Are you telling me you don't have hope?"

"That's different."

"Why?"

"Because I'm not other people, Becky. I have the knowl-edge and ability to do something, and I am. But I'm not telling everyone about it. It gives them false hope and puts more pressure on me to live up to people's unrealistic expec-tations. It doesn't help anyone."

"So, what? You're saying you don't believe you can do this? Because if that's the case, why bother? Why drag us halfway across the country if you think it's pointless?"

"I'm not saying that. I believe I can do this, but that doesn't mean I will. I'm a realist. I hope for the best and prepare for the worst."

"And what do you think these people are doing, Will? Jesus! Look around you. Everyone here is prepared for the worst. Supplies are scarce. There's the constant fear of a Tristar patrol coming along and taking advantage of them. They've had to make peace with the fact that this is just their life now. I'm telling the stories of GlobaTech's rebellion and of your own journey to every camp we come across because it shows them there are some who haven't given up. There are some who are trying to do what's right, no matter what. They need this."

"I understand that, Becky."

"Then stop acting like you have to avoid the responsibility of inspiring people. Like it or not, that's exactly what you're doing. Don't you see that? Remember that camp we stayed at last week? On the outskirts of Augusta? The women there were being harassed, and in a couple of cases *abused*, by one of the regular Tristar patrols. What happened?"

Roach glanced at the ground. "We stayed there until the patrol came around and I killed them all."

"Right. And what happened after that?"

"You know what happened after that."

"You're right. I do. I saw every single one of those refugees flock to you like it was the Second Coming. The women you saved cried in your arms, Will. They were still talking to each other about what you did as we were leaving, and you're going to stand there and tell me you're not inspiring people? Do you know what your problem is?"

He shook his head. "I know you're about to tell me."

"You've distanced yourself so much from other human beings, you've completely forgotten how to be around them. How to interact with them. You don't know how people think and feel anymore. Honestly, there are times when I think you're a robot. Just... devoid of any—"

Roach's gaze flicked to something he saw over her shoulder. A second later, he grabbed her arm and marched her toward the back of the camp, walking with fresh urgency.

Becky hurried to keep up with him. "Hey, what are you doing?"

"A Tristar truck just pulled over by the camp entrance. Must be a supply drop-off." They stopped in the far corner, just past where the kids were moments earlier. He pulled the hood of her coat over her head, then did the same with his own. "Thanks to your stories, it's safe to assume any patrols are on the lookout for us. We need to lie low."

She quickly finished her hot dog. "I'm pretty sure it's all the Tristar patrols you've killed that will have gotten their hackles up."

He smiled weakly. "Semantics."

A few people close by moved over to them, forming a larger group around them, hiding them from view. Some of them stood quietly, sipping hot soup from a large mug, warming their hands. Others spoke among themselves. It looked natural, as if they were behaving like Roach and Becky weren't even there.

Glancing from beneath his hood, through the crowd, Roach watched patiently, observing the movements and routines of the Tristar patrol. There were six men in total. One stayed behind the wheel, while four others unloaded the supplies and wheeled them on carts. The last man coordinated the effort, stepping inside the borders of the camp and directing where the delivery should be left.

As the last of the crates was dropped off, Henry approached the Tristar coordinator.

"Where's the rest of it?" he asked, pointing to the five crates now stacked just inside the entrance to the camp. "Last week, you sent eight crates. This won't be enough."

The Tristar guard shoved him away and rested his hand on his sidearm. "Hey, back up, or I'll put you down."

Henry kept his distance, holding his hands up in clear resignation. "But this isn't enough to feed all of us for a week."

"That sounds like a whole lot of your problem. We need to make all these deliveries earlier and faster because some of you people have decided it's a good idea to try attacking our patrols. You wanted out of our camps. You wanted to set up your own. You did. You should be grateful we're giving you anything at all."

Without realizing, Henry took a step forward as he continued his protest.

"You can't do this to us! You're supposed to be helping, not—"

The Tristar guard shoved him again, harder this time. Henry stumbled backward and fell hard to the ground. The guard drew his weapon and took aim, holding it steady.

"I said... back up! This is your last warning. Next time you threaten me, I'll shoot you. Understand?"

Henry remained silent.

At the back of the camp, Roach's whole body tensed. Becky felt it and placed a hand on his arm.

"Don't," she hissed. "This isn't the time."

He snapped his gaze to her. "They're taking advantage of

these people, Becky. They're assaulting them for no reason. They can't get away with it. I won't let them."

She shuffled in front of him, being careful not to move too much and draw any attention to them. "Patrols are one thing, but this is a supply run. They're already penalizing these people. You interfere now, it could cost them everything. There's no real danger here. You have to let this one go, Will. Please."

He tensed even more, to the point where his body shook and his jaw ached. Then he unclenched his fists and sighed. "Fine."

"Thank you."

A few moments passed. The Tristar supply truck left without further incident. Only once it was out of sight did the group move. Roach pushed through them and made a beeline for Henry.

He was just getting back to his feet, with the help of an elderly couple, when Roach neared him.

"Are you okay?" asked Roach.

"Yeah, I'm fine," replied Henry reluctantly. "Hurt my pride more than anything."

"I'm sorry. I should've done something."

Henry waved the comment away with his hand.

"You'd have only made it worse if you did. I'm fine, honestly." He glanced over at the delivery. "I'd best get that packed away."

Roach watched him leave. He was angry at himself for not doing more, despite knowing why he couldn't have.

The old woman who had helped Henry appeared at his side. He turned to her. She smiled at him. It warmed her expression, lighting up her brown eyes, which had no doubt forgotten more than he himself had ever seen.

"That's your sister, isn't it?" she asked him. "The one who has been telling us all those wonderful stories."

He nodded. "It is."

"So, you're the one she talks about? The man who used to work for Tristar but is now fighting back for us?"

"I am. They betrayed me, and I've been hunting them since long before all of this happened."

She took his hand in hers and patted it softly. "Please... tell me you can stop them. Tell me you can help put an end to this... suffering. You and those people who used to work for GlobaTech."

Her eyes began to mist with tears. Roach held her gaze, not really knowing what he could say that would help.

He caught sight of Becky, standing a little away from them with a group of refugees, all looking on and listening. She stared at him, shaking her head almost imperceptibly. A silent demand to not answer with the realism he was so fond of.

Roach took a deep breath and looked back at the old lady. "I promise you I'll either stop them or die trying. This is more than just a personal vendetta now. Someone needs to stand up. Someone needs to say, 'Enough.'"

She smiled, forcing tears to escape down her face, which ran along the narrow canals in her frail skin.

"No one should be in your position. I'm sorry you've found yourself underneath the weight of this burden, young man. We cannot ask any more of you than you have already given us. Too many of us are too scared or too weak to do anything except exist anymore. But you..." She smiled again. "You give us hope. May God be with you."

Roach nodded his gratitude, and she walked away.

Becky moved over to him, grinning. "See? You can be human when you put your mind to it."

He rolled his eyes. "Yeah, yeah. Listen, we should stock up on whatever food and water these people can spare, then hit the road. We have a long walk ahead of us."

Becky rested her head against his shoulder and sighed. "Don't we always, big brother?"

18

ADRIAN HELL

November 16, 2020

Ruby's driving the black Escalade we borrowed from a Tristar patrol three weeks ago. Well, I say *borrowed*... we stole it from them. Well, I say *stole*... we killed them and just kinda took it. Whatever. It's big enough for all of us, and we were sick of traveling in separate vehicles.

Rayne and Link are arguing in the back like a pair of kids. Something about legroom. Behind them, Jessie is sprawled out on her own seat, eyes closed, hands clasped behind her head, no doubt listening to their inane banter.

I glance sideways at Ruby, who looks back and smiles.

"You okay?" she asks.

I nod. "Yeah. Just thinking how all these roads look the goddamn same. This entire country has merged into one continuous stretch of tarmac."

"I know what you mean. I imagine there's a little more variety near the cities."

"Probably. Guess we'll never know."

Like most people who don't live in a large city, we tend not to go near them. Too many patrols. Too much risk. I hate it, but we have to play it smart right now.

Mostly.

Ruby is in contact with Julie. Maybe once a week, they connect and exchange updates. We know where they are and what they're doing. Similarly, they know how we're doing our part to help.

See, GlobaTech operatives are moving around the U.S. in packs. There are around two hundred groups in total, each containing a hundred or so men and women. Twenty thousand well-trained operatives sounds like a lot, and it is, but not compared to the quarter million-plus Tristar has. They're trying to find out what they can use to fight back, and they're trying to do it quietly.

I, on the other hand, am not.

Early on in this shit-show, I told the team that we weren't going to hide. GlobaTech had a clear idea on how to approach this, right from the beginning. So did Roach, albeit a much different one.

The team and I were on the fence. I saw the benefits of both strategies. GlobaTech's plan was smarter but would take much more time to get a result. Roach's was a little more direct but carried with it additional risks, which not everyone was comfortable with.

I decided we would compromise.

We're trying to track down Brandon Crow, and we're making as much noise as we can along the way. We're small enough to hide but dangerous enough to do some serious damage if we put our minds to it.

I know word gets around—and not just among the refugees. All the talk of rebellion is great, but I'm only concerned about what Quincy Hall is saying. His focus is primarily on me because he knows what I'm doing, and I'm making damn sure he knows where we are. This way, he's not paying as much attention to the others, which buys them some time.

Plus, it keeps us entertained.

"So, you think this tip-off we got is legit?" asks Ruby.

I shrug. "Who knows? It would make sense, at least geographically, for Crow to be heading this way. Guess we'll find out soon enough."

"Y'know, considering this asshole is moving around in a convoy of three huge, heavily armored, well protected juggernauts, he's surprisingly hard to find."

I chuckle. "Especially given how empty the interstates are nowadays, yeah."

"That's a pretty good point," says Rayne, behind us. "You would think someone might've noticed him by now."

"Someone probably has," I counter, shifting in my seat to look back at him. "Thing is, normal folks won't say anything for two reasons. One, they're most likely in the cities, where I imagine most of his routes take him, and they won't want to jeopardize the borderline normal life they have. And two, chances are most of those people won't know what they're looking at if they did see him.

"Now, the refugees... *they* know how this wicked new world works. We've all seen that firsthand. But people in their position... they see *that* much Tristar heading their way, they run and hide. Plus, we ain't exactly got access to all the fancy satellites and spy networks and shit we used to have. Hence why it's like trying to find a fart in a jacuzzi."

Ruby screws her face up. "Oh, Adrian... gross!"

Rayne and Link laugh. Jessie sighs.

I shrug. "What? I'm just saying."

"Well, work on your metaphors. Jesus."

"Technically, that was a simile."

"Whatever. *Technically*... it was disgusting."

I grin as she sticks her tongue out at me.

The vehicle falls silent. I go back to staring out the window, watching the world rush by. The last solid lead we got on Crow's whereabouts was from an incredibly cooperative Tristar patrol we met in some deserted, backwater town in South Dakota. Before Link tore his throat out, the last remaining guard told us Crow was heading for Nebraska. One of his routes usually took him through Omaha and down I-29, toward Missouri.

Omaha is where I was born. I haven't been there in... Christ... almost thirty years now. While the guy didn't sound like he was lying with his last words, there's a risk we were fed some well-rehearsed bullshit. However, given it's where I grew up, we decided as a team it was fate's way of saying this is a lead worth pursuing.

And so, here we are, ten or so miles outside the city limits.

The interstate is quiet. Most refugees stick to their camps, and people from the big cities have no real reason to venture too far from them anymore. Only people you really see on main stretches of road like this are—

"Ah, guys?"

I look back at Jessie, who's staring out the rear window. Rayne and Link do the same.

"What is it?" asks Rayne.

"We might have some company," she says.

"Oh, no..." says Ruby. "We *definitely* have some company."

I turn to her and see the frustration on her face. I follow her stern gaze and look ahead. There's a Tristar roadblock coming up. Two vehicles are parked nose-to-nose across the width of the road. Presumably eight guys—four in each.

"Okay," I say. "We've got two vehicles ahead. Jessie, is it just the one behind?"

"That I can see," she calls back.

"Okay. So, three vehicles... let's assume four assholes in each one. No mounted fifty cals, which means these aren't the armored variety."

Jessie spins around to face forward and leans on the seats in front of her. "I get to use Dizzy?"

I smile. "You get to use Dizzy."

"Yes!"

She high-fives Link, then starts fumbling inside the large gym bag beside her. She takes out a thick, metal briefcase, which she rests on her lap and flicks open. Inside is a combat drone, remotely piloted by a portable console that's also kept in the case. It's bright red, with four mini rotors and a payload that would make most Navy destroyers blush.

We call it Dizzy.

She begins prepping it for flight.

I reach behind me and take out one of my Raptors. I check the mag and knock the safety off.

"Usual drill?" asks Link.

"I reckon so, big guy," I reply. "Jessie, tell me when you're ready."

"Any minute..." she replies.

I look over at Ruby. "You good?"

She glances over and smiles. Ruby has a beautiful smile. She always has. It lights up her face and any room she happens to be standing in at the time. But this smile isn't one of those smiles. It's a smile I've seen more and more of these last six months.

It's her Stonebanks smile. The crazy smile she perfected

for the character she sometimes needs to play when shit gets real.

I grin at her. "Yeah, you're good. Sexy bitch."

She stares ahead and slowly puts her foot to the floor.

"Jessie?"

"Ready!"

"Let her fly."

In the back, she buzzes her window down and flies the drone outside, using the tablet with the flight console on it. I watch it zoom past us, toward the roadblock ahead.

"In position," she confirms.

I nod. "Fellas."

Link and Rayne lean out of their respective windows, aiming two of the many assault rifles we acquired from previous encounters with Tristar at the vehicle behind us.

"We're ready, boss," says Rayne.

"Hit 'em."

Jessie taps the screen. "See ya, bitches."

A thin trail of smoke appears behind the drone as a small missile fires from beneath it. A heartbeat later, the roadblock ahead disappears in a thunderous explosion.

As it does, Link and Rayne open fire, peppering the vehicle behind us with bullets. It swerves to avoid the gunfire, then slides to an abrupt halt.

"Inside!" shouts Ruby.

They duck back inside. Ruby steers into the middle of the road and bursts through the wall of fire and metal carcasses ahead at full speed. She slams on the brakes and turns a one-eighty, causing the tires to screech as we stop.

Link, Rayne, and I get out. They each take a side of the road. I move around the vehicle and lean against the hood. A moment later, Ruby steps out, taking aim with my other Raptor behind the cover of her open door. Jessie has climbed out the back and up onto the roof, kneeling and aiming her own weapon directly ahead.

I'm holding my gun low. Patient. They'll follow us through. They always do.

A couple of minutes later, the vehicle that was pursuing us pushes through the gap Ruby made in the flaming wrecks. They slow to a stop. Kill the engine. And wait.

If this were a western, there would be tumbleweeds rolling across the street.

Finally, all four doors open, almost in unison, and the remaining patrol gets out. They're dressed head to toe in black, all armed with Tristar-issue SMGs.

"Put them down," I shout over. "This isn't a fight you're going to win."

The guard who was riding shotgun lowers his gun and steps forward.

First one to move or talk is in charge. Always.

He looks back at his men, gesturing with his hand for them to lower their weapons too.

They do.

"You're Adrian Hell," he says to me, stopping halfway between his vehicle and ours.

I smile. "I am. And you're a Tristar piece of shit."

He ignores me. "You won't get away with this. You think we didn't call for back-up before following you?"

"Oh, I'm counting on it. Gives us more people to kill."

The guard scoffs. "When I bring Mr. Hall your head, he's going to give me a medal."

I frown. "You know he's not empowered to give you medals, right? He's not *actually* the president. He also pretty much disbanded every branch of the armed forces, which was the only organization that handed out medals anyway.

Trust me, I got a few of them myself back in the day. The point is, *Skippy*, you ain't gonna get shit."

"We'll see about that, you sonofabitch."

His arm twitches. The slight movement indicates his intention to fire at me. That was all we needed.

Rayne and Link open fire and take out the three men standing behind ol' Skippy here. They drop before they ever knew what hit them. The last man standing spins around, stares in horror at his fallen comrades, then turns back to me. Slowly. He drops his gun and raises his hands.

Rayne moves in from my left and kicks the gun away, then steps back, keeping the guard covered. Link moves back to our vehicle. Ruby steps around the door to my side. She leans into me, smiling seductively as she slides the Raptor she had back into the holster I'm wearing behind me.

"Thanks, sweetie."

She kisses my cheek. "Any time, handsome."

From above, I hear Jessie making fake retching noises.

"Now, now," I call back without turning around. "Jealousy doesn't suit you."

"I'm not jealous," she replies. "Just nauseated."

I smile. "Ah, I think you're a little jealous."

Ruby punches me.

I look at her. "What? She's more likely to be jealous of me, not you."

She holds my gaze, then smiles. "Damn straight."

"Still just nauseated, you guys," says Jessie.

The guard shakes his head. "You people are fucking insane."

I push myself away from the hood and walk toward him. "Quite possibly. But here's the thing, my little *Plant Pot* —these last few months have been a little shitty, and that's kinda your fault. Not like there's an abundance of thera-pists to go and talk to anymore, so I deal with it by going back to what I know. And what I know is killing fuckwits like you."

I nod to Rayne, standing behind him, who knocks the guard's helmet off him with a sharp jab of his rifle butt. I immediately press the barrel of my own gun to the guy's newly exposed forehead.

"We heard that Brandon Crow's monster truck show is rolling through here. That right?"

The guard shook his head. "I-I have no idea."

"Really?" I look over at Rayne again. "He has no idea."

Rayne shakes his head. "Well, shit. I guess we should let him go, then."

"I guess we should. Except... that's, what? The ninth? *Tenth* time someone in his situation has said they don't know something."

"At least."

I look the guard in the eye. "And you know what? They *always* knew something. So, you're gonna tell me if we're on the right track. Then you're gonna impress me by telling me something I don't know because you want to be helpful."

To be fair to the guy, he's holding eye contact with me. Most people in his position would've pissed their pants by now.

"And if I do," he says. "Will you let me go?"

I pause for a moment, then lower my gun and smile. "Sure. Why not? It's nearly Thanksgiving. We're still doing that this year, right?"

He nods eagerly, which is hilarious.

"Mr. Crow should be passing through Omaha later today," says the guard. "We were told to run extra patrols along the route."

"And do you have details of all the routes he takes?" asks Ruby, moving beside me.

He shakes his head. "No. No one does. We get the call usually a couple of hours before. That's it, I swear."

I nod. "Okay. I believe you. So, tell me something I don't know."

"Like w-what?"

I shrug. "Surprise me."

He looks around, in every direction except at me.

Whatever he says will be bullshit. I can see it in his eyes. He's trying to think of something impressive, which means he doesn't already *know* something impressive. He's simply going to lie to try and save himself.

Worth a try. Anything we can learn is useful. We always pass new intel over to Julie too.

He doesn't answer.

I shake my head. Rayne and Ruby step away, knowing what's coming.

"Time's up, sweet cheeks."

"No, wait! I can tell you—"

I raise my gun and pull the trigger. The bullet drives through his skull and out the other side, taking some bone and brain with it. The impact drags his body to the ground hard.

I turn without a second thought and walk back to the Escalade. Jessie and Link are already inside. Ruby is climbing in behind the wheel. Rayne catches up to me as I open the passenger door.

"Hey, Adrian, do you really think we're still doing Thanksgiving this year?" he asks.

I stare at him blankly, then frown. "How do you not fall down more?"

"What? I'm just saying. After everything that's happened, it'll be nice to celebrate something."

"Uh-huh. With what? You gonna have roadkill and stuffing on a sandwich?"

He rolls his eyes. "Man, you're such a downer..."

"Yeah. Who would've thought being forced to spend six months on the run like a fugitive from three hundred thousand armed assholes all desperate to shoot me would be one of my things?" I open my door. "Get in the car."

A minute later, we're back on the road to Omaha, comforted by the knowledge that we're probably heading in the right direction.

If we can finally catch up to Brandon Crow, maybe we can put an end to all this...

19

ROACH

November 16, 2020

They had been walking most of the day. It was late afternoon, and the sun was already disappearing, allowing the evening's gloom to take over.

Roach and Becky had stayed mostly to the sides of highways and interstates. It kept the route straight and simple. Also, given how light traffic was nowadays, it made spotting Tristar patrols a lot easier.

"My feet are killing me," said Becky, with a frustrated huff of breath.

Roach glanced down. "You're wearing heels. What do you expect?"

"They're not heels. They're boots. Boots you wear for walking. They're sensible. It's not like I'm wearing stilettos. Also, bite me."

He let slip a small smile. "It's too early to hunker down for the night, but we'll stop at the first camp we find, okay?"

"Thank you."

"Where are we, anyway? I haven't seen a road sign for a few miles."

Becky rummaged in one of the pockets of her thick winter coat and took out her cell phone. She loaded the GPS, slowing her pace while it connected.

"I think we're approaching Concord," she said. "That's good going. Huntersville is almost eighteen miles back."

Roach nodded. "We should make it to Greensboro by the end of the week."

"Maybe we could try hitching a ride once we get a little closer to civilization? Save our legs."

"Yeah, maybe. It puts whoever stops for us at risk, though, especially with all the roadblocks set up on the outskirts of the main towns and cities."

"I know, but at this rate, it'll be Christmas before we make it to D.C. I'm tired, Will." Her phone beeped at her. "I also need to charge this somewhere soon. The battery's on less than fifteen percent."

"Okay. Turn it off for now. We don't need it just yet anyway."

She did and shoved it back in her pocket. Then she adjusted the strap of the large bag she had over her shoulder, pushing it behind her a little.

"I need to charge my laptop too. I should post another blog soon," she said.

"Whatever you need."

Becky glanced sideways at her brother, watching his fixed, hard expression. He didn't blink much, which she thought was strange. His breathing seemed measured, as if he only took a breath when he absolutely needed to.

"Will, can I ask you something?" she said after a few minutes.

He shrugged. "Sure."

"If you had never questioned that order and stayed working for Tristar, do you think you would be fighting on the other side right now?"

Roach looked at her and frowned. "Is this for one of your blog posts?"

She shook her head. "No. It's for me. I'm curious."

He took a deep breath and stared ahead, fixated on the space a few feet in front of him as he thought about his answer.

"Honestly? No. I'm all for doing the job and walking a morally questionable line at times, but wrong is wrong. If it wasn't that, it would've been something else. I wouldn't have stayed with Tristar long enough to be around when all this started."

Becky smiled. "I figured."

"What made you ask?"

"I was just thinking. It's not always easy to step up and do the right thing, especially if doing so puts you at risk." She reached over and linked his arm with hers, leaning into him as they walked. "The more people we meet, the more I realize how special you are, big brother."

"Yeah? How's that?"

"Because the more I see people react to my blog... see how they treat you when we arrive somewhere... the more I realize this isn't one of those humbling times where you get to say, *'I'm just doing what anyone would've done.'* Very few people would choose to do what you're doing, Will. You're a real—"

"Don't say it..."

She looked up at him and grinned. "Hero!"

Roach rolled his eyes. "Don't call me that. I'm not a hero. I'm just... doing what needs to be done, same as a lot of people."

"Do you hate *hero* as much as you hate *Roach?*"

He sighed and glared at her. "Not quite."

"Y'know, Ray had a point. It's a pretty badass nickname. I can't believe you haven't rolled with it before now."

"I don't want a nickname. I don't like being that familiar with people. Besides, a roach is a bug. There's nothing badass about something you step on."

"Yeah, but a cockroach is the only thing that would survive a nuclear holocaust. Something that difficult to kill is kinda cool. Anyway, you introduced yourself to Adrian Hell as Roach. What makes him so special?"

"That was different."

"Why?"

"Because looking into his eyes was like looking in a mirror. I'm not saying we're going to hang out and drink beer together, but I saw the way people acted around him... how they talked about him and to him. I could tell he and I are basically the same person. What, you think Mister and Missus Hell named their child Adrian? No— it's a moniker. My guess would be it was bestowed upon him, rather than something he chose himself. Out of everyone in that room that day, I had a feeling he was the only one who would truly understand me and why I was there. It made sense to me for him to know me on that level."

Becky was silent for a moment, then smiled. "That was actually kinda sweet. And I get it. You're Will, my brother. But Roach is... someone you need to be. A persona that helps you separate the good in you from the bad."

He raised an eyebrow. "Yeah, something like that."

They walked in silence for a few minutes, remaining huddled together as the temperature continued to drop.

"That's going in your blog, isn't it?" he asked finally.

She smiled. "Showing your human side will really help people connect with you."

"I don't want people to connect with me."

"Well, tough. That connection is how this blog will keep working and inspiring people."

Roach was about to protest, but lights in the distance caught his attention. He squinted in the early dusk. At first, he thought they were headlights, which most likely would've been a Tristar patrol. But as the closer they got, he realized it wasn't a vehicle.

There was a refugee camp beside the interstate.

He pointed to it. "Looks like we might have a place to rest."

Becky saw the lights and sighed with relief. "Oh, thank God!"

"Can't wait for another roadkill hot dog, huh?"

She hit his arm. "Gross!"

He smiled. They both picked up the pace, motivated to push through the aches and fatigue by the promise of pending respite.

It took them a little under ten minutes to reach the border of the camp. They slowed as they approached, having learned from experience that caution is usually required.

There weren't any barriers along this stretch of highway. The tarmac simply stopped, and the dust and gravel began. There was no shelter for miles around. What few trees there were stood barren and thin, sickly with winter.

The campsite itself looked like a test tube, with a wide arc of tents at one end, all facing the road and focused on a large campfire. Forming the sides were makeshift stalls wrapped with tarpaulin, which displayed basic food and tools.

Close to the road was a food truck. The rattle of a generator broke the silence of the oncoming night, and the fluorescent lights pierced the veil of dusk. A small line gathered in front of it, filled with the muted chatter among the people of the camp.

An older man saw them approaching and walked to greet them. Roach eyed him warily. He looked good for his age, but he figured his fifties were long behind him. His body looked a little thinner than maybe it should be, which made his winter clothing seem bigger than it was.

The man smiled as he neared them. "Howdy, folks."

Becky smiled back. "Hi."

"And what brings the two of you through our part of town?"

Roach cleared his throat. "Just passing through on our way to Greensboro. Wondered if you had a little food and water to spare? We won't take up too much of your time or resources, but it's been a long day, and we would appreciate the chance to rest."

The man patted Roach on his shoulder. "Say no more, son. You're both welcome here as long as you need."

"Thank you," said Becky. "That's really kind of you."

He turned and walked back to the crowd by the food truck, beckoning them both to follow. As they entered the boundaries of the camp, more people looked over as they noticed the new arrivals.

"These fine folks are passing through," announced the man. "I said they were welcome to stay as long as they need."

There were murmurs of agreement and acceptance. People began to walk over and introduce themselves, extending their hands casually and nodding polite greetings.

"The name's Billy," he said when the curious crowd has dispersed. "Billy Newton. Folks here tend to call me Old Bill. Truth be told, I ain't the oldest here, but they seem to look up to me, so I take it as an authority thing rather than a slight about how old I look."

He chuckled to himself.

Becky smiled. "Well, Billy, I don't think you look old at all."

He pointed to her, smiling. "I like this one! She's a keeper, all right!"

Roach held back a smile. "She's actually my sister. You can have her."

Billy roared with laughter. Becky looked offended, although Roach knew she wasn't. She hit his arm playfully.

"Will! Jesus..." she exclaimed.

Still laughing, Billy turned toward the food truck and shouted, "Can you spare me two bottles of water and a couple of burgers there, Jimmy?"

The man behind the counter, who was wearing a dirty apron and glistening with perspiration, nodded. "Sure thing, Billy. Gimme two minutes."

He looked back at them. "I like you folks. This is a long, lonely stretch of road you've found yourself on. Don't see too many new faces along here. You're heading to Greensboro, you say?"

"We are," said Roach. "Like I say, we're passing through."

"Uh-huh. And where are you passing through to, if you don't mind my asking?" He saw Roach's hesitation and immediately held his hands up in apology. "I'm not meaning to pry, son. You won't cause offence if you tell me to mind my business, I promise."

Becky smiled warmly. "He's just a little skeptical. That's all. We try to stay under Tristar's radar, so the less people know about us, the less at risk they are should anyone come asking."

Billy nodded. "I see. And why would Tristar come asking for you, exactly?"

Becky glanced at Roach for approval, which he gave in the form of a slight nod.

She fixed Billy with a wry smile. "Because they're not really a fan of my cooking blog..."

Billy frowned, confused. But then his eyes grew wide as the realization of who they were hit him.

He pointed at Becky. "You're..." Then he looked at Roach and took a small step back. "Which means you're... holy crap!"

He spun around to face everyone who was standing nearby.

"Folks! We got... you're not gonna believe this... come meet Rebecca and Roach! I'm being serious. Come on now!"

The crowd stampeded to surround them. Word of the commotion quickly spread around the small campsite, and soon everyone was standing with them. Some were smiling and laughing. Others had tears in their eyes.

Becky leaned close to her brother. "This is why I write my blog, Will. This, right here."

He rolled his eyes as his mouth curled into a resigned smile. "Yeah, yeah. Okay, hotshot. Don't let it go to your head."

The two of them were ushered into the camp. While he hated to concede any point, Roach had to admit that seeing the way people treated them... he was beginning to understand why Becky wrote that blog of hers.

He was beginning to see that hope still existed.

20

ADRIAN HELL

November 16, 2020

We entered Omaha about a half-hour ago. I felt it the second we did. It hit me like a foreign heat when you first step off an airplane. It was tangible.

It felt like home.

I haven't been here in almost thirty years. The last time was for my dad's funeral. I joined the CIA a few days after, and the rest is history, I guess. But despite the fact that I was only here for eighteen of my forty-eight years, it still feels like home to me.

The city itself looks normal. The streets are packed with traffic. The sidewalks are busy. Life goes on. Looking at this place, you would never know anything had happened.

But there's a Tristar patrol on every other street corner. Nothing is as it used to be.

"I have a bad feeling about this," mutters Link behind me.

"You get a bad feeling about everything," counters Rayne. "It's probably heartburn."

"Nah, man. It's the fact that we're driving through a city in a stolen Tristar Escalade."

"It's not stolen," I say. "It's just on indefinite loan."

"Right. Which makes all the difference..."

The windows are tinted, but they still slide low in their seats. Ruby is sitting upright and tense behind the wheel. I reach over and rest my hand on her leg.

"Just act normal," I say, trying to offer her some comfort. "Drive like everyone else and head away from the center. We'll be fine."

"And if we get stopped?" she asks without looking over.

I shrug. "Then I start shooting, and you drive a little faster."

She shakes her head and smiles. "Well, at least you've thought this through."

Realistically, Tristar patrols aren't going to stop one of their own on a busy street. They don't strike me as a sociable bunch.

We navigate the flow of traffic without issue. There's a comfortable silence inside the vehicle. We've spent so much time together over the last six months, we've become like family. We're so used to each other's company that the need to fill every silence with conversation has long since gone.

Outside, thick gray clouds cover the sky, signaling the end of another winter day. The heater's blasting around the car, so it's comfortable in here. But outside is a different story. Here in the Midwest, it's hovering around ten degrees right now. Or, as some meteorologists call it... fucking cold. That's why Jessie has a pile of thick coats stacked next to her. We agreed a while ago it was best to prepare for the winter when we got the chance. We grabbed these from a Goodwill we passed a couple of weeks back.

Ruby guides us away from the busy center, heading west along the highway, toward I-80. We figure if Crow is heading this way from Lincoln, that's the road he'll be coming in on.

The office buildings and high-rises soon fade away, revealing more of the dull skyline. Jessie mentioned yesterday how Roach's sister wrote about a winter that feels like it won't ever end. Looking out at the world right now, I know what she meant. I can't remember a time when it wasn't cold and harsh and miserable.

Ruby drives around an intersection, then exits left off the highway, taking us south. It starts to open up; there are hardly any buildings or people, just refreshingly busy roads and...

"Hey, pull over, would you?" I say to Ruby. I point to the side of the road. "Just here."

I feel everyone shuffle and tense, immediately on edge. They think I've seen something they haven't.

She does, without question. I climb out the moment the engine dies. I dig my hands into my pockets and hunch my arms to my body, instantly struggling with the drastic change in temperature. The others follow me outside, hustling to get their coats on. Ruby appears next to me, holding mine out for me. I take it gladly and shrug it on as I stare through the metal railings that line the street.

"What is it?" she asks. "Are you okay?"

I gesture inside the fence with a nod. "This is Omaha's National Cemetery. My parents are buried here."

"Oh, my God..." she whispers. She moves close to me and links my arm. "Are you okay?"

"I am. It's just weird being here. I knew I would feel it, coming back to my hometown and all, but I didn't consider the possibility of coming *here*. Now that we are... it's hit a little harder than I thought."

Rayne walks over, turning his collar up against the sharp chill. "Hey, everything okay? What's going on?"

Ruby looks at him. "Adrian's parents are buried here. We're gonna need a minute."

He holds his hands up and nods. "Hey, say no more. I get it. Take all the time you need, boss."

"Thanks, Adam," I say without looking over.

He walks back over to the others, no doubt explaining why we're here.

"You wanna go inside?" asks Ruby.

I turn to her. "Honestly? No. I'm not good with this type of thing."

"But?"

I smile. "But... I know I have to. It's been too long, and God knows how long it'll be until the next time."

"You want me to come with you?"

I step away and take her hand, squeezing it in mine. I trace my thumb across the back of her hand, amazed at how warm and smooth her skin feels, despite the cold.

"Thank you, but I think I need to go in there alone." I glance over her shoulder at the others. "Besides, someone needs to stay here and watch the kids."

Ruby smiles. "Go do what you gotta do, handsome."

She kisses me, then walks over to the team. I shove my hands deep in my pockets, hugging my coat around me. I head for the entrance—a small gate just a couple of hundred yards away, set into the fence.

Inside, the skeletal trees paint thin lines against the sky. The remains of frozen leaves litter the path, and the grass is sprinkled with frost. I navigate the cemetery as if I come here every day, instinctively knowing where my family rest.

The cemetery is huge, and it takes me a few minutes, but I finally see the landmark I recognize—a large, chipped statue of an angel, easily ten feet tall. It's covered in moss, but it's still one of only a few tombstones in here that's this big or grandiose. My parents share a grave right next to it.

I stop in front of it and stare down at the ground. The names of my parents, along with two of the most important dates I will ever remember, are etched into the damp, weathered stone.

I stare at my father's date of death. New Year's Eve, 1990. I'll never forget the day I found out. It was the same day I was awarded the Purple Heart and the Silver Star. Just a skinny, beat-up kid, lying in a hospital.

I crouch in front of the grave and clasp my hands in front of me. I wince as my knees crack under the duress of the winter chill.

"Hey," I say quietly. "It's me. I don't have any excuses for why I haven't visited before now. If I'm honest, I didn't intend to visit today. Fate just happened to bring me this way, I guess. But I wasn't going to pass by without coming to see you."

I close my eyes and smile, listening to the peace surrounding me. The rush of the wind and the occasional bird are the only sounds. I could be a million miles from anyone right now.

I stare at the tombstone again and place a hand flat on the ground.

"Dad, I never thanked you for making me join the Army. I know I resented you for it at the time, but it paved the way for the life I've had, and I never got the chance to thank you. It hasn't been the easiest life. I mean, some of the things I've seen and done... they would have you guys rolling around down there. But for better or worse, this is the life I've had. There's very little I would change, and I owe that to you."

I take a deep breath, which stutters in my chest as emotion looks to take over. A single warm tear stings my cold cheek. I quickly wipe it away.

"Mom, we never really knew each other. It feels cruel not to acknowledge you, but the reality is you never got the chance to do anything for me. I guess the only thing I can say to you is... Dad did his best with me. I was a handful as a kid. I know that. He did a great job with me, and you would be proud of him.

"Whether you would be proud of me is a different story. I've led a complicated life. I've done things many people would disagree with. Bad things. Incredible things. But... despite all the pain I've caused, despite all the people I've lost, I still believe I did them for the right reasons. I lost my wife, my daughter, my best friend, and countless other innocent people because of the life I chose. I just hope that one day, when I'm lying there with both of you, people will understand. If there's anyone left to come and visit me, I hope they remember the good I tried to do, not the bad things I did along the way.

"I've never really taken the time to think about my legacy. To think about what I'll leave behind. But I'm *your* legacy, and I hope you both know that I did the best I could. The world's in a tough spot. I played a part in that. I know I did. No one's really sure how all this ends, or if any of us will even be around to see it. I've never been afraid of dying. I've never thought about what happens when we do. I guess all I know for certain is that those who love us will miss us. I miss you both, and I hope when my time comes, there's someone around to miss me."

I kiss my hand and press it against the tombstone.

"One way or another, I'll see you both again. I promise."

I slowly stand, taking in every detail and refreshing my memory of my parents' resting place.

I blink away tears and stare blankly ahead, across the expanse of graves and to the world beyond. I try to appreciate the peace and the quiet. I know there is little of both in my immediate future.

I'm glad I did this. I almost didn't, but now that I have, I realize just how important it was to—

"Sonofabitch..."

On the other side of the cemetery is I-80. It's far enough away that the noise of the traffic doesn't carry over, but it's close enough that I can see the vehicles speeding along it.

Three huge, dark Juggernauts zoom past, dominating my view, accompanied by two Tristar patrol vehicles.

I don't believe it.

That's Brandon Crow's convoy.

I look down at my parents' grave. "I'm sorry. I love you both, but I gotta go kill somebody."

21

BRANDON CROW

November 16, 2020

Brandon Crow leaned forward, spreading his palms on the surface of the desk to steady himself against the natural sway of the moving vehicle. Beside him, Jay stood with her arms folded across her chest, staring at the same screen Crow was.

The convoy of Juggernauts was Hall's idea. Instead of having a stationary command center to oversee all the Tristar forces in the U.S., he told Crow to arrange a mobile one. He believed a moving target was hard to find and even harder to hit. It was one of the few times when Crow unequivocally agreed with his superior.

Both he and Jay had spent months living on the road. The fleet of huge trucks travelled the country along a cycling series of predetermined routes. Each one took three to four weeks to complete and included scheduled stops to refuel and resupply.

The trucks themselves were a feat of modern engineering. The trailers had two levels. The lower one housed all the equipment and, at any given time, up to ten Tristar operatives. The upper level had simplistic accommodation and cooking facilities. Operatives served in four-week shifts, rotating each time the convoy stopped.

Crow and Jay, however, essentially lived on them.

On a raised platform at the back of the lower level, Crow's desk overlooked the array of computers and workers. He was surrounded by monitors, which hung from the ceiling on adjustable arms. A laptop rested in the middle of it, with a two-way radio fixed beside it, used to communicate with the drivers of the trucks.

Crow studied the screens intently, taking note of the plethora of detail each one provided.

Meanwhile, Jay quietly studied him. His ragged, unshaven jawline. The consistent lack of a tie. The untucked shirt. She recognized the look of a man who had burnt out long ago.

She leaned forward and mimicked his stance, leaning into him slightly so that her whispers could be heard.

"Brandon, are you okay?" she asked.

"I'm fine," came his curt response.

She pointed to the monitor he was currently fixated with. "You've been staring at that screen for fifteen minutes. Nothing on it has changed. Maybe you should take a break?"

He snapped his gaze to her, staring at her with the same intensity he had afforded the screen seconds earlier.

"I said I'm fine," he hissed. "I don't have time to rest."

Jay stood straight and looked at him. Her expression lacked any emotion. She simply maintained eye contact until he looked away.

He gazed down at the desk between his hands and let out a heavy sigh. "I'm sorry."

"Don't apologize to me," she said softly. "Talk to me. I'm more than just your hired gun, Brandon. You know that."

"I know. I'm just tired." He casually gestured to the monitors around them. "Everything is going well. Our numbers are growing almost daily as we recruit more people from the old military. We're up to almost four hundred thousand now."

Jay nodded. "That's good."

"There's almost zero crime nationwide. The number of reported incidents of rebel activity is low. The public are just... getting on with things. Exactly like Hall predicted."

"And you've heard nothing from him?"

Crow scoffed. "No. It's a miracle he's found nothing to berate me for. But apart from the daily report on GlobaTech sightings and the odd skirmish here and there around the camps, even *he* seems appeased."

"So, cut yourself some slack." Jay turned her back on the truck and rested against his desk, leaning in again to talk discreetly. "You need to stay strong in front of these people. You're single-handedly running the largest private military force the world has ever seen. The second anyone sees you faltering, the control and the power you have will disappear."

He looked at her. "Have they been talking?"

"No. And if I heard anyone say anything that might undermine you, I'd slit their throat."

He smiled at the gesture of twisted endearment. "Thanks."

"Fuck what Hall thinks, okay? And fuck what he says. He couldn't have done any of this without you. He might be sitting in that office, but you're the one who's really running this country. You're the one with the power. Remember that."

Crow stood straight, taking a deep breath and puffing out his chest. He looked out at the rest of the truck. Men and women in Tristar's dark uniform worked feverishly behind the banks of computers, all focused and dedicated to a singular goal, as Crow had instructed.

He nodded to himself. He was in charge, and he didn't need to prove himself to anyone, least of all Quincy Hall. He was Brandon fucking Crow.

He looked back at Jay, who was smiling at him. She admired the man she knew he was... even if he forgot sometimes.

"What about you?" he asked. "How are you doing? I can only imagine how difficult being cooped up in here with me must be for you."

She shrugged. "I won't lie—I want to be out there, heading up a patrol, fighting back against GlobaTech wherever I can. Or that bastard, Roach."

"I know you do," he replied sympathetically. "But even now, I think it's too dangerous."

She raised her eyebrow at him. "You don't think I can handle myself?"

"I'm not saying that at all. We both know you can handle yourself better than anyone. I'm saying there's no way you're not one of GlobaTech's primary targets. Or Roach's, for that matter. He's a relentless sonofabitch, that one. If you head out into the wild, you'll be hunted."

Jay cracked her knuckles. "All the more reason I should be out there hunting them first. If we take out Roach or GlobaTech's high command, you'll win permanent favor with Hall."

Crow raised an eyebrow. "Hmm. We could conquer the

entire world in the name of Orion, and Hall would still find a reason to be pissed at me. Look, I know you have scores to settle. Especially with Julie goddamn Fisher. But that will come in time. Our patrols are picking up GlobaTech personnel and sympathizers every day. We'll find them eventually. Besides, the only real concern we have at the moment is Schultz's little pet project."

"What? This... Blackstar? Brandon, please. There's, like, five of them."

He turned his body to face her directly. "Assumption is the mother of all fuck-ups, Jay. Those five people have done more damage to Tristar than anyone from GlobaTech. They've made no secret about being on our tail. They've taken out countless patrols, and they're not hiding, which is cause for concern."

"Why?"

"Because everyone else is. By our latest estimates, GlobaTech have close to twenty thousand men scattered around the country. It's a fraction of what they have trapped outside our borders, but it's enough to do some serious damage if they put their minds to it. Why are all those people hiding from us, yet these five assholes are making as much noise as they can? Why do they want us to find them? What are they planning? What do they know?"

"Probably nothing."

"No, you're right. It probably *is* nothing. They're likely just bored. Or they've realized it's only a matter of time before we find them and kill them, and they have some deluded idea of going out in a blaze of glory. But I don't like taking chances. So, until we know more, I'm not risking you being out in the open."

Jay nodded slowly. "Fair enough. But I swear to God,

Brandon, if I don't see some action soon, I'm gonna tear this Juggernaut apart."

He smiled. "Patience, my butterfly. All in good time."

The two-way radio beside him crackled with static, followed by the distorted hiss of urgent words.

"Sir, this is Cab Two. Come in!"

Crow reached for it and held it to his mouth, frowning. "This is Crow. What is it?"

"Sir, we're under attack."

Crow and Jay exchanged a glance. "We're... what?"

"We're under attack. I just got word from Cab Three. One of the rear patrol vehicles has been taken out."

"How many?"

"Sir?"

"How many people are attacking us?"

"I'm getting word it's one vehicle, sir. Four, maybe five assailants."

He looked at Jay again. "Speak of the devils."

She smiled back at him with evil intentions. Her eyes burned with life and fire.

Crow held her gaze as he spoke into the radio. "Tell all vehicles to maintain the present course and speed. I'll handle this."

"Y-yes, sir."

He tossed the handset onto the desk.

Jay was standing ready, holding her gun in her hand.

"Well, well. Looks like Blackstar finally found us." He nodded to her. "Go get 'em."

22

ADAM RAYNE

November 16, 2020

The Escalade fish-tailed across the road as Ruby made a hard right, putting them roughly a quarter-mile behind the convoy.

Beside her, Adrian grabbed the handle by the door to steady himself.

"Try not to kill us before we give this prick a chance, yeah?" he called over to Ruby.

She didn't take her eyes of the road. "Shut up and let me drive."

He nodded and smiled to himself. He wanted her focused and pissed. That was the most effective version of Ruby in a fight, and that's who was driving.

"Holy shit, we found him!" said Rayne from the middle row of seats. "After all this time... I can't believe it."

"Believe it," said Adrian. "Now get your head in the game. We gotta assume we're only getting one shot at this, so make it count."

"What's the plan, boss?" asked Link, who was sitting beside Rayne.

Rayne looked over at him. "Well, I think we—"

Adrian shifted in his seat, turning to look back at the others.

"Pretty sure he was talking to me," he said.

Rayne's shoulders slumped forward a little. "Shit. Right. Sorry, boss."

Adrian ignored it, as did everyone else. Rayne meant nothing by it, and he knew the others knew that too. But that didn't stop him from feeling embarrassed. The truth was, he still wasn't used to working alongside Adrian in big situations like this.

"Ruby's going to nudge the back end of the rear security vehicle, forcing it to stop without damaging it too much," said Adrian. He glanced over at Ruby. "Without damaging it too much... okay, baby?"

Again, her unblinking stare didn't leave the road ahead. "Do you want me to be pissed at you? Because I can do two things at once, y'know."

Adrian smiled again.

"Yes, you can." He ignored Jessie's groans of protest in the back. "When it stops, we hit the vehicle hard. Take out everyone inside it, quick and deadly. Then Link and I will use it to catch up to the middle truck. Odds are that's where Crow is most likely to be. You three, take out the other rear patrol vehicle, then see about stopping the trucks."

"Should I use Dizzy?" asked Jessie.

Adrian shook his head. "No. Not this time. We don't have time for you to prep it, and you wouldn't make a dent in these Juggernauts anyway. It's more effective to disable the security vehicles one by one. Then we can think about the trucks."

There was a murmur of agreement as the team began prepping their weapons.

"We're almost within spitting distance of the rear vehicle," said Ruby. "No way they haven't seen us. You'd best be ready back there."

Adrian looked at Rayne. "Once we've hit this first vehicle, I want you to take point with Ruby and Jessie, okay? Hit hard, hit fast... cause as much of a distraction as you can to take the focus off me and Link. Got it?"

He nodded. "You got it. Listen, just then, I didn't mean to—"

Adrian held up a hand. "I know. Don't worry about it, okay? Get your head in the game."

"It is."

Everyone readied their weapons.

"Here we go," said Ruby.

With the needle pushing seventy, they approached the last vehicle of the convoy, then moved alongside it. As the hood drew level with the rear wheels, Ruby hit the brakes and turned left, nudging the back end of the Tristar Jeep.

At these speeds, it didn't take much.

They slid to a halt and watched as the Tristar vehicle spun out and skidded off the road.

"Go!" shouted Adrian.

Everyone hustled out of the Escalade, weapons levelled, fingers on triggers. They swarmed the Jeep, surrounding it before anyone inside had a chance to react. They opened fire, shattering every window and riddling the Tristar guards inside with bullets.

It took less than a minute for them to drag the dead bodies from the vehicle. They checked them for spare ammunition, then Adrian and Link climbed in. Link sat in the driver's seat.

Rayne and Jessie ran back to their own vehicle and climbed in. Ruby watched as Adrian and Link sped off, once again in pursuit of the convoy. She then moved around and slid in behind the wheel of the Escalade, gunned the engine, and did the same.

"So far, so good," said Jessie from the rear seat.

Rayne nodded. "Same again on the rear vehicle, okay? Except this time, Ruby, don't stop. And Jess, you and I will shoot out the tires and disable them. I don't want to waste time stopping to clean up. We need to keep close to Adrian and Link and support them. These assholes aren't gonna run after us."

"You got it," said Ruby, once again focused on the road.

It didn't take long to catch back up with the convoy. Ahead, they saw Adrian and Link pulling out into the other lane, trying to draw level with the middle truck.

"Get ready," said Rayne.

He and Jessie leaned out the broken windows, weapons ready. As they got within a few feet of the next Jeep, they opened fire, hitting both driver's side tires. They ducked back inside as Ruby yanked the wheel to the right, tapping the rear of the Jeep with the front of their Escalade.

The effect was the same as before; the Jeep spun out to the side of the road. Except this time, because of the two shattered tires, the rubber melted away as it slid, causing the metal inner rim to spark across the tarmac.

The Jeep flipped and ignited. It landed on its roof and exploded in the dirt beside the interstate.

"Holy shit!" shouted Jessie, laughing with disbelief.

Ruby glanced in her rearview. "Well, that worked…"

She slammed her foot to the floor, desperate to close the gap between them and the first truck in the convoy. She lined them up with the rear doors and leaned forward slightly, looking up through the windshield at the towering behemoth in front of them.

"Not sure what we're supposed to do now," she said.

"I don't think hitting the back end will do much good," added Jessie. "That thing's a beast."

"We should focus on—*shit!*"

Ruby swerved with shock as Jay jumped from the roof of the rear truck and landed on the hood of the Escalade. The two of them locked eyes as Jay gripped the roof for balance.

Time froze. Ruby stared into Jay's dark, hateful eyes for the first time, immediately understanding why GlobaTech and Roach had so much trouble with her in the past.

Jay stared back, bemused by the shock on the face of the woman she was supposed to be intimidated by.

Ruby recovered and slammed the brakes.

Jay's eyes went wide as she flew from the vehicle. She landed hard on the unforgiving interstate and rolled to a stop several feet away.

"What the fuck happened?" yelled Rayne.

"Pretty sure we found Crow's pet killer," said Ruby, catching her breath. "Come on."

The three of them rushed out of the vehicle, but Jay had already recovered. As Ruby moved around her door, she was met with a stiff boot to the face. It connected cleanly and sent her to the ground, dazed.

Jessie and Rayne moved around the Escalade, approaching from both sides.

Jay turned to deal with Rayne. She stared at him, grinning like a demon set free from Hell. She stepped close to him, swinging her elbow at his head. He was slow to react. His attempt at blocking it was ineffective, and the blow connected flush with his temple, sending him staggering backward and eventually dropping him to one knee.

Jay took a step forward, moving in for the kill.

"Hey!" shouted Jessie.

Jay turned to look back at her, her eyes narrowing as she assessed her next target.

Jessie switched to a loose boxing stance. "Let's see what you got, bitch."

Jay smiled and ran toward her. She threw a couple of hard shots, which Jessie blocked and deflected before countering with a couple of her own. The last one got through. The stiff jab connected with Jay's face. It did little in terms of pain and damage, but it gave her cause to hesitate.

"Not as easy when people are ready for you, is it?" said Jessie.

Jay shook her head. "No. But it's *way* more fun!"

She charged at Jessie again, preemptively ducking low and jabbing her in the side of her gut. As she doubled over the side, Jay followed up with a downward forearm shot to the face, which Jessie caught the full force of. She dropped to one knee and brought her right arm up, preparing to defend herself from the inevitable follow-up.

Jay bore down on her, like a wolf hunting its prey.

Jessie waited. When she saw Jay wind up the next shot, she spun around, driving her own forearm into the side of Jay's knee. She buckled on her front leg, falling unceremoniously to the ground in front of Jessie.

Both women were on their knees, scrambling to get a grip on each other's throat. They hammered down punches on each other, trading shots and hoping for an advantage.

As Jessie managed to get a grip of her throat, Jay let out a visceral scream. Her wide eyes burned with inhuman fury. She lunged forward, driving her forehead into Jessie's face. The headbutt took her by surprise, and she fell away.

Jay shuffled backward, creating a little distance while she got to her feet. She never took her eyes off Jessie, who was still dealing with the cobwebs from the hard shot to her face.

Jay stood upright, smiling menacingly. She took a step toward Jessie but stopped when she felt the gun barrel press against the base of her skull.

"Don't," said Ruby. "As much as I want to ask you some questions, don't think for one second that I won't paint the road red."

Jay discreetly shifted her feet, preparing to spin around. But she never got the chance. Instead, she relaxed her body and held her hands out to the side as Rayne appeared in front of her, his own gun trained on her with unwavering aim.

"Enough," he said to her.

He held a hand out for Jessie to reach up and take, which she did gladly. He hoisted her to her feet without taking his eyes or his gun off Jay.

Jessie recovered and retrieved her own weapon, then moved to cover Jay. They had her pinned against their Escalade, with guns aimed at her from three directions. She wasn't going anywhere.

"Now," said Rayne, "you're going to answer some questions."

Jay looked at him, raised an eyebrow, and smiled challengingly. "Am I?"

Ruby stepped forward and slammed the butt of Adrian's Raptor into the side of her head. "Yes."

"Where's Brandon Crow heading on those trucks?" asked Rayne.

Jay glared at Ruby, then turned to him. "Wherever the fuck he wants."

Jessie inched closer. "Who hired you to kill the president of Paluga six months ago?

Jay looked at her and frowned. "Jesus, are you still going on about that? After everything that's happened, *that's* what you want to know?"

Jessie shrugged. "Humor me."

Jay thought for a moment. Eventually, she sighed. "Fine. It doesn't really matter now anyway. Orion told me where to go and who to shoot."

"Why?" asked Ruby.

"Who knows?"

Rayne took a deep breath, trying to bury his frustration. "Okay. What about the advanced weaponry and munitions you used to carry out that hit? Where did they come from?"

Jay smiled. "Tristar manufactured them."

"Bullshit."

She shrugged. "Think whatever you want. There's a lot more to those guys than people realize. It's amazing what you can do with a little money behind you."

"How did Orion and Tristar manage to do all this without anyone knowing?" asked Jessie.

Jay shook her head. "No idea."

Ruby moved to her side and placed the barrel of her gun against her temple. "Stop lying to us. You're Brandon Crow's right-hand bitch. There's no way you don't know everything he does. Tell us how Orion did this."

Jay leaned away, creating a little distance from the gun, and stared at her with disdain. "Orion has been planning this for years. Brandon was only told what he needed to get Tristar ready. He's not privy to Quincy Hall's plans, and neither am I. Anyway, it doesn't matter. There's no going back from this now. There's no stopping it."

"I wouldn't be so sure of that," said Rayne. "GlobaTech

are stronger than you think. We're going to find a way to take this country back."

Jay scoffed. "GlobaTech won't do shit. Do you think we don't know everything that pathetic little *rebellion* is doing? They're nothing. And neither are you."

She practically spat the words out. He noted the venom in the way she spoke and believed she was dedicated to what was happening right now. He had to believe she was always willing to die for it, which would make further inter-rogation difficult. He had to wrap this up and get as much as they could before they put her down.

Rayne shrugged. "Oh, I don't know. They managed to stop that coup in Paluga with far less manpower than they have at the moment... despite the best efforts of Tristar's finest. What makes you think—"

"Oh, please! You think anybody cared about that piss-ant country? Orion orchestrated that whole thing. They gave the Palugan military men and weapons to help them stage that poor excuse for a coup."

Ruby, Jessie, and Rayne all exchanged a glance of concern.

"If they didn't care, why get involved at all?" asked Jessie.

Jay looked at her and smiled. "Practice. It doesn't take a genius to figure out that if something like that happens, GlobaTech gets the call for help. We wanted to see what we were going up against. And it turns out... the answer is: not much."

Rayne took a step back, keeping his weapon trained on her but looking away, processing everything she had told them. She had no reason to lie to them, which meant the extent of what they were up against was even worse than any of them realized. Orion had used Paluga as a test run to force GlobaTech into action, to show them what they were capable of. They then used that to execute their larger plan, knowing exactly how to beat GlobaTech before anyone even knew they were in a fight.

But something still didn't sit right with him.

He looked back at Jay. "Why tell us all this?"

She shrugged back at him, still acting oblivious to the guns trained on her. "Why not? Six months ago, yeah, if this came out, there would've been global ramifications on everyone involved. Orion and Tristar would've been sanctioned and shut down overnight—kinda like GlobaTech almost was. But now... who's left to give a shit? We run the country. There's no military, no GlobaTech, and the federal agencies answer to Hall. It's not like you're going to arrest me. And before you start trying to threaten me, if you were going to kill me, you'd have done it already. I've given you some information. Chances are, I know more, right? But I'm not saying another goddamn word until you take me to see Julie Fisher."

Rayne looked at Ruby and Jessie in turn.

He hated to admit it, but Jay made a good point.

23

ADRIAN HELL

November 16, 2020

We speed up alongside the convoy. I hear a thunderous explosion behind us. I glance back to see a fireball swirling into the sky. A moment later, I see the Escalade swerve into view, then move back behind the truck, out of sight.

"Everything okay?" asks Link.

I smile. "Not for Tristar, by the looks of it."

"You got a plan for actually stopping these things?"

"No. Do you?"

"What? I'm following you!"

"Really? I was following you."

Link glances over at me, frowning. "Please tell me you're fucking with me."

I grin. "Yes. Yes, I am."

"Jesus. So, seriously, how do you intend to stop this convoy?"

"I don't."

I climb back into the rear seat and open the door on the

passenger side. The noise of the wind is deafening. I grimace as I feel its chill biting at my cheeks.

"What the hell are you doing?" shouts Link.

"Just get me alongside the middle one," I shout back. "I'll do the rest."

There's a loud bang. I look around to see one of the rear doors on the middle truck swinging open, having just slammed against the side.

Huh. Well, that's fortunate. I hadn't figured out how I was going to get inside, but this works perfectly. Why are they inviting me in?

I look up in time to see a pair of legs disappear up and over the cab of the third vehicle.

Looks like Ruby and the others are about to have some company.

I'm sure they'll be fine.

"Move us closer," I shout.

We must be doing at least eighty alongside this convoy. It's a good job the roads are quiet.

I stare down at the blur of tarmac, watching as the gap between us and the giant wheels of the middle truck narrows.

God, I hope this works.

I guess the only comfort is, if it doesn't, I probably won't know about it.

Not that *that's* much of a comfort.

I brace myself, staring at the rear door, watching the motion and timing of its swinging.

This is a bad idea.

I shift my right leg back a few inches, preparing to launch myself.

This is a really bad idea.

Satan, do you mind?

Hey, it's my job to make you do violent shit when you need to. I'm not here to convince you to go all Fast and Furious *on Crow's collection of Hot Wheels, okay?*

Yeah, well... shut up.

I jump out of the Jeep...

...and grab one of the metal poles that forms the outer locking mechanism of the rear door of the truck.

"Oh, shit!"

I start swinging back and forth. My left hand instantly throbs from gripping so hard. No way I could've done this with my right.

The door swings shut, leaving me dangling from it and staring at the driver of the truck behind it, which is maybe ten feet away.

Hmm.

I smile and flip him off.

Come on, take the bait, asshole...

The truck accelerates. I hear the growl of its huge engine as it closes the gap.

Bingo!

He's going to try to squash me, but if I do this right, I might just be able to...

I kick my legs up and rest them on the hood of the third truck, which gives me additional balance and relieves some of the pressure on my hand. I quickly spin myself around, then push myself away from the door, just for a split-second. The door flies open, and I springboard through the gap, turning in midair so that I land on my back inside.

Ugh!

Which I did.

Which hurt.

Fuck.

I push myself up and scramble to my feet, turning to face the interior of the truck.

Oh.

I stand uneasily against the natural sway of the vehicle and stare into the eyes of nine Tristar guards, all sitting at workstations and consoles lining the sides of the large trailer. At the far end, leaning on his desk, is Brandon Crow.

Sonofabitch. We actually found him.

Now to get to him.

I move forward, which prompts the guards to hustle to their feet. The nearest one to me is on my left. He's barely out of his seat as I reach him. I don't hesitate or even break stride. I lean forward and to the side, swinging my elbow and forearm down in a wide arc. I connect with the side of his head, which sends the guard backward, bouncing off his computer and onto the floor.

Well, that's one.

The rest of them hesitate, standing by their desks with their hands hovering over the sidearms holstered to their thighs.

"Okay," I call out. "Who's next?"

Their collective gaze shifts to something behind me. I frown and look over my shoulder. The third truck has backed off, leaving enough space for a Jeep full of Tristar guards to slot in between. Men from inside it are filing out and climbing onto the hood, preparing to jump in behind me.

Shit.

Looks like Satan will get a chance to do what he's paid for after all.

I don't have a lot of moves to make here. My only real chance is to close the gap between me and Crow and hope the new arrivals are less willing to fire at me if the bodies of their colleagues are between us.

Here goes nothing.

I lunge forward and head for the next guy along, who is on my right. I grab the straps of his combat vest and spin him around, then plant a stiff punch on the side of his face.

As he's falling, another guard across from me steps forward, reaching for his gun. I lean back on the console and lash out with my lead leg, kicking his hand away from his holster. I push myself toward him, grab his throat, then force him back. I reach behind me for my own gun. I bring it around, tuck the barrel up underneath his combat gear, and fire two shots at close range into his stomach.

He slumps back against the console behind him.

I spin around and start shooting. Mostly to buy myself some time and distance, but I'll take any kills I can get along the way.

Three more men fall in the chaos.

I hear the click of an empty magazine.

No time to reload.

I slam the butt into the nose of the next guy along, then immediately divert left and kick the guy standing there in the balls. As he doubles over, I bring my knee up and smash it into his face, dropping him.

I think there may be a few left behind me, but they're all taking cover under their desks. They won't do anything now. They had their chance, and they chose to hide.

Pussies.

I place a foot on the first of two steps that lead up to Crow's raised platform and stare at him.

"You're a hard man to find," I say to him.

He shrugs. "You're a hard man to kill."

"I do my best."

"So, now what, Adrian Hell? Are you here to take me into custody on behalf of GlobaTech?"

An arrogant smile spreads across his face. He has a glint in his eye, like he thinks he knows something I don't.

Prick.

I'd say this guy was beaten but didn't know it, but he looks as if he was beaten weeks ago. Unkempt hair, dark stubble, ruffled shirt, dark circles around his eyes... this guy is hanging on by a thread. Must be tough running the militia that's holding the country hostage.

Let's see if I can alleviate some of his stress.

I shake my head. "I think the time for shit like that has long since passed, Brandon. You think I've been hunting you to *capture* you? No. I've been searching this entire country for you to *kill* you."

He nods toward my gun, which I'm still holding. "Such a shame you're out of bullets."

"And if you think I need bullets to kill you, you really haven't been paying attention."

I take another step but feel myself tugged backward. It catches me off guard, and I fall heavily to the floor, clutching hopelessly at nothing but air on the way down. I land hard, and I'm immediately swarmed by three, maybe four guys. I see nothing except a flurry of feet, all scrambling to bury kicks into my body.

I turtle up, bringing my knees up to my chest and my arms up to protect my head as best I can. I wince as a few shots get through.

Oof!

That one knocked the wind out of me—Jesus!

I need to find a way out of this. I need to get to my feet, first of all. Then I can think about fighting back. It's an enclosed space, which might work to my advantage, but lying here isn't going to end well.

I try to grab someone's foot, but they're kicking me too fast. I need to—

"Hey!"

"Who's that?"

"Get him!"

Huh?

I tilt my head and look up toward the doors.

Link is tearing through the second patrol, launching them out onto the interstate.

One of my attackers leaves to join his friends. Not that it'll do them much good.

There's just two on me now. I can handle two.

I grab the nearest ankle and twist, forcing the Tristar guard to overbalance. He falls into his colleague, buying me valuable seconds. I wait until the first guy is on the floor beside me, then grab the heel and toe of his boot and twist sharply. Even with the noise from outside and the ruckus behind me, I hear the joint snap.

Grim but necessary.

I hustle to my feet as the second guy recovers. He moves unsteadily toward me and throws an awkward right hook, which I block easily. I jab him in the gut, then swing my arm up, connecting a solid shot with his jaw. He drops—not out cold but out of this fight—leaving my path to Brandon Crow clear.

I glance behind me to see Link still holding his own against the four—no, *five* remaining Tristar guards.

He'll be fine.

I look back at Crow. Credit to him, he appears unfazed by the fact that there's no longer anyone standing between us. I step up onto the platform and move around the desk, standing face to face with him.

Crow smirks. "Not gonna ask me how Orion was able to plan all this? Or how Tristar was able to position themselves to take over the U.S. in less than three days?"

I shake my head slowly, never breaking eye contact. "I don't care. I'm here to kill you. It's kinda my thing. I was hoping to find your pet psycho here too. I was originally drafted in to take her out, so it would've been nice to kill two birds with one stone. I'm guessing that was her running along the truck behind us?"

Crow nods, smiling. "It was. I'm sure by now the rest of your team will be dead."

"Unlikely. Respect where it's due. Wherever you found that maniac, she's impressive. Held her own against a few people I know to be tough bastards. But she hasn't faced anyone like my team before. She'll either be dead or spilling her guts. Either way, we win."

"You think finding me will change anything?"

"I do, yeah. Word is, you coordinate everything from here. I know Hall's type. Not one to get his hands dirty. So, he'll delegate it all to the first poor schmuck in the pecking order who craves the approval he never got from an absent father." I gesture to him with my hand. "And here you are."

He scoffs. "You think you know everything, don't you?"

"I know enough."

"You really, really don't."

Crow lunges at me, grabbing me by the throat and landing two stiff shots to my face.

Man, he's fast!

I wasn't expecting him to put up much of a fight at all, let alone be competent.

I clamp my shoulder to my cheek, trapping his hand,

then twist my torso quickly. It breaks his grip and sends him backward a couple of steps. He flexes his hand, loosening up after almost having his fingers snapped.

I move into him, faking a throat grab of my own before launching a flurry of well-placed body shots. I connect with most of them—hard punches that dig into the ribs and gut, knocking the wind from him. He doubles over, exposing the back of his neck. I drive my elbow down onto it, landing on the base of his skull and sending him crashing to the floor.

Crow recovers quickly. He turns onto his back and punches the side of my leg, causing it to buckle under my weight. I fall backward, but I reach out and grab the handrail of the small staircase leading to the upper level.

He gets to his feet the same time I do. We stare at each other for a second, then charge like two raging bulls. Our arms flail together, desperately looking for an opening that will give one of us an advantage. We throw each other against the back wall, then across into the desk.

I hit the back of his chair and lose my footing, which allows him to force me back against his desk. Crow steps in close, pinning one of my legs in place with both of his. He then bears down on me, hands around my throat, using his weight to hold me in place. I feel his thumbs fighting against my own desperate grip, searching for the spot just beneath my Adam's apple. If he locks his grip in and presses down there, I'm finished, and we both know it.

My teeth are gritted together, and each breath seethes out of my mouth. My jaw aches as I try to tense every muscle in my head and neck to combat the hold he has on me.

I begin punching his arms and hands and wrists... anything I can do to get a moment's reprieve and fight back.

...

...

...

It's not working.

I look into his eyes. They're wide and filled with hatred. His face is contorted with rage. He's trying, with every fiber of his being, to kill me.

I feel my efforts weakening. Breaths are getting harder to take. My vision is blurring.

I turn my head to the side, trying to alleviate some of the pressure. If I can just get a few good, deep breaths, I might be able to power through and...

And...

Damn. My eyes are getting heavy.

I stare up again. Crow's smiling like a lunatic.

"You're not so tough, Adrian!" he shouted. "I expected more from you. Maybe you're just past your prime."

Yeah, maybe I am. But when my number's up and the person who has it comes calling, I can guarantee they'll be better than Brandon... fucking... Crow.

Beside us, among the disturbed clutter of his desk, I can see a portable hard drive.

Huh. I bet that's useful.

Not as useful as what's next to it, though...

I grab one of Crow's wrists with my left hand and start pulling. I reach across with my right, stretching my fingers out to try and grab...

Almost... got it...

THUD!

Got it.

I smash a thick, glass paperweight into the side of his skull. Crow flies away and crashes to the floor, reeling.

I roll away from him and lean on the desk, coughing and gasping for air.

I look over and see Crow already on his knees. A thick

stream of blood is pouring down the side of his head. He's reaching up for the desk drawer nearest to him.

There's a gun in there, isn't there...

I push myself upright and stamp down onto his face, knocking him back to the floor.

"Stay down, for fuck's sake," I say to him.

I fumble with the wires and various USB connectors, then manage to detach the hard drive. I tuck it inside my jacket and look over at the door. Link is dispatching the last couple of guards.

"Link, where's our ride?" I call over to him.

He glances back at me, grimacing. "We're walking home, boss. Sorry."

As he throws one of the guards against the side of the truck, he looks outside. I see his shoulders slump forward a little. He then turns back to me.

"We gotta go," he says.

I sigh, which hurts way more than it should. "Reinforcements?"

He nods. "Yeah."

"How many?"

"Enough."

That's all I need to hear to know it's time to leave. I don't have the time nor energy to finish Crow off. I look down at him. He's moving slowly and groaning a lot. He's done, at least for now.

I hope this hard drive has something useful on it because that's all we're getting from this.

I stagger over toward Link and look outside. The third truck has closed the gap behind us again. There are two more Tristar Jeeps running alongside us on the right.

"Grab a gun," I say to him.

He does, then looks at me. "Now what?"

I frown and nod to the outside. "Now shoot something!"

Without thinking, I run and jump through the open trailer door. I tuck my knees up to my chest in midair and crash into the windshield of the third truck.

"Fucking Christ!" I hear Link yell behind me. Then he starts shooting.

I roll away to my left, dropping the seven or eight feet down to the road. I land hard and feel something pop. Possibly my shoulder. I let the momentum roll me away to the side of the road until I eventually stop, lying flat on my back. I lift my hands to my face, mostly to check that my arms aren't broken.

"Ah! God...dammit!"

My right shoulder is dislocated. Fuck!

There's a lot of blood on my hands—grazes from the fall, most likely.

I lift my head. Up ahead, I see Link dive from the second truck, landing about as badly as I did.

I rest my head back and stare up at the dull, winter sky, gasping in deep, painful breaths.

I gambled on the backup patrols not following us. I could have easily been wrong, but I figured after our attack, their priority would be getting Crow safe and away from me.

I close my eyes, comforted by the fact that it appears I was right.

After a few minutes, a huge shadow looms over me. I open my eyes to see Link looking down at me, smiling. He holds out his right hand, which I take with my left. He hoists me effortlessly to my feet.

"You're fucking crazy, man," he announces.

I smile weakly.

"Like, I've seen and done some crazy shit in my time, but you... you're literally insane."

"Thanks. Listen, could you do me a solid and put my shoulder back where it's supposed to go?"

"Huh?" He frowns, then looks at my right arm, which is hanging significantly lower than it should be. "Oh, damn!"

"Yeah. Just, y'know, count to three and—ah! Fuck!"

He just grabbed me and popped it back into place.

"What happened to counting to three?" I shout.

He shrugs. "It would've taken too long."

I slowly rotate my arm, getting the blood flowing and checking the movement.

"Yeah, well... that hurt."

"Come on," he says. "We should head back to the others. That convoy's long gone."

"Yeah."

We set off walking along the side of the interstate. Not a single car passes us.

"Is Crow still alive?" asks Link after a moment.

I nod. "He is."

"Did you at least kick the crap out of him?"

"I did."

"Not an entirely wasted trip, then?"

I smile, then reach inside my jacket, rummaging for the hard drive. I'm praying it's still in one piece.

I take it out and look at it.

It is, thankfully.

"I managed to steal this," I say.

"What is it?"

I look over at him. "It's a chicken sandwich, Link. What do you think it is?"

He rolls his eyes. "I meant is it useful?"

"I hope so. I was too busy being choked to death to check before I took it."

"Are you always this sarcastic after a fight?"

I shrug. "Yeah. But I'm also this sarcastic *before* a fight."

"True."

We carry on walking in silence for almost ten minutes before we see the others up ahead.

"Uh-oh," says Link, pointing. "That doesn't look good."

We run the last couple of hundred feet until we reach them. Jessie is sitting on the road, leaning against the damaged front bumper of the Escalade. Rayne is leaning forward, hands resting on the hood, looking unhappy. Ruby is leaning back against the driver's door, arms folded across her chest.

She looks over as we approach, then moves to meet us. She throws her arms around me as she reaches me.

"Are you okay?" she asks. "What happened? Did you get him?"

I step away and shake my head. "He's still alive, but he won't forget the day he met me."

I hand the hard drive down to Jessie, who takes it with a questioning look on her face.

"I stole this. See if it's got anything on it that we can use."

She gets to her feet and nods. "I will, first chance I get."

"What happened here?" asks Link, looking around at the broken glass and bullet casings littering the road.

"We met Jay," says Rayne. "She's a real peach."

I look at Ruby. "What happened?"

She looks down for a moment, dejected. "We had her, Adrian. She told us a lot of things I know Julie and Globa-Tech will find useful."

I nod. "Okay. Then what?"

"Then she stopped holding back," says Jessie, before Ruby has a chance to speak.

I raise an eyebrow. "She took out all three of you?"

Rayne nods. "Like a hot knife through butter. I've never seen anything like it."

"Where is she now?"

"Another patrol picked her up," says Ruby. "I'm guessing they were on their way to you."

I nod. "Yeah, two more Jeeps arrived just as Link and I were making our escape. She must've been in one of them."

Everyone regroups and forms a loose semicircle in front of me. They all look beaten and tired. Their faces are covered in dirt and blood.

"Okay, look," I begin. "We might not have managed to kill Crow and his psycho sidekick, but this isn't a loss. We've worked for six months to find this asshole, and we did. That means we'll find him again. Wherever he's heading in that convoy, he's licking his wounds and thinking twice about every move he intends to make. Today, we showed him he's not invincible. We proved we can not only find him but attack him and beat him. That will affect him, and it'll affect his boss."

"Doesn't feel much like we beat anybody," says Jessie. "Kinda feels like we lost more than he did."

I snap my fingers and point to her. "Hey, that's not how we think, understand? We don't lose. We either win or we learn. You've encountered this Jay now. You know exactly what you're dealing with. By the sounds of it, everything Roach and Ray told us didn't do her justice, but that's okay. We know for next time. Meanwhile, I had my hands around Brandon Crow's throat, and Link singlehandedly took out close to fifteen guys. Not to mention we stole that hard drive. We hit them hard today. It might not feel like it, but this is a win. In fact, it's the biggest win we've had in months. So, lift your heads, stand tall, and get ready for the next fight. Understand me?"

Everyone nods and mutters their agreement.

"Good enough. Now come on. Let's get the hell out of here."

We all climb inside what remains of the Escalade.

I look at Ruby as she starts the engine. "Once Jessie's taken a look on that drive, you should reach out to Julie and Jericho and the others. Let them know what's happened."

She nods. "I will. Are you okay?"

I wave my hand dismissively. "I'm fine. Just... feeling it a bit."

"Yeah," she says, offering a comforting smile. "Think there's a lot of that going around right now."

We drive away, heading in the opposite direction to the convoy, in search of the nearest town.

24

ROACH

What remained of the afternoon had passed by quickly. Becky regaled the camp in Charlotte with one of her stories. Roach sat beside her quietly, uncomfortably eating a burger and trying to avoid eye contact with everyone who stared at him in awe. Instead, he observed the people gathered around the campfire with them. Friends and families gathered together, laughing and talking, connecting in a way that humans had all but forgotten how to do before T-Day.

Roach felt comforted by it. As much as he wanted to shut the world out, he wasn't as detached from people as Becky made him out to be. When his journey was over, he hoped people would know that he fought back for moments like this.

Becky's words faded into the background. Roach had heard all the stories before. He knew the importance of what she was doing. He knew this was as much for her as it was for everyone else. She impressed him. The strength she had developed over the last six months, compared to when she first broke down in the alley where Tristar took her, was staggering.

Roach was so distracted by his own musings that he almost didn't see the black Jeep pull over at the side of the highway, next to the camp.

He heard it before he saw it. He looked over and saw five Tristar guards, dressed head-to-toe in black, carrying silenced SMGs. They bled into the surrounding night like deadly shadows.

Roach pulled his hood up over his head, then tapped Becky's arm. She saw him, saw his hard expression, then saw the Tristar patrol. She pulled her hood up too. Everyone around the campfire scrambled to their feet. Most moved to meet the patrol. The ones who stayed ushered Roach and Becky off to the side, standing around them to hide them from sight.

From beneath his hood, Roach stared at the patrol, watching. His jaw was set. His gaze was unblinking and burned with rage.

Silence descended on the camp like a heavy blanket.

Billy made his way over to the patrol. "Can I help you, gentlemen?"

One of the guards stepped forward to meet him. He pointed at the food truck. "This mobile food outlet isn't authorized. Only supplies provided by Orion are allowed in these... *camps*."

The last word was said with a disdain which he made no effort to hide.

Another man stepped to Billy's side. "All we're doing is cooking the food you give us. What's wrong with that?"

"Are you?" said the guard. "How do we know that? How do we know you're not moving from camp to camp, feeding people more than they're allowed? You people are rationed for a reason."

"Look around," said Billy. "We don't have a vehicle. What do you think we're doing? Pushing it?"

The guard pointed at him. "Watch yourself, old man. Are you in charge of this camp?"

Billy nodded.

"Then I'm ordering you to shut this operation down. Right now."

"And what if we don't?" asked the guy next to Billy. "You can't get away with this. It isn't right. It isn't fair. You shouldn't—"

The guard stepped back, leveled his gun, and tapped the trigger. A three-round burst erupted from the suppressed barrel and tore through the refugee. His body dropped straight to the ground. In the faint glow of the nearby lights from the food truck, the gravel around him turned dark.

Gasps and short cries of fear rippled around the camp.

Roach instinctively took a step forward.

Becky grabbed his arm. "Be careful, Will. It's too risky to get involved. We need to stay off Tristar's radar as long as we can. That's *your* rule."

"I know," he hissed. "But shit like this is why we're fighting in the first place. They just killed someone for no reason. That can't stand, Becks. I won't allow it."

She held his gaze for a long moment, then let go of his arm.

He stormed across the campsite, pushing through the thin crowd until he was standing beside Billy, staring at the armed guard. He held his hand out in front of Billy and looked across at him.

"Step away, Billy," he said. "I'll take it from here."

"And who the fuck are you?" asked the guard.

Roach slowly removed his hood. "I'm the man you think you are."

"Whatever, asshole. Move." He took a step toward Roach, raising his gun until the barrel was inches from his chest. "Unless you want to wind up like your friend down there."

Roach stepped closer, so his body was touching the barrel. His eyes never left the guard's.

"Make me."

Behind him, the other four members of the Tristar patrol shifted restlessly. They exchanged looks of uncertainty and moved their fingers inside the trigger guards of their weapons.

The guard smirked. "Are you... are you serious? Last warning, dipshit. Move or be moved."

Roach raised an eyebrow. "See, that's your biggest mistake."

The guard frowned. "What is?"

"You waste time with warnings."

He stepped to the side and thrust the heel of his hand into the guard's nose. He felt the cartilage buckle beneath the impact. A burst of gunfire twitched as the guard reacted.

Roach stepped back in front of him, spun him around, then charged forward, using the guard as a shield. None of the other Tristar operatives fired, for fear of hitting their colleague.

When he was just a few feet away, he thrust the guard into the group and charged at the one standing farthest to the left. They all wore tactical helmets, so blows to the head were restricted. He lunged for the guard's throat, gripped it tightly, then slammed his fist into his face. Once. Twice.

The third blow sent him to the ground. Roach dropped to a crouch, scooped up the SMG, and swiveled on the spot.

Everything was happening too fast for Tristar to react. They hadn't expected any resistance.

Roach squeezed the trigger repeatedly, firing controlled bursts into the group of Tristar operatives. The stuttering symphony of gunfire filled the air, despite the suppressors. Bullets punched into the bodies of the remaining three guards, sending them sprawling to the ground, landing on top of the first guard he spoke to.

Roach relaxed, holding the SMG low, aimed at the ground beside him. He looked down at the guard next to him, who was stunned and nursing a bloody nose. He adjusted his downward aim slightly and squeezed the trigger, sending the remaining rounds of the magazine into his body at devastatingly close range.

Roach stood, dropped the gun by his feet, and walked slowly toward the last surviving member of the patrol. The one who had killed a refugee for no reason. He leaned forward, grabbed the clasps of his armor, and hoisted him to his feet with ease. He ripped the helmet off, then used it to smash his face with another hard blow before tossing it aside.

The guard staggered and stumbled, grunting with pain. Roach stayed on him, making sure he remained standing. He held him in place and stared into his eyes.

"These people are protected by the rebellion," he said. "And more importantly, they're protected by *me*."

The Tristar guard laughed, exposing his bloodied mouth. "So, what? You're gonna send me away with a message to leave these people alone? You think you can scare us? GlobaTech's little rebellion won't last. And I know who you are, *Roach*. That's right. I see you now. You're a traitor and a coward. You'll be dead before dawn. When word of this gets to my superiors, Mr. Crow himself will send more men here to kill you."

Roach narrowed his gaze and tilted his head slightly. "Huh. And who, exactly, is going to tell your superiors?"

The guard's smile faded. His eyes widened with growing panic as he realized he wasn't going to be left alive to deliver a message.

He *was* the message.

Roach expertly grabbed the guard's jaw and neck, then jerked his body counterclockwise, letting the momentum carry his arms where they need to go. The sickening crack of the guard's neck snapping echoed around the campsite.

He let the body drop to the ground. He stood for a moment, taking deep breaths, forcing the adrenaline to slow and return his heart rate to normal.

Billy appeared by his side. A moment later, Becky and a few others joined him.

"Thank you, son," he said to Roach. "We'll move the bodies. Don't you worry—it'll be like they were never here."

Roach looked up at him. "I'm sorry for putting you at risk. But I couldn't risk letting them hurt any more of you. I should've saved your friend…"

Billy stepped in front of him and pressed a finger to his chest. "Now you listen to me, young man. Don't you ever blame yourself for things like this. This wasn't *your* doing. You're a hero. Do you hear me? You're a goddamn hero."

Becky moved to Roach's side and threw her arms around him.

"Will, are you okay? Are you hurt?"

He shook his head. "I'm fine, I promise."

She stepped back to look at him.

He smiled, trying to offer her some comfort. "They never stood a chance."

She relaxed and nodded, then stepped to the side to speak with the refugees standing with them.

Billy took Roach's arm and guided him away in the opposite direction.

"Your sister's a hell of a woman, Roach," he said. "Her stories... that blog of hers... you should be proud of her."

Roach nodded. "Thank you. I am."

"And I don't just mean her stories of those GlobaTech folks, either. Sure, those guys might be the future we need, but the things she says you've done for folks like us... that's what helps us sleep at night."

"I'm just doing what I can."

Billy nodded. "I know. Want some free advice from someone who's been where you're going, son?"

"Of course."

"See, I've known men like you before."

Roach smiled politely. "That right? And what kind of man am I, Billy?"

"The kind of man who says he's searching for peace, yet he can't stop himself from looking for the next war to fight."

He shrugged. "All I wanted was to be left alone. The fight came looking for me, and I did enough to make it leave again. But now... the fight's everywhere. I wouldn't be able to look myself in the mirror each night if I didn't fight back."

Billy nodded. "Well, then here's my advice—a lesson learned the hard way by a man much older than you. Don't deny who you are. Say whatever you want to the rest of us. Play into your sister's stories, by all means. But don't lie to yourself. You don't want to be alone, son. You want peace, and they ain't the same thing. You won't find peace until you *believe* there are no more wars to fight. But take a look around you, Mr. Roach—that ain't happening any time soon."

Roach could tell Billy knew exactly what he was talking about. He could see it in his eyes. His gaze was saddened by burdens of the past.

Billy continued. "But you ain't gotta be alone, and you ain't gotta protect us as much as you might think. All this shit tonight... this was the right thing to do, no matter how many casualties it might cause. Ignoring the fight won't bring you peace. It will bring you torment. Embrace who you are. Run toward that unspoken urge to stand and fight. Peace will come when the time is right. But a man like you, in times like these... that's exactly what people like us need, Roach. Don't run from it. Please."

Becky appeared next to them. Her bag was over her shoulder, and she was carrying another, smaller bag, which she held up for Roach to see.

"We've been given some supplies," she said, smiling. Then she held up a set of car keys. "And it was suggested to us that we borrow the ride Tristar just abandoned."

Roach shrugged. "Yeah. That will help with the journey. We'll need to ditch it before we hit D.C., though."

"Of course." Becky tuned to Billy. "Thank you for your hospitality and for offering to clean this mess up. I'm really sorry this happened."

Billy smiled and gave her a hug. It was the kind of hug a grandparent gives a grandchild as they're about to leave for college.

"After everything the two of you have done for us, it's the least we can do. I was just saying to your brother here, keep doing what you're doing, kid. We'll be watching."

Her cheeks flushed, stinging the skin in the fresh, winter air.

Roach extended his hand to Billy, who shook it gladly.

"Thank you," he said.

Billy nodded. "You remember what I said to you, son."

"I will."

Roach and Becky turned and headed for the Jeep. He climbed in behind the wheel, started the engine, and flicked the headlights on. Becky got in beside him and immediately slouched into the comfortable seat.

With the heater on, she was asleep within minutes of them driving away.

Roach glanced at her, balled up on the seat next to him. He smiled. He was happy that, for now, she was safe and warm.

Then he stared at the dark road ahead as Billy's words cycled through his mind. He had to decide if he should stick to his own plan and play it safe, which had gotten them this far... or embrace the side of him Becky was trying to show the world, which might be the only thing that would get them over the finish line.

25

JERICHO STONE

November 17, 2020

Seven figures crouched beneath the trees that lined the road leading up to the Cincinnati Art Museum, where Collins had scouted the day before. Shadows within shadows shrouded the team in near-total darkness. The winter chill penetrated their bones, despite their layers of protective clothing.

"Whose dumbass idea was this?" whispered Collins, shivering as he knelt on the cold, hard undergrowth.

Beside him, Jericho rolled his eyes. "Pretty sure it was yours."

"Aye, well... since when did ya start listening to me?"

"Will you two shut up?" hissed Julie, from the other side of Jericho. "It's cold, I'm tired, and I don't want to listen to you two bickering like a pair of schoolgirls. Now when's the patrol due?"

Next to her, along the line, were four GlobaTech operatives. The one closest to her, a fresh-faced but experienced former soldier called Roberts, pressed a button on the side of his watch to illuminate the face.

"Should be any time now, ma'am," he said.

Julie winced in the darkness. She had punched people before now for calling her *ma'am*. But she let it slide. They had bigger issues to deal with.

She looked along the line at the faint outlines of her friends and colleagues. All of them wore thick, black, weatherproof clothing over their tactical gear. All were armed with suppressed pistols.

They had spent the last twenty-four hours lying low, resting to ensure they were fresh for the attack. Julie knew they needed some good fortune and hoped this attack would yield some. She had to move her people on from the city soon and didn't want to leave empty-handed.

Away to their left, the rumbling of an engine faded into earshot.

"This is it," said Jericho. "Wait for my signal, then we make our move as planned."

There was a murmur of agreement from everyone.

The glare of the headlights bounced into view. It was one of the Jeeps with a mounted fifty cal on top. The patrol vehicle turned onto the street, making its way up the slight rise to complete its circuit of the museum.

Then Jericho saw the second vehicle behind it.

He cursed to himself. "Ray, there are two vehicles!"

"Aye, I see that, Jerry!" he replied. "Shit! I watched this route for nine hours. Every time, there was only one. What do we do?"

"We proceed as planned," said Julie, before Jericho had a chance to reply.

She felt the tension immediately.

"If that's a problem for anyone, speak now. Otherwise, get ready. Nothing needs to change. We're just surrounding two vehicles instead of one."

Jericho set his jaw and closed his eyes, taking slow, deep breaths. He was trying to steady his heart rate, to calm himself and prepare mentally for the violence he was about to enact.

He opened his eyes again as the two vehicles were almost level with them.

"Go," he said.

The line of GlobaTech operatives burst from cover, weapons raised and aimed at the windows. They fanned out quickly and surrounded the patrol with practiced precision. Collins and Julie quickly shot the men standing behind the guns on each vehicle.

The patrol stopped. The stutter of the idling engines drowned out the silence of the still night.

"Out of the vehicles, slowly," said Jericho firmly.

No one moved. In the gloom, he could see the men inside the vehicles exchanging uncertain glances. There were still four in each vehicle. He knew this wasn't going to be an even fight. He knew one of them was worth ten of Tristar.

Jericho holstered his weapon and moved toward the lead car. He grabbed the handle and the reinforced wing mirror of the front passenger door. With considerable effort, he tore it from its hinges.

He discarded the door as if it were made of paper, then reached inside and dragged the passenger out of the vehicle, forcing him to his knees. He took out his weapon again and placed the barrel to the man's head, then looked inside at the driver.

"I'm short on time and even shorter on patience," said Jericho with an icy, almost eerie calm. "Out of the vehicle. *Now.*"

The driver and other passengers opened their doors and slowly exited the vehicle. The Jeep behind them remained still. Julie made her way around the hood to confront the driver. The circle of GlobaTech personnel stepped back, widening their perimeter, giving themselves a better angle to cover the patrol.

As Julie reached the driver of the first vehicle, the doors of the second vehicle flew open. The men jumped out with weapons raised.

Everyone scattered as the second patrol opened fire. The night was alive with the rattle of gunfire. The idea of running for cover didn't occur to Jericho. He scooped up the armored door like it was nothing and held it upright, crouching slightly behind it. He turned and ran toward the guards nearest to him.

He slammed into the nearest man, pinning him to the Jeep behind his makeshift shield with incredible force, causing him to drop his automatic rifle. He then spun clockwise and drove the back of his fist into the side of the next man's head, sending him flying into the side of the vehicle, then crashing to the ground.

Jericho lifted the door away, then punched the guy trapped behind it hard in the face, as if he were trying to punch through the side of the Jeep itself. Consciousness abandoned the guard instantly. He slumped to the ground and fell to the side, landing next to his fallen colleague.

The GlobaTech team traded shots from cover. Julie shielded herself behind the body of the first driver. She held him close, controlling his neck and resting her gun barrel to the side of his head.

Jericho flew over the hood of the second Jeep, twisting to bring his legs out in front of him. He planted the sole of his boot into the second driver's chest, sending him flying away. As he landed, he grabbed the remaining passenger from the second vehicle by the straps of his combat gear and lifted him clean off the ground. He slammed him twice into the side of the vehicle, then tossed him away.

The gunfire stopped.

Without pausing for so much as a breath, he strode toward the fallen driver and smashed his boot into the man's face, knocking him out. He then turned his attention to the nearest passenger from the lead vehicle, who dropped his gun and held his hands up immediately. His eyes were wide with fear.

Jericho ignored his pleas of surrender. He placed one of his shovel-like hands on the side of the man's head and slammed it into the side of the vehicle, knocking him out cold. He glanced over the hood at the two remaining passengers on the opposite side. Both held their hands up as the GlobaTech team emerged from cover and surrounded them, weapons raised, fingers on triggers. Collins stepped toward them.

"Nice and easy, fellas," he said, pressing the barrel of his gun into the driver's back. "Don't get any bright ideas, and ya might make it through this."

The two guards exchanged a resigned look.

Jericho tore the other driver from Julie's grip by his throat, then pinned him to the side of the Jeep.

"I want information!" he snarled through gritted teeth. "I want to know where Brandon Crow's convoy is, and I want to know where you're holding President Schultz."

The man's eyes were so wide, it looked as if they were ready to simply drop out of his skull.

"I-I don't know, I s-swear!" he cried.

Jericho pulled the guard toward him, then slammed him back again. "Don't lie to me!"

The man's eyes misted with tears. The sound of trickling water was quickly accompanied by the stench of urine.

"I-I'm sorry!" screamed the guard. "I don't know anything."

Again, Jericho slammed him against the vehicle.

"Bullshit!"

Julie stepped toward them and placed a hand on his shoulder.

"Jericho..." she said softly.

He ignored her, continuing to glare into the fearful eyes of the Tristar guard. "This is your last chance. Give me something, or I'm going to rip you in half!"

"N-no, please!" he begged. "Wait, I... I might know something. Just please, let me go."

Jericho relaxed his grip.

The man tried to back up, despite being pinned against his vehicle, desperate to put some distance between him and the hulking maniac in front of him.

Across from them, two gunshots echoed in the night. Everyone looked over as the guards dropped to the floor. Collins was standing a couple of feet away, weapon still raised, smoke still swirling from the barrel.

He looked up at Jericho. "Sorry. They got a bright idea. Carry on."

Jericho looked back at the driver, who had lost even more color in his face.

"Talk," he said.

The guard took a deep, quivering breath. "Look, I... I don't know if this is what you're looking for, okay? But I've heard talk of a top-secret location... some kind of strategic site used by Orion. A few of the patrol leaders have spoken about it. I heard them at headquarters more than once."

Julie frowned. "Where is it?"

He shook his head. "I-I don't know exactly. I swear I don't. But I'm sure I heard someone say Wyoming. Like, an old Air Force base or something. One of the guys was bragging about having been there a few months ago. It might be bullshit. You know how guys are, bragging to sound good in front of the boys and all that... but I honestly think there's something there. I just... I don't know what." He looked at Jericho. "I don't know if it's what you're looking for, but it might be something. That's all I know, I swear!"

Jericho held his gaze, staring through the terror in the man's eyes and looking straight into his soul. He could tell if a man was lying, especially under such duress. But he didn't think he was. He saw a man who was genuinely scared he might die. And rightly so. But he wasn't lying.

Jericho nodded. He slowly released his grip of the man, then lunged forward and drove his forearm into the man's face, knocking him out. The guard slid to the ground.

He turned to Julie. "First solid bit of intel we've had in months. You're welcome."

He walked past her and away from the stationary patrol. He needed some distance from what had just happened, to stem the flow of adrenaline and calm himself again.

Collins made his way around the vehicle to Julie's side. He watched Jericho pace away up the road. He then looked down at the unconscious guard.

"Did he just make a grown man piss himself?" he asked.

Julie shook her head with disbelief. "Yes, Ray. Yes, he did."

"Jesus. That man's a goddamn monster. Maybe we

should point him in the direction of the White House, then tell him Quincy Hall insulted his mother. This shit would be over by the morning."

Julie chuckled and walked away. Collins followed her a moment later. The team regrouped a little farther up the road, away from the patrol. Jericho idled over and rejoined them.

"Ya good, big fella?" Collins asked him.

He nodded silently.

Roberts approached them. "What are we going to do with the patrol? We can't just leave them there."

She looked at Collins and Jericho in turn. Both nodded their silent agreement to the horrible, unspoken question.

She looked back at the operative. "Load the bodies inside the vehicles, then torch them. No survivors."

He nodded once. "Yes, ma'am."

As the rest of them walked away, Roberts headed back to the vehicles. He rounded up the other operatives, and they set about stowing the dead and unconscious bodies in the Jeeps.

Once the road was clear, four operatives quickly pulled the pins on a grenade, tossed them inside the vehicles, then sprinted to catch up with the others.

Jericho looked over his shoulder impassively as the two vehicles exploded, illuminating the dark night with a bright orange and red glow. The heat from the blast carried over to them. He closed his eyes as it rushed across his face, relishing the momentary reprieve from the cold.

"That's going to attract some attention," said Julie. "We should get out of here."

The team jogged back to their own vehicles, which were parked off the road, closer to the museum.

"Do you believe what Pee-Pee Pants told us?" asked Collins.

"I think so," replied Julie. "Jericho seemed to, which is good enough for me. We need to verify what he said before we get excited, and I know just the person to ask."

26

JULIE FISHER

November 17, 2020

Julie sat alone in the office of the asphalt plant, listening to the rush of the Ohio River outside. The lapping of the water was almost serene. She found herself staring off into space, a million miles away from the horrors of her daily life.

It was almost noon. Upon arriving back at their makeshift camp, many of them had gone straight to sleep, exhausted from the attack and coming down from the adrenaline rush.

But she hadn't. She couldn't rest. Not after what they had done.

The door to the office opened. Jericho walked in, holding a steaming cup of coffee. He placed it on the desk in front of her with a comforting smile.

"You okay?" he asked.

Julie took a deep breath and reached for the coffee, welcoming the warmth of the cup in her hands. She felt her mouth open and close, but no words came out.

Jericho watched her for a moment, then turned to close the door.

"Ray said you didn't sleep after we got back," he said. "What's on your mind, Jules?"

She looked up at him, narrowing her eyes. "What do you *think* is on my mind?"

He shrugged, ignoring the uncharacteristic confrontation. "I don't know. That's why I'm here. Talk to me."

Jericho took a seat opposite her. He leaned forward on the desk, clasped his hands together, and watched her patiently.

Julie mirrored his body language. She stared into the coffee cup, swirling it around in her hand, watching the liquid dance inside.

She sighed. "I just... I can't believe things have gotten this bad. We should've seen this coming, Jericho. I mean, look at us. Look at what we've been reduced to. Killing already-defeated enemy soldiers in cold blood in the streets. What example are we setting to the people we're supposed to be fighting for?"

Jericho remained patient and impassive. "This is war, Jules. It's us or them—that's the only way you can look at it."

"But doesn't this just make us no better than the enemy?"

Jericho shook his head. "War is about winning or losing. That's it. What we did this morning makes us *better* than the enemy, because we walked away and they didn't. We're fighting for our lives, and we're the underdogs here. Any chance we get, we have to use the most extreme measures to show our strength. It gives the enemy something to think about. Morals don't have anything to do with it. The enemy doesn't have any, and we can't afford to have them, either. They're a weakness that will get us killed. End of story."

"But what difference does any of it make when we're outnumbered ten-to-one, and the bad guy is sitting in the Oval Office? The entire country is against us. It's like we're running in quicksand. We're fighting with everything we have, and we're getting nowhere."

Julie sat back in her seat. She drained the coffee, then pushed the empty cup away from her across the desk.

She and Jericho had been through a lot together. They had seen every side of each other. They knew each other's strengths and weaknesses. They understood what made each other tick. Jericho saw what Julie was going through right now. He had never seen it in her before, but he knew what it was because he had experienced it himself more than once.

There came a point in every soldier's life when they questioned what they were fighting for. When their back was against the wall, they couldn't help but think about what put them there. About what they could have done differently. About whether they still believed in the reason they were fighting in the first place. It happened to him not so long ago in Paluga.

Jericho reached across the table and held out his hand, inviting Julie to take it. She leaned forward and placed her hand on top of his.

"The entire country is *with* us, Jules," he said. "Don't you see that? Our rebellion is inspiring people. You've heard the whispers between the citizens that secretly help us. What we're doing matters. And the stories of Roach... man, whatever he's doing, it's sure as hell working. That guy's become a campfire legend across the country."

Julie smiled. "Yeah, his sister's a great reporter."

"The few have always controlled the many through fear. That's how the world works. The way to win is to keep showing people there's nothing to be scared of. That's when the grip of the few weakens, and they lose."

"And you think what we're doing is achieving that?"

Jericho nodded. "I do. Let me tell you something. Two thousand years ago, a Roman citizen could walk the face of the earth, free from the fear of harm. People the world over knew the wrath of the Roman Empire would be devastating, should anyone lay a finger on one of its citizens. We need to put that same fear into Orion and Tristar. It's all we have. They strike one of us, we come back with the fury of the gods and lay waste to an entire platoon of their guys. I'm a soldier. All I know is how to fight. When things are *this* bad, you have to retaliate first. Overreact in frightening ways. Show the larger enemy that one of you is worth ten of them. That will show the people that the enemy is only human. It takes the fear away. That's how we win."

Julie sat back, smiling with surprise at how good Jericho's point was.

"Thank you, Jericho. Y'know, you say you're a soldier, but you're much more than that. You're a born leader, whether you like it or not."

He shrugged. "I do what I have to. That's all."

"I'll tell you what else. That little speech you just gave me right there... it made you sound more like Adrian Hell than he does."

Jericho stood and leaned against the wall next to him, folding his arms across his chest.

"No, I'm not," he said.

"You are, and you know it," countered Julie.

He fell silent and stared at the floor, frowning. He felt angry at the idea anyone—especially Julie—would compare him to... *him*. Then he thought back to when they were all standing in Buchanan's office six months ago. How Adrian acted, how he spoke, the things he said. Had this fight turned him into the very thing he hated Adrian for being?

Conflict did things to people. It could change them. It could also show people who they really were. He remembered what Adrian had said to him, shortly after the attack had begun. He had said war was his thing... and then immediately fell in line and followed orders, despite their history. He put his ego aside and acknowledged not only his own shortcomings but other people's strengths.

Maybe Julie was right. Maybe the two of them weren't all that different, and maybe that wasn't a bad thing.

He shook his head.

And all it took was a nationwide invasion for him to see it.

Still, that didn't mean he had to like it.

Julie's cell phone rang, breaking the silence in the room and pulling Jericho out of his own thoughts. She took the phone from her pocket, placed it on the desk, and answered, putting it on speaker.

"Fisher," she said.

"Julie, it's Ruby," came the reply, slightly distorted through static. "How are things?"

"Hey. You're on speaker with me and Jericho. We're doing okay. Lying low. How's everything on your end?"

"Oh, you know. Same old, same old. We do have some news, though."

"Yeah? Us too, actually. I was going to call you later today. You go first."

"We... ah... we finally caught up with Brandon Crow."

Julie and Jericho looked at each other, their eyes wide with shock and hope. "You did? Where?"

"Just outside of Omaha. We met his special friend too."

Julie frowned. "You mean Jay?"

259

"I do." She huffed down the line. "She's really something, isn't she?"

Julie smiled. "We did warn you. Have you got her?"

Ruby sighed. "No. We *had* her, but she fought her way free."

Julie glanced away. "Damn it..."

"However, she told us a few things you might find interesting."

"Such as?"

"She admitted it was Orion who put her up to the hit on the Palugan president. And she confirmed that the fancy bullet she used was manufactured by Tristar."

"Holy shit!"

Jericho sat on the edge of the desk and leaned forward a little, putting himself closer to the phone. "Do you believe her? Why would she admit that now?"

"I asked her the same thing," said Ruby. "She was pretty dismissive about it. Said there was no reason not to. Not like we can do anything to punish the people responsible anyway."

He rolled his eyes. "Yeah, fair point, I guess."

"Did she say anything else?" asked Julie.

"We asked her how Tristar and Orion were able to do what they did without anyone knowing. She explained that Paluga was basically a trial run for all of this. To test Tristar's manpower and to force you guys to play your hand and show them what you're capable of."

"Jesus Christ..."

The door to the office opened, and Collins stepped in.

"Everyone okay in here?" he asked.

Julie nodded to the phone. "We've got Ruby on the line."

He smiled and closed the door, then walked over to the desk. "Hey, Ruby. How ya doing, love?"

"Not bad, Ray. And you?"

"Aye, I'm okay. Ya missing me so much, ya just had to call, eh?"

She tutted loudly, causing a hiss of static. "You know Adrian's not above shooting you, right?"

He chuckled. "Ah, me and him are tight. He wouldn't do that. W-would he?"

Julie and Jericho smiled at each other.

Ruby laughed. "Probably not, but I wouldn't test that theory by flirting with me."

"Aye, fair."

"So, attacking the convoy was a bust?" asked Julie, changing the subject.

"Not completely," replied Ruby. "Adrian and Link managed to get inside one of the trucks and confront Crow."

"Are ya serious?" said Collins. "That's awesome!"

"Is he dead?" asked Jericho hesitantly.

"No. By all accounts, Crow put up a hell of a fight. Adrian had to fight through eight or nine Tristar guards to get to him, then the two of them almost killed each other."

"How is he?" asked Julie.

"A little beat up but okay. And it wasn't a completely wasted trip. He managed to snatch a portable hard drive from Crow's computer. Jessie spent all night decrypting it."

"That's great," said Julie. "Anything interesting on it?"

"Tons. We hit the goddamn jackpot, guys! It had details of cryptocurrency wallets, with combined holdings of almost half a billion dollars. That must be how they're funding all this."

"Jesus, that's a real chunk o' change," said Collins.

"It sure is. Jessie checked the access logs of the wallets. We figured the only people who would access the money would be the people in charge. We found only two IP addresses."

"Can you track them?" asked Jericho.

"We can and we did," said Ruby. "The first, we weren't able to pinpoint the exact location for, so we're figuring that's Crow's mobile convoy."

"Makes sense," said Julie. "What about the other one?"

"Well, that's the interesting thing. It was in New Texas. More specifically, Fort Hood."

The three of them looked at each other, all surprised by the revelation.

"Is Fort Hood still a thing?" asked Collins.

"Yup," confirmed Ruby. "Jessie's a real hotshot with computers. She hacked into your old satellite network and used it to look at the area."

"And?" asked Jericho.

"And it's a busy place. Teeming with Tristar assholes, power lines, and—most importantly—fuel pumps. We think that's where Crow's convoy refuels."

Julie got to her feet and leaned forward with her hands on the desk. "Ruby, this is really great work. Do you have any idea how often they go there?"

"We think so. Jessie checked the access logs on the hard drive for when the two main IP addresses logged on. It's a pretty consistent pattern—both access the wallets once a day, one about fifteen minutes before the other. However, every five weeks, like clockwork, there's one day where only one IP address accesses the drive."

"The one at Fort Hood, right?" said Collins hopefully.

"Correct. We think Crow's Juggernaut convoy heads there to refuel every five weeks."

"Sounds to me like hitting Fort Hood should be our

number-one priority," said Jericho. "Do you know when Crow's next scheduled to be there?"

"Based on the log history... four days from now."

Silence fell in the office. The three of them looked at each other with a renewed sense of hope and purpose in their eyes.

Julie nodded to them both. "Ruby, I think it's time we regrouped. We should discuss hitting Fort Hood together. This is the first real piece of actionable intel we've had in six months. We need to do this right."

"I agree," said Ruby. "We're heading out of Nebraska in the early hours tomorrow. We'll head south and link up with you."

"Okay. Let's meet in Canton. It's a small town about an hour east of Dallas. It's far enough away from Fort Hood that we're unlikely to attract too much attention but close enough to make our move when we're ready."

"Okay. I'll let Adrian know. Hey, didn't you say you had news too?"

"We do. We're in Cincinnati right now. We took out a couple of Tristar patrols a few hours ago. One of the guards mentioned something about Orion using a strategic location in Wyoming. No one really knows what for. It's all rumors and hearsay among the Tristar patrols. But we think it might be where Hall's keeping Schultz."

"Damn. If you're right, this could turn the tide of this whole thing," said Ruby excitedly. "That's great news. How can we help?"

"The guy told us it was an abandoned Air Force base," explained Jericho. "We figured Jessie might have some idea where it is."

"Quite possibly. She was awake all night working on that drive, so she's catching up on some much-needed rest now.

I'll ask her when she wakes up. We can give you what we have tomorrow when we meet up."

"Sounds good," said Julie. "Thanks, Ruby. I'll message you the location to meet. We'll see you there tomorrow night."

"Perfect. Take care until then, guys."

"You too."

Julie ended the call, then looked at Jericho and Collins in turn.

"Well, that was unexpected," she said.

Jericho nodded. "We just went from down on our luck to maybe having two ways to end all of this in about ten minutes. Not a bad day's work."

"We need to be ready for this. Ray, go and tell the others to prepare to move out within the hour."

Collins frowned. "During the day? Isn't that a bit risky?"

She shrugged. "It is, but we have no choice if we want any chance of reaching Canton by nightfall tomorrow."

He nodded. "Ya got it, boss lady."

He turned and left.

Jericho smiled at Julie. "You feel better now?"

She rolled her eyes. "Yes, I do. Thank you for... y'know... everything you said before."

He waved the gratitude away. "Hey, it's what we do. We can only focus on one battle at a time. The war will take care of itself."

"Well, if ours and Ruby's intel all checks out, the war might just be coming to an end."

"Let's hope so."

Julie walked around the desk and put her arms around Jericho. It was a quick embrace, a final moment of comfort. He kissed the top of her head, then they left the office.

They had work to do.

27

BRANDON CROW

November 17, 2020

The convoy rolled through the streets of downtown Chicago, along the predetermined route. The gigantic motorcade caused chaos at large intersections, and traffic was backed up for miles, but no one complained. No horns blared. No one stood beside their vehicle, angrily shaking their fist at the passing trucks.

This was Tristar.

They had regrouped and recovered following the attack the day before, then proceeded along their route as if nothing had happened. They had a schedule to stick to, and they were already behind.

In the back of the middle truck, Crow stood behind his desk, staring down at the surface as he tried to mask his anger. On the screen in front of him, Quincy Hall shouted and snarled from behind his own desk in Washington. His face glowed red with rage.

"Damn it, Brandon! How could you let this happen?" he bellowed.

Crow looked up wearily. "All due respect, Mr. Hall, I didn't *let* anything happen. They attacked us, and we did our best to defend ourselves."

"How in the hell did they even find you?"

"I don't know. Our routes are known to only a select few, and I trust none of them said anything. My guess is they've been tracking us for months and just got lucky. It's not like they have anything else to do."

Hall sighed and shook his head. "You're supposed to be crushing this pathetic little rebellion of GlobaTech's..."

Crow shrugged. "This wasn't GlobaTech. This was Adrian fucking Hell and Schultz's little pet project. They hit us hard from out of nowhere. We fought them off. The Tristar escort did their job. There's been no sign of them since."

There was a pause.

Crow glanced at Jay, who was standing beside him, out of view of the webcam. She looked like she had been in a fight but showed no signs of fatigue. Cuts and bruises covered her face and arms. Her expression was hard, displaying more frustration and fury than usual.

Crow sympathized with her. He knew exactly what she was thinking right now. He felt comfort and relief in it. He wanted her pissed. He wanted her desperate to fight. That was when she was at her most deadly.

He also suspected part of her anger was directed at how Hall was speaking to him, not that there was anything either of them could do about it.

"Did they get anything?" asked Hall eventually.

Crow huffed with hesitation. "Yes, they..."

He looked away, knowing the ire what he was about to say would draw.

"Spit it out, Brandon," barked Hall. "Christ."

Crow looked back at the screen, holding Hall's gaze. "Adrian managed to snatch one of the network drives from my computer as he ran away."

Hall didn't say anything. The thin line his lips formed grew tighter as he narrowed his eyes. His breathing was labored.

"Which one?" he asked after a long silence.

"Mine," answered Crow begrudgingly.

"You mean, the one with our crypto holdings and patrol routes on it?"

He sighed. "Yes."

Hall slammed his palm down on the dark surface of the Resolute desk. "Goddammit, Brandon! How can you be so fucking useless?"

"Useless?" He shook his head. "Quincy, I fought off the best assassin in the world. I'm lucky to be alive."

Hall leaned forward. "That, Mr. Crow, is something we agree on."

The call ended.

Crow was left staring at a blank screen. He furrowed his brow, trying to subdue a level of anger he didn't know could exist. Such was his rage following yet another chastising from the White House, his whole body shook.

Beside him, Jay saw his reaction. Her own frustrations subsided, replaced with the engrained instinct to protect the man to whom she owed everything. She looked up, staring out at the expanse of the trailer before them. The Tristar technicians who were killed yesterday in the attack had already been replaced. Much like the morbid fascination with passing a car crash, every person at every console was looking toward the desk at the end, unable to turn away.

Jay made sure to make eye contact with every one of them before speaking, so they could see and understand how serious she was.

She took a step around the desk, then pointed to the staircase in the corner, leading to the upper level. "All of you, leave. Now."

There was a flurry of movement as everyone rushed for the stairs. Jay watched until the last person was out of sight above them, then she turned back to Crow. She didn't say anything. She just wanted him to know that he had the freedom to talk.

He slammed both fists down on the desk. "Who the fuck does he think he is, speaking to me like that? I put him in that fucking office. Me!"

Jay moved to his side and placed a hand tentatively on his shoulder.

"I know," she said. "So, what do we do now?"

Crow took deep breaths, looking around at nothing in particular until he calmed down enough to speak rationally.

"The drive he took was heavily encrypted, so it should be useless to them," he said. "However, just in case they're smarter than they look, we've got people looking at securing the crypto wallets."

Jay nodded. "Okay, so let's assume the money is safe. What about the patrol routes?"

Crow sighed. "When we stop to refuel, I'll work out some new ones. Then they can waste their time looking for us in the wrong place. That's an easy fix."

"Okay. Do you think they will come after us again?"

"I don't know. Most likely. He's a persistent bastard, that

Adrian. I want him on the top of your list. I want you to find him and kill him."

Jay smiled. "Consider it done."

"He's not to be underestimated. Nor is his team. If they have the drive, there's a chance they can hack it and use it." He thought for a moment. His gaze darted across the desk as his mind calculated as many outcomes as he could think of. After a minute, he turned to her. "I want you to go and head up the security detail on Schultz."

She took a step back, frowning. "Why? I belong with you. Especially now... you need me here."

Crow shook his head. "I'll be fine. But think about it. I don't know how they did it, but they managed to find us. There's nothing to say they won't try to do it again."

"And if they do, I'll be ready for them."

"I'm not their endgame, Jay. Whatever GlobaTech, or Adrian, or that bastard Roach is doing, their goal is Hall. They get him, this is over."

"That's his problem."

Crow smiled. "I agree. But my problem is maintaining the control Tristar has over this country, and that control will disappear completely if GlobaTech manages to rescue Schultz."

"Do you really think they will find him?"

He shrugged. "They found us. I honestly didn't think they would do *that*. So, I would rather not take the chance. Go and make sure he remains hidden and secure. You get so much as a sniff of GlobaTech within fifty miles of him, you unleash hell. Understand?"

Jay nodded reluctantly. "Fine. I don't understand why he's even still alive. Hall killed the V.P. on day one. We should've done the same with Schultz."

"He's alive because at some point, when Orion has done

what they set out to do with this country, we're going to have to deal with the outside world. And when that day comes, no one will recognize Hall's authority except us. Legally, Schultz is still the president, so we need him for the next step."

"Okay. I'll go. Are you sure you'll be okay on your own?"

Crow nodded. "We'll be arriving in Texas to refuel in a couple of days. That's the safest place in this country right now, outside of D.C. After that, we'll be on new routes, and they'll never find us again."

They looked at each other for a moment, then smiled.

"Go," he said to her. "Take one of the patrols with you. I'll call ahead and tell them to expect you. I'll make sure they understand you'll be in charge of the facility upon your arrival and that your word may as well have been spoken from my mouth."

"How long do you want me there?"

"For now, until I say otherwise. I'll send additional patrols to the areas surrounding where they attacked us. Once we've tracked them down and dealt with them, you can come home."

"Are you not worried about GlobaTech?"

Crow shook his head. "They haven't done anything of note this whole time. Apart from Adrian Hell's attack yesterday, the only other thing we've heard of is Roach taking out a couple of patrols. As frustrating as that is, he's alone and, as best as we can tell, heading for Washington. What can he do? Besides, he'll be dead soon enough anyway."

Jay looked away.

Crow placed his hands on her shoulders. "Don't worry. It'll all be okay. I promise."

She smiled weakly, then walked away, heading for the doors of the trailer. Crow picked up the radio on his desk and called through to the drivers, instructing them to pull over the first chance they got.

A few minutes later, he watched as Jay climbed out of the trailer and disappeared with one of the escorting patrol vehicles.

He slumped heavily into his chair as the people from above cautiously returned to their workstations. Resting his elbow on the arm of his chair and his chin on his hand, he stared blankly ahead, lost in thought.

He had lied to Jay.

He had told her if Hall fell, GlobaTech won, and this would all be over. But that wasn't true.

If Hall was captured or killed by the rebellion, it wouldn't change anything. Hall was a mouthpiece. He was nothing more than the PR department for what was ultimately Tristar's takeover of the United States. Sure, Orion funded everything in the beginning, but they were past needing handouts to operate now. It was Tristar's men and women who occupied the streets of the country. It was Crow's leadership of Tristar's forces that kept everyone under control.

If Hall fell, Crow knew he would inherit the dynasty by default. He knew he would run it much better than Hall ever did.

He smiled to himself.

Maybe GlobaTech's endgame could use a helping hand, he thought.

28

ROACH

November 17, 2020

Roach and Becky took I-85 from Greensboro and headed northeast, then turned off on I-95 and continued north toward Richmond. They dropped back down onto Route 460 just outside Petersburg and followed that all the way to the border of Windsor, Virginia. They ditched the stolen Tristar vehicle in the early hours, choosing to walk the last few miles to avoid any unwanted attention.

Unfortunately, they had stumbled upon a small Tristar patrol parked at the side of the highway not long afterward. There was no way around them without attracting their attention, so Roach was forced to deal with them preemptively. He had stocked up on weapons and ammunition before he and Becky carried on, eager for rest and shelter.

As the morning progressed into afternoon, the winds grew stronger, carrying with them a bitter chill that penetrated the most stoic of all-weather clothing. Both Roach and Becky hunched against it, their collars turned up to protect their necks and cheeks.

"I'm r-r-really missing that h-h-heater," said Becky, shivering involuntarily.

"I'm missing a lot of things," replied Roach, muttering mostly to himself.

They passed a road sign welcoming them to Windsor. It was one of the smaller communities that had been almost completely overrun by Tristar troops following the takeover. Roach knew it was a risk passing through, but they needed to keep going north and had to give Richmond a wide berth. Heading into a larger city would always be too risky for them. This way added valuable hours to their journey but also offered slightly more safety.

They entered the town limits, then immediately moved away from the road. They headed behind a gas station on their left, seeking cover from any prying eyes. They moved along the back wall, crouching and eventually stopping beside a large dumpster.

"Let's just take a minute," said Roach, looking around them.

Becky squatted beside him. She leaned back against the wall and crossed her arms, hugging herself to stay warm.

"Don't take too long," she replied. "I can feel frostbite setting in."

Roach rolled his eyes. "Drama queen."

Becky responded with an exaggerated sigh. "Asshole."

He smiled to himself and surveyed the nearby area. The back of the gas station faced a small suburban estate. The streets were lined with Tristar vehicles, which he assumed belonged to patrols that had taken over the residences.

"No easy way past *Orion Row* over there," he said without looking around. He failed to hide the dejection in his voice.

"We might have to make a run for it, move from building to building, and see if we can find a path through. We heard talk of a camp here, right?"

No answer.

"Becks?"

Still nothing. Then he felt her move beside him. He looked around to see her staring away in the opposite direction, her eyes wide and her mouth clamped shut.

"What is it?" he hissed.

Becky flicked her head in the direction of her gaze. He looked over and saw three Tristar guards walking along the sidewalk on the border of the suburbs, maybe thirty feet from them.

"Stay down and stay still," Roach whispered. "We're not in their periphery."

They both held their breath, watching as the three men ambled along the street. They were talking among themselves, paying little attention to the world around them.

They drew level with Roach and Becky. If they looked to their right, they would have seen them as clear as day. But they seemed focused on the road ahead and with each other's conversation.

The Tristar guards continued past. Neither of them moved until the men had turned the corner, putting their backs to them. Only then did Becky dare to reach over and hold out her hand for her brother to take.

He did, feeling her cold skin against his own.

They both let out a heavy sigh.

"That was close," whispered Becky.

"Yeah, a bit too close," agreed Roach.

He wasn't afraid of a Tristar patrol twice that size, let alone three men with no visible weaponry. The trio on their own wasn't the problem. The issue was the hundred-plus friends they undoubtedly had in nearby houses, who would have descended on them within minutes.

Roach knew if they had been spotted just then, it would have been over for them both.

"Oh, my God!" shrieked Becky. She immediately clamped her hand over her mouth.

Roach snapped his gaze to her again. A little girl was standing next to them, looking at them curiously, with wide eyes and an innocent face.

Roach twisted to face her properly. "Hey there."

The girl smiled. "Hi."

"Are you... are you okay?" he asked her. "Are you lost?"

She shook her head slowly.

Becky recovered from the fright. "Are your parents nearby, sweetie?"

The girl nodded. She then turned and walked away, back toward the road leading into town. At the corner of the gas station, she paused to look over her shoulder at them. She beckoned them to follow with her small, gloved hand.

Becky and Roach looked at each other and shrugged.

"Unless Tristar started recruiting out of third grade, I think it's safe to say we're better off following her than staying here," observed Becky.

Quietly and carefully, staying low, they followed the girl. She moved with fearless speed, back across the highway and toward a school on the opposite side.

Roach and Becky followed, always aware of their surroundings, wary of any nearby Tristar patrols. But they saw none. They continued after the girl as she traced an experienced path through the town, keeping them hidden from the eyes of their enemy.

A few minutes passed before they stepped out from a narrow alley and came face to face with a small hotel on the far side of town, close to where Route 460 left Windsor behind and continued east toward Suffolk.

"This way," said the girl quietly.

They jogged across the road and followed her up the steps and into the hotel. It was a simple building, a far cry from the five-star establishments in the city. The reception area was small and unmanned. A circular desk dominated the left side as they entered. Roach and Becky slowed their pace, unfastening their winter coats as the welcoming heat indoors flowed over and through them.

The girl ignored the front desk and walked through a set of double doors. She headed along a corridor where the first set of rooms were, then disappeared inside one of them on the left.

The doors to all the rooms stood open. People lined the hallway; some stood alone, while some fussed over the young and the elderly alike.

Becky tugged at Roach's sleeve to get his attention.

"I don't believe it," she said quietly. "*This* is the refugee camp."

He nodded. "It's a better setup than many of the camps we've seen. That's for sure."

A young man who looked barely old enough to drink stepped away from the wall and moved toward them. He wore a thick sweater and waterproof pants. A few whisps of hair lined his otherwise unblemished face.

"Oh, my God. You're him, aren't you?" he said.

Roach and Becky exchanged another look. Seeing her smile only added to his confusion.

He looked back at the young man. "Who do you think I am, kid?"

A wide grin crept across his face. "Yeah... you're Roach, the plague of Orion!" He looked across at Becky. "And you're his sister, the storyteller! Becky, right? Oh, man—I love your blog. I tell everyone about it! I'm Tim. Tim Byrd."

Becky's cheeks flushed with color, bringing some much-needed warmth to her face. "Thank you, Tim! Your support means so much to me, honestly."

He turned a quick circle in front of them, then walked backward away, just ahead of them. "This is so cool. You guys are, like, heroes! Come in, come in!"

Roach raised an eyebrow. He looked over at Becky, who simply shrugged, unable to hide the look of bemusement on her face.

Tim turned and ran ahead of them along the hallway.

"They're here! They're here!" he shouted. "Everyone... it's Roach! He's here!"

Roach took a deep breath, attempting to hide his discomfort.

He leaned over to Becky. "You and your big mouth."

They reached the end of the hallway. Tim gestured to the right, where an older woman stood, leaning patiently on the doorframe of the room. He then continued left, announcing their arrival to anyone who would listen.

They watched him go, then looked back at the woman. They wavered awkwardly on the spot, unsure what to make of everything.

The woman gave them a warm smile and stepped to the side, gesturing past herself, into the room.

"I'm Mary," she said. Her voice was soft and sounded younger than her looks suggested. "My husband, Frank, is inside. Please, make yourself at home. You'll be safe here. *They* don't come in. They just leave our scraps at the door outside."

Becky followed Roach into the room. The bed had been

replaced with a sofa, a couple of armchairs, and a coffee table, making it look more like a living room.

Frank sat in one of the chairs, watching them as they entered. He cast a wary gaze over them, then got to his feet gingerly. He pushed past them without a word and closed the door, shutting out the gathering crowd in the hallway outside.

"Heard you got yourself into some trouble on the way into town," he said bluntly.

Mary tutted. "For God's sake, Frank. Can you at least try to be nice?"

Becky frowned. "How do you know that? I haven't spoken to anyone..."

Frank took his seat once more. Mary moved past them and stood in the middle of the room by the wall, between the sofa and the chairs, still smiling.

Roach looked at them both. He figured they were just south of sixty. They were probably regarded as leaders in the camp.

"We have scouts," said Frank. "People who risk their lives to gather information on Tristar. Helps us stay one step ahead of those bastards."

"And why would you need to do that?" asked Roach.

Frank leaned to the side and reached into his pocket. A second later, he pulled out a GlobaTech badge and flashed it to them.

"For the rebellion," he announced proudly.

"Has anyone from GlobaTech been through here recently?" asked Becky.

"We got a few of them resting up here. Got caught out a few weeks back by a patrol. Some made it. Some didn't." Frank looked at Roach. "And what are you doing here?"

Roach was quick to pick up on the underlying hostility in his tone.

"Heading to D.C.," he said, as blunt as Frank had been with him.

"And what do you plan to do when you get there?"

Roach glanced at Becky before answering, giving her a chance to protest his intended honesty. She didn't react.

"I'm gonna march to the front door of the White House," explained Roach. "And when Quincy Hall answers, I'm going to break his neck. Put an end to all this."

Frank scoffed and looked away. "You dumb sonofabitch..."

Roach frowned. "Excuse me?"

Mary stepped over and looked at Roach regrettably. "Ignore Frank. He's... agitated."

"Goddammit, Mary, I'm not agitated—I'm pissed off!" snapped Frank. He looked back at Roach. "I support the rebellion. I believe in them. They ever come here looking for help, I'll give them the shirt off my back. But you..." He pointed an accusatory finger. "Hell, I've heard the stories. Sure, you've taken out a few of those bastards. Big deal. You think what you're doing is helping anybody? You think those tales you tell folks do anyone any good? All you're doing is endangering anyone you come into contact with. You wanna get you and your little sister here killed, be my guest. But if you had an ounce of human decency in you, you'd keep your ego trip away from the rest of us."

A tense and claustrophobic silence fell inside the room.

Becky wasn't sure where to look. Roach shifted his weight restlessly back and forth between his legs. Mary smiled apologetically but didn't speak.

"You have one hour," said Frank finally. "Freshen up, get

some food and water, whatever you have to do. Then I want you out of here."

He pushed himself out of his chair and strode past them as if they weren't there. He yanked the door open and stormed out into the hall, pushing through the small crowd outside.

Mary looked at each of them. "I'm sorry. He's not usually like that. This is... it's hard. The way things are nowadays, it takes its toll on people. It's just his way is all. Take your time. Stay as long as you need. It's okay."

She nodded and left before either of them could respond, closing the door behind her, leaving them alone in the room.

Roach looked at his sister and tilted his head slightly. "Well, *that* went well."

Becky's shoulders slumped forward. The look on her brother's face wasn't difficult to read. Frank's words had hurt him, and she knew it.

She moved over to him, placing a hand on his arm. "Will, I—"

He shrugged her away. "No, Becky. This... this is *exactly* what I was trying to tell you. This is the *exact* reason why I didn't want you telling stories about us to everyone you meet. It doesn't give them hope. It makes them angry. It reminds them of how shit everything is, and it puts pressure on me that I don't need."

Becky glared at him angrily and jabbed his chest with her finger. "Hey! You can't let one disgruntled old man shit on everything you've done for the people of this country. Think of how far we've come, Will. We've literally travelled the full width of this country, on foot, for over six months. We've been able to do that because you've killed countless Tristar men along the way. I tell people about everything

Julie and her team and GlobaTech are doing. About everything Adrian and his team are doing. I tell them everything *you're* doing. People want to know. They *need* to know that someone, somewhere is doing *something*. We've travelled almost three thousand miles, Will. After a while, people started to recognize us. Word of what we're doing travels faster than we do, and that's a good thing. That's an *amazing* thing."

Roach shrugged. "Yeah, I guess."

"Not everyone is going to be singing and dancing, but that has nothing to do with us. We're just easy targets because we're... well... I guess we're, like, celebrities now, right? We're high profile. Easy to pin blame on someone everybody knows."

"Maybe you're right. Maybe what we're doing is helping to inspire people, despite ol' Frank here. But that doesn't change the fact that he made a good point. Where we go, shit follows. We can't stay here."

Becky sighed. "You want to keep moving."

It was a statement, not a question.

He nodded. "It's another few hours until nightfall. We're maybe three days out from D.C. We should find somewhere quiet to spend the night, away from any camps."

Becky was disappointed, but she knew he was right.

"Okay," she said. "We'll take a half-hour here to freshen up and get some supplies, then we'll move on. You want me to check in with Julie? Or Adrian?"

Roach shook his head. "No. Whatever they're doing, it isn't working. Otherwise, we'd have heard about it. They didn't want to help us, so they're on their own... just like we are."

She went to reply, but she stopped herself. She knew Roach was hurting after Frank's reaction. He was doubting himself and their crusade, despite all the positivity they had seen along the way. She knew it wasn't the time to get into a debate.

They left the room and found Tim standing there, smiling. He gave them some extra clothing, some water, and a couple of protein bars. Becky thanked him for his help and hospitality.

They passed Mary and Frank on their way out, who were standing by the doors that led into the reception area. Mary wished them well. Frank said nothing.

As they reached the entrance, Becky felt a tug on her arm. She looked around to see the little girl who guided them there in the first place.

"Well, you're a little ninja, aren't you?" she said with a smile.

The girl giggled. "I like ninjas."

Becky laughed. Even Roach failed to suppress a chuckle.

"There's a small camp a couple of hours that way, by the next big city," said the girl, pointing east. "They have tents and food and a big fire pit. Everybody sits around it at night. You can maybe sleep there, if you want."

Becky knelt in front of her and placed her hand gently on the side of her face. "You're an extraordinary little girl. Thank you."

She giggled again. "You're welcome."

"Can I ask your name?"

"Josie."

"It's a pleasure to meet you, Josie. I won't forget you."

The girl threw her arms around Becky's neck and squeezed. Then she turned and ran into Roach's legs, reaching around to squeeze him around his waist.

He grimaced at the impact but recovered and placed a hand around her.

She then ran away, disappearing through the doors and down the hall, leaving them alone in reception.

Outside, the sun was low. The burnt orange sky was losing its color by the minute as the night closed in.

Roach nodded toward the doors. "We should get going."

"Yeah, we have a couple of hours' walk ahead of us, apparently," replied Becky.

They headed outside and turned left. Within minutes, the small town of Windsor was behind them. They walked along the side of the road, zigzagging to avoid the revealing glare of the streetlights.

"It was cute watching you cuddle little Josie," said Becky after a while.

Roach said nothing. He looked over at her and rolled his eyes.

Becky grinned. "Yeah, we should head back this way when all this is over. Maybe you could have a tea party with her. She could braid your hair."

He shook his head. "Becky?"

"Hmm?"

"Shut up."

29

ADRIAN HELL

November 18, 2020

We pull over behind the abandoned gas station on I-20, just outside the town limits of Canton. There's nothing around for miles. The crunch of the gravel under our tires is amplified by the darkness outside.

The drive took us the better part of a full day. We stopped to eat and rest along the way. Ruby and I alternated driving. The kids were asleep in the back for most of the journey.

It was weird heading down here. I haven't been near Texas since I watched Cunningham flatten it three years ago. I guess I never really processed what I left behind.

Ruby can read me like a book, which I'm both touched and frustrated by. At one point, she said I looked as if I had something on my mind. We talked about the life I had here. The bar; my dog, Styx, friends like Sheriff Raynor... and, of course, Tori. She listened patiently. It was nice and it helped.

I'm certainly feeling better about being here than I did twelve hours ago.

We had to divert a little to avoid Dallas. While much of the city is in the early stages of reconstruction, it's still populated and was crawling with Tristar patrols as a result.

But we made it.

The headlight beams swing around as we turn and come to rest on three pairs of legs standing close to the wall.

The five of us climb out of the Escalade and stretch out the cramps after a long ride. Ruby leaves the engine running and the lights on, illuminating the otherwise pitch-black world around us.

We form a line and approach Jericho, Julie, and Collins, who are huddled together for protection against the frankly awful temperature.

"You couldn't have picked somewhere indoors to meet?" I ask, smiling.

Julie shakes her head. "No, I chose somewhere Tristar is unlikely to find us instead."

"Oh. Well, you know for next time..."

A momentary silence falls on us, then smiles and laughter break out. Handshakes and fist-bumps are exchanged all around. Then Jericho steps in front of me. We stare at each other as a palpable tension fills the air.

Everyone else takes a step back.

I don't break eye contact. I don't move.

Neither does he.

Seconds feel like hours.

Then he extends his hand. I shake it. He nods. I nod back.

Everyone breathes a sigh of relief, which accumulates into a large cloud of steam in front of their faces.

"How are you guys holding up?" he asks me.

I smile. "Oh, you know... just enjoying the vacation. Doing some sightseeing. And you?"

He shrugs. "Same. Although, some of the hotels have been a real let-down."

We smile at each other.

Collins appears between us and puts a hand on each of our shoulders.

"How long's it been since the gang was all together, eh?" he asks.

"Too damn long," says Link. "Nice to see some friendly faces."

Julie moves beside Ruby, her arms folded over her chest. "It's been one hundred and ninety days since all of us last stood together."

"Not that you're counting?" says Rayne, grinning. "Anyway, where's the miserable one?"

"Roach?" says Jericho, shrugging. "We don't know. Not heard from him or his sister in weeks."

"Well, whatever he's doing, it's working," I say. "I don't know exactly how far word of him has spread, but folks in Missouri were talking about 'the guy walking alone to the White House.' He's apparently been taking out Tristar patrols left and right."

"It's amazing he's managed to stay off their radar this long," says Collins.

"Probably easier with it being just the two of them, to be fair," offers Ruby.

Julie takes a step forward, into the center of the group.

"Look, as nice as it is to catch up, we need to focus on why we're here." She looks over at Jessie. "What can you tell us about this base in Wyoming? Anything?"

Jessie nods. "I'm pretty sure I know which one it'll be. There was a base there, now listed as abandoned, that was secretly used for testing experimental aircraft in the eighties and nineties. I can't remember the official name of it, but people just called it The Nest. It was closed for real about fifteen years before I joined the Air Force, but people still liked to talk about it. Word was the place was enormous, built into a mountain. Very difficult to get to, which I guess was the point."

Julie looks at Jericho and Collins. "That sounds exactly like the kind of place Orion would hide Schultz. Hitting that is our endgame. If we can rescue Schultz, it could inspire the military and government acronyms to step up and fight back. It could bring about the end of all this."

Rayne shakes his head. "Ah, I dunno. The military's pretty much decommissioned at this point, right? Hall's been using Orion to fund the local and state police. The FBI, CIA, et cetera will follow the White House no matter what. From what we've seen, yeah, a lot of people support what we're trying to do, but when it comes down to it, it's unlikely that all of these folks are going to risk upsetting the new status quo. Orion control the airwaves, the news, and the people. They're keeping the public in line. I'm not sure Schultz being back will change that."

Julie glances away. Her lips purse together and her brow creases. Her breath is rapidly steaming in front of her face.

She looks back at Rayne. "Y'know what? I don't need you shitting all over the best chance we've had of ending this. This rebellion is ours. GlobaTech's. And what we do next is *my* call. You can either get on board or get out of my way."

I step forward and look at Julie. "Hey, take it easy. He has a point, and I think maybe you're too caught up being *Princess Leia* to see that. Everything we've been doing so far is all well and good. You guys have been gathering intel and support, we've been making noise and pissing people off, and Roach has... well... been doing whatever he's been doing. But even *if* we got Schultz back, think about it—if you combine the GlobaTech forces still inside the U.S. with all of the able-bodied refugees across the country, you've *maybe* got enough of a force to fight Tristar in one of the big cities. *One.* That's not enough to topple the Orion regime. It just puts all our eggs in one basket and leaves us—and the people who have supported us—open to swift and deadly retribution. Despite what Roach thinks, realistically, we can't just storm the capital and hope for the best."

Silence falls again.

Ruby looks at me and raises an eyebrow. I shrug slightly. I'm not letting anyone berate a member of my team. I don't care who it is.

Link, Jessie, and Rayne shift nervously on the spot. Collins has moved to their side and is doing much the same. Jericho remains beside Julie, as I would expect, but he's not saying anything. Perhaps he doesn't agree with his girlfriend but won't say anything because he doesn't want to argue on the ride home.

Julie looks to the ground and says nothing.

Jericho steps forward and nods to me. "What do *you* suggest we do?"

I look at him, surprised. It's a genuine inquiry. There's no animosity.

I hadn't actually thought of an alternative strategy. But one quickly comes to me.

I shrug. "We need to be logical about this. You want to cut down a hundred-foot oak tree, you don't just go for the stump at the bottom, do you? That's several feet thick and too difficult to cut straight through. What you would *actually* do is carefully climb to the top and trim it, branch by branch, working your way down. That way, when you get to the bottom again, you're not faced with a stubborn, hundred-foot oak. You have a weakened ten-foot stump that falls with no effort at all."

Everyone around me is exchanging unsubtle looks of shock and disbelief, like they never thought I could make such a concise and, frankly, brilliant point.

I'd be offended, but it's too damn cold.

"We can't win this fight with one knockout blow." I gesture at Jericho. "Even with *Hercules* on our side."

Julie nods slowly. "You're talking about Fort Hood..."

"I am. If Crow's convoy truly *is* the all-important mobile command center controlling every Tristar patrol across the country, we need to take it out. Cripple that, and the patrols are blinded and weakened... as is Hall himself."

Ruby claps her hands together, catching up with the thought process. "Then we try and get Schultz, which will be much easier if they can't see us coming."

Collins nods. "Aye, and then maybe... *maybe*, there will be enough blood in the water that we can make the stand we need to."

Link, Jessie, and Rayne all look at each other, shrugging and nodding their approval.

Julie holds out her fist to me, which I bump. It's an unspoken apology. Not something she needed to make, but I respect the hell out of her for making it anyway.

"Okay, then," she says. "Your intel puts Crow at Fort Hood two days from now, right? So, we hit it in two days. What are we looking at?"

Jessie clears her throat. "The whole place is kinda similar to how Santa Clarita was—barracks, armories, vehicles, lots of bodies... and a large refueling station. The base is in the center of a small town, so we would need to make our way through several scattered Tristar patrols to get to it. Once inside, we're looking at a much larger, more concentrated force protecting the place."

"That doesn't sound all that fun," says Collins.

"Yeah," adds Link. "Not to rain on the parade, but how the fuck can the eight of us take down an entire military base that's crawling with bad guys?"

I turn to look at him. "We don't have to. We're not trying to take out Fort Hood and everyone in it. We're trying to take out Brandon Crow and his convoy. All it needs is one grenade next to a gas pump, and that's the ball game. Sure, if we can also disable some vehicles and kill a few bad guys along the way, even better. But that's not the mission."

"You got a plan for how we're going to do that too?" asks Jericho.

I look over at him and smile. "As a matter of fact, I do."

"Since when?" asks Ruby.

I shrug. "Since about five minutes ago."

She shakes her head. "Jesus..."

Jericho gestures to me. "Let's hear it, hotshot."

"Okay. We need to do it quietly. A small force can sometimes be more effective than a large one. If we knock on the front door with every GlobaTech operative for ten miles, it'll make too much noise. We'll be lucky to get out of there alive, and if we did, there would be nowhere to hide. We've lasted this long by keeping off the streets, out of the major cities, and relying on the kindness of strangers. We can't risk losing our ability to keep fighting just because we're making a stand."

"That's all well and good, matey," says Collins. "It makes perfect sense, what ya saying. But it doesn't tell us how ya think we can infiltrate a place like that on our own."

I reach into my pocket and take out a quarter. I turn to

him and show him my hands. I place the coin on the palm of my left hand, then make fists with both.

"Where's the quarter?" I ask him.

He nods to my left hand. "I just saw ya put it in that hand."

I shrug and open my left hand. It's empty.

Collins frowns.

I open my right hand and show him the coin.

"The subtle art of misdirection, my good friend," I say, grinning as I flip the coin over to him.

Behind me, Ruby scoffs. "Since when have you ever been subtle?"

I look around at her. "A good point. Well made. But let me ask you this: have I ever been caught, except when I wanted to be?"

She sighs and looks away. "No."

"Exactly."

"What are you saying?" asks Jericho.

"I'm saying we create a distraction." I look at Julie. "How many guys do you have?"

She frowns. "In total?"

"Yeah. In the States, in total, right now."

"I don't know, exactly. A little over twenty thousand."

"Can you get word to all of them quickly?"

"I can. What are you getting at?"

"They're all in groups, scattered around the country, right? So, over the next forty-eight hours, I want those groups to start making some noise. Openly protect the camps. Hit the Tristar patrols. Rush the streets of the major cities. But nothing too drastic. We want lots of tremors, not one big earthquake."

Julie nods along. "All those little distractions flag up to

Hall and Crow. They think GlobaTech is finally making a stand, so they focus on trying to put out all the fires..."

"...and we sneak inside Fort Hood while they're not looking and wait for the convoy."

"Then what?" asks Collins.

I shrug. "What do you think? We blow the shit out of it and make enough noise on the way out that those assholes think there's a hundred of us. That's where we want the earthquake."

Jericho smiles. "And when all eyes turn to Texas, we can quietly make our way out the back door and do the same thing in Wyoming."

I nod. "That's the idea."

He shakes his head. "Huh. That's... that's actually bat-shit crazy enough to work. In fact, that's almost exactly what I would do, thinking about it."

Julie clears her throat with a dramatic *ahem*. Jericho looks around at her, and she raises her eyebrow at him, which he reacts to by rolling his eyes. It looks like an *I told you so* situation.

Whatever.

I don't know what it's about, and I have no desire to ask.

"So, this is it?" asks Rayne. "This is where we fight back."

"I reckon it is," I say to him.

"About damn time."

"I second that," says Ruby.

Julie looks around at all of us. "Those bastards think they beat us. They think T-Day was the start and the end of this war. But they're wrong. This shit ain't over... we were just pausing to catch our breath. Now they get to see we're not people you should fuck with."

I smile. Exactly what I was going to say.

She's a hell of a leader. I'll give her that.

"Should we try and get word to Roach?" asks Link. "He always said he was heading for D.C. If he knows what we're planning, he might come and help us... or at least coordinate whatever he's doing."

"I'll try his sister," says Julie. "We have her number. It's been radio silence from them for a while, so I wouldn't count on their involvement here. But I'll let her know what we're planning."

"What's he hoping to accomplish on his own, exactly?" asks Ruby.

Jericho shrugs. "I don't know. But the guy's capable. We know that. He thinks he can get to Hall. Not much else anyone can do. He has trust issues and doesn't know how to rely on other people. It's not perfect, but I get it. I was the same way before GlobaTech."

He pauses, then turns his body to face me, ignoring the others. He looks me in the eye and takes a deep breath. "Look, while we're here, I just want to say..."

Is he... is he going to apologize to me?

I'm so surprised, I actually take a step back.

Jericho continues. "...I still don't really like you."

The air sizzles with immediate tension.

I step forward again and plant my feet. I honestly can't tell if he's going to hit me or hug me. I'm prepared for either.

He sighs. "But... I never thanked you for saving my life in Colombia. Given the circumstances, you had every right to leave me there to die."

Huh.

I let his words sink in. Strangely, I don't have any urge to be a dick to him. This is a genuine turning point between the two of us. And the fact that he did it with everyone here... I can't help but admire that. I'm not sure I could have —or would have—done the same.

I shake my head. "You don't need to thank me. Even in those circumstances, I still believe that if the situation were reversed, you'd have done the same for me. I said it to you then, and I'll say it now: I'm not the enemy. I'm really good at the worst things, but I've always been on the right side when shit hits the fan. I don't know how to be any other way."

For the second time since we got here, Jericho extends his hand. And for the second time, I shake it gladly.

"I guess things worked out in the end," he says. "At least for a little while."

I nod. "Exactly. I mean, you got a metal head and a fancy new eye. You're like the Terminator. Oh, or the Six Million Dollar Man! Please tell me Josh called you *Lee Majors* at least once."

Collins and Rayne laugh. Julie and Ruby shake their heads and smile to each other. Link and Jessie just roll their eyes.

Jericho sighs. "For the first two months after I was back on my feet, he would say, 'We can rebuild him' whenever I walked into the room."

I burst out laughing. "That's my boy."

"Come on," says Julie. "We have two days to plan exactly how we're going to end this shit. You two can hold hands later."

With nothing left to be said, the GlobaTech trio turn and head back toward their vehicle, which is parked next to the gas station. The five of us return to ours. I climb inside, relishing the hot air that's been pumping out this whole time. I flex my hands, trying to get some warmth back into them. This weather really plays havoc with my old injury.

Collins is driving. He pulls away. We follow close behind.

"So, do you really think this is it?" asks Jessie from the back. "Is this the beginning of the end?"

I think for a moment. "Honestly, I don't know. I *do* know this is the best shot we've had since this shit happened. And if anyone can make it work, it's the people in this car and the people in front of us."

Link nods. "Damn right."

COOKING WITH REBECCA
RECIPE: THANKSGIVING PREPARATION

Published: November 19, 2020 by Rebecca R. | 334k comments

Listed: *Uncategorized.* **Tags:** *None.*

In one week, we celebrate Thanksgiving. It doesn't feel like there is much to be thankful for right now. 2020 is the year the world changed.

At least, it did for us.

Thanks to Orion's control of the media and the sanctions it's placed on all our communications, cell phones can no longer call international numbers. Websites and social media platforms censor much of what is being posted around the world. What information they *do* put out there is nothing but fake news—TV reports and newspapers spinning the facts to make all of this seem like anything other than what it is.

Those of us with our eyes open see the true horror of what has become our everyday life. Unfortunately, many people still willingly ignore the oppression and continue with their lives, accepting the harsh new realities without question.

However, outside the walls of this fortress that our nation has become, our allies around the world are still living in ignorance of what we're going through. Quincy Hall told them that the U.S. is taking extreme measures to combat the most extreme threat of domestic terrorism our country has ever faced. He thanked world leaders for their offers of support but asked that they respect our decision to close our doors and deal with this ourselves. And they believed him because it's the same message he's feeding us, and there's a media embargo preventing any contradictory reports making it to air or to press.

Right now, the world is looking at us the same way they have looked at North Korea for so many years.

Their issues, their problem. Nothing to do with us.

We must understand what this means. No help is coming. Our borders are closed.

We are on our own.

Many of us have friends and family trapped outside of our borders. The toll this is taking on us mentally and emotionally is great. But remember this: we still have each other.

That's what I'm thankful for. As we have shown time and time again in the last six months, our kindness toward each other undermines the control Orion has over us. Like Paul Newman in *Cool Hand Luke*, we keep getting up, we keep helping each other, and we keep fighting back.

There's something else we should all be thankful for: GlobaTech.

As many of you know, my brother and I are periodically in contact with the leaders of the rebellion. We knew them on a personal level, albeit briefly, before all of this started. I wouldn't say we were all friends, but if there's something important, Julie Fisher herself will reach out to me.

And yesterday, she did exactly that.

I cannot give you specifics, but over the next 48 hours, you can expect to see an increase in GlobaTech's presence across the country. Julie and her people believe they have an opportunity that could finally tip the balance of power away from Orion. The first step is for GlobaTech forces to finally emerge from the shadows and begin taking the fight to Tristar. It won't be easy. It *will* be dangerous. But this is what they have been fighting for—what we have all been *hoping for*—ever since this whole thing began.

My brother and I have been on the move a lot more recently, so there has been less time to safely stop and post my blog. But I promise you, as soon as I have more information, I will let you know. For now, please hold everyone who is fighting for us in your thoughts and prayers. And above all else, please be safe out there. Do not take any unnecessary risks. Continue to live your lives carefully and within the rules Orion has laid out for us, at least for a little while longer.

Remember: in the coming days, if you see anyone from GlobaTech, go back to your homes or your jobs—anywhere you feel safe. Just keep off the streets. GlobaTech's not looking for your help anymore. They're looking for a fight.

30

QUINCY HALL

November 19, 2020

Quincy Hall sat at the head of the long, smooth oak table in the White House Situation Room. He rested his elbow on the arm of his chair and his cheek wearily on his fist. In front of him, lining both sides of the table, sat members of the new National Security Council. Gone were any military liaisons and agency directors; they had been replaced by members of Orion's board and Tristar's high command, who had assumed responsibilities previously carried out by secretaries and generals.

The secretary of defense and the vice president had been forcibly and publicly removed from office. The secretaries of energy and the treasury remained, along with security advisors from Homeland Security and the NSA.

Finally, at the end of the table on the right, as far away from Hall as was possible, sat Elaine Phillips, the secretary of state. It took concentration and effort to make sure the disdain she felt about being there didn't creep onto her face.

She felt partly responsible for everything that had happened. She had been a proponent of swearing Schultz into office following President Cunningham's death three years ago. She had also sat on the committee that had tried its best to dismantle GlobaTech and everything Moses Buchanan had worked for, based on the misinformation campaign created by Orion. The guilt kept her awake most nights.

But she was smart enough to sound convincing when asked where her loyalties lay. She said whatever she needed to in order to keep her position, believing the time would come when GlobaTech would need her help. It was her continued duties as secretary of state that kept her in the room.

She looked over at Hall. "Before we get started, Mr. Hall, have you read the report I sent to you yet?"

Hall didn't look up. He adjusted his tie and straightened the sleeves of his expensive suit, like he had all the time in the world. Then he took a cigar from his inside pocket and held his lighter to it, sucking and turning it slowly as the end gradually lit. He took a satisfying drag and blew the light gray smoke into the air.

"I've been busy," he said eventually. "Bullet point it for me."

Elaine fought to hold back a sigh of impatience. "It was a brief detailing how best to integrate the country back into the global community once your mission here is complete. Including how to appease the allies we're alienating with each day that passes."

Hall finally turned his attention to her. "That isn't your concern. I will deal with that when the time is right."

She pursed her lips together. "Respectfully, it *is* my concern. I'm the voice of this administration's foreign policy.

I'll be heavily involved in the talks with world leaders when this is over."

Hall shook his head. "This isn't an administration, Elaine. It's a dynasty. And you're here because I was assured your advice and counsel is valuable. You will not, at any point, speak on my behalf to anyone."

Elaine went to reply but thought better of it. She knew a lost cause when she saw one.

Hall looked at the man sitting to his immediate left. "Now explain to me again why I'm here. What's the problem?"

Dan Thomas was the youngest member of Orion's board of directors. He was the director of marketing for Europe and the Middle East. Now he found himself out of his depth, delivering security briefings to his boss, who had assumed control of the country.

His fresh, unblemished features masked his age. He was forty-one, although he looked like he was in his twenties. His hair was styled into a comb-over. His inexpensive suit was a sickly beige. His hands shook as he opened the file in front of him.

He swallowed hard. "Okay, um, sir. There have been reports of increased rebel activity, which is causing concern for many of the central command posts across the country."

Hall nodded. "Acts of rebellion are nothing new. Is this really what you called me down here for?"

Thomas took a deep breath. "But sir, this isn't your average skirmish near a refugee camp, nor a sighting of GlobaTech movement. This is—"

Hall let out an impatient sigh and glared at him. "This is what? Spit it out, goddammit."

"Sir, this is bigger than that. This is activity on a level we haven't seen before. Reports coming in show that attacks on our patrols have increased five hundred percent in the last thirty-six hours."

Hall's eyes narrowed. "Five *hundred* percent? What's changed?"

Thomas shook his head. "We don't know. Nothing, as far as we can tell. There has been no increase in reports of issues with the outlying camps, nor in sightings of people on our most wanted list."

Hall gestured to the monitor mounted on the wall opposite him with his cigar.

"Show me," he said.

Thomas looked over to one of the Tristar guards stationed in the corner, behind the computer there. A moment later, a map of the United States flashed up on the screen. There was a scattering of red dots across it.

"Sir, this is a snapshot of every reported encounter with rebels across the country, as of two nights ago." He nodded to the technician in the corner. A second later, the screen changed. "And *this* is as of two hours ago."

There were no longer any dots visible. Large areas of the map were now simply colored red.

Hall leaned forward slowly in his chair; his gaze transfixed on the screen. The graphic of the country—*his* country —was more red than not. The increase in rebel activity looked significantly greater than five hundred percent.

Others looked at the screen, shocked by the visual, but they were more concerned with what Hall's reaction would be.

Hall could see the expressions on their faces, but he ignored them. He stared at the display as his mind cycled through the plethora of information he had about the state of things out there. He knew people, especially refugees, were probably helping GlobaTech and hoping they didn't get caught. He also knew Tristar would follow their orders and deliver a swift and decisive punishment to anyone caught aiding GlobaTech personnel.

GlobaTech had been relatively quiet for a long time. A few instances popped up here and there, but any issues Tristar patrols faced were largely caused by the assassin, or Tristar's former asset and his interfering little sister.

Thomas had said nothing had changed. But one thing had.

Hall clenched his jaw until his teeth ached.

"Brandon fucking Crow," he muttered.

"Sir?" said Thomas, frowning.

Hall looked at him. "You say nothing has changed, yet three days ago, that fucking assassin attacked Crow's convoy and stole a hard drive from him. And now all this is happening. You can't possibly be dumb enough to think this is a coincidence?"

Thomas swallowed hard again. "N-no, sir."

Another member of the board, a woman named Melinda Bates, was sitting to Hall's right. She leaned forward to get his attention.

"Mr. Hall, could this not simply be a reaction to the gradually decreasing public opinion? It's no secret that approval ratings are declining. Perhaps this is something that's been building up for a while and has simply come to a head. The attack on Mr. Crow's convoy could just be the catalyst... the straw that broke the camel's back."

"I don't care about approval ratings. I'm not seeking re-election. I understand people might not like it, but they will learn to. My mother used to say, '*Prevention is better than a cure.*' That's because medicine, while it helps, usually tastes like shit. Well, it's too late to prevent what's already happened to this country. *We* are the cure, Melinda." Hall pointed to the screen with his cigar. "They might not like how it tastes, but it will make things better. Until then, they can all suck it up like big boys and girls. The news cycles will continue to manage expectations and craft the right message, just like we planned. So, no, public opinion might not be sky-high, but it's where we expect it to be, and it certainly isn't the cause of *this*. No... this is because of the attack. I'm sure of it. The assassin is up to something."

Thomas shuffled through some papers in another file. "Sir, the last reported incident involving Blackstar—before the attack on Mr. Crow—was just outside of Omaha. Two patrols were taken out. Before that... there had been nothing since mid-October. It doesn't look like he's working toward anything. They're just running, like GlobaTech are."

Hall shook his head as he looked back at the screen. "No. No, that's not it. Look at the map. Tell me what you see. All of you, look."

All heads turned and looked at the map. An uneasy silence fell over the room, like a fresh blanket descending across a new bed.

It was Elaine Phillips who spoke first. She didn't want to, but she saw what she figured Hall had seen, and it would look out of place if she didn't comment.

"The increased attacks are widespread," she observed. "Markedly increased almost nationwide. Everywhere... except New Texas."

Hall nodded toward her. "Exactly. Thank you, Madam Secretary. At least someone here is paying attention." He then looked around the room, once again pointing to the screen with his cigar. "All these reports of violence and attacks on Tristar patrols started after that piece of shit, Adrian Hell, hit Crow's convoy. That's not a coincidence. That means he's up to something. Possibly coordinating with GlobaTech. Seeing as there is an increase everywhere except New Texas, I would suggest he's planning something there. Any ideas?"

Melinda thought for a moment, then looked at Hall with panic in her eyes. "Isn't Fort Hood where Crow refuels?"

Hall nodded. "It is. Blackstar will try and finish the job they started in Omaha, and they're going to do it in Fort Hood." He looked across the room at the man who served as Tristar's liaison, Jacobs, who spoke for Brandon Crow in his absence. "Get word to Fort Hood to prepare for an attack. And send more men there."

"How many?" asked Jacobs. He was a tall, thin man with a weathered face and a thick, graying beard.

"As many as you can. The more, the better." Hall looked at Thomas. "When's Crow due to refuel there next?"

Thomas quickly sifted through more paperwork in front of him. "Tomorrow, sir. He'll be there tomorrow."

Hall turned to Jacobs. "Use patrol centers local to the base. They will get there faster." He then looked back at Thomas. "Get me the asset on the phone."

"Miss Tevani?"

"Yes. She needs to know where her target is going to be. This seems like the perfect opportunity for her to carry out some long-overdue retribution."

Hall smiled to himself. He patted the cigar with his finger, sending ash scattering across the table in front of him.

"GlobaTech think they're smart. They think they still have some hope of fighting back. They think their assassin friend will help them. They know nothing. They lost six months ago. They just haven't admitted it yet." He turned his attention to the room. "Increase patrols in the areas with the highest concentration of rebel activity. If GlobaTech attacks persist, start shooting any refugees nearby until they get the message. The assassin and his team will be dealt with tomorrow. This should all be over inside forty-eight hours. Then we can get back to work."

Hall stood without ceremony and left the Situation Room. The security detail followed him out, leaving the rest of the room in a sullen silence.

At the back, on the right, Elaine Phillips stared at the surface of the table and sighed. She felt like she should be doing more to help GlobaTech. But deep down, she knew there was nothing she could do that wouldn't compromise her own safety and that of her family.

But now good people were about to die. Innocent people. All in the name of a cause they didn't believe in.

She wouldn't be sleeping tonight. Her conscience wasn't going to allow it. As far as she was concerned, any innocent blood that was spilled in the coming days was on her hands.

31

JERICHO STONE

November 20, 2020

The crisp, pre-dawn air carried with it a bitter wind. Navy blue streaks lined the starless night sky. In near-total darkness, three shadows moved quickly across the open grasslands, approaching Fort Hood from the north.

Jericho, Julie, and Collins were wearing identical winter coats, which were jet-black and lined with fur, resting just above the knee. The hoods were pulled up over their heads. Their all-weather tactical combat pants and boots were also black.

Their GlobaTech-issue *Negotiators* were holstered to their thighs. Assault rifles hung over their shoulders by straps.

The last forty-eight hours had been productive. Together with Blackstar, they had formulated a plan to attack the base and take out Crow's convoy. It had been unanimously agreed upon as the only sound strategy they had available to them. They had triple-checked every detail and invested in three burner phones—one for each team—so they could coordinate the attacks without fear of being traced.

Adrian and Ruby were coming in from the east. They were passing through the border town of Killeen before heading into the residential part of Fort Hood, known to be still occupied by civilians. Rayne, Jessie, and Link were approaching from the southwest. They moved past the now-abandoned regional airport and circled around to enter the base from the west.

The trio of elite GlobaTech operatives were aiming directly for the base itself. They assumed that most of the Tristar populous would be camped in the barracks there. They also knew from satellite imagery that the fuel pumps were in the center of the base, so they were heading directly to where Crow and his convoy would be arriving later in the day.

The plan was to sneak inside and plant explosives under the cover of darkness, then hide out until the convoy arrived. They would attack hard and fast from three sides, taking everyone by surprise. The plan was to kill Crow, destroy the convoy, then set off all the explosives and disappear in the chaos.

They had parked roughly four miles north, on a dirt track behind an abandoned training facility, and made the journey on foot. They jogged at an easy pace, mostly to keep warm.

"I'm dressed as an Eskimo and have been running for almost an hour," observed Jericho. "How the hell am I still cold?"

Julie sighed. "Because you're a pussy who hates being cold."

Collins laughed.

"Who *likes* being cold?" said Jericho.

"Most people are indifferent to it," countered Julie. "They just deal with it because it's unavoidable. But you moan about it all the time."

"No, I don't..."

She looked over at him. "Really? What about last year, when we went to Montreal to protect Ulysses Hyatt? You complained the whole time we were there."

"That's because September in Montreal makes this—" He gestured around them. "—feel like Hawaii, and I was wearing a T-shirt."

Collins laughed again. "Not wishing to side with ya missus here, Jerry, but if ya went to Canada in the fall and didn't think to at least take a sweater, ya only have yaself to blame."

"*Thank* you!" said Julie.

"So, it's like that, is it?" scoffed Jericho. "Both of you ganging up on me. Well, let me tell you, if you—"

Julie slid to a stop and held a hand up, signaling for the others to do the same.

She dropped to a crouch. "Up ahead. You see that?"

Jericho and Collins did the same, following her sight line. There was a faint light glowing in the near distance. Shadows moved around it. People.

"Is that a Tristar patrol?" asked Collins.

"I doubt it," said Julie. "Not in the middle of nowhere at this time of night. What would they be looking for?"

Jericho looked at her. "Us?"

Julie and Collins looked back at him silently.

He shrugged. "What? Why else would they be out here?"

Julie shook her head. "No. No way they know we're coming. And even if they did, who would be crazy enough to approach a heavily fortified base, out in the open, in freezing temperatures, at night?"

Collins huffed. "Aye. Who, indeed?"

"Come on," she said. "Let's check it out. Low and slow."

They made their way toward the light, maybe a quarter-mile away. Their sidearms were drawn, held low and ready.

As they neared, the light revealed three people huddled together, not moving, staring down.

"Civilians," whispered Julie. "Be careful. We don't want to spook them and draw attention to us."

Julie, Jericho, and Collins waited until they were no more than twenty feet away, then stood upright and spread out. They holstered their weapons and held their hands out to the sides, as a gesture of peace.

"Excuse me," Julie called out. "Is everything okay?"

The three figures spun around. The two men and a woman, dressed for the weather, quickly clung together. The woman gasped, but one of the men clamped his hand over her mouth.

"Quiet!" he hissed.

The other man stepped in front of them and looked along the line as they approached.

"Who are you?" he asked tentatively. "What are you doing out here?"

Jericho stepped to meet him. "We could ask you the same question."

The man eyed him warily. "Are... are you Tristar?"

"No. We're GlobaTech."

The man looked back at the people with him, who muttered their surprise to each other.

"What are you doing?" asked Julie, moving to Jericho's side. "It's not safe out here, no matter what time it is. Not this close to the base."

"We're refugees," said the man. "We live in Killeen. The whole town is pretty much a camp nowadays."

"What about Tristar?" asked Collins. "Where are they?"

The man looked at him. "They took over the base months ago. All the barracks and the surrounding residential areas."

"Christ..." muttered Collins.

"How many?" asked Julie. "Do you know?"

The man shrugged. "I don't know. Maybe five hundred. Maybe more."

Julie glanced at Jericho, a silent look of concern.

Jericho looked back at the man. "Seriously, why are you out here?"

The woman stepped forward, to the man's side. Tears were visible on her face in the faint glow of the fire they had started. Clean streams etched into the dirt on her face.

"I'm burying my son," she said flatly, then walked away again.

Jericho nodded to Julie, who followed the woman to offer comfort. Collins lingered nearby.

Jericho turned away, gesturing for the man to follow him.

A few paces away from the others, Jericho stopped. He folded his arms across his chest as he looked at the man.

"What happened?" he asked.

The man hesitated, then sighed with resignation. He glanced to the ground, as if ashamed or embarrassed by what he was about to say.

Jericho was quick to notice. He placed a comforting hand on the man's shoulder.

"Hey, it's okay," he said. "We can help. You're safe with us, I promise."

The man nodded. "Thank you. I... I just don't know how things got this bad, y'know?"

Jericho smiled to himself. "Yeah..."

"The name's Kevin. Kevin Nicholls. That's my sister, Helen, and her husband, Paul. A few days ago, a Tristar patrol passed through Killeen. I'm guessing they were on their way to the base. Anyway, they started causing trouble. They... they raided a couple of stores, destroyed everything, and called anyone nearby *refugee scum*. Helen and Paul were walking down the street with their son. The patrol saw them and... one of the guards, they... they grabbed her. Started pushing her around, joking about how they would... do things... horrible things."

Jericho felt every fiber of his body tense. He took a deep breath. "Then what happened?"

Kevin continued. "Paul, he... he did what anyone would've done. Of course, he did. He pulled Helen away and confronted the guard, who immediately pulled a gun on him. Their son... my nephew... Timothy, he was only nine. He... stepped in front of his dad, just as he had seen his dad do for his mom a minute earlier, y'know. Started yelling at the guards to stop and leave them alone. This guard, he shoved Timothy away like he was nothing. Sent him flying to the ground. Paul grabbed the guard, started trying to beat on him. But there were, like, eight of them. He had no chance. The guard punched him, raised his gun, and fired. But Timothy... he had gotten back to his feet and rushed to his dad's side. He... he took the bullet, right in the chest. He died instantly. Helen was screaming and crying. Half the town saw it happen, including me."

Jericho tried to swallow the anger that was consuming him.

"I'm sorry," he said.

Kevin shook his head. "And do you know what that patrol did? They looked at each other, shrugged, and the one who fired just said, 'Whoops.' Then they walked off like they had just stepped in dog shit." He looked Jericho in the eyes. "You say you're GlobaTech, right?"

Jericho nodded. "I am. The name's Jericho."

"You have to help us, man. You have to stand up to these guys. You have to stop them. Take our country back. This has to stop..."

Kevin's voice cracked as emotion took over. Tears began to flow freely down his face.

Jericho took another deep breath, partly to subdue his own emotion. The anger, he could deal with. But Kevin's story had gotten to him, and he felt a genuine sadness for his loss. Tragedy like this happened everywhere, every day. But hearing it from someone, seeing how it could affect an individual... a real person, not just a statistic... it made it all seem more real.

"That's why we're here," said Jericho finally. "These next couple of days, if everything goes to plan, a lot of things are going to change. I promise you."

Kevin smiled weakly through his tears. He reached for Jericho's hand and shook it without being asked. "Thank you. What you guys are doing for us... for all of us... you don't know what it means. Thank you."

Jericho nodded. "Come on. Let's go check on your sister."

The two of them walked back to the others. Julie was standing with Helen, comforting her. Collins and Paul were standing opposite them, with the fire and the shallow grave between them.

They looked over as Jericho and Kevin approached.

"Jerry, this is Helen and Paul," said Collins.

He nodded. "Yeah, this is Kevin. He... told me why you're all out here." He looked at Helen. "I'm truly sorry for your loss."

She nodded gratefully, silently.

Paul looked at each member of GlobaTech in turn. "Hey, ah, is *he* here?"

They each exchanged glances of confusion.

"Is who here?" asked Collins.

"The one people call Roach. I know he and his sister travel all over, telling stories of how GlobaTech are fighting back. Her blog is so great. The fact they risk their lives to spread word of the rebellion to refugee camps is incredible."

Collins smiled. "Aye. Those two are really something..."

"He's been sticking up for people in camps for months," continued Paul. "Fighting off patrols and everything. Is he here? He's a legend. I would love to meet him."

Jericho looked at Julie, who simply shrugged. He then looked at Paul.

"I'm afraid he's not," he said. "We're here on a GlobaTech mission. Roach is... well, he's taking the fight to Tristar in his own way."

"I heard a story a couple of nights ago," said Kevin. "Some people in the bar were talking about how he took out an entire Tristar patrol up in Charlotte. They were trying to close down a food truck in a settlement, and he killed them all."

Jericho smiled. "Good for him."

"Was there any talk of where he was heading?" asked Julie.

"Word is, they stole the Tristar truck and set off for Virginia. That was... four nights ago, now."

"That's really helpful. Thank you. And we're sorry again for what happened to your family. Please take care out here, okay? Stay clear of the base."

Kevin nodded. "We will. Thank you. You folks look after yourselves too, okay? We need you."

"We will."

Jericho shook Kevin's hand. "Take care. It was nice meeting you. I'm sorry it was under such tragic circumstances."

Kevin nodded and moved over to his sister and her husband, keen to get back to their mourning.

Collins and Julie rejoined Jericho, and the three of them continued toward the base. They still had over two miles to go, and they would soon be racing the sunrise.

Jericho shook his head with pleasant disbelief and smiled. "That sonofabitch has almost made it to D.C."

Collins laughed. "Aye. Part of me kinda figured he would, y'know? Fella's too stubborn to let Tristar beat him."

"Agreed," said Julie. "I'm happy for him. For both of them. Becky's stories are really helping keep this country together right now. I wish he would've worked with us a little more. Coordinated his efforts. Perhaps that would've made what we're about to do a little easier. But still... maybe there's some hope after all."

Jericho didn't comment further. His thoughts were on the task that lay ahead. He hoped the others had made it to the base safely. He felt frustration and anger on behalf of Helen, Paul, and Kevin. He knew there was little to no chance of finding the specific patrol responsible for Timothy's death. The only way he could think of was to tear the whole base down with his bare hands and kill everyone, just to be safe.

He smiled to himself.

Not the worst idea.

32

ADRIAN HELL

November 20, 2020

It took me almost an hour to finish hiding the dead bodies inside the abandoned plane. There were three—a small Tristar patrol wandering around the airfield north of Killeen, Texas. They were in our way, so... you know how *that* goes.

We arrived a few hours ago, under cover of darkness, at roughly the same time everyone else was getting into position. The airfield was no longer used, and a couple of small aircraft stood like statues just outside the hangars. Ruby and I broke into one and got a couple of hours' sleep. We woke to the sound of these three assholes walking around outside.

Ruby had insisted on taking them out, citing general frustration and the urge to practice as her reasoning. I understand that. And it's not like she isn't capable. Of course, she is—as evidenced by the three dead bodies.

But it was daylight—just after nine—and therefore riskier to engage than it would've been a few hours before.

But there wasn't anyone else around, so if we kept it quiet, we would be fine.

And we were.

She took them out effectively, brutally, and—if I may say so—gracefully. Yet, for some reason, *I'm* the one who had to drag the dead bodies across the tarmac, carry them up the steps, and hide them in the fuselage of the plane we had slept in.

Go figure.

We planted an explosive inside, on the engines, as planned. We left straight after, beginning the mile-long walk toward East Lake, near the south entrance of the base inside Fort Hood. It was a bright day but cold. To our left, we could see the low skyline of Killeen in the mid-distance.

"Seriously, how long did it take you?" says Ruby, smiling. She's been enjoying teasing me about being tired after moving the bodies earlier.

It's been a long walk.

I look over at her, breathing deeply. "Ruby, I have two words for you, and the second one is 'off.'"

She laughs. "I'm just trying to keep you focused. Quit sulking."

Truth is, I recognize and appreciate the effort. Today is a big day. Everyone needs to be at the top of their game if this is going to work. I focus better when I'm not thinking about the task at hand too much. Overthinking leads to hesitation, and hesitation will get you killed. Josh always understood that, which is why people thought we were crazy when we joked around during a mission.

Ruby understands that too. It's one of the many reasons I love her.

"How are we doing for time?" I ask her.

She checks. "We're good. Everyone else should be in

position now. Just a matter of waiting until the convoy arrives."

"I hope he hurries up. Otherwise, we'll freeze to death."

She looks over at me, shaking her head. "You sound like Jericho, always complaining about being cold."

"Okay, first of all, it's *painfully* cold, so my complaints are justified. Second of all... shut up—no, I don't."

Ruby laughs. "Oh, you *so* do. And he sounds like you. The way he was talking the other night, it's like you two are brothers."

I roll my eyes. "I'm sure he would love to hear you say that."

"It's true. Julie thinks so too."

"And how would you know?"

She shrugs. "Girls talk, dumbass. I guess one good thing to come out of all of this is that you two buried the hatchet... and it wasn't in each other."

I smile. "Yeah, well, to be fair, the issue was all his to begin with. Although, I'll admit it's nice to have him fighting beside me. That guy's a monster."

We continue on and reach the outer fence of the base maybe ten minutes later. There wasn't any sign of any Tristar patrols along the highway, and there's no one around guarding the entrance to the base at the north of the town.

"Bit quiet, isn't it?" notes Ruby.

I shrug. "I dunno. Maybe. Crow will likely arrive with some patrols protecting him. I imagine most of the patrols use the base as their headquarters, right? They'll either be out patrolling or further inside, waiting for their boss to show up."

"Yeah, I guess."

She doesn't sound convinced, but it's too late to worry about that now.

We walk along the side of the fence until we reach an opening. We step inside and run across to the first bit of cover we see—a concrete barricade lining the road through the base. We crouch behind it.

"Where's the fuel station?" I ask.

Ruby frowns at me. "Seriously, how bad is your memory?"

"What? I'm just checking we know what we're doing."

She sighs. "According to Jessie's satellite recon, the convoy is going to come in from the west, which will have it pass by the rest of the team. It will refuel to the north of the base, near where Julie and the guys should be."

I nod. "Okay. We should check in with the others and make sure they're ready."

Ruby takes out her burner phone and hands it to me. I quickly type out a text.

We're in position at the south entrance. How are you looking?

I send it to Julie and Rayne.

A couple of minutes pass, then the phone vibrates.

"Who is it?" asks Ruby.

I open the message.

"Julie," I say. "They're hiding out to the north. All their explosives are in place. They have eyes on the fuel station. She says there's a lot of Tristar presence up there. More than we anticipated."

"Shit."

I shrug. "It doesn't change anything. They don't know we're here. Whether it's five or five hundred, once that convoy goes up, they won't have a clue what to do. We'll sneak out the back and blow everything else on the way, just like we planned."

The phone goes again.

"Adam?" she asks.

I read the message.

"Uh-huh. They're by the west entrance, hidden behind some buildings. They will see the convoy coming, and they're close to the fuel station. They're ready."

"He say anything else?"

"Only that he's seeing a lot more Tristar assholes than we thought we would."

Ruby sighs. "Adrian, something doesn't feel right here."

"It's fine, like I said."

She slaps my arm. "Don't dismiss me!"

I hold my hands up and nod. "Okay. Okay. I'm sorry. I'm just trying to reassure you, that's all."

"I'm a big girl, Adrian. I don't need reassuring. I need you to open your eyes. Something is wrong. This place was not *this* busy two days ago on the satellite feeds."

She's right. It wasn't.

"Maybe this is just how it gets when His Highness is due to visit," I suggest.

She thinks for a moment, then shrugs. "Yeah, maybe."

"Look, that has to be it. It's the only thing that makes any sense. We've done everything right so far. This is a solid plan. No one knows we're here."

"If that's the case, why have so much additional security when this place, Crow's routes, the refueling timetable... all of it is supposed to be a secret. Why protect something no one knows about?"

Good point.

I shrug. "We know about it. Maybe they're just paranoid. All those stories of rebellion are getting to them. In a way, it's a good thing. Shows it's working."

"And what if it's not just paranoia? What if they know we know? What if they're expecting us?"

I reach over and rest my hand on her leg, feeling the

coldness of her skin through the material of her pants. "They don't know. How could they?"

"We figured this out from the drive you stole. Maybe they figured out we would find what we did."

"I don't think they're that smart, but even if they are, it still doesn't change anything. If they know we're coming, they will be expecting a huge show of force from GlobaT-ech. No way they think eight of us are going to attempt this. Plus, everything not nailed down within a half-mile radius is rigged to go up like the Fourth of July at the press of a button. That will send them into a panic, thinking they're being attacked from all sides. Exactly like we planned." I shift slightly to face her. "Look, I understand your concern, and I do share it. But don't worry, okay? We'll be fine. Today's the day when things change, I promise."

Ruby nods and smiles. "Okay. Thank you. I guess I just—"

The phone vibrates.

I open the message. It's from Rayne.

"What is it?" she asks.

I look up at her. "It's showtime. The convoy just drove through the west gate, toward their position. Here's hoping they were able to attach the bombs as it rolled past."

"Yeah, there's too much at stake for them to not hold up their end of this."

"I trust them. The convoy will be moving slowly once inside the base. They could easily keep up on foot. If they stick to the driver's blind spots, they should be able to get the explosives in place on the rear Juggernaut. We pick the right moment, that's all it'll take. Come on."

We keep to the perimeter of the base and make our way north, pausing behind each building to avoid being seen by any patrols.

It's been a while since I've been on a military base. I forgot how organized everything looks. The grass is so short, it appears artificial. Everything is clean and maintained, even now, with no military personnel on base. I wonder if Tristar has been keeping up with the chores.

The main road stretches around the interior of the base, acting as a barrier between the central buildings and the outer circle of barracks and armories. After a few minutes, we see the fueling station up ahead. The road branches off, creating an additional loop around it. All three of Crow's trucks are parked in a semicircle, taking up almost all of the space.

Ruby's just ahead of me. We stop behind the last building on the right side of the base and peer around the corner.

"That... is a lot of guards," whispers Ruby.

"Yeah. Yeah, it is," I reply absently.

Shit. That *is* a lot of guards. It looks worse than either Julie or Rayne described. There are two ten-man patrols with the convoy; one is stationed at either end. Beyond the fuel pumps is a row of buildings, maybe thirty feet back. That must be where Jericho and the guys are. If it is, they're screwed. There are at least forty Tristar guards lined up in front of the buildings, all facing the convoy, alert with weapons ready.

Just in front of us—maybe ten... fifteen feet away—is another patrol. Another ten guys. I can't see the opposite side, but I suspect Rayne and the others are seeing something similar.

"There he is," says Ruby, nodding toward the convoy.

I look over and see Crow walking alongside the trucks. He's talking with a Tristar guard as others busy themselves around them.

"No sign of that crazy bitch who was with him. Jay." Ruby huffs. "I fucking owe her."

I place my hand on her back. "We'll get her. Don't worry. One step at a time."

I feel something behind me and freeze. My body tenses as I hold my breath.

"What's the move?" asks Ruby, still staring out at the convoy.

I don't answer. I'm not sure I can.

"Adrian, what should we do? We can't stay here. It's too risky. Someone might see us."

I sigh. "Yeah... it might be a little late for that."

She turns around and looks behind me. Her eyes go wide. I haven't looked, but I know there's at least one guy standing there because he's pressing the barrel of his gun to the back of my head.

Another appears behind Ruby. He shoves her with his gun, causing her to almost overbalance.

"Both of you, on your feet," says a voice behind me. "Slowly."

We stand. I look apologetically into Ruby's eyes. She stares back at me the same way.

I turn around to see one guy standing there, dressed head to toe in black, with the Tristar logo displayed on his body armor.

I smile. "Would you believe me if I said I was looking for the restroom?"

He jabs me with the gun. "Weapons. Toss them."

"Huh. Guess not."

We both throw the Raptors to the ground beside us.

"Let's go," says the guard.

We're marched out from behind the buildings, toward the mass gathering of assholes by the trucks.

"You got a plan?" says Ruby quietly.

I shake my head. "Nope. You?"

"Nope."

"Good times..."

Crow looks over as we approach and smiles. It's a smug grin, laced with the arrogance of someone who believes they've already won.

Prick.

"Nice to see you again, Adrian," he says. "And so soon after our last meeting. How are you?"

I shrug. "Fucking cold. You?"

He continues smiling. "I've never been better."

I point a finger at the bruising around his right eye and on his cheek.

"Sorry about that. Looks painful."

He shrugs. "It's nothing. You should see what I'm going to do to the other guy."

I roll my eyes. "Right..."

"It's over, Brandon," says Ruby. "And when I'm done with you, I'm going to find that psycho bitch you keep on a leash and finish her too."

He looks to her. "We haven't been formally introduced. You must be... Ruby, right? The assassin's girlfriend. I think I'll make you watch as I flay him."

She takes a step toward him, her expression twisted with rage. The two guards standing with us rush in front of her and aim their guns at her head.

I move to her side and grab her arm, pulling her back a couple of steps.

"Easy, Ruby," I say to her. "Now isn't the time."

"That's right, Ruby," says Crow. "Listen to your man, like a good girl."

I close my eyes for a second and let out a heavy sigh. Then I look over at Crow.

"This might not be the right time, but trust me, you really don't want to push your luck."

He laughs. "Right. So, tell me, are you two here alone?"

I nod. "Yes."

"Really?"

"Uh-huh. It wasn't hard to figure out where you would be with that hard drive I took from you. Fair bit of cash on there too. That will come in handy when all this is over."

Crow holds my gaze. "So, where are all your friends?"

"What friends?"

"Your team. Those interfering bastards from GlobaTech. That traitor and his irritating little sister."

I shrug. "No idea. We split up days ago. They all went off to cause you as many headaches as possible."

He ambles toward us, stopping in the middle of the road. "Right. You two snuck in here to do... what, exactly?"

"Kill you," says Ruby.

"Ah, I see. Well, that's a good plan. It certainly makes sense. But you're lying to me, which isn't very nice."

"Am I?"

Crow grins again, lifts his hand, and snaps his fingers. "Yes. You are."

There's a flurry of movement ahead of us and to the left. The groups of guards forming the perimeter around us all shift to the side, making room for even more Tristar assholes to join in.

The new arrivals on the left are escorting Rayne, Jessie, and Link at gunpoint. The ones in front of us, walking past the trucks, have Jericho, Julie, and Collins, also at gunpoint.

No one has any visible weapons on them.

"Shit..." mutters Ruby.

Everyone is ushered together where Ruby and I are standing. The guards close around us again.

Christ, there must be over a hundred of them...

The two trios move to our side and turn to face Crow.

"Hey, folks," I say casually. "How's it going?"

Everyone ignores me.

"They knew we were coming," says Rayne with desperation in his voice.

"Ya think?" replies Collins offhandedly.

"How?" asks Jessie. "No way they traced my hack."

"I think we're past the stage where any of that matters," I say. "Don't you?"

Jericho is looking around. I can see the cogs turning behind his eyes. The crazy sonofabitch is planning how to fight his way out of this. I smile to myself. A man after my own heart.

I glance down the line to my left and catch Rayne's attention. "Hey, Adam..."

He looks back. "What?"

"Did you do what you were supposed to do before they caught you?"

He smiles and winks at me.

I nod gratefully. "Good man."

"Just say when, boss."

Crow walks toward us, flanked by eight guards. One for each of us. His arrogant swagger is infuriating, but it doesn't mask the slight limp he still has. That was either me or Roach. Either way, I hope it fucking hurts.

We're standing in a line, staring at an overwhelming Tristar force, not sure what to do next.

Talk about déjà vu.

Ruby and I are in the middle. On my left is Jessie, then

Rayne, then Link. On Ruby's right is Jericho, then Julie, then Collins.

Crow stops in front of Julie. He straightens to his full height and width, puffing his chest out like a king.

"Well, well. If it isn't Julie fucking Fisher. The leader of the resistance. The rebel queen herself. I am honored."

She spits in his face. "Honor that, dipshit."

He wipes his cheek, nodding. "Okay. I guess I owe you that one. You, I'm going to leave alive. Jay wants the pleasure of killing you."

"Lucky me."

He walks along the line, then stops in front of me.

I raise an eyebrow. "Go ahead. Say something funny. I'll do more than fucking spit on you."

Surprisingly, he doesn't say anything. He just smiles. Again, he's acting like he knows something I don't. I hate when people do that. Especially if it turns out they're right... and I'm getting a bad feeling about all this.

He carries on, stopping in front of Rayne.

"So, you're in charge of your little team in the field, are you?" he asks.

He doesn't answer.

"Yes. You're the protégé." Crow glances at me. "Well, Adam... everything you've been doing for the last six months meant nothing. This attack was futile. But I guess it was inevitable. Sooner or later, you were going to make a mistake. When I deliver the heads of eight of the ten most wanted to Quincy Hall, he'll mount them on spikes outside the White House, and your rebellion will be dead."

He paces away, then turns to face us all. "Now where are the other two? Roach and his sister. Anyone?"

Collins shakes his head. "Honestly, fella, we have no idea. And that's not me saying I wouldn't tell ya even if I knew... none of that. Six months ago, we all went one way, and he went the other. We don't know where he is. But I'm sure he'll say hello soon. He's friendly like that."

Crow scoffs. "Well, we both know *that's* not true. I made that stubborn piece of shit, and I will damn well unmake him. But for now, I guess the eight of you will have to do."

The men flanking him all raise their guns and aim at us.

"Leave the GlobaTech bitch alive," says Crow, looking at his men. Then he turns his attention to us. "Any last words?"

I raise my hand. "Actually, yeah, if you don't mind?"

"How did I know *you* would be the one with something to say?"

"What are you doing?" hisses Ruby beside me.

I turn at her and smile. "Winning."

I look at Link and Jericho in turn, making sure they look back at me. We exchange a short, silent conversation, which I hope to God they understand.

Then I take a step forward, separating myself from the others, and look at Crow. "I just wondered why you thought what we did here was futile?"

Crow frowns and looks around, confused. "You can see the hundred and fifty Tristar soldiers surrounding you, right?"

I shrug. "Ah, they don't mean shit. Bottom line, Brandon, when we blow up your little convoy over there, Tristar is blind. Then GlobaTech's gonna sweep in and take back the country, and all this ends."

He laughs. It's exaggerated to make a point that he thinks what I just said is silly. He threw his head back and everything.

Such a dick...

"And how, exactly, do you plan on doing that, hmm?" he asks.

"Real simple. See, we—"

Crow holds his hands up. "Wait, wait, wait. I almost forgot! Before you say anything, Adrian, I have a little surprise for you."

I frown.

He's grinning. "I think you're really going to like this. Are you ready?"

I throw my arms into air and shrug. "Anything to delay you shooting me, I guess."

He looks behind him, over to the first truck in the convoy. I follow his gaze. The group of guards over there is looking at something I can't see. Then they start stepping back, as if making way for something.

Or someone.

I see a pair of legs between the gap in the fuel pumps. I see heels.

A woman.

I see Crow still grinning out the corner of my eye.

The woman walks into view. Behind me, I hear Ruby gasp.

My eyes go wide. Now I know why he looks so happy. I don't believe it...

I shake my head with disbelief. "Miley?"

She strides confidently toward us and stops beside Crow. She looks at me with her dead eyes. I see the same hatred in them I saw back in Tokyo.

"Hello, Adrian," she says.

"I don't understand. I thought you were dead. I mean, I literally blew you up."

She takes a step toward me. "No. You blew up my boat. I swam to safety. Nearly froze to death in the water. Worth it, though."

I rub my eyes. "I don't... why are you here?"

She produces a gun from behind her and holds it menacingly at her side. "I've been living in your old penthouse in Tokyo. I built my own empire from what remained of Kazawa's. I'm now the head of one of the most powerful Yakuza families in all of Japan."

"Well, good for you. That still doesn't explain—"

"How do you think I found you in the first place?" she asks.

I shrug. "A result of you being angry for five years, wasn't it?"

"No. I was told exactly where you were by my employer."

My eyes go wide again. "Orion..."

"Yes. Mr. Hall often uses me for work he would rather didn't make it onto his news cycles."

"Sonofabitch..."

Crow steps to her side and sneers at me. "It made sense to bring her in again when the time was right. To finally get rid of one of the biggest thorns in Orion's side."

Miley shrugs. "Well, he's not wrong."

She points her gun at me. Her finger moves inside the trigger guard. The barrel is aiming right between my eyes.

I can't believe this is it. After everything we've been through. Everything *I've* been through. This is how I go out. Unbelievable.

I see the corner of her mouth twitch. It's a miniscule movement that doesn't quite make it into a smile.

I close my eyes, embracing the inevitability of it all.

BANG!

I shudder. A chorus of gasps and exclamations sound out behind me.

...

...

...

Why am I still alive?

I open my eyes in time to see Crow's lifeless body fall to the ground. Miley's facing him. Smoke is twirling from the barrel of her gun. Tristar guards are looking at each other, unsure of what to do, as if they weren't expecting her to kill Crow.

Join the club!

Miley looks over at me, smiling.

I frown. "What in the Kentucky fried *fuck* is going on?"

She walks toward me, unconcerned by the restlessness around her. "You only get away with letting Mr. Hall down for so long. He hired me to kill him."

"And now you're going to kill me?"

She walks a slow circle around me, ignoring everyone else around us. "Well, I wasn't told to. But I wasn't explicitly told *not* to, either."

She slams the gun into the side of my head, sending me down to one knee. She then takes a step back and delivers a vicious kick to my chest, knocking me backward.

She stands over me, gesturing wildly with her gun. "You took everything from me! *Everything!* I'm going to kill you, Adrian. I'm going to fucking kill you. But first..."

She strides over to Ruby and grabs her by the hair, dragging her over to Crow's body. I push myself slowly up to my feet.

She holds Ruby close to her, pressing her gun into Ruby's side. "First, I'm going to make you watch as I peel the skin off your girlfriend's bones! I'm going to bathe in her blood, Adrian. I'm going to take away everything you hold dear in this world. *Then* I'm going to kill you. And oh, it'll be slow. Do you understand me? You're going to *suffer!*"

I believe her.

She hasn't changed a bit.

I look into Ruby's eyes. She believes her too.

This wasn't exactly how I wanted this to play out, but I have to make a move now, or Ruby's dead.

"There's only one problem with all that, Miley," I say.

Her eyes narrow. "And what's that?"

I gesture to everything around us. "You don't have enough backup to get away with it."

She frowns and shakes her head. "Are you... are you serious? You're outnumbered almost twenty-to-one. You're unarmed. You're trapped. You're finished."

I hope Jericho and Link are ready.

I shrug. "You know what else we are?"

"Enlighten me."

I smile. "Not alone."

On cue, a concerto of explosions fills the air. The cold, bright sky darkens with thick smoke as bombs all over the base go off, one after the other, like a violent drum solo. The ground beneath our feet shakes.

Tristar guards scatter in all directions, taking aim and preparing for an assault by GlobaTech troops.

Seconds later, more bombs go off in the distance, all the way back to the airfield Ruby and I passed through.

Miley screams. "Get them! Kill them all!"

Ruby dives free from her grip. Miley spins around in a crazed circle, searching for a target.

Everyone rushes into action, wrestling with the nearest guards to get themselves a weapon.

I make a beeline for Miley, striding with purpose and bad intentions through the chaos. She sees me too late and turns in time for her face to meet my fist.

"You *don't* touch Ruby!" I yell as the punch connects. "Ever!"

The impact takes her off her feet, sending her flying

backward. The gun falls from her grip. I ignore it and stalk toward her again. I've dealt with her before. I know I can't give this bitch an ounce of room, or she'll have me.

Miley looks up at me. Her cheek is split open from the punch, and blood is flowing freely down her face.

I fall forward, landing heavily on top of her with all my weight, and grip her by the throat. I steady myself on one knee as she grabs my wrist with both hands. But she's too late. I've got her. I squeeze hard. Her cheeks instantly fill with color, and her eyes begin to roll back in her head. Her legs kick and flail with panic.

I keep squeezing.

Then I punch her. I hammer my fist down into her face, busting her nose. And again. This time, I dislocate her jaw. And again. Her right eye swells shut almost instantly.

And again.

And again.

And again.

My teeth are gritted together so hard, it feels like my ears are bleeding. I rain down blow after blow, determined to beat the life out of her for everything she's done to me.

I stop only because my hand feels broken.

As I stand, Jessie and Link appear next to me.

"Oh my God..." gasps Jessie, looking down at what's left of Miley Tevani.

Link puts his hand on my shoulder. "Adrian, we gotta go. We took out a bunch of Tristar guys in the blasts and some more in the confusion afterwards, but our window for getting out of here is getting smaller."

The others regroup on us, squeezing off bursts of gunfire from stolen weapons.

"Are ya good?" asks Collins.

He glances at me, then at Miley.

"Jesus, fuck!" he exclaims. "Forget I asked."

"We gotta go, Adrian," urges Jericho. "Like, right now."

Ruby walks toward me, holding Miley's gun. She stares at me. I know what I must look like. I look like a demon, and that's unnerving to a lot of people.

But not to her.

She places her hand on the back of my head and leans forward, resting her forehead against mine. For just a second, the noise of the world fades away. Nothing exists except the two of us, in a surreal moment only Ruby and I could ever understand.

The sound of coughing pulls us back to the chaos. We look down to see Miley's left eye wide open; the ghostly white conjunctiva shines through the crimson mask that has consumed what remains of her face. She's a mess. The horrifying sound of her rasping bores into my brain. She's a nightmarish vision of suffering, and I did that to her.

The gaze of her eye rests on me. Her lips move, but no sound comes out. Only blood.

BANG!

BANG!

BANG!

Ruby just put three rounds in her. Two in the chest, one in the head.

The last one obliterated her skull.

She's dead.

"Let's go," she says.

We both turn and head after the others, but I remember something that stops me in my tracks.

"Hang on," I say to her.

She frowns. "For what? Adrian, we need to get the fuck out of here right now."

I hold my hands up. "Just... one minute."

335

I turn and run back through the chaos and gunfire, toward where Ruby and I were captured. I slide to a stop behind the building and scoop up both my Raptors. I quickly reload and start shooting anything that moves as I run back to her.

She's staring at me with disbelief. I don't care. Josh got me these guns. I'll be damned if I'm leaving them behind.

I toss one to her as I reach her side, and we both continue shooting as we set off after the others, who are sprinting for the west gate.

I see them ahead.

I glance back to see how much distance we've put between us and the convoy.

Hopefully enough.

"Adam! Now!" I shout.

A moment later, there's a thunderous explosion, followed by two more in quick succession, like rolling waves.

I feel the heat on my back, despite being far enough away to not be affected by the blast.

That was the convoy going up, taking all the fuel with it.

The others have stopped beside three Tristar vehicles parked at the side of the road. Ruby and I catch up to them, gasping for breath.

"Everyone good?" I ask. "No one hurt?"

There's a unanimous murmuring to signal they're all fine.

"What the hell happened back there?" asks Julie. "Who *was* that?"

"That..." I say, still trying to catch my breath. "...was the crazy bitch who tortured me on the internet in Tokyo. Apparently, she was working for Orion this whole time."

Ruby shrugs. "I mean, not so much anymore..."

"Yeah, I saw," says Julie. "Look, we gotta get out of here.

Once those bastards realize we don't have any reinforcements, they will be on our tail in seconds. We know what we need to do. We split up and take different routes to Wyoming. We'll meet back up in two days, okay?"

Everyone nods their agreement.

"I'm going to arrange for a GlobaTech squad to link up with us en route, so we have some additional support when we arrive. It's gonna be a long drive, especially if we have to avoid going through major cities. Take care, everyone."

Handshakes and fist-bumps are exchanged all around. Then we all climb into our vehicles. Jericho, Julie, and Collins set off first, followed a few moments later by Jessie, Link, and Rayne.

Ruby and I are last to leave. She's driving. I lean out the window and fire aimlessly until I run out of bullets, deterring the few Tristar guards who gave chase from continuing their pursuit.

I duck back inside and relax back into my seat. Ruby's driving hard, trying to put as much distance between us and Fort Hood as we can.

I let her drive. Now isn't the time for talking. I close my eyes. Crow's dead. The convoy's gone. As are several Tristar patrols, thanks to our explosives. And as an unexpected bonus, Miley is dead too. For real, this time.

Today was a good day. Our plan worked, we survived, and we dealt a huge blow to the enemy. And if our hunch is correct, in a couple of days, we'll have freed Schultz. Then, maybe, we can start taking our goddamn country back.

COOKING WITH REBECCA
RECIPE: THE PERFECT TURKEY

Published: November 21, 2020 by Rebecca R. | 393k comments

Listed: *Uncategorized.* **Tags:** *None.*

Step 1 — Preparing the Turkey

In my last post, I told you about GlobaTech's plan to turn the tide in this war and what they hope will be the first of many knockout blows to Orion and Tristar.

Today, I'm happy to say I can share more information with you. But first, you need some background.

The man in charge of all the Tristar forces that control this country is Brandon Crow. He was the CEO of Tristar Security before all of this. He reported directly to Quincy Hall and coordinated every single Tristar patrol in the country. He did so by traveling in an armored convoy, consisting of three gigantic Juggernauts that function as a mobile command center. They moved constantly on top secret routes, to reduce the chances of anyone being able to find them and attack them.

For months, it has been the mission of a dedicated group of rebels known as Blackstar to do just that. And four days ago, just outside of Omaha, Nebraska, they did.

While Brandon Crow was able to escape, valuable data was stolen from the convoy during the attack. This information provided Julie Fisher and her elite GlobaTech operatives with all they needed to mount a significant assault against a tactical Tristar location.

Before they could do that, however, they needed a distraction that would create a window of opportunity large enough to allow them to execute this plan. That is why there was increased GlobaTech presence in cities and towns over the last 48 hours.

With Tristar distracted, eight brave men and women launched an attack on Fort Hood, New Texas. They risked their lives to not only destroy the convoy, but to also kill Brandon Crow and a significant number of Tristar mercenaries in the process.

Make no mistake. It's a tragedy when any life is lost, but we are at war. Tristar guards have needlessly killed hundreds of thousands of Americans since T-Day. We have no choice but to fight fire with fire.

GlobaTech has dealt a crippling blow to the enemy. Tristar's now effectively blind, with no real command structure in place. This means we all have a better chance of helping each other and the refugees still suffering on the outskirts of our towns and cities.

But this doesn't mean it's any safer out there.

Tristar is like a wounded animal, which means they are more likely to lash out than before. Julie Fisher is concerned that Tristar patrols may start going to greater lengths to prove their point to civilians. There may be retribution, especially in the refugee camps. Crow might be gone, but

Hall is still in charge of everything. Tristar may actually become more dangerous than ever now, especially if there is no structure or coordination to their actions.

GlobaTech has a plan. Yesterday was the first step. They are now working on the next. They believe the end is in sight. If yesterday was the warning shot across the bow, then what comes next will sink the whole ship.

Step 2 — Roasting the Turkey

My brother and I have been travelling across the country for six months, with the singular goal of reaching our nation's capital. Thanks to the overwhelming support and kindness of you all, as I post this blog, we are due to hit Washington, D.C. tomorrow.

We made it!

You know my brother about as well as anyone by now. Even if we haven't crossed paths with you, I've worked hard to make sure you have heard his stories.

I know what he wants to do in Washington. He wants to confront the man who did this to all of us. He wants to wrap his hands around Quincy Hall's throat and beat an apology out of him. Then he wants to kill him and put an end to this.

It's hard to argue with his logic.

But realistically, we can't exactly knock on the front door of the White House and start swinging... as much as Roach would like to!

I've always urged my readers to stay safe and not put themselves in harm's way—not even to help GlobaTech. I know anyone fighting for the rebellion would rather struggle themselves than endanger one of you by accepting your help. But there's something in the air now. It genuinely feels like things are changing. Maybe the events of the last

24 hours—and those to come—will trigger a second wave of oppression, locking in our fates for generations to come.

But maybe they won't.

Maybe this is when we show the enemy that tyranny has no place in the modern world. And if that's the case, then we need your help.

There is a refugee settlement inside Franklin Park. That's where we're heading. My brother won't say anything, but I will. When we arrive, I will ask every able-bodied man and woman to stand with us. I will ask that word is sent across the city for anyone else who wants to fight to join us. If we attack a single patrol, they will fight back. If a single camp stands up, they will be pushed back down. But if an entire city stands up, they cannot be ignored. Hall knows the power of the media better than anyone. I don't believe he will simply gun us all down, and he definitely cannot ignore such a large, united voice.

There is no third option for him that I can see.

If he does either of those things, this country will riot. Right now, half a million controls 300 million, and they do so through fear. But if the majority suddenly push back... what is that minority going to do? Hall won't risk a nation-wide rebellion. He has enough problems with the 20 thousand-strong movement that exists already. He will have to hear our voices. He will have to listen to us.

Our forefathers created the second amendment so that the people of this country could rise up against an oppressive government. That sentiment was great 200 years ago. In modern times, the government has one of the largest and best trained militaries in the world and a drone program and satellites. But Quincy Hall doesn't have those things. He decommissioned the military. He has his own men on the ground. That's it. Maybe in this new world, we don't need weapons to fight back...

Maybe we just need a voice.

Tomorrow, my brother will stand before the White House, and he will speak up. And knowing him like I do, he will either make Orion listen, or he will give his life trying to.

If ever there was a time to stand up, this is it.

Roach has fought for all of us, risking his life more times than I could ever write down. I am asking you, please, just this once, to fight for him.

Fight for all of us.

33

ROACH

November 22, 2020

Franklin Park stood half a mile northeast of the White House. It had long been a haven for the city's homeless population, even before the country was lost to Orion. Now close to a hundred and fifty refugees camped there. With tents and stalls lining the square path that encompassed the central fountain, it looked more like a fairground.

All around it, the nation's capital bustled about its normal life. Traffic flowed, people hurried to and from their jobs... life carried on.

Roach and Becky had arrived as the sun was beginning to peek up over the horizon. The camp had ushered them inside, welcoming them like celebrities. Few pleasantries had been exchanged. Both were tired, and they were soon shown to a tent in the middle of the camp, where they could rest. They were asleep within minutes.

It was almost noon when Roach awoke. He felt stiff but

rested. He had grown accustomed to sleeping on thin mattresses and feeling the hard ground beneath him every night, but that didn't make it any more comfortable.

He emerged from the tent, squinting until his eyes adjusted to the daylight. The first thing he saw was Becky walking toward him. Her hair looked frazzled, and the dark circles beneath her eyes suggested her few hours of sleep had been similar to his own.

"Hey," she said, stopping beside him. "How are you feeling?"

He shrugged. "Tired. You?"

"Yeah. Same."

Roach looked around. Franklin Park was certainly one of the livelier camps they had stayed in. A little overcrowded, perhaps, but a solid community. People were bustling around them, happily lost in their own world of activity.

"This place feels different," he said after a moment.

Becky frowned. "In what way?"

"I don't know. Just different. Everyone seems busy. In most camps, people just tend to exist. But here, they all look like they have a purpose."

Becky dismissed the comment with a casual wave of her hand. "You've never been comfortable with people treating you like a hero or a celebrity. It's the same everywhere we go. The two of us showing up often lights a fire under people's asses, y'know. Besides, I can imagine the people here have more to worry about than other camps, given where they are."

Roach thought for a moment, then shook his head. "No, that isn't it. I noticed it when we arrived earlier too. There was... I don't know... excitement in the air. Like they were expecting us."

Becky held his gaze for as long as she could but looked away after a few seconds. She pursed her lips together and winced.

Roach sighed. "What did you do?"

"In my last blog post, I told people this is where we were heading."

Roach took a step back. "You did what? Why?"

"Well, because I—"

"No, Becky. No. You had no right to put these people in that position. It's reckless, and it puts everyone here in danger. We both heard what that old timer said in Windsor. Wherever I go, shit follows. Giving the enemy a head's up as to where we're going to be is crazy!"

Becky scowled and pointed a finger at him. "Hey! Frank was one man. And by all accounts, he was pissed at everything anyway. He doesn't speak for all refugees in this country, and we've met plenty who think you're a goddamn hero. Rightly so, I might add. Me telling people we were coming here makes no difference. First of all, Tristar and Orion have had six months to find my blog, and they haven't. No reason to think they're going to now."

"That isn't the point. You—"

"I haven't finished. Second, look where we are, Will. We made it. We made it all the way to D.C., and we did so relatively unscathed. There's nowhere left to go. This is our endgame, right? The fact we're here is part of our story. Literally millions of people have followed our journey from the beginning. You think I'm not going to tell them when we reach the final chapter?"

"That may be," he said stubbornly. "But there's still a difference between arriving here quietly and calling ahead of time so they can prepare the welcome wagon. You're right; we made it to Washington. But this city is the epicenter of

Orion's control, and it's the most dangerous place we can be right now. What if someone had seen us? Hmm? What if we were spotted coming here, and that led someone in Tristar to figure out this entire camp was helping us? The consequence for these people would be deadly, and that would be on us."

Becky shook her head. "You're missing the point, Will. I didn't tell everyone to arrange fanfare. I wanted to give them hope. To say, *'Look what two people managed to do... imagine what two hundred can do.'* These people stood up and helped because they want to. They believe in the rebellion. In you. One month ago, I'd have agreed with you all the way. But this is it. There's nowhere left to go, Will."

Roach fell silent. They stared at each other, walking the line between stubborn siblings and a genuine argument. After a moment, Becky turned away.

"I just need a few minutes on my own," she announced.

She paced away to explore the camp, wandering from group to group, introducing herself, asking how people were... exactly like she had done a hundred times before. But for the first time in a long time, she found it difficult to talk to people. No one had shown much interest in listening to her stories. It had taken her by surprise a little and had left her feeling like a spare part. But now, as she sat with a couple of other women by the foot of the John Barry statue, watching a large huddle of refugees follow Roach's every footstep, she understood why.

As she had said to Roach during their heated exchange, her last blog post was the final chapter in the story she had been drip-feeding to millions of Americans over the last six months. Now that she had told people where they would be and what Roach intended to do, there were simply no more stories left to tell.

"You should be over there with him," said one of the women beside her with a friendly tone. She was a young woman, maybe a few years her junior. She nursed a small child close to her body. "Not letting him hog the limelight."

Becky shook her head, smiling politely. "No, I've played my part. This has always been his journey. His crusade. I wanted to make sure people knew what he was doing, y'know? I thought it might give them hope to know some-one's fighting for them."

The woman to the other side of her nodded. She was black, much older than her, with a kind face and weathered skin. "What the two of you have done... what you've risked... it's nothing short of a miracle. And it *did* give people hope. Folks around here, all they talk about are those blog posts of yours. Girl, the things you've seen and done... we ever get through this, you should publish that shit!"

Becky laughed. "I think I'm a bit young to publish my memoirs."

The woman with the baby chuckled. "Becky, your stories are more like dystopian fiction."

"Yeah, I guess they probably are. George Orwell, eat your heart out, huh?" She paused. "I'm sorry. I never asked your name."

The woman smiled. "Amanda."

Becky turned to the other woman.

"Florence," she said, unprompted. "People call me Flo."

"It's great to meet you both," said Becky, smiling. She looked back at Amanda. "If you don't mind my asking, how old is your baby?"

Amanda bounced her child in her arms lovingly and smiled. "She's five months old."

"So, she was born after T-Day? How did you..."

She nodded. "She was born at George Washington

University Hospital, just down the street. I won't ever defend Tristar or anything that awful man in the White House has done, but they were good to me the day my daughter was born. My water broke right over there by the fountain. People ran out to get the attention of a passing patrol. It's not like we're short of them around here. The men came into the camp, helped me into their vehicle, and drove me straight to the doors of GW. The doctors and nurses there were amazing. They knew I was a refugee. They offered to hide me inside the hospital, to keep me there without charge."

Becky frowned. "Why didn't you stay?"

"I didn't want to put them in any danger. All healthcare facilities are guarded, and they're not allowed to give sanctuary to refugees—only to treat them. I figured there was a chance Tristar would come looking for me when I didn't reappear in the camp. Besides, the people here have become like family to me. I knew I would be looked after. Me... and little Isabella here."

Becky smiled, feeling a swell of emotion that made her eyes mist over.

"That's a beautiful name," she said. "I'm sorry she was born into such an ugly world."

Amanda shook her head. "Don't be. I'm not. This world was never perfect. If it wasn't this, there would be something else that I would need to protect her from. My parents were born right here in D.C. in the fifties. They grew up during the Civil Rights Movement. My grandparents grew up during World War Two. Now I'm going to raise my daughter through all this. No matter your generation... there's always something. You just gotta do the best you can and look out for one another. That's what I'm going to make sure Isabella grows up understanding."

Becky stared at her with admiration, watching as she fussed over her little girl, who was just beginning to stir from her nap. It was that strength, that spirit, that she hoped everyone shared.

Just then, a man came running over to them, pushing through a gathering crowd.

"You'd better come quick," he said to Becky through heavy breaths.

She scrambled to her feet. "What is it?"

"We... we just captured a Tristar guard! He walked into the camp and surrendered to us. We grabbed him and took him to your brother."

Becky looked across the camp and saw a large crowd had gathered by the fountain. Without a word, she sprinted toward it, assuming Roach was at its center. She might not be able to do much, but if anyone could stop her brother from tearing that guard's head off, it was her.

She pushed her way through. Roach was standing there, arms folded, staring down at the Tristar guard, who had been forced to his knees before him.

She eyed the guard up and down. He was unarmed. His pale expression, wide eyes, and visible sweat suggested that he was understandably terrified. Then she looked at her brother, who seemed to be displaying an uncharacteristic amount of restraint.

Becky frowned. "What happened?"

Roach glanced up at her, then nodded toward the guard. "This guy just walked into camp of his own accord, unarmed, and asked to see me."

"Why?"

He shrugged. "I was waiting for you before I asked him."

They looked at each other. The corner of his mouth

flicked up into a gentle smile. She took a deep breath and smiled back.

As with most siblings, that was all it took to put a disagreement behind them.

Roach turned his attention back to the guard. "I have questions, and you're going to answer them. If you refuse, or if I think you're lying, I'm going to drown you in this fountain and dump your wet body on the steps of your boss's new home. Do you understand?"

The guard nodded urgently.

"Good. Why are you here?"

The guard swallowed hard, looking around at the dozens of pairs of hate-filled eyes focused on him. "I... I want to help."

Roach raised an eyebrow. "Not the best start."

He reached down and grabbed him by his throat.

"No, wait, wait, wait!" pleaded the guard.

Becky stepped forward and placed a hand on brother's arm. He took a breath and relinquished his grip.

"Go on," he said reluctantly.

The guard wiped sweat from his eyes. "I came here alone. I didn't bring a weapon. Why would I do that if I were lying to you? I want to help you. I... I need to."

He stared at the ground in front of him.

"How can you help us?" asked Becky. "And why now?"

"Look, I didn't sign up for this, okay? Everything that's happening. None of us knew this was coming. Most of us, we... we do what we're told because we're scared not to. But I ain't the only one who thinks this ain't right."

"And you just don't have a choice, right?" scoffed Roach. "Just like the rest of us."

The guard looked at him. "You think Orion treats us any differently than they treat you people when you step out of line? I've been... I'm new to this, okay? I've been stuck behind a desk this whole time. Yesterday, we all got deployed to the streets, after GlobaTech's attack on Mr. Crow. I've been out here twelve hours, and I... I just can't... this is horrible!"

A tear escaped down his face.

Roach regarded him impassively. "Why come here? Why ask to see me?"

"More importantly," said Becky, "how did you know we would be here?"

The guard smiled humorlessly, as if offended she had to ask. "You think you're the only ones who know your stories? We hear everything you refugees say. We know who Roach is. We know everything he's done, and we see the hope he gives these people. Sure, to many of us, he's nothing more than the ultimate notch on the ammo belt. But there are some, including me, who admire him. If one man will go to such lengths to fight back against a force the size of Tristar, what does that say about us, huh? How bad must we be to invoke that kind of reaction?"

He looked up at Roach and held his hands out to the side, as if emphasizing how vulnerable he was.

"Please, I don't wanna go back there. They will kill me after this."

"I might kill you anyway," replied Roach flippantly.

The guard nodded. "Yeah, maybe you will. Honestly, I wouldn't blame you if you did. But I'm literally on my knees here. I'm begging you... show me mercy. Let me join you. Let me help you."

"How, exactly, can you help me?"

"Tristar knows you're here," he said flatly.

"How?" asked Becky.

The guard looked at her. "Because of you."

She held a hand to her mouth and gasped. "My blog..."

Roach and Becky looked at each other as murmurs of concern rippled throughout the camp. Their eyes grew wide, silently acknowledging that the guard's statement simultaneously validated both sides of their arguments earlier.

He nodded. "Orion's analysts found it. They know you're coming here, and Tristar is preparing to attack. They're cordoning off the city one block at a time as we speak. That's why I came when I did. To warn you."

"Next time, maybe open with that," said Roach.

"I needed you to know I wasn't lying first. Otherwise, what would be the point?" He slowly got to his feet. The crowd backed away, giving him and Roach more space. "You have to run. All of you. Roach, if you go now, you can get out of the city safely. I can guide you past our patrols. Live to fight another day. But if you stay here, I can promise you, you're going to die... and maybe these people will too."

The tension mounted as uneasiness swept through the camp. Refugees all around exchanged looks of worry and fear.

Becky stepped close to her brother, once again placing a calming hand on his arm.

"Will, maybe we *should* leave," she said. "This guy has a point. If they know we're coming, they'll send an army here to kill us. If we die now, after everything we've done, after all the stories people have heard... it will crush the rebellion."

Roach stared blankly, silently at the ground beside them. He looked at the base of the fountain, fixated on a spot where water had seeped through and stained the brickwork. He found himself drawing comparisons to it. Orion had built this regime that encompassed the country, shielding it from the rest of the world. But there were cracks in it, and hope was beginning to seep through. From him. From his sister. From GlobaTech. If it kept going, those cracks were going to get wider, and eventually, the foundations would crumble, and the water would flow freely once again.

"Roach?" urged Becky.

He shook his head.

"No," he replied quietly.

"What?"

He looked at her. "No. I'm not running."

He turned and looked out at the gathered mass of refugees, who were all staring back at him with a mixture of hope and fear on their faces. They looked to him for answers.

They looked to him to lead.

Roach stepped up onto the edge of the fountain and pointed to the Tristar guard.

"This man put himself at risk to come here and warn us that we're in danger," he said, raising his voice to be heard over the noise of the world around them. "That took courage. He says we should run, that our enemy is coming here, and we should live to fight another day. That decision is up to you. You're a family, and this park has become your home. I'm the one who brought the danger to your door. But I'm not running. I've come too far to turn back now.

"There's a saying: *'If you don't stand for something, you'll fall for anything.'* I came to this city to take a stand. For the longest time, I wanted nothing but peace. I played my part in what Tristar has become, and I fought them to walk away. I wanted to separate myself from the world and atone for my own sins, but that time is over. Those days are gone. I've traveled this country looking for a fight, and I'll be damned if I'm backing down now. Tristar might know I'm here, but I can promise you this—they don't know who I am. Quincy

Hall is sitting across the street right now, thinking he knows everything about me. Well, their biggest mistake is thinking I'm still the person *they* created... that I'm still standing where *they* left me. I came here to show them exactly who the fuck I am, and nothing is going to stop me."

Becky watched her brother in awe. She felt a swell of pride as she saw him finally embrace the person she and so many others had been telling him he's become.

One of the refugees moved to her side, stopping in front of Roach. He was a tall man, thick-set and bearded, wearing a plaid shirt with the sleeves half rolled up, despite the temperatures.

"Then I'm going with you," he announced.

"Me too," said a woman from behind.

Becky looked over her shoulder to see Flo standing there, tall and proud.

Roach shook his head. "No. It's too dangerous. I can't ask you to—"

"You're not," said the man, cutting him off. "I'm volunteering."

The noise among the crowd grew as more and more people stepped forward, raising their hands and shouting their support.

Roach looked at them all, rushing to stand by his side. He took a deep breath, which quivered in his chest.

He stared down at the first man who spoke. "Please. I can't put you all in danger."

The crowd fell silent. The man looked around, then back up at Roach.

"We listened to you, so now you listen to me," he began firmly. "We've all heard the stories. We've all read your sister's blog. We all know what's happening out there. We know about GlobaTech's rebellion and everything they're doing to put an end to this. But all that... it's happening somewhere else. It's like... it's like when someone tells you how far away the sun is. The numbers are so great, they don't seem real. That's the rebellion. To many of us, the scale of this fight is too big to really mean anything to us.

"But you... your fight... *that's* something we can understand. That's what gives us hope. That's what inspires us to help GlobaTech and fight back against Tristar. You're one man, Roach. One man who set off on a journey across the country to pick a fight with the schoolyard bully. You did that on behalf of everyone who couldn't. And now you're here, man. You're face to face with the enemy. Hell, I don't know what you intend to do. But I know you're fighting for all of us. What gives any of us the right to do anything less than the same?"

Becky wiped away a tear from her eye.

Roach stepped down and moved in front of the man. "What's your name?"

"Cooper. John Cooper."

Roach extended his hand. "You're a good man, John Cooper."

Cooper shook it and nodded.

"Listen to me, John. I have an idea, and I'll need your help."

"Name it."

"I want you to round up every capable man and woman, okay? Then I want you to gather every weapon you have. Those who want to stand with me, I want half of them to stay back and protect those who are not able to fight. The rest, including you, will be with me." He looked over at the Tristar guard. "How long do you think we have until they come for us?"

The guard shrugged. "I'm sorry. I honestly don't know. I

left the moment we got the order to prepare for the attack. That was about an hour ago. So, you maybe have another hour. Maybe less."

Roach nodded and turned back to Cooper. "You have thirty minutes. Not a second more. Be ready to send everyone who isn't with us out the north entrance to the park. Send them away to the nearest secure building. Offices, libraries, restaurants... anywhere public, anywhere normal. Hide there until this is over. Understood?"

Cooper nodded. "You got it."

There was an instant flurry of movement and urgency as people began rushing around with renewed purpose.

Becky moved to Roach's side as he began to walk away, but the guard tapped his shoulder.

"Listen, Roach, I... I know you probably don't trust me, but I really do want to help. I want to fight with you. Please."

Roach looked at him. "Are you sure? I appreciate what you did for us, but if this doesn't work, and we're captured, they will kill you. You know that, right?"

He held his gaze for a moment, then nodded. "I do. And I don't care. Enough is enough."

Roach regarded him for a long moment. "What's your name?"

The guard smiled weakly. "Kevin."

"Okay, Kevin. Go and help Cooper."

Roach looked around to see Becky smiling at him.

He raised an eyebrow. "What?"

"I'm so proud of you, Will."

He shifted uncomfortably. "Thanks."

"Billy was right about you. This is who you were always supposed to be. A leader."

"Well, I don't know about that. I might be preparing these people to die."

"They don't care. Don't you get it? They know that. But they want to stand with you anyway. You inspire them. That's what great leaders do."

He sighed, then shook his head. He smiled as he put his arm around her. "You and your goddamn stories."

34

JULIE FISHER

November 22, 2020

The small fleet of vehicles sped along the highway that cut a path through the mountains of northern Wyoming. Tall, steep cliff faces lined both sides of the road, looming over it like towering guardians.

The sky was darkening. Low clouds fought to hide what remained of the sun. As natural light faded, the temperature dropped.

In the lead vehicle, Julie drove, silently focused on the long, straight road ahead. Beside her, Jericho was wedged into his seat, struggling for comfort. His mind was equally focused on what lay ahead. Behind them, Collins sprawled across the seat, staring out at the imposing scenery, trying his best not to think of anything at all. They were dressed in GlobaTech uniforms—black and red combat gear beneath insulated jackets lined with Kevlar.

Behind them, two SUVs followed, full of GlobaTech

operatives who had driven up from Denver to join the attack.

At the back, Adrian Hell and his team followed.

Up ahead, the road began to gently dogleg to the left. At the same time, a sharp, unmarked turn appeared on the right.

Julie slammed her brakes on. She turned and slid to a halt across the intersection, facing the road to the right. The sound of tires screeching rippled back along the line as the others did the same. They all stopped in a rough line, completely blocking the road.

Everyone climbed out of their vehicles, drawing their weapons as they regrouped in the middle of their roadblock.

"Is everything okay?" asked Ruby.

"Yeah, everything's fine," replied Julie. "I think this is it. I almost missed the turn-off."

The eight of them, along with the eight GlobaTech operatives, all looked down the road. Julie grabbed a pair of binoculars from the back of their vehicle and placed them to her eyes.

Everyone looked at her expectantly.

"Well," she said with a sigh. "I think it's safe to say we're in the right place."

She passed the binoculars to Adrian, who had moved to her side. He looked through them.

"Fuck me," he muttered.

Leading away to the right was a narrow two-lane road. Concrete blocks on both sides formed a border along it. A couple of hundred feet farther down was a chain-link fence on wheels, blocking the full width of the road, positioned beside a small security post.

Beyond that, the road continued, leading toward an impossibly huge mountain. It stretched across the full width of his sight line. A large tunnel was carved into the base of it. Small groups of armed guards stood on either side of the barrier in front of the tunnel. Off to the sides were several guard stations and outposts, all manned.

Looking upward, walkways ran along the side of the mountain, in front of large observation windows. Thin trails of steam danced into the air from vents built into the top of the mountain, too high up to be visible from the ground.

Adrian handed the binoculars over to Jericho, then looked around at the group.

"That place is a goddamn fortress," he said.

"So, what do we do?" asked Rayne.

Julie stepped away from the group, then turned around to face them.

"There's only one way in or out," she began. "That's along *this* road. There's really only one thing we *can* do."

"Storm the gates," said Jericho.

She nodded. "It's not ideal, I know, but if we do this right, we stand a good chance of making it inside."

Jericho looked at Adrian. "You and your team follow my lead, okay?"

Adrian shrugged. "I'll do whatever you want if it means I'm standing behind *you* when we run at these bastards."

Jericho ignored him. He moved to Julie's side and looked out at the group in the middle of the highway.

"Here's what we're gonna do," he began. "I want four teams of four. First two teams are in the vehicles. Vehicle one, you'll hit the gate. Vehicle two will follow up and take out the guards in the checkpoint. The rest of us will follow on foot. We'll move along the road, using the vehicles for cover, and fight our way to the entrance of the base. Once there, we'll move into two teams of eight and sweep the first floor of the base. We'll then take each floor above us as a whole unit until we find the president. Questions?"

People shook their heads, murmuring their understanding of the plan.

"Good." He looked at the GlobaTech operatives. Eight men. All strong and capable. "Two teams. Take the vehicles. Get ready to move."

He then looked at Collins. "Ray, I want you with Blackstar."

Adrian and Ruby walked over to where Julie and Jericho were standing, at the front of the crowd.

"So, it's the four of us?" observed Ruby.

Julie nodded. "If and when we find Schultz, he stays in the middle of us until he's in a vehicle and we're clear of this place. Understood?"

Adrian and Ruby both nodded.

"Get all the weapons and ammo you can carry," said Jericho. "Something tells me you're going to need them."

He watched them walk away, then turned to face Julie.

"You okay?" he asked.

She let out a heavy sigh. "Yeah."

His eyes narrowed. "You sure?"

She smiled at the fact that he could see right through her. "This is it, Jericho. If Schultz is in there, this is our one shot to get him back. Was it the right call, playing this the same way we played Fort Hood? I would feel much better if we had fifty guys backing us up."

Jericho took a breath, taking a moment to choose his words carefully. He understood it was a fine line between honesty and inspiration.

"I think we all would," he said eventually. "But that's not possible, so we go with what we have. We know what our operatives are capable of. We know what the three of us are capable of. And honestly, if I could pick anyone outside of GlobaTech to have beside me in the trenches, I'd be hard pressed to find anyone better than Adrian and his team—and you know that's not easy for me to say."

Julie looked around, watching the others busying themselves by their vehicles, readying their weapons and preparing for war. Then she grabbed Jericho's arm and pulled him to the side, turning herself so that her back was to the others.

"Look me in the eye and tell me you think we can do this," she said. "If you do, I'll believe you."

He held her gaze without hesitation. His expression hardened. His eyes narrowed slightly. His jaw locked.

"I *know* we can do this," he said. "But let me ask you this, Jules. Do *you* think you can lead us through those gates? Because you ain't following me—I'm following you, as I always have. I'm the soldier. You're the leader. I believe we can do this because I was trained for half my life to never think anything else. But if you want me to follow you into Hell, *you* gotta make *me* believe you believe it too."

"I do. I told you, I just—"

"No, Julie. This isn't you and me now. This is GlobaTech. This is *war*. Do you understand me? I don't follow you because I love you. I follow you because I respect you and because I believe in you. Don't think something just because I said it. You tell me... do *you* think we can do this? Because if you don't, I'll tell everyone here to walk away right now. Anything less than one hundred percent here, and we die."

Julie took a step back from him. She took a breath and pushed her shoulders back. She planted her feet defiantly and stared into his eyes. She felt anger boiling inside her. How *dare* he suggest she wasn't up for this! They wouldn't be there if it wasn't for her. She had stepped into the role as leader of this rebellion when no one else would. She commanded every GlobaTech operative in the country for six months. She was responsible for the lives of every man and woman brave enough to fight back.

She clenched her fists until she felt the color drain from her knuckles. This was the man she loved. How could he think she wasn't up for this? How could he possibly think—

Her eyes softened. The rest of her remained stubbornly furious, but her eyes saw what he was trying to do.

Jericho smiled. He saw the moment the penny dropped for her.

There was a fine line between honesty and inspiration.

"Yeah," he said quietly. "You believe it."

"Bet your ass," she replied, then turned to look at the others.

They were ready. Each of them was wrapped up against the weather. Each of them held their weapons ready. They all looked to her.

Julie nodded toward them. "All right, listen up. You know the plan. You know the mission. Anyone you come across in there who isn't our president is an enemy. You shoot to kill, then you move on. The longer this takes, the more chance there is of us still being here when reinforcements inevitably show up. Make no mistake, people. Today is the most important day of your life. We either go down in history, or we go down bleeding. Personally, I intend to be around to see the look on Quincy Hall's face when President Schultz walks back into his office and slaps the shit out of him. Now let's go!"

Everyone rushed to their positions. The two vehicles full of operatives gunned their engines in unison. The two teams formed behind them.

Adrian and Jericho stood side by side between Julie and Ruby, a couple of steps behind them.

Adrian looked over. "Never thought I'd be standing next to you in a fight."

Jericho looked back. A half-smile crept across his lips. "Funny how things turn out, I guess."

"Yeah. Imagine if you had stood with me in Colombia? None of this would've happened."

Jericho's smile disappeared. His expression became deadpan.

Adrian nodded. "Too soon? Yeah, it was too soon. My bad."

Jericho made a show of chambering a round in his *Negotiator*. "Try not to get in my way. Be a shame if I were to accidentally shoot you."

Adrian smiled. "Ah, you wouldn't do that. You're too good to get me confused with the bad guys, aren't you?"

Julie turned around. "Will you two knock it off?"

Adrian shrugged. "I'm just making sure the big guy has his game face on. That's all."

The first vehicle accelerated away, tires screeching, and left rubber on the road. The second followed a moment later. Everyone else set off running after them, weapons raised.

The first vehicle burst through the gate at speed, tearing it easily off its hinges. It slid to a halt as the two Tristar guards inside the security booth stepped out and took aim.

The second vehicle gunned its engine and mowed the guards down. Their bodies bounced unceremoniously off the hood, flying away into the concrete barriers. It then stopped beside the first one and waited for the rest.

The two groups ran past the booth and the bodies without looking.

"Do you think they got a call off?" shouted Jessie.

Ruby looked over. "I think it's unlikely to matter if they did or not."

The vehicles set off along the road, fast enough to make good progress toward the base but slow enough that the people on foot could keep pace with a comfortable jog.

Up ahead, they saw a flurry of activity. Tristar guards ran back and forth along the entrance. More filed out from within.

"I'm gonna go out on a limb and say they know we're here," said Rayne.

Julie looked across. "Jericho, Ray... explosive rounds on my order."

Adrian watched Jericho chamber a special round into his weapon.

"What the hell are those things?" he asked.

"Dual-barrel, DNA-coded handguns, explained Jericho. "We call them *Negotiators*. Secondary barrel fires special ammunition—explosive rounds, incendiary, even EMP."

Adrian looked at his own Raptor. It was a beautiful weapon. A posthumous gift from Josh. One of a matching pair. Ruby had the other. It was an amazing gun, but it didn't fire grenades...

"Hey, can I get one of those?" he asked.

Jericho smiled. "Maybe when you're older."

"Oh, but all the other kids have one..."

As they approached the entrance, the scope of what they were facing become clearer. Easily fifty men lined up behind portable barricades, all heavily armed. The groups behind the vehicles ducked low as the enemy opened fire, peppering the road and the vehicles with bullets.

"Jericho, left; Ray, right!" shouted Julie. "On three..."

...

...

...

"Three!"

In unison, Julie, Ray, and Jericho popped up from behind their own cover and fired. Each special round found its mark. The explosions were significant but contained. The sound thundered and echoed around the mountains. Bodies flew as fires raged in front of the base's entrance.

Half the enemy's force disappeared in an instant.

"Go!" yelled Julie.

The vehicles shot ahead, then slid to a halt side-on as the road opened out in front of the giant entrance to the mountain. The GlobaTech operatives piled out and provided covering fire while the others caught up.

"You ain't getting paid by the hour," shouted Jericho over the stuttering cacophony of gunfire. "Clock's ticking."

To his right side, Link and Rayne pushed forward, guns raised and locked in their grip, synced to their eyeline. They zipped back and forth in short, controlled movements, firing in bursts and dropping guards with each engagement. Jessie and Collins backed them up, finishing off the guards they didn't kill before they could retaliate.

Julie and Ruby reached the first vehicle and dropped to a crouch behind it. Adrian and Jericho were a few steps behind. They moved around it and swept across the left side of the resistance. Bullet after bullet... headshot after headshot... the guards fell until no one remained.

They all looked across the entrance in time to see Rayne dispatch the last guard on the other side.

They quickly regrouped in the middle and looked ahead, dwarfed by the large tunnel entrance. The mouth loomed over them like a giant creature about to feed. Inside quickly became enveloped in darkness.

Julie examined it and spotted the security cameras almost instantly.

"We're on TV," she said. "Someone's watching and knows we've made it inside. You know your teams. You know your mission. Stay focused. Eyes open. Let's move."

As they moved ahead, they were blinded by flashes of light from deep inside the mountain base. Countless bursts of gunfire erupted in front of them, providing glimpses of the men waiting for them within.

"Take cover!" yelled Jericho.

But they saw them too late.

The first three GlobaTech operatives flailed backward and fell lifelessly to the ground; their weapons flew away as they landed. The rest dove to the sides, away from the entrance, seeking cover behind the abandoned Tristar barricades.

Link felt a bullet punch into his shoulder. The impact spun him around, and he grunted as he fell hard at Rayne's feet.

"Link!" shouted Jessie, rushing to his side.

She crouched next to him, firing blindly at the entrance to provide cover, so he could scramble away to safety.

Adrian heard her and looked over. His eyes went wide as he saw Link.

"How bad is it?" he called out.

"It's a scratch. I'm fine!" shouted Link. "Just shoot these bastards!"

Everyone concentrated their fire on the entrance, hitting it from both sides. Another group of Tristar guards tried to rush out and ambush them. The crossfire took the first wave out, cutting them down as they emerged from the tunnel.

Another two GlobaTech operatives were lost before the flow of enemies from within ceased. Everyone recovered, reloaded their weapons, and moved to the sides of the entrance.

Julie looked across at Link, who was favoring his left shoulder.

"You gonna be okay?" she asked.

He nodded. "It was through and through. Just hurts like hell. I'll be fine."

"Okay. Let's move in. Take it slow, keep to the sides, and shoot anything that moves."

Inside was wide enough for a small vehicle to drive through. The floor was dark, smooth concrete, blackened by patches of moisture and damp. The high ceiling wasn't visible in the gloom. Running along each side of the tunnel was a raised platform. The walkways led to metal doors with dimmed wall lights next to them, positioned at irregular intervals.

Julie, Jericho, Adrian, and Ruby made their way up the couple of steps and along the left platform. One of the remaining three GlobaTech operatives covered the rear. She had sent the other two across to Collins and Blackstar, to help compensate for Link's injury.

"Keep it tight," Julie called out. "Watch these doors as we go along."

The hurried stomping of their collective footfalls echoed along the tunnel, as if carving a path for them to follow. Ahead, the entrance opened out; the area was bathed in a pale, fluorescent glow.

There was no sign of movement. No visible cameras, either, although none of them believed for a second that they weren't being watched. Given the level of protection they had seen so far, there was little doubt left that Schultz was in there somewhere.

As they neared the end, Julie stopped and held up a fist,

signaling for the others to do the same. She looked around, then turned to Adrian.

"You and Rayne scout ahead," she said.

Adrian nodded, then signaled to Rayne to follow him with a sideways nod of his head. The pair moved to the middle of the tunnel and moved ahead, weapons aimed and ready, covering the angles on both sides.

Julie watched them as they approached the opening. They split up, each taking a side and disappearing out of sight of the others. A couple of minutes passed in relative silence. There was a low, distant hum from the air conditioning system that ran throughout the mountain.

"Come on. Come on..." she muttered impatiently.

Then they heard it.

A single gunshot resonated around the cavernous interior of the mountain, somewhere in the distance.

Everyone tensed. Ruby adjusted her grip of the Raptor she was holding.

"Be ready," said Julie. "Spread out and find cover."

On both sides, they moved down the steps and spread across the width of the tunnel. Jessie, Link, and the two operatives from the right. Julie, Ruby, Jericho, and the third operative from the left. Two lines. Four crouched in front. Four stood behind. Feet planted, body braced, weapons ready.

Then they waited.

Five seconds passed.

Ten seconds.

Fifteen.

The faint sound of quick footsteps faded into earshot. Then voices. Two, in unison.

"Shit, shit, shit, shit!"

Sirens began to wail as Adrian and Rayne appeared

around their respective corners at full speed. Both slid along the floor to a clumsy stop beside the lines of defense waiting.

They looked at each other, then at the group.

Julie raised a questioning and accusatory eyebrow at Adrian.

He shrugged. "Whoops."

Automatic gunfire rattled to life from the left and right, sparking against the concrete floor.

"What did you do?" shouted Ruby over the noise.

Rayne scrambled to his feet and moved away to the side. "In my defense..."

"Shut up and shoot!" screamed Julie.

Tristar guards appeared from both sides. Groups of five or six swarmed into view, painfully unaware of what was waiting for them.

The group unloaded their weapons at the new arrivals, killing them all within a matter of seconds. The bodies fell with a loud, collective thump. Weapons clattered on the ground. Silence returned.

"Are you two okay?" asked Julie. "What the hell happened?"

Adrian got to his feet. "This ground level is like a wheel. There's a big central control hub, with spokes in six directions coming off it. Inside the hub are stairs and an elevator. We saw one guy on his own, so we went to take him out..."

"And he wasn't alone?" offered Jericho, rolling his eyes.

Adrian shook his head. "Not even a little bit."

Rayne walked over toward Link, ignoring Julie's questioning. He had sat back on the steps of the walkway. His eyes were glazing over.

"Yo, Link, are you good?" asked Rayne.

The inquiry prompted the others to look over. As Rayne reached his friend, Link fell forward into his arms.

"Oh, shit, Link!"

He guided him to the ground as the others gathered around them.

Link was holding the bullet wound on his shoulder and breathing heavily.

"Move your hand," urged Rayne. "Let me see."

Link shook his head slowly. "Why? You're not a... a doctor..."

"Damn it, would you move your fucking hand? Jesus!"

Eventually, he did.

Rayne's eyes went wide. "Oh, shit..."

Despite Link's vague and dismissive report earlier, it was anything but a scratch. The round had punched a hole straight through his arm, taking a chunk of flesh from above his considerable bicep. While it wasn't inherently bad on its own, it had caused significant blood loss.

Julie looked to the nearest operative. "Get that cleaned and wrapped. Then two of you take him back to the vehicles."

Link let his head loll to the side, so he was staring up at Julie. "I ain't sitting... this one... out. I'm good. I just need... a minute."

Julie went to reply, but Jessie stepped in. She placed a hand on Julie's arm—a silent instruction that she would handle it. Then she crouched beside Link.

"We're gonna be okay, Link," she said calmly. "We need to move quick and quiet here, and you're no use to us like this. However, when we get out of here, we're likely going to be coming in hot. With you and your new buddies here waiting outside, engines running, we've got the additional fire support we'll need to make our escape. We need you out there, okay?"

Link's head lazily turned to the other side. He stared up at Rayne, his eyes silently pleading for reasoning he could agree with.

Rayne smiled apologetically. "Jessie's right, big guy. Right now, you're more use to us out there. Y'know, as long as you don't faint like a little girl."

Link smiled weakly. "Help me up, so I can kick your ass..."

Two GlobaTech operatives carefully hoisted him to his feet. One of them threw his good arm over his shoulder. The other leveled his weapon and looked back at Julie. "I'll get him out safely, boss."

She nodded back. "Thank you."

As they walked away, the rest gathered themselves and quickly searched the nearby pile of dead bodies for spare ammunition.

"Show me this command hub," Julie said to Adrian. "See if we can shut these goddamn alarms off."

He led them to the left, following the wide arc of the corridor until they reached the control room. The large square room in the middle housed monitors that were linked to the security feed throughout the base.

They stepped inside.

Julie looked at Collins. "Wait out here. Watch our six, okay?"

"Aye." He nodded. "No problem, Jules."

He turned away, immediately checking all visible directions for any sign of movement.

Inside, Jessie had already sat behind the large console that dominated the north wall of the room. Her hands glided over the keyboard like a concert pianist. A moment later, the alarms shut off. The deafening silence left in their wake was momentarily unnerving.

Julie moved to her side and pointed to the bank of security monitors to the right.

"Let's see what we can see," she said.

The rest formed a semicircle behind them, clambering to see the screens.

Jessie moved a hand to a small joystick beside the keyboard and began moving the cameras. She cycled through the feeds, sweeping the areas displayed on the monitor for signs of life.

The first couple of feeds showed groups of men on floors above them, running and moving into position outside the doors of elevators.

Julie looked behind them. The door into the room was on the west wall. Built into the wall opposite was a bank of three elevators. To the right, on the south wall, was a stairwell. Wide, metal steps with thin railings covered in wire mesh ran up to the other floors.

She looked back at the monitors. "Looks like we're taking the stairs, folks."

Jericho leaned forward and tapped one screen, which showed a small group of Tristar guards crowded around a stairwell from a short distance away. "Where's that?"

Jessie moved quickly, navigating the system until she found the answer. "Sixth level. South side."

"Not as busy there," said Jericho. "Could give us a head start, at least."

"Maybe," said Julie. "But we still need to find Schultz."

The room fell silent as Jessie worked the console. Adrian and Ruby exchanged nervous glances. Rayne handled his own impatience by gazing absently around the room, noting the sickly, pale yellow walls and flooring that looked as if it had been taken straight out of a hospital in the seventies.

"Got him!" announced Jessie after a few minutes. "That's him, right there."

Everyone focused on the screen she was pointing to. It was a clear feed of a man sitting side-on to the camera feed, clearly restrained to his chair. The room appeared otherwise empty. A large observation window was behind him.

"Where is that?" asked Julie.

"Twelfth level," she said. "That's the main control room."

Julie turned to face the room. Everyone stepped back and looked at her.

"This is it," she said. "We'll try to get a clear idea of how many bad guys there are and how much real estate there is between us and our target before we make our move. But this is it, guys. President Schultz is here."

Everyone looked at each other, unable to hide their excitement.

Julie glanced at Jericho, who smiled at her. She returned the gesture, then checked the magazine of her weapon.

"Let's go get him."

35

ROACH

November 22, 2020

The group stood beneath the trees along the south side of the park, looking over at the White House. Twenty men and women stood with Roach. Twenty more were gathered at the far side, preparing to escort the rest of the camp to safety.

Roach looked out across the intersection of 14th and I. The street and sidewalks had emptied in the last twenty minutes. He was trying to calculate Tristar's next move. Clearly, the defecting guard was right—an attack was coming. He didn't know enough about the city to figure out where it would be coming from.

Cooper stood to his right, armed with a crowbar, waiting patiently.

Roach turned to him. "You know this city well?"

Cooper nodded. "Lived here for the last ten years."

Roach pointed toward the intersection. "If we head

along there and cross H Street, that leads us to New York Avenue, right?"

"It does. That'll lead you straight to Pennsylvania Avenue."

"Any idea where the nearest Tristar outposts are?"

He shook his head. "No idea. There are so many patrols on the streets here, it's like they're part of the scenery. You never see them coming or going. They're just there."

Roach nodded and fell silent. His eyes darted left and right as his brain accessed everything Tristar had ever taught him and everything he had gleaned from the mercenaries and former soldiers he had worked beside. He had to figure out the best and safest route to the White House.

Standing on his left, Becky shivered. She shifted her weight between each leg, eager to keep moving.

He looked at her. "Do you think there will be any news outlets nearby? Reporters? Hell, even civilians, I'd take at this point."

She shook her head. "Honestly, Will? I doubt it. Hall controls most of the media. It's not going to be like it was when an *actual* president was in there. They've clearly set up roadblocks on the roads around here. The city is a ghost town now. We're on our own."

Roach took out his own gun and checked the magazine. It was full, and he had one spare in his pocket. He glanced behind him at the rest of the group. Most were armed with melee weapons—baseball bats, iron bars, wrenches. Only a couple had handguns.

He repeatedly tensed his jaw muscles and ground his teeth, lost in thoughts that were marred by frustration.

What am I doing? he thought. *I'm going to get these people killed.*

He looked back across at Cooper. "Okay, we head toward

H, then take New York Avenue. It looks like the roads are empty, so we stick to the middle of the street, as visible as we can be. The more people see us, the safer we're likely to be. Hall is unlikely to risk another PR disaster by attacking civilians without provocation."

Cooper eyed him warily. "Are you sure?"

He shrugged. "Educated guess. We make it to the White House, we create a scene, start a protest... whatever it takes to get people's attention."

"Say we do that. Say the man himself comes out to confront us. Then what?"

Roach held us gun up. "Then I put a bullet between his eyes."

"And then what? All this is just... over?"

"Maybe. Maybe not." He tucked his gun back into his waistband behind him. "But I know Brandon Crow is dead, so if Quincy Hall dies too, there's unlikely to be a competent successor ready to take his place. Tristar will be in disarray. They will be confused. Maybe it gives the people with the power to take this country back a window of opportunity."

Cooper sighed. "Look, man. I'm with you, okay? I believe in what you've been doing. But this seems to be riding on a lot of ifs and maybes."

Roach shrugged again. "That's all we have. It's all we've had since day one. But someone needs to take a chance. Someone needs to stand up, play the odds, and do something that might put a stop to this."

"And that's you, huh?"

"I don't see a line of volunteers itching to do it for me."

"You're a crazy bastard, Roach." Cooper chuckled, deep and guttural. "But I'm with you. Better to die on your feet than live on your knees, right?"

"Something like that. Although, if we could avoid dying at all, that would be nice."

"Yeah. Right."

Roach turned to Becky. "Go tell Kevin and the others to move out. The same goes for all of them—keep to the streets, stay visible, find the first signs of civilization beyond Tristar's patrols, and stay there."

She nodded. "Okay."

As she turned to walk away, he reached for her arm. When she looked back at him, he looked into her eyes.

"I want you to go with them," he said.

Becky pulled her arm free and took a defiant step back. "What? No! This is my fight too, Will. The safest place is by your side. It always is. After all this, I'm not—"

"You are. This is not up for debate, Rebecca. I need you to stay with the refugees and get to safety. I can't do what I need to if I'm worrying about you. If you're out there with me, it puts a bullseye on you, and I can't have that. Not anymore."

Her expression softened. "But I—"

"No buts, please. Get out of here, get safe, and make sure that whatever happens next, you tell the story of this day to as many people as you can. That's how you can help, okay? Please. For me."

She sighed, relenting. "Okay. But you come and find me when this is over, Will. I mean it. You come back to me, okay?"

He placed his hand on her shoulder and smiled. "You know I will. Now go on."

Becky threw her arms around his neck, squeezing him tightly. She held onto him for a full minute before finally releasing her loving grip. Then she turned and walked away, heading across the park without looking back.

Roach watched her go for a moment, then turned back to look at the intersection ahead of them.

"You okay?" asked Cooper.

"I'm fine," he replied bluntly. "Let's go."

Without another word, Roach stepped off the grass and onto the sidewalk. He didn't bother to look before heading out into the middle of the road and moving toward 14th Street. Behind him, he heard the group of refugees following him.

They moved along the street, passing between a hotel and the university building. A vicious wind whipped around them; its howling echoed in the deserted streets. It seemed to intensify the closer they got to their destination, as if the elements themselves were trying to deter them.

They continued along 14th, crossing the intersection with H.

Cooper looked around, staring up at the tall buildings. "Man, this is creepy as shit."

Roach didn't respond. There was something almost post-apocalyptic about walking through an empty city. But having passed through many towns in the last six months and experienced the same thing, it wasn't as noticeable to him.

"This is New York Avenue up ahead," said Cooper. "We go right here. It'll take us straight to the White House."

Roach nodded, but again, he didn't answer. He was focused on what might lie ahead. He was concerned by how quiet it was. Tristar had clearly set up blockades throughout the city, ensuring the area around the White House was devoid of people and traffic. But if it were him, he would've lined the streets with Tristar patrols. He wouldn't have let them get out of the park. Why wasn't there any Tristar presence? If they knew where he was, what were they waiting for?

He tried to clear his mind. He figured he would find out soon enough.

They reached the next intersection and headed right, along New York Avenue, toward 15th Street. Ahead of them, he could see the U.S. Treasury building.

They turned left and made their way along H Street, past the hotel, toward where Pennsylvania Avenue cut across them.

Roach turned and held up a hand, signaling for the group to stop. They gathered around him expectantly.

"This is it," he said. "The White House is on the other side of this building. We head along Pennsylvania from here, and it puts us on Quincy Hall's doorstep. There will be a significant Tristar presence there. Remember, defend yourselves if any patrols get too close and try to attack you, but do not provoke them. As far as all of you are concerned, this is a peaceful protest. They have automatic weapons, which your socket wrenches will offer little protection from. We protest, we make noise, we try to get Hall to show his face. I'll do the rest. Understood?"

Murmurs of agreement rippled around them.

Roach nodded and set off walking again, heading for the barricaded entrance to where the statue of General Sherman stood tall. He made it three steps before he heard a low noise somewhere nearby.

He stopped and looked around, holding his hand out to the side for the others to see.

"Everybody, stay where you are," he said.

Cooper was beside him. "What *is* that?"

"I don't know. Movement of some sort."

The sound was carried on the wind and distributed easily around the otherwise silent streets.

"Tristar?" asked Cooper.

"Maybe," replied Roach.

"What do we do if it is?"

"Exactly what we talked about."

He looked to his left, back along Pennsylvania Avenue, away from the White House and toward the old mayor's office. Just in view was a group of people. They were too far away for him to be sure of their numbers but close enough to tell they weren't Tristar.

Roach watched as they got closer. He frowned when he could make out their faces.

"Sonofabitch," he muttered. "They're civilians."

The group relaxed and spread across the street, looking on as another thirty people approached them. A man and a woman were leading the pack. They made a beeline for Roach when they saw him.

"You're Roach, right?" asked the woman. "Ah, Will?"

Roach raised an eyebrow, quickly looking the couple up and down. Both seemed of similar age and maybe a few years older than himself. Both were dressed in business attire.

There was only one reason she would know to call him Will.

"Becky sent you, didn't she?"

The woman nodded. "She was with a group of refugees who came seeking shelter in our office building, over on the corner of 11th and M. She told us you were here and what you were planning to do."

The man took a step forward. "We want to help. We want to stand with you. The more of us there are, the better the chance of that sonofabitch Quincy Hall listening to us, right?"

Roach nodded. "That's the idea."

"Then we're with you," said the woman. "No matter what. Enough is enough."

"This could be dangerous. I can't guarantee your safety."

The man scoffed. "Have you not been paying attention these last six months? No one can. We're done being afraid of Tristar."

Roach couldn't resist a small smile. "Fair enough. We stay together. Coordinate your people. Stay as visible as possible, okay? We need to—"

A loud rumbling, like distant thunder, seemed to be coming from every direction.

"How many more of you are there?" asked Roach.

The woman shook her head. "None. This is it."

"Shit." Roach turned to address the refugees who came with him. "I want you all to be ready, okay? I don't know..."

His words trailed off as he caught a glimpse of what was approaching behind them. Vehicles. Jeeps. Black. Four of them.

Tristar.

He spun around, looking ahead, all the way down to Constitution Avenue. More vehicles. Easily six or more, heading toward them.

The others saw the approaching Tristar patrols. Restlessness and panic took a hold of the group. Roach didn't say anything. He let them deal with it however they felt like they needed to. He was too busy doing the math.

Ten vehicles. Probably four men in each.

Tristar wouldn't send forty guards to secure fifty refugees. Especially knowing one of them was him.

They would send a hundred.

Roach's eyes narrowed. Where were the rest?

"This isn't right," he said quietly. "There should be more of them."

Cooper looked at him, eyes wide with disbelief. "Are you serious?"

The vehicles slowed to a stop. Tristar guards hustled out, weapons raised, and formed a wide semicircle that covered the full width of the street and sidewalks.

The new arrivals quickly turned, looking back the way they had come. Standing in their path was another large Tristar presence, easily thirty-strong.

Roach figured they must have been waiting inside a nearby building. Pinned in on three sides, he turned to look over at the gated entrance to Pennsylvania Avenue, which led to the White House. He felt his shoulders slump involuntarily forward as more Tristar guards appeared there, swarming as if from nowhere to box them all in.

Cooper nudged his arm. "Well... are you happy now?"

Roach ignored the obvious sarcasm. The truth was, he felt a modicum of relief that the Tristar guards were acting how he would expect them to. If they hadn't, he would've been more concerned that they were becoming less predictable. Still, he wasn't blind to the fact that things had turned bad a lot sooner than he assumed they would.

Ahead of them, a lone guard stepped forward and fired a short burst from his assault rifle into the air in a loose arc. The chorus of screams from the refugees and civilians was short-lived as surprise quickly gave way to fear.

"This city is currently under lockdown due to suspected rebel terrorist activity," shouted the guard. His voice boomed in the silence. "For your own protection, I am ordering you all to leave this area immediately."

No one moved.

Roach's gaze locked on the guard who spoke. His fists clenched. His feet were planted, and he was leaning forward slightly, like a sprinter in their starting blocks, preparing to charge forward.

He felt angry. At Tristar. At Orion. At Hall. At the world. But mostly at himself. As he stood there, surrounded by innocent people who were only in danger because of him, he began to see how futile his crusade truly was. He realized the others had been right. Julie, Jericho, Adrian... they had all expressed their reservations about the idea of going after Hall directly, right out the gate.

But he didn't listen because he didn't want to trust other people and their opinions. He wanted to do it alone. His way. But where had that gotten him? He had spent six months trekking to Washington. He had been here less than six hours, and he was already finished.

"You are surrounded and outnumbered," said the guard. "If you do not disperse immediately, we will make you. This is your only warning. Failure to act now will leave us no choice but to assume you are a part of the rebellion and to treat you all like terrorists."

Cooper's grip tightened around his crowbar, flexing his forearm.

"Easy," whispered Roach.

Cooper ignored him and stepped forward. "Go to Hell! We are all citizens of this country, and we have a right to be heard. We demand to see Quincy Hall!"

The guard didn't respond. He glanced over to one of his colleagues on his left, standing near the crosswalk. The other man gave a small nod, then raised his weapon and fired without warning or hesitation. A burst of bullets tore through Cooper's chest. His arms flailed in the air, sending his crowbar flying away. He fell to the ground as if in slow motion, landing awkwardly and heavily.

"No!" screamed Roach as the body thudded to the ground.

Again, an initial outburst of shocked screams quickly died. The silence that followed was haunting.

Roach took a step forward, pulling the first guard's attention onto him.

The guard smiled. "Well, well... look who it is, boys! The rumors were true. We're in the presence of a celebrity. Tell me, *Roach*, where's that lovely sister of yours, eh?"

He took another step forward.

The hundred-plus Tristar guards all did the same.

The refugees and civilians huddled closer together in the middle of the street, forming a large group behind Roach. He looked behind him to check on everyone.

They looked scared.

"Last chance," shouted the guard. "Refugees, return to your camps. Civilians, return to your homes and your jobs. Walk away and you will not be hurt. But understand that *this man—*" He pointed to Roach. "—is a known terrorist and a wanted criminal. By staying here, you are admitting your own involvement in rebel activities. That carries with it a harsh sentence, which will be carried out immediately. Do I make myself clear?"

Tristar had them all boxed in. Roach stood a few paces away from the others. He looked around, turning a slow circle as he assessed his situation. He was easily thirty feet away from anyone in a Tristar uniform, in any direction. If he tried to rush any one of them, he would be cut down before he made it halfway.

He forced himself not to think about the people who had followed him there. Perhaps it was selfish of him, but if today was to be his last, he didn't want anything else weighing on his conscience. His own anger and regret were already enough.

The air sizzled with tension. No one moved. He could feel the nervous energy behind him. He wanted to say something to make them feel better. To make them believe it would be okay. But in that moment, words failed him.

The guard made an exaggerated gesture with his arms, symbolizing his lack of patience. He began walking slowly toward Roach, shaking his head.

"Look what you've done, *Roach*. Look what your actions and your sister's stories have done. They've given these people a false sense of hope, which has led them to willingly endanger their lives just for a chance to stand beside you. It's pathetic, really. We're trying to give you people a better life, and this is how you repay us. Seriously?" He pointed his finger at Roach again, stabbing the air. "Understand that what happens next is on you."

Roach stepped back, putting himself closer to the group. "Don't hurt these people. Let them go. I'm the one you want, right? I'm the trophy your boss wants for his wall. Take me to see him, and we'll end this between us. But don't hurt the people you say you're here to help."

His words fell on deaf ears.

"You all had your chance," said the guard, shaking his head. He looked around at the small army of Tristar personnel surrounding them. "Take them."

Three sides of the enclosure swarmed toward the center as one. They went for the group, pushing and jostling them away to the side of the street, using their guns as leverage. People started screaming and shouting. Some of them gallantly fought back. Men stepped in front of the women and threw wild punches. A couple of Tristar guards were knocked to the ground in the chaos.

Roach watched in horror, rooted to the spot. Not one of them came for him. He knew he should help. He wanted to, so badly. But he couldn't move. All he could do was look on as close to one hundred armed mercenaries assaulted a group of civilians with impunity. And he was to blame for it all.

The anger boiling inside of him finally took control from the self-pity, and his senses cleared. He turned to look at the guard who had given the order, who was already staring at him, smiling. He took one step toward him, then gunfire erupted behind him. He spun around to see three refugees from the Franklin Park camp drop to the ground. They were dead before their bodies hit the tarmac.

Silence fell on the world.

Roach stared with wide eyes. His mouth hung open with disbelief.

The remaining civilians were ushered away without further incident by a group of guards, along Pennsylvania Avenue and away from the White House. The noise of their protests died down as they disappeared from sight. Roach watched until he could no longer see them, then turned back to stare at the guard, unable to hide the defeat from his face.

The enclosure came together again, forming a smaller circle around Roach now that forty of them had gone. He looked around, once again turning a slow circle. He estimated there were sixty men, all armed. On three sides, they were all around twenty feet away. Ahead of him, the main guard and his team were closer to forty feet away.

Too far to charge. Too close together to push through.

He had no options. No moves. No way out.

Roach took deep breaths, trying to remain calm. He had never been afraid of dying, but then, he had never truly faced death. Not like this.

He knew this was it. He was going to die.

His breathing began to slow as he regained control.

He smiled to himself and shook his head.

"So goddamn close," he muttered.

He locked eyes with the main guard, who was standing directly in front of him, slightly ahead of the others. Maybe twenty-five feet away.

"Fuck it," whispered Roach.

He drew his gun and took aim with both hands, pointing the barrel squarely at the guard's face.

The guard laughed, prompting a ripple of laughter all around them.

"Are you... are you serious?" he asked. "How many bullets do you have in that thing? Because if it's less than ninety, you're making a huge mistake."

Roach shook his head. "I only need one."

"Why? Are you taking the coward's way out? That'll give your sister something to blog about, wouldn't it?"

"What's your name?" asked Roach stubbornly.

The guard frowned. "What?"

"If you're the one in charge here, I want to know who I'm talking to."

"The name's Myers. I'm a senior operator for Tristar, and I oversee all the patrols in D.C."

Roach nodded. "Okay, Myers. I didn't come all this way to leave empty-handed, so if I'm going to die here, you can bet your ass I'm taking you with me."

"Wow. I feel so special, honestly. But you'll be dead before you get your shot off. Take a look around, Roach. You had a good run. You walked from California to Washington.

You killed a bunch of our friends along the way. You became... what? Some kind of folk hero. It's all terribly impressive. But it's over. Our orders are to deliver your head to Mr. Hall."

Roach's finger slid inside the trigger guard. He glared ahead, feeling the anger boil inside him and the icy grip of fear around his chest. He didn't want to die. He wasn't ready. There was still a war to fight.

He wasn't ready.

He wanted to see Becky one last time, to tell her that he loved her and was proud of her.

He wasn't ready.

Myers was right. He would never get the shot off. He could see the restless twitching all around him in his periphery. That realization... that acceptance of defeat made his anger boil over.

He raised his gun and let loose a guttural roar as he emptied the magazine at the sky. He screamed until he heard the repeated clicking of a hammer hitting an empty chamber. Then he launched the gun toward the guard in front of him. It clattered and bounced and slid to a stop a few feet away from him.

Myers watched impassively. "Well, *that* was dramatic."

Roach stood tall and held his head high. Each breath he took moved his shoulders. He looked to his sides, noting the impatience and arrogance in the men surrounding him.

He clenched his fists.

"You want me?" he shouted. "Come and get me!"

He stepped back into a fighting stance and waited. No one moved.

"Come on! What are you waiting for?"

Myers nodded to a guard standing on Roach's left. He stepped forward, pushing his rifle behind him; it hung on his shoulder by its strap. He took out a pair of plastic hand ties from his belt.

"Don't be an asshole," he said. "Let's go."

Roach waited until he was within arm's reach. Then, without warning, he lunged toward him, driving his fist into the guard's throat.

The guard's eyes bulged in their sockets. His panicked breaths came in nightmarish rasps. As his hands clutched at his throat, Roach drove his foot through the side of the guard's right knee, breaking his leg. He began to fall to the ground. Roach took a step back, lining up his shot, then swung a stiff right hook. It connected flush with the side of the guard's face, dislocating his jaw.

He collapsed to the ground, unconscious and broken.

Roach stepped away and turned back to Myers. He gestured for him to come closer with his hand.

"I've got nowhere else to be, shit-for-brains," he said defiantly. "Who's next? Come on!"

Myers felt his composure leave him.

"What are you waiting for?" he screamed, his face contorted with rage. "Get him!"

Roach took a breath and once again unleashed a visceral roar. He didn't wait for anyone else to approach him. He set off running toward Myers.

He didn't expect to be taken alive. He no longer expected to see another sunrise.

Maybe this was the moment his life had been building toward.

Maybe this was who he was destined to become—a man whose journey would live on as the stuff of legend, in a time when history was rewritten.

Maybe he *was* ready.

Myers's eyes grew wide at the sight of Roach charging

toward him, screaming his primal war cry. He was a man who had accepted death and, therefore, had nothing else left to lose.

Roach's heart was pounding in his chest. Sweat dripped from his brow, despite the winter temperature. As he bore down on Myers, his only thought was of his sister. Wherever she was, he hoped she was safe. He hoped she would continue telling her stories. He hoped she would make sure what he did here would help inspire people to stand and fight.

A single gunshot shattered the air around him, forcing him to duck instinctively and slide to a stop in the middle of the road. It was loud. Much louder than normal. It was a high caliber round. A sniper rifle, maybe.

He brought his arms up over his head, waiting for his body to register the impact. He didn't want to suffer in his final moments. He felt nothing. For all he knew, he was already dead.

Then he saw Myers drop to the ground in front of him. A small hole was visible in the right side of his head. The left side was completely removed.

Roach frowned. "What the hell?"

All eyes, including his, looked around to find the source of the noise that was beginning to register with him. Movement. Lots of it. All around.

Slowly, he got to his feet. Everyone in a Tristar uniform was ignoring him. From way back along 15th Street, he saw a tank rumbling slowly toward them, surrounded by men in fatigues.

Military fatigues.

From his right, approaching from the direction the refugees were taken minutes earlier, more men approached. More military fatigues.

From behind, where Myers's body now lay, even more men approached, accompanied by an armored Humvee and an open-top Jeep.

Roach smiled. Then he laughed.

Close to two hundred U.S. infantry soldiers were descending upon them. Tristar didn't even think about resisting. They dropped their weapons at the mere sight of the U.S. military.

Soldiers pushed through the Tristar patrol and dragged Myers's body out of the way. The Jeep nosed through and came to a stop a few feet away from Roach. Both passenger side doors swung open, and two familiar faces climbed out. Faces he hadn't seen in a long time.

"Sonofabitch..." he said.

Moses Buchanan walked over to him, wearing a thousand-dollar suit and a million-dollar smile. Beside him, Kim Mitchell kept pace, her hands thrust into the pockets of an ankle-length overcoat.

Buchanan stopped in front of Roach and extended his hand.

Roach shook it gladly. "We thought you were dead."

Buchanan smiled. "I missed you too, Mr. Roachford."

He nodded a courteous greeting to Kim, who smiled back.

"Seriously, where have you been?" he asked.

Buchanan looked around and watched for a moment as the Tristar guards were rounded up and escorted away by the soldiers. Then he looked back at Roach and took a deep breath.

"The medical facility I was taken to after we lost Santa Clarita saved my life. They recognized me and kept me hidden until I healed. I spent some time watching this country suffer. Then I watched as the rebellion grew. Then

I started reading your sister's blog. How is she, by the way?"

Roach nodded. "Safe, I hope. I sent her away with some of the refugees before coming here."

"I'll make sure our boys here find her."

"Yeah, what's with the Army? I thought they were decommissioned by Orion?"

"Just because the military was retired, that doesn't mean all the men and women who served suddenly disappeared," said Kim. "Julie Fisher rallied the GlobaTech troops. We rallied Uncle Sam's. Turns out, everyone was itching to get a little skin in the game."

"Well, I can't fault your timing. You saved my life. Thank you."

"We were watching," said Buchanan. "We were just waiting for the right moment. I hope we're not too late to help the others, either."

Roach frowned. "The others?"

Buchanan nodded. "Miss Fisher, Adrian Hell, and the rest are all trying to rescue President Schultz as we speak. I figured they might need an assist."

"Really? That's some timing."

"It is. Imagine how coordinated this would've been if you had been working with them this whole time?"

Buchanan raised an eyebrow that forced Roach to momentarily glance away. He fought to keep the look of shame from his face.

After a moment, he turned back, frowning. "So, wait. You just sat back and watched while refugees were killed? Why the hell didn't you intervene earlier?"

"Because if we did, there would've been fifty innocent lives in the crossfire, not one. I figured you were the main prize here. Sooner or later, you were going to be separated from everyone else. And when you were, we made our move. It wasn't like I was sitting there with popcorn, Mr. Roachford."

Roach shook his head. His expression hardened. He was angry, despite knowing Buchanan was right.

"You were prepared to die, weren't you?" said Buchanan, after a moment.

"I was."

"Well, I'm glad you didn't."

Roach relaxed. "Yeah. Me too."

Buchanan turned to look at the barrier that blocked access to Pennsylvania Avenue to the west and the path beyond it, which led to the White House. Roach did the same, standing beside him. Around them, a small group of soldiers gathered, holding their weapons loose and ready.

"Now," said Buchanan, looking over at Roach, "let's go take our fucking country back."

36

ADRIAN HELL

We step out of the elevator onto the sixth level of the base, moving in pairs. Julie and Jericho are up front. Collins and Rayne are behind them. Jessie and the last remaining GlobaTech operative are next. Ruby and I bring up the rear.

The floors in this base are semicircular in shape, with either a large room or multiple smaller ones in the center. Each floor narrows in width the higher we get. We've also discovered they account for around twenty-five percent of the base's actual size.

The rest?

The biggest goddamn hangar I've ever seen in my life!

"We're clear," says Julie.

We all move into the middle of the corridor. It stretches away from us in both directions. No sign of any movement.

"So, there's another set of stairs on the south side, which should give us an easier climb up to the twelfth, right?" I ask.

Jessie nods. "Yeah."

"Okay, so, one question: which way is south?"

Everyone stares at me like I'm an idiot.

I shrug. "What? I'm more of a *left and right* kinda guy."

Collins chuckles. "How the hell have ya lived so long, matey?"

"Do you not have a compass with you?" asks Julie.

I shake my head. "No, I left it back in my tent, along with my flashlight, knitting needle, and my fucking ukulele."

"But you know which direction the sun rises from, right?"

"I do. However, we're standing inside a fucking mountain, and Mother Nature didn't see fit to install a skylight, so..."

Jericho reaches into a side pocket of his pants and pulls out a flashlight. He waves it at me and smiles.

I roll my eyes. "Oh, well, *of course* you have one, you goddamn boy scout. Did you earn a goodie-two-shoes badge to sew onto your sleeve too?"

He flips it upside-down to reveal a compass embedded in the base of the grip. He studies it, then looks at me. "We go right. Happy now?"

"Yes, thank you. See? Wasn't that easier?"

There's a collective sigh. The group sets off walking right, along the corridor.

Jessie hangs back and moves to my side, then leans close. "To be fair, I only knew it was the south side because it said it on the screen."

I look at her and raise my eyebrow. "Why didn't you say something to back me up?"

She frowns. "What, and risk looking stupid in front of everyone? Nah, I'm good, thanks."

"No loyalty," I say, shaking my head. "I'll remember this for your next performance review."

"Bite me, old timer."

She smiles and flips me off, then moves up and falls in line with Collins.

Ruby is on the other side of me, smiling to herself.

"What?" I ask her, feigning offense. "You wanna say something smart too?"

She laughs. "Not at all. But be honest—you're a little proud of our girl right now, aren't you?"

I hold her gaze for a moment, then look forward and sigh heavily. "Yeah..."

The corridor is wide, with entrances to rooms on either side of it. The floor is the same dark concrete as below, with the same dark stains scattered across it, like rotting patchwork.

We spent a little time in the control room downstairs figuring this out. We saw the opportunity to get up here to the sixth. We pulled up some schematics on the console and plotted the path of least resistance all the way to the main control room on the twelfth. That's not to say there won't be resistance, but if we're quick and quiet, we might avoid any major confrontations.

So far, so good.

"The stairs are just up ahead," says Jericho. "Be ready. Ray, you and Rayne cover the rear."

Collins and Rayne hang back. They turn, raise their weapons, and walk slowly backward, making sure we're not followed or ambushed. Julie and Jericho press on ahead, scouting to make sure there are no surprises.

Ruby, Jessie, this GlobaTech guy, and I are grouped together in the middle.

I look over at the operative. "Hey, buddy. I'm sorry—I

didn't catch your name."

He looks at me. "It's Stevens, sir."

I give him a curt nod. "Adrian."

He smiles awkwardly. "Yeah, I... I know. You were something of a legend around GlobaTech, sir."

Ruby stops in front of him, glaring at him. "Now, why on earth would you go and tell him a thing like that?"

Stevens looks at her, confused. "Ah, I'm... sorry?"

I wave her away. "Oh, don't listen to her, Stevens. She gets jealous when people refer to my notable and, frankly, God-like status. How long have you been with GlobaTech?"

"Six years. I was with Miss Fisher and Mr. Buchanan in Washington when Tristar first attacked us."

Julie walks back toward us. "We're clear. Let's go."

I nod at Stevens. "When this is over, you and I are having a beer, understand?"

He smiles. "Yes, sir."

I catch up to Julie and the others.

Behind me, I hear Ruby say to Stevens, "Please don't encourage him. He's bad enough as it is."

"Now, now, dear. Envy doesn't suit you," I call back over my shoulder.

"No, but shooting people does," she replies bluntly.

Jessie is beside me, smiling. I look at her. "She has a point there."

"Are you finished?" hisses Jericho.

I shake my head disapprovingly at him. "It seems someone earned their party-pooper badge too."

He stares at me with a deadpan expression. "I really hate you. I hope you know that."

I smile. "Ah, that's just the adrenaline talking. You'll be fine once you kill a couple of bad guys."

He walks away and sets off up the stairs. Julie is close

behind. Jessie and my new friend, Stevens, follow them. Ruby goes next. I look behind us, waiting for Collins and Rayne to catch up.

"We good?" I ask as they pass me and start climbing the stairs.

"Aye, we're good," says Collins. "This level looks clear."

As Rayne draws level with me, I tap his arm with the barrel of my gun.

He stops and turns to look at me.

"You okay?" he asks.

I shrug. "Anything about all this seem a little... *off* to you?"

His eyes narrow. "Boss, we have just infiltrated an Air Force base so big that you could fit Alabama inside it to rescue the president of the United States, who has been held here for the last six months by a rogue paramilitary outfit that took over the country. Everything about this is off."

I nod. "Exactly. So... where the fuck is everybody?"

"What do you mean? We saw on the monitors. They're gearing up in front of the elevators on every level."

"Right. And Tristar's just *that* stupid that no one's thought to cover the last six flights of stairs leading up to their VIP hostage?"

He looks around. "Are you saying you think this is a trap?"

"I'm saying Julie and Jericho are understandably looking at the bigger picture of rescuing Schultz and what that might mean for Orion's reign. Collins and Stevens are following them, obviously. Jessie is being Jessie. You're not blind. You know how capable she is, but you also know she's always trying to prove herself... to prove her worth. She's fighting the big fight to show that she can. Ruby... well, she's likely just worrying about me. But I also know she's itching for a fight."

Rayne looks away, staring into space, thinking. I tap his arm again to regain his full attention.

"Listen to me, Adam. One day, I'm either going to retire or die. When that day comes, you're going to take over running this thing. I'm not saying I'm perfect, but there's a reason I'm still alive after all the shit I've been through. Sometimes you have to look at the big picture, sure. But other times, all that matters is what's in front of you. Ever heard the saying, *'You can't see the wood for the trees?'*"

He shakes his head.

"It means you're so focused on looking for one thing, you can't see all the other things around you. You know I respect the hell out of GlobaTech, but I'm worried they're thinking about the battles ahead and not paying attention to this one. I need you to see what I see."

Rayne takes a breath and nods. "I understand, boss. I'll make sure I watch out."

"Good man."

As we turn to continue climbing, Ruby appears in the stairwell.

"Are you coming?" she asks.

Rayne shakes his head. "No, it's just how I'm standing."

He grins at her eye roll.

I try to suppress a laugh because it'll get me in trouble for *being gross.*

We jog up the stairs and quickly catch up with the others as we pass the eighth level. We know the elevators are on the opposite side to us. We also know that's where all the bad guys are. Apparently, Tristar think all rebels are lazy and wouldn't dream of taking the stairs.

I sigh.

I don't like this.

I should say something.

But would Julie listen? Would Jericho? Collins might, but how much do they listen to him?

We follow the stairs around, climbing to the ninth. Rayne has moved ahead and is now beside Jessie, so I'm directly behind Ruby.

Even in shapeless combat pants and a long, thick winter coat, she's an absolute vision. I smile as my eyeline levels with where I know her ass is underneath all the clothing.

Simple pleasures.

She glances behind her and sees me smiling.

"You okay back there, champ?" she asks sarcastically.

"Just enjoying the view," I reply.

"What view? You can't see anything. I'm dressed like an Eskimo."

"True. But first of all, you still look sexy as hell. And second, I know what's under there, so I can use my imagination."

"Christ. Will you focus?"

"I am focused."

"On something besides my ass."

"Oh." I sigh. "Fine."

I can't have any fun.

I move around the ninth floor and start the climb up to the tenth. I get to the top of the first flight, where it levels out before the second flight that leads to the next floor. As I turn off the stairs, I happen to glance back over my shoulder, at the small, open vestibule.

There's a man standing there, staring at me.

He isn't moving. He's not even blinking. He's not armed that I can see. He's wearing a lab coat with the Tristar insignia on the breast pocket. His skin is a dark tan. His eyes are wide as he stares right at me.

Honestly, it's creepy as shit.

I see his back foot move slightly.

He's getting ready to run.

"Hey, come here!" I hiss.

He inches uncertainly away from me.

I take a step back down toward him. "Hey, move and I'll kill you."

I raise my gun and take aim. The barrel's pointing right between his eyes.

His mouth hangs open. His hands are trembling as he raises them.

But he's still moving backward.

"I don't wanna do it, but I will," I continue. "Get over here right now, and I promise I won't shoot you."

He takes another step back.

Fuck. I'm going to have to shoot him.

See, the thought had occurred to me that perhaps we weren't heading into a trap. Perhaps Tristar's not stupid. Perhaps they're just doing exactly what anyone would do if they thought they were under attack. We killed everyone outside and everyone on the first floor. Then we disabled their security feeds. The damage we've done, you would think there was a hundred of us, not eight. Maybe they just assumed GlobaTech are hitting them with everything they've got, and they're digging in, expecting an over-whelming force and not a small group of bloodthirsty lunatics.

So, if I shoot this guy, it will bring everyone on this level —and likely the ones immediately above and below—to our position, guns blazing. Then we're fucked.

He takes another step back.

I rest my finger on the trigger.

Two Tristar guards, dressed in black and holding SMGs, appear at his side.

"What the hell are you doing?" asks one of them.

The other follows his gaze and, a second later, locks eyes with me.

I sigh.

Fuck.

I fire three rounds in quick succession, putting a bullet in the middle of each of their foreheads. A moment later, alarms begin to sound again.

I thought we had shut them off...

I run up to the tenth, where the others are waiting for me.

"What happened?" shouts Julie.

"Someone saw me," I say. "I had no choice."

"Goddammit!"

I push through them and continue up the stairs. "Come on! We don't have much time. We need to get to Schultz. We secure him, defend that control room as best we can, and hope Link and your boys do something heroic outside."

I sprint up the stairs, taking two at a time. I hear the others quickly follow behind me. I don't even look at the floors as I pass them. If there's no one there now, there soon will be. I don't need to hang around to see it.

Eleventh floor.

I'm breathing heavy. Exertion and adrenaline.

Definitely too old for this shit.

And... twelfth.

Here we go.

I step out into the corridor. I hear the crunching thud of multiple boots moving at speed. A moment later, I see Tristar guards appear to my left.

I drop to my knee and start shooting.

"Contact!" I shout.

I clip a couple of them, but more keep coming. Six, seven... ten—shit! I step into a doorway to my right. It's not deep, but it offers me more cover than I had standing in the open.

I reload and keep shooting as the others file out behind me. The sound of gunfire echoes and bounces around, amplified by the cavernous interior. The walls are literally the inside of a mountain. The acoustics in here are wicked.

"Contact!" shouts Jericho behind me.

Another guy drops in front of me. I think that's five. Jessie and Rayne are behind the wall in the vestibule by the stairs, shooting in the same direction I am.

"How many?" I shout over.

"I see four," replies Jessie.

I look behind to see more coming along the corridor. Collins is crouched behind a couple of metal containers stacked against the outside wall. He sporadically pops up from cover to fire at our group of bad guys. The others have sought what cover they could and are dealing with the new arrivals.

We can't stay here.

I look at the door I'm leaning against and try the handle.

It's locked.

Of course, it is.

I empty another magazine.

"Reloading," I call out.

"They're down," confirms Rayne.

I chamber a new round and step out of cover, gun held out in front of me, ready for anything.

I edge around the near wall, moving around the gentle bend in the corridor, limiting my own exposure in case there are more guards ahead. Rayne and Jessie move up alongside me.

It looks clear.

I turn to Rayne. "Go and tell Jericho to fall back to me. We're clear here."

He nods and heads back.

"How are you for ammunition?" I ask Jessie.

She holds up her assault rifle. "One mag left for this. One in and one spare for my pistol. You?"

"One spare after this one. A straight-up firefight isn't sustainable." I gesture to the dead bodies littering the floor around us. "Grab a couple of those SMGs and as much ammo as you can carry."

As we do, the others appear at full speed.

"We got more incoming," yells Julie.

"A lot more!" adds Collins.

I grab an SMG and toss it to Ruby as she passes me. I do the same for Rayne and Stevens.

"Let's go," I say to Julie as she draws level with me. "We can't stay here. We need to find Schultz."

We continue along the corridor, occasionally pausing to fire back and slow down our pursuers. We reach the middle of the corridor, the tip of the arc of the semicircular layout. Another corridor runs across us, leading into what must be the control room.

"This is it," says Julie. "We move in and spread out on my mark. Secure the room, free Schultz, then dig in while we regroup. Ready?"

We are.

Bullets punch into the wall close to my head. I look back and raise my Raptor, quickly killing the two guards who had chanced their luck by following us.

"Any time you want, guys," I say.

We form two lines, one on either side of the door. Julie and Jericho are first. Then Collins and Rayne. Then Jessie and Ruby. Then me and Stevens.

The double doors are metal, with thin panes of frosted glass above the pull handles.

"Go!" shouts Julie.

She and Jericho yank them open. There's a hiss as they're pulled faster than their automatic hinges are designed for.

We file in, one after the other with experienced efficiency, then spread out to the sides, weapons raised. Stevens and I turn and back into the room, making sure no one tries to blindside us. Happy we're clear for now, I turn around and take a proper look at the room.

It's huge and oval. A large window dominates the far wall, which seems to look out over the enormous hangar below. There's a large table in the middle, with a thin bank of computers along one side of it. The walls are lined with consoles and monitors. We entered from the south, but there are doors built into the walls in the northwest and northeast corners too.

The most distinguishing feature, however, is that the room's empty.

"I don't get it," says Rayne. "Where is he?"

"Did they move him when the alarms went off, maybe?" offers Ruby.

There's a noise behind me. I turn back to see the doors closing. As they shut, there's a suction noise, followed by a loud, mechanical click.

Oh, no...

I move to them and try to push them open.

They don't move.

"Ah, guys..." I look around. "We're locked in."

407

"What?" says Jericho.

He marches over to me, holstering his weapon. Without breaking stride, he slams his shoulder into them. The impact almost shakes the walls, never mind the doors. But they don't budge.

He steps back, then lunges a heavy kick forward, planting his boot between the handles. Again, nothing.

"I wouldn't waste your time," says a voice behind us.

We all spin around to see President Schultz standing by the northeast door. He looks tired. He's lost weight in his face and body, and not in a healthy way. His torn and tattered suit is hanging off him.

Behind him, pressing a gun to his head is...

Is...

What the hell?

It... it can't be...

Everyone in the room reacts, raising their weapons and taking aim at the new arrivals.

"Let him go, Jay," says Julie. "It's over."

Jay? *That's* Jay?

It can't be.

Ruby takes a step toward them, on my right. "You're looking at a lot of people who owe you, bitch. You want a chance to get out of this alive, you need to move away from the president right now and call off your Tristar dogs outside."

The woman smiles at her. It's an evil, almost inhuman grin.

"Wow, you guys are stupid," she says.

I can't take my eyes off her. I don't understand. *That's* who has kicked the crap out of almost everyone in here? *That's* who killed the president of Paluga? *That's* Brandon Crow's bodyguard?

That's Jay?

How?

The northwest door flies open, and Tristar guards file inside. They circle around us, outnumbering us two to one. Each of us has two guns aimed at our heads.

"Drop your weapons," says Jay. "Do it now."

With little choice, everyone does.

I don't. Mine isn't raised anyway. I'm gripping it tighter than I've ever gripped anything in my life, but it's held at my side. I'm not sure I could lift it now if I wanted to.

I step slowly, absently, into the middle of the room. I brush past Ruby without even realizing she's there.

"Adrian," she hisses. "What are you doing?"

Her words register but sound distant. My eyes are locked on the president's captor. On the woman with the gun. On Jay.

The room is deathly silent. I feel everyone watching me, but I don't care. I'm just trying to understand.

I stop at the side of the table in the middle, maybe ten feet away from Schultz.

The gun moves away from his head and aims at me. The dark eyes behind it stare through me like I'm a stranger.

But she isn't a stranger to me.

I drop my gun to the floor and put a hand over my mouth. My heart is beating so fast, it's as if it's trying to punch its way out of my chest.

"Is there a problem?" she says to me.

I shake my head slowly.

"I... I don't believe it," I say quietly.

"Adrian, stand down," says Julie behind me.

I ignore her.

I swallow hard. The gun isn't moving. It's as steady as this mountain and pointing at my chest.

Her eyes narrow, as if unsure of my next move.

I take a breath. "Janine? Is it... is it really you?"

For a split-second, her eyes grow wide. Then she fires.

The bullet hits my body like a wrecking ball. I'm thrown backward and hit my head on the—

37

ADAM RAYNE

Adrian's body fell hard to the floor. Chaos descended in the moments that followed. The sound of gunfire exploded around the room.

Julie dove toward President Schultz, pushing Jay away from him and sending her stumbling backward against the nearby door. She then dragged Schultz to the floor and placed her body on top of his.

"Stay down, sir," she yelled. "We've got you."

Everyone else rushed to close the distance between them and the nearest Tristar guard, knowing the safest place was beside the allies of the people shooting.

Jericho was standing by the door they had all entered through. He grabbed the Tristar guard closest to him by the throat and effortlessly slammed him down to the floor. He heard the mechanical click beside him as the door unlocked. Immediately, his gaze snapped to the opposite corner of the room. He and Jay locked eyes, staring at each other for a fleeting moment. Then she ran from the room via the door behind her.

Jericho tried the door next to him. It opened.

"Guys, let's go!" he shouted.

In close quarters, despite the difference in numbers, it became a much more even fight.

Rayne dealt with the two guards in front of him with brutal efficiency. He delivered a stiff kick to one guard's knee, which broke his leg. He grabbed the other around the back of the head, clasping his hands together in a clinch and pulling him forward. At the same time, he brought his knee up. One connected with the other, and the guard dropped to the floor, unconscious, with a broken nose.

He looked over at Jessie, who had just thrown a guard to the floor and snapped his arm. All around him, Tristar guards were dropping, seemingly lost without the ability to shoot.

In no time at all, every guard had been disabled and dropped.

Pausing only to recover their own weapons, Julie, Ruby, Jessie, and Stevens hustled President Schultz to his feet, then marched him toward the exit. Jericho held the door, firing periodically out into the corridor to deter any reinforcements and buy them some time.

Rayne and Collins rushed to Adrian's unconscious body and hoisted him upright. Collins draped one arm around his neck. Rayne quickly bent to scoop up Adrian's discarded weapon and tucked it behind him, then did the same with the other arm.

"Ready?" asked Rayne.

Collins nodded. They each placed an arm around Adrian's waist. Then, with a gun in their free hand, they struggled out of the control room as Adrian's feet dragged limply across the floor.

"I'll cover your six," said Jericho. "Head for the nearest elevator."

They all followed the corridor back around the perimeter of the control room, dispatching the few Tristar guards they came across between them. There was no sign of Jay.

They reached the bank of elevators on the twelfth level. The doors to one of them were just sliding closed. Rayne caught sight of Julie, who nodded a silent *we got this* before beginning their descent.

Rayne bashed impatiently on the call button.

"Come on, come on... fuck!" he seethed.

Collins fired along the corridor that continued past them, dropping a Tristar guard that had appeared there.

Jericho reached them. "It's clear for now, but that won't last. The others get clear?"

Collins nodded. "Aye, they got the first elevator. Jerry, what the hell happened back there?"

He shook his head. "Damned if I know, but now isn't the time. Our only priority is getting Schultz to safety."

The doors slid open as the elevator arrived.

"Finally!" exclaimed Rayne.

He and Collins dragged Adrian inside. Jericho followed and hit the button for the first floor. The doors began to close as more Tristar guards appeared down the corridor. They opened fire. Everyone pressed themselves against the sides of the carriage. Bullets pinged and sparked off the metal doors as they shut.

As they began their descent, they heard a groan. The three of them looked at Adrian as his head began to loll and nod.

"Wh-what happened?" he muttered.

"Take it easy, fella," said Collins. "We're getting ya out of here, okay? Just hang in there, buddy."

"Did we... did we get him? Schultz."

"We did," said Jericho. "He's with Julie and Ruby. He's okay."

Adrian raised an eyebrow for a second, then blacked out again.

"He's wearing a vest, right?" asked Rayne.

Collins quickly checked. "Aye, he is. Took a nasty blow to the head on the way down, though."

"He'll live," said Jericho, "provided we get out of here in one piece. How are you for ammo?"

"I'm fine, so long as no more than three bad guys come after us," said Rayne.

"Make every round count," said Jericho.

The elevator slowed to a stop as it reached the first floor.

Jericho looked at the others. "Let's go."

The doors stuttered and screeched as they slid open, resisting against the stiff mechanisms. The sound of exchanging gunfire greeted them.

Jericho led the way; Rayne and Collins grappled with Adrian's dead weight behind him. They made their way out of the security hub and around to the left, heading for the tunnel that would lead them outside.

As they rounded the corridor, they heard shouting over the gunfire.

"Get down!"

Jericho slowed. That was Julie's voice.

He glanced behind him. Collins looked back and nodded, having also heard it.

"Go," he said. "We're right behind ya, Jerry."

Jericho sprinted on ahead.

Rayne wheezed with exertion. "Man, I sure wish Adrian was awake for this."

"Aye," said Collins. "The fella's handy in a fight."

"No, I just mean because he's fucking heavy..."

"We're almost there. If we can make it out of here with Schultz in one piece, that'll be a good day's work."

"One step at a time. We need to—shit!"

Bullets whizzed past their heads from behind. Collins dropped to one knee and turned, letting Adrian's body fall to the floor as he opened fire at the small squad of Tristar guards that had appeared there.

Rayne dragged Adrian's body to the side and returned fire. He caught one of the guards in the leg. Another in the stomach. Collins rushed to his side. A stream of automatic gunfire tore across the floor inches from where he had been kneeling.

"Bollocks! There's too many of the bastards back there," he said. "We gotta get out of here."

Ahead, Rayne and Collins could still hear the shooting from whatever skirmish the others were facing. They were crouched against the inner wall of the main hub, at the point where the wide corridor doglegged left.

Collins continued to shoot back at each Tristar guard who edged around the corner after them.

"We're pinned in," he shouted. "We can't make a run for Jerry and the others. We'll bring all these assholes with us."

Rayne fired and took out a guard who had just appeared. His weapon clicked empty.

"Fuck, I'm out," he said.

"I'm getting there," said Collins. "Shite."

"How many are there?"

"I don't know. Five or six, at least."

Rayne stared down at Adrian. He watched his mentor

and friend as he breathed slowly, blessed with unconsciousness during the violent chaos of their attempted escape.

"What would you do?" he muttered. "What would Adrian Hell do right now?"

Collins fired until the hammer came down on an empty chamber.

"That's me done," he announced dejectedly. "Got another two of them. Think there's four left. They all have SMGs. It won't take long for them to realize we ain't firing back no more. Got any bright ideas over there?"

Rayne didn't reply. But he had an idea. It wasn't great, but he knew it was exactly what Adrian would do right now.

He reached behind him and drew Adrian's Raptor from his waistband. He held it for a moment in his hand, feeling the balance and admiring the intricate craftsmanship of the weapon.

Then he looked over at Collins. "Get to the others. Help them any way you can. I'll handle this."

Collins frowned. "Are ya crazy? And what about ya boss? We can't just leave him."

"We won't. Trust me. Just go."

Collins held his gaze for a moment, then let out a reluctant sigh.

"Ya mad bastard," he muttered. "Both of ya. Mad as a bicycle."

Collins stood and ran toward the tunnel.

Rayne watched, knowing the sight and sound of him going would attract the attention of the remaining patrol taking cover around the corner. He crouched, poised, ready to move. He held the Raptor with both hands.

"They're running!" shouted one of the guards. "Let's get after them!"

Rayne smiled to himself.

Fucking amateurs.

As the men appeared around the corner, he dove to his left. Mid-air, he fired twice, hitting the first guard squarely in the chest with both rounds. He landed and rolled with the momentum, coming to a stop on his back in the middle of the corridor. From there, Rayne emptied the magazine into the remaining three guys. He watched them drop, then rested his head back, flat on the floor, and stared up at the high, natural ceiling of the mountain base.

He let out a long sigh, which shivered with adrenaline. Then he looked to his right, staring over at Adrian, who was lying beside the wall.

"Man, being you sucks."

Rayne scrambled to his feet, tucked the empty Raptor behind him, then moved over to Adrian. He struggled to pull him upright, then grabbed a wrist and positioned Adrian's left arm over his neck. He then bent his knees, hooked his arm around the crook of Adrian's left knee, and hoisted him into a fireman's carry.

"Come on, boss," he grunted. "Let's go home."

With small, quick steps, he continued along the same corridor he and Adrian had run along earlier, toward the mouth of the tunnel. When he reached the others, he found them all standing around the final Tristar guard left alive from their own attack. Ruby stepped forward and put a bullet in the guy's head, then looked around at Rayne.

"Oh my God, you're okay!" she exclaimed.

"I'm fine," he replied. "I've got him. Let's just get out of here."

Schultz was flanked by Julie and Jessie, looking disoriented and disheveled. Jericho led the way along the tunnel, with Stevens beside him. Ruby and Collins let

Rayne go ahead of them, then they followed, covering their backs as they headed toward the near-dark skies outside.

They were almost to the entrance when more gunfire erupted behind them. Ruby and Collins both glanced back to see a swarm of Tristar guards running after them. There were too many to count from a distance.

"Run!" yelled Ruby.

Nobody bothered to look around or question why. They just broke into a sprint and moved as fast as they could toward the exit.

Schultz stumbled and fell to the floor, his legs buckling beneath the exertion.

Julie and Jessie lifted him to his feet without breaking stride.

"Almost home, sir," said Julie. "You've got this."

The cold night wind hit them as they burst out of the tunnel at varying speeds. The sound of gunfire behind them echoed around the tunnel.

But they had no time to celebrate. They slid to a halt and bunched together as they realized they were not alone. Fifty-plus men surrounded the entrance to the base in all directions. All were armed and dressed in dark blue camo fatigues.

"What the..." said Julie.

Before anyone could react, two squads broke away from the large group and took up position on either side of the tunnel. They opened fire, wiping out the pursuing Tristar guards within seconds. The sound of automatic gunfire echoed around the mountains, amplified in the quiet evening air.

Julie quickly made sure Schultz was okay before walking over to Jericho's side. The two of them exchanged a confused look. Ruby and Collins joined Jessie, forming a loose triangle around President Schultz.

"You okay, sir?" asked Ruby. "Can you walk?"

Schultz nodded vacantly. "I'll damn well walk out of here. What's going on here?"

"I have no idea. Just stay here."

Rayne shuffled over to Stevens, still holding Adrian on his back.

One of the men surrounding them stepped forward and moved in front of Julie. He wasn't young. Perhaps early fifties. He was clean shaven, although his face was weathered and battle worn. He saluted, then nodded a curt greeting.

"Miss Fisher? I'm Lieutenant Colonel Hickson, Special Operations Command, United States Air Force. I heard you needed some help."

She frowned. "I mean... yeah, but... heard from who?"

Lt. Col. Hickson smiled. "Mr. Buchanan sends his regards."

Julie's eyes went wide. She dropped her gun and cupped her hands over her mouth as she gasped.

Jericho placed a comforting hand on her shoulder, then looked at Hickson. "Buchanan's alive?"

Hickson nodded. "Yes, sir. He's in Washington, helping your colleague—a Mr. Roach?"

Jericho smiled and shook his head. "That sonofabitch made it. Unbelievable."

"Yes, sir. They have support on the ground from some of our brothers in the United States Army and Marine Corps. My understanding is they're moving to take back the White House. About time too." He paced over to the president, stopped in front of him, and saluted. "Damn good to see you, Mr. President."

Schultz nodded weakly. "Good to see you too, son. Where have you boys been hiding?"

"Wherever we could, sir. Just biding our time. Mr. Buchanan has been working to keep us involved."

"Well, I think we all owe that man a drink."

Rayne shuffled past them all, toward a Humvee. The passenger door was open. Link sat with his body turned, his feet planted on the ground.

Rayne rested Adrian on the ground, propped him up against the wheel, then bumped fists with his teammate.

"How are you holding up?" he asked.

Link gestured to his freshly bandaged arm. "Not bad. I was in and out for a little bit, but then these boys showed up and brought the Band-Aids. I briefed them on what you guys were doing and facing in there. Another ten minutes and they were fixing to come in and get you."

"Yeah, these guys are a sight for sore eyes. And Buchanan's alive, which is great news." He paused. "Glad you're doing okay, man. We missed you in there."

"I missed being there," said Link. He nodded to Adrian. "What happened to him?"

Rayne sighed. "*That* is a long story. Keep an eye on him, will you?"

"Sure thing, man."

Rayne walked over to Julie and Jericho. He placed a comforting hand on Julie's shoulder. "You must be relieved to hear Buchanan's okay?"

Julie nodded, wiping away the thin stream of tears cascading down her face. "Yeah. Yeah, I am. When we left him in Santa Clarita, not knowing if he was going to live or die... that was one of the hardest things I've ever had to do."

Jericho took her hand and squeezed it in his. "We'll see him soon."

Collins, Ruby, Jessie, and President Schultz paced over to join them. The group stood together quietly for a moment.

It was Schultz who eventually broke the silence.

"I can't thank you folks enough for what you did back there," he said. "You have done this country a hell of a service."

Jericho nodded. "Let's hope today is the day everything changes."

Julie cleared her throat. "Speaking of which... do we know what happened with Adrian back there? He seemed to know Jay. Does that mean she *was* an assassin, like he suspected?"

Everyone instinctively turned to Ruby.

She shrugged. "I... I honestly don't know. She's not an assassin. She was..."

"He called her Janine," said Collins. "Who's that?"

Ruby sighed. "Janine was his wife. She was killed thirteen years ago by a crime boss who was looking for revenge after Adrian killed his son. At least, we thought she was."

"Ya telling me Jay, the psycho bitch queen from Hell who has kicked our asses more times than I care to admit, is Adrian's *wife*?"

"I'm saying he seemed to think so."

"I don't understand," said Schultz. "Why didn't he say something earlier? Hasn't he been tracking her for months?"

"He was, sir," said Jericho. "But think about it. He and I are the only ones who hadn't actually seen her face until today. The photo we had of her, from that New York surveillance tape, wasn't great. You guys only knew it was her because you had met her before."

"Okay," said Julie. "But that doesn't explain why he thinks she's his dead wife. What is it, some kind of PTSD thing?"

Ruby shook her head. "No. It wasn't that. I saw it in his eyes. He wasn't confused. He knew her. I think... I think that actually *was* her."

"How is that possible?" asked Collins, with a notable hint of panic in his voice.

"I don't know," said Julie. "But now isn't the time. We need to get the president back to Washington. The Air Force can secure the base. It's theirs anyway."

As the group dispersed, Rayne moved to Ruby's side and nudged her shoulder gently with his.

"Hey, you okay?" he asked.

"I'm fine," she said, smiling politely. Then she nodded toward Adrian, who was still unconscious on the ground beside Link. "It's him I'm worried about."

38

ROACH

November 22, 2020

Buchanan, Roach, and a squad of seven U.S. infantry entered the White House via the entrance to the West Wing. Buchanan was familiar with the route, having had many meetings there with Schultz in the past. Ahead of them was a security desk, currently unmanned. A metal detector was positioned next to it, covering the only way past and into the building itself.

Buchanan stopped and turned to the others. "Now listen up. Hall will be in the Oval Office and will likely be surrounded by heavy security. Understand that not everyone working in the White House will be employed by Tristar. Many of the people here are innocent, so check your fire."

"Are you sure he's in the office?" asked Roach. "Would they not have moved him to a secure room or bunker the moment you showed up outside?"

Buchanan shook his head. "Honestly, Mr. Roachford,

423

there are few rooms in this building more secure than the Oval Office. Hall will have barricaded himself inside and stationed every Tristar guard within a mile of this place outside the doors."

Roach nodded. "Fair enough. What about the Secret Service?"

Buchanan shrugged. "What Secret Service? He isn't the president. All the security here is Tristar."

"Are you sure?"

He smiled. "What do you think I've been doing all this time, Mr. Roachford? Trust me. He'll be there."

"Okay. Let's go."

Buchanan nodded to the sergeant in charge of the troops with them, and the group set off for the Oval Office. The alarms sounded as they moved through the metal detectors, which was unavoidable but of little consequence now.

They moved across the lobby, which was divided into sections by the positioning of the furniture. Doors to the left, right, and ahead led to other areas of the White House.

Roach looked around quickly, taking in the high ceilings and their chandeliers, the black and white tiled floor, and the large paintings hanging on the wall like a gallery. He had never been to the White House before. Even under the current extraordinary circumstances, the moment and sense of occasion wasn't lost on him. It was a unique place, intimidating and awe-inspiring in equal measure. Roach couldn't imagine being in a position where he could ever get used to this place. He certainly wouldn't *want* to ever be in that position.

This world, of politics and occasion... that wasn't him.

Buchanan led them to the left, moving along the corridor that took them past the Roosevelt Room. The door to the Roosevelt Room opened, and a man looked out. He wore glasses, which magnified his wide, fearful eyes. His tie was loose around his collar, and his shirt was damp with sweat.

The soldiers stopped and snapped their attention toward him, weapons raised. Roach lowered his own gun, holding a hand up to signal for everyone to stand down.

"Are you with the Army?" asked the man. "The a-a-actual Army?"

Roach nodded. "We are. Listen to me. We have taken back the capital, okay? Orion's rule is over. The only thing left to do is get the man in charge and put a stop to this once and for all."

The man held his gaze for a moment. Then his breathing stuttered, and his shoulders shook as emotion took over. He broke down in tears, his hands covering his mouth.

"Are you serious?" he said between whimpers.

"I am." Roach tried to look past him, into the room. "How many of you are in there?"

"There are... fifteen of us. No one from Tristar. We all worked here before all this. Mostly in the press office."

"Okay. Stay here. Keep this door closed and locked and stay quiet. Understand? There's about to be a whole lot of fighting, and I don't want you getting hurt."

He nodded. "Thank you. Thank you so much. I can't believe this is almost over..."

Roach placed a hand on the man's shoulder and tried to offer a comforting smile. "We need to be able to do our jobs without worrying about civilians. If you can call around to other offices, tell your colleagues to do the same, okay? Stay down. Stay quiet. When this is over, the military will come for you."

He nodded again and headed back into the room, shutting the door behind him. Roach waited for the sound of the lock clicking into place before turning around. When he did, he saw Buchanan watching him. They exchanged a nod.

"Come on," said Roach.

They continued along the corridor, toward the Cabinet Room at the end.

"The Oval is on the right," said Buchanan.

Just then, Tristar guards appeared in front of them, swarming out from both sides of the corridor. Sixteen in total formed a loose line, blocking their way.

"Contact!" yelled one of the soldiers.

Buchanan and Roach dropped to one knee and opened fire. The group of soldiers around them did the same. The Tristar force fired back. Glass shattered around them. The sounds of repeated, dull thuds as bullets punched into the walls and doors filled the air.

One by one, the Tristar guards dropped to the floor, critically wounded or dead, until only a handful remained. The soldiers moved forward, screaming orders and demands of surrender. The firing stopped. The Tristar guards put down their weapons and raised their hands, knowing the fight was lost.

Buchanan and Roach moved up and headed to the right, toward the Oval Office. Stationed outside it were two more Tristar guards, standing on either side of the northwest entrance. Both men fired two rounds, dropping the guards between them. They took up position on either side of the door and waited for the troops to join them.

When they did, no words were exchanged. No orders needed to be given. Buchanan simply nodded to the sergeant, who silently counted down from three with his hand, then kicked the door almost off its hinges.

The troops quickly moved inside, shouting and firing as they swept through the room, securing the other entrances and taking out any guards inside. It took less than thirty seconds to take the Oval Office.

Buchanan and Roach stepped calmly inside and looked around. The military had formed a semicircle around the room. All seven soldiers aimed their weapons at the man sitting calmly behind the Resolute desk.

Quincy Hall.

Buchanan and Roach moved in front of the desk.

"It's over, Quincy," said Buchanan. "You've lost."

Hall smiled. "Have I?"

"The capital is ours. Brandon Crow is dead. If they haven't already, my people will soon have President Schultz in their custody. This is over. Orion is done. You're done."

Hall held his gaze, then smirked and shook his head. "You people. You'll never change. You're your own worst enemies. Always have been. Can't you see what I was trying to do here? I gave you all a practical alternative. A new way of living in this world that would've guaranteed a better way of life for this country for generations to come."

Roach frowned. "What? By installing a privately funded police state and killing anyone who disagrees with you? By making millions of Americans homeless and treating them like prisoners? Doesn't sound like a better way of life to me."

Hall had been staring at Buchanan with a deep loathing in his eyes, but he tore his attention away and focused it on Roach.

"I've been wanting to meet you for a long time, Mr. Roachford," he said. "You were a constant thorn in Crow's side, which meant you were a constant thorn in mine. I want you to know, I hate your stinking guts, and I will dedicate my life to ending you."

Roach held his gaze, unwavering and impassive.

"Okay. Good luck with that." He glanced back at one of the soldiers. "Get this piece of shit out of here."

Buchanan stepped forward. "Not so fast. I want some answers first."

He raised his gun and took aim at Hall, who watched with a defiant smile of bemusement on his face.

"Before you stand trial for the hundreds of war crimes you've committed, you're going to answer my questions," said Buchanan. "First of all, stand up. That isn't your chair."

Calmly, Hall did as instructed. He raised his hands slightly and stepped out from behind the desk. Buchanan followed him with his gun, never taking his eyes off him.

"What would you like to know, Moses?" asked Hall. "Want some tips on how to run a multi-billion-dollar company properly?"

Buchanan ignored the quip. "No. Firstly, I want to know why, fourteen months ago, Tristar killed six of my men in Nova Scotia and stole sixteen million dollars that we had confiscated from a criminal."

Hall shrugged. "I have no idea what you're talking about."

"Don't bullshit me, *Quincy*. I know exactly how long Orion has owned Tristar. There's no way you weren't already planning this back then. That means you told them to steal that money. What use is sixteen million dollars to a company that already has billions?"

Hall said nothing. He simply stared at Buchanan with a mixture of disdain and disregard.

"In fact, while we're on the subject of money," continued Buchanan, "why were Tristar people trafficking black market weapons when they clearly manufacture their own?"

Still nothing.

Roach let out a taut breath. He stepped over to Hall, placed a hand on the back of his neck, then slammed his face into the dark, polished surface of the desk. He held it there, keeping Hall bent over, and put his gun to the back of his head.

"I'm not as nice as he is," he said calmly. "Or as patient. I also have no interest in seeing you stand trial. Answer his questions, or I'll shoot you."

Hall grunted as his face was squashed against the desk. "Okay! Okay!"

Roach let him back up and stepped away.

Buchanan glanced over and gave him a small smile.

Hall held his nose, which was bleeding, and fixed Buchanan with a hard stare.

"It was too early to risk exposing the link between Orion and Tristar," he explained. "To keep the illusion of autonomy, we instructed Tristar to secure their own funding. The fact Brandon Crow chose to do that at the expense of Globa-Tech wasn't ideal, but the chain of events it set in motion were inevitable, so we adjusted things to accommodate your involvement."

"Hang on," said Roach. "What about the tech that was stolen from Cambodia?"

Hall shrugged. "What about it?"

"I almost died because of that mission. GlobaTech operatives actually did. Was that just another attempt to piss GlobaTech off?"

Hall didn't answer.

Roach stepped forward again and placed his gun against Hall's temple. "Were you not paying attention a few moments ago? I'd be happy to remind you."

Hall sighed. "That tech was needed to help us develop the propulsion technology that we have since weaponized."

"The bullet used in Paluga..." said Buchanan.

"Among other things, yes. Ultimately, Moses, we have been playing you for a long time. Ever since you took over, in fact."

Buchanan frowned. "What?"

"Oh, yes. This plan has been in place for years, but with Josh Winters in charge of GlobaTech, we knew they would be too formidable an adversary to combat back then. He was a very knowledgeable man, that one. A once-in-a-generation mind who knew far more than he ever let on. Believe me, I know. We spent a lot of time and money discovering many of his secrets over the years, in case we ever needed to forcibly remove him from the equation. Thankfully, that preposterous Order of Sabbah did it for us. When you took over... oh, it was as if Christmas had come early!"

Roach watched as Buchanan's body language changed. Every fiber of him visibly tensed. His calm, calculating exterior vanished, replaced by anger and... embarrassment, perhaps? He lowered his gun and stepped away, recognizing when someone was about to start swinging.

Hall grinned. "See, *you*, Mr. Buchanan... you are no Josh Winters. I told you when we first met, you don't belong in this world. You have no business spearheading a machine like GlobaTech. You're no use for anything besides shining my goddamn shoes, you worthless, pathetic, ni—"

Buchanan swung his fist with an almighty amount of force. It connected squarely on Hall's jaw, sending him tumbling to the plush blue carpet. He didn't move.

"Shine that, you racist bastard," he spat.

Buchanan flexed his hand, trying to get the blood

flowing to combat the stinging of the blow. He turned away and perched on the edge of the desk, staring off into space.

Roach walked over and stopped in front of him. He smiled briefly. "I bet that felt pretty good."

Buchanan looked up at him and smiled back. "Hurt like hell, if I'm honest. But it was worth it. This war, we've all been fighting for six months. *That* war just then... I've been fighting it my whole life. And do you know what? As CEO of GlobaTech, I'm one of the most powerful people on the planet. Nobody talks to me like that anymore."

"Fair enough."

"I'll be honest with you, though, Mr. Roachford. It's a little frustrating to think that, no matter how far we come as a society, as a country... we still have a long way to go, y'know?"

Roach nodded. "I agree. Maybe today we've taken the first step."

Buchanan got to his feet. "I think maybe we have. We'll get that sorry sonofabitch out of here and check in with Julie. They should know what's happened here."

"No problem. I should leave anyway. I need to find my sister and make sure she's okay."

"Of course. Pass on my regards to her."

"I will. Thank you."

"You given any thought to what you'll do next?"

Roach shook his head. "All I've thought about for six months is this moment. Figured I would think about what happens after it if I made it that far."

Buchanan gave him an understanding smile. "Well, we took the White House back and essentially shut down Tristar, but this is far from over. There's a lot of cleaning up to do and a lot of rebuilding after that. I could sure use your help."

Roach didn't hesitate. "I'm done here. All the politics and fixing the world and hunting down Tristar to bring them all to justice... that's your fight. Not mine. This is over, and so is my part in this. I think it's time I got back to being alone."

Buchanan held his gaze. "I hope you don't think you still have things to atone for, Mr. Roachford. I know where you came from. I know some of the things you did. But you didn't pull the trigger on any of my people, and you were left for dead in Cambodia yourself. I'm telling you here and now, as far as GlobaTech is concerned, your slate is clean. By all means, go and start a new life somewhere, but please, for your own sake, don't isolate yourself unnecessarily. You have nothing to punish yourself for."

Roach took a deep breath and extended his hand, which Buchanan shook.

"I appreciate you saying that. Thank you," said Roach. "But my answer remains the same. Let's say you're right, and I don't need some kind of self-imposed exile, I still have a lot of freedom to catch up on. I've never really had any up until right now. If my life can truly start over now, I want to go and live some of it for a while."

"Well, then I wish you all the best. That's the least you deserve."

"Likewise."

"But just remember, Mr. Roachford, you were instrumental in bringing down this reign of tyranny. The things you did, the journey you embarked on, the hope you and your sister inspired in others while we faced the darkest days of our history... they won't ever be forgotten. I won't allow it."

Roach glanced away, feeling as awkward and uncomfortable as he always did when receiving praise.

"Thank you," he said after a moment. "I—"

His words caught in his throat as time slowed to a standstill. So many things began to happen, and he was seeing them all at the same time. His mind was working so quickly to process everything, it was as if the world itself had stopped.

Over Buchanan's shoulder, he saw Hall using the desk to climb back to his feet.

Beyond that, ropes dropped into view through the glass doors on either side of the presidential seal behind the desk.

To his left, he saw the dark shapes of Tristar guards piling into the room from the corridor outside.

Hall reached inside one of the desk drawers.

Guards began sliding down the ropes outside.

More noise to his right indicated that additional Tristar guards were entering the office through the other doors.

Bursts of gunfire broke out around the office behind him as the military began to exchange with the new arrivals. Roach looked all around, confused by the sudden flurry of activity.

Over the chaos surrounding him, a single gunshot sounded, louder than everything else. Roach flinched as his world momentarily turned black. He stepped back, reeling, unaware of how close he was to the gunfight behind him.

He shook his head and brought has hands up to his face. He wiped away a layer of thick liquid. He blinked hard as he stared down at his blood-soaked palms.

Confused and alarmed, he looked up to see the wide, haunting eyes of Buchanan staring back at him. It was as if they were glowing against the darkness of his complexion. Just above them, in the middle of the forehead, was a gaping hole, bordered by a deep crimson ring of torn flesh.

The lifeless body of Moses Buchanan fell forward,

crashing unceremoniously to the floor. Quincy Hall stood with his arm outstretched, still pointing the smoking barrel of a pistol in front of him. A sick smile twisted across his bruised face.

The doors behind him burst open, and two teams of Tristar guards rushed in. They paid no attention to Roach, who was frozen to the spot, his eyes locked on Hall's. The guards swarmed around Orion's leader.

"Sir, we need to get you out of the capital right now," said one of them.

Hall was dragged away, surrounded by the patrol as he was ushered outside.

The world sped up to its normal speed.

Roach regained his senses. He looked down at Buchanan's body, which lay crumpled at his feet. He had no words.

He felt nothing.

His entire body was soaked with shock and overcome with a primal anger that superseded any other thought or emotion. Everyone around him was dead.

He raised his weapon and set off in pursuit of Hall. He burst out through the door and onto the front lawn in time to see Hall being hustled onto a waiting chopper. Some of the guards with him turned and started shooting. Roach dove away to his left, seeking cover behind one of the thick marble balustrades that bordered the outside of the Oval Office.

The shooting continued until the wheels of the helicopter left the ground. The second it stopped, Roach jumped to his feet and ran out. He unloaded his weapon at the chopper as it gained altitude and peeled away from the White House. Around him, the Tristar guards had been either neutralized or distracted by the military as U.S. soldiers continued to secure the presidential grounds.

Roach continued firing until the hammer slammed down on an empty chamber. He dropped his weapon and raised both arms, clasping his hands behind his head. He took deep, emotional breaths, watching in horror as the helicopter grew smaller and smaller, eventually disappearing in the descending dusk of Washington's skyline.

The White House was reclaimed. Tristar forces were being driven from the capital. Orion's grasp on the country was removed. But Quincy Hall had escaped, and Moses Buchanan was dead.

In that moment, Roach had no idea what the fallout of this would be. He didn't know where to begin trying to understand the consequences of what had happened, nor what it meant for the country moving forward. The only thing on his mind was the terrible feeling that wouldn't go away.

This war was only just beginning.

39

JERICHO STONE

The silence in the room was thick, like winter fog. The mood was somber. The victory was hollow. No one could lift their head and look toward the future. The recent past pulled their eyes to the floor.

The last thirty-six hours had been a whirlwind. Reports from across the country flooded in of local and state police arresting Tristar guards. Of the military shutting down outposts. Of refugees being welcomed into cities without fear.

President Schultz walking back into the White House did exactly what people hoped it would.

It changed everything.

Now, in the Oval Office, for the first time since the fall of Santa Clarita, everyone had gathered together.

Almost everyone.

Schultz stood behind his desk, clutching the drip stand beside him. A bag of saline solution hung from it, feeding into him intravenously via the cannula in the back of his hand. His prolonged captivity in the Wyoming base had left him malnourished and suffering from dehydration. It would take time for him to get back to full health. Nonetheless, he stood stoically in his office, trying to remember what it was like to be in control.

On his left, Jericho, Julie, and Collins stood in a line, hands clasped behind their backs. They each wore empty expressions. Their eyes stared blankly in front of them, as if exposing the part of their souls that would never again be complete.

Ahead of him was Blackstar.

Rayne, Jessie, Link, and Ruby stood together, patient and out of place, tired and lost. Link's arm rested in a sling, and his shoulder was heavily bandaged.

On one of the sofas in front of them, Kim Mitchell sat quietly, staring at one of the many bloodstains that still decorated the carpet through darkened eyes.

Standing slightly farther back against the far wall, were Roach and Rebecca. She clutched her brother's arm tightly in her grip, imparting the love she felt for him while seeking comfort from knowing she would never let him leave her again.

He also saw Roach's distant gaze, unwaveringly fixated on the floor in front of his desk.

Then there was Adrian.

He stood alone, separated from the others, leaning against the door to the right of the desk, arms folded across his chest. Schultz watched him for a moment. He couldn't begin to imagine what must be going through that man's mind right now. His entire world had been turned upside-down. Everything that man was stemmed from the knowledge that he had lost everything that made him who he used to be. Now that knowledge counted for nothing.

For the first time in a long time, Schultz found himself wishing he still had Josh Winters around. Between them, they had rebuilt GlobaTech. Then, when Schultz took office, he and Josh had closed the gap between the government and the private sector, working together to fix the world after 4/17.

What he wouldn't give to have that man here to help him rebuild again. He also imagined Adrian felt the same way.

He cleared his throat. Everyone focused on him. Everyone except Adrian.

"We all know winning one battle doesn't win the war," he began. "But the battle we won did change things. For all of us. Forever. There is much work to be done to get this country back on its feet. That's all that matters now. Politics be damned. But I just want to take a moment to say... thank you, to everyone in this room. Your rebellion kept the people of this country united in the face of an unimaginable enemy. I wouldn't be standing here without the efforts of each and every one of you. I—and this country—owe you all a debt we can never repay."

Jericho took a deep breath. "What's next, sir? How can we help?"

Schultz looked over at him. "Well, son, Orion might not be in this building anymore, but they aren't dead. Quincy Hall has gone to ground. Our priority is finding that son'bitch and seeking justice for his crimes."

"What about Orion?" asked Becky. "Much of their media presence was legitimate. Obviously, their board was corrupt, and their illegal activities will presumably be stopped, if they haven't been already. But what about the news?"

"All of their assets are being seized by the FBI," said Schultz. "I don't care how legitimate they were. Orion's media empire is finished. I'll make goddamn sure of it."

Rayne raised his hand.

Schultz shook his head. "Jesus Christ, son. Are you still doing that?"

He lowered it again sheepishly. "Sorry, Mr. President. Still not entirely sure how to act around you if I'm honest."

"I don't give a damn, son. What is it?"

"Okay. Well, what's going to happen to Tristar? They had a lot of troops in this country, right? They all gotta go somewhere. I guess what I'm asking is, can Blackstar help with the clean-up?"

Schultz nodded. "Don't worry about your place in all this. Your team is needed now more than ever. I put you together to fight the battles others couldn't. A lot of high-ranking members of Tristar's security force will likely have valuable information. I want the bastards found and brought in. Understand?"

Rayne nodded. "Yes, sir."

"Ah, speaking of people's place in the grand scheme o' things," said Collins. "What about us? Is GlobaTech even still GlobaTech?"

Schultz looked over at him. "That's a question I can't answer for you right now, Mr. Collins. For now, I want the three of you to work with Blackstar. Our focus going forward is to—"

"Goddammit!" shouted Julie. She placed her hands on the back of a nearby armchair and flipped it over in the middle of the room.

Her outburst took everyone by surprise.

Schultz remained calm. "Miss Fisher, listen to me. You—"

"No, *you* listen to *me*," she said firmly, stepping past Jericho and moving to the edge of the desk. "We risked our lives to save you, while others risked their lives to get your capital back. Buchanan's blood is still on your fucking floor, and all you can do is stand there and talk about what comes next, as if it's suddenly business as usual. Can you not stop for one goddamn minute to remember the people who *aren't* here?"

Jericho stepped to her side and put his arm around her.

"He's fucking dead!" she screamed. "He's dead, and no one cares about anything he did for us!"

Jericho pulled her close to him and embraced her. He felt her body shake as six months of emotion poured out of her. He knew what Buchanan meant to her. She had lost her father shortly before the Palugan crisis and had now lost her father figure after leading a rebellion in his name.

Silence fell again.

There were no words.

For over five minutes, no one spoke. The sound of Julie's heart breaking over and again filled the room.

Only when she had calmed down did Roach step forward. He tugged himself from his sister's grip, moved past Ruby, and approached the desk. He stood almost exactly where he had two days ago.

He clenched his jaw until his teeth ached, subduing the emotion that boiled within him.

He glanced around the room before settling his gaze on Schultz. "Look, I, ah... I know there's a lot going on. A lot to think about. I'm not looking to get involved. But you've tasked everyone in this room with finding members of Tristar who might have information about Hall and what he has planned next, right?"

Schultz nodded.

"Well, is no one going to address the elephant in the room?" When no one replied, he turned to Adrian. "We all know who is most likely to have information on Hall. What are *you* going to do when Jay's brought in?"

Adrian flicked his gaze up from the floor and focused on Roach. There had been a full debrief yesterday, while Schultz was being treated in hospital. Between them, they had filled in his blanks from Wyoming and brought Roach and his sister up to speed.

"Her name's Janine," he said quietly.

"Whatever, Adrian. She's a stone-cold psychopath, and she's the best chance we've got of finding Hall. She can hold her own against most people in here, so when we find her, she's going to put up a fight."

Adrian pushed himself away from the wall and stood inches away from Roach.

"No one is going to look for her," he said with an icy calm. "I'll find her. I'll talk to her."

"That's a bad idea, son," said Schultz.

Adrian took a step back and looked over at the president. "Excuse me?"

Schultz saw the look in his eyes and swallowed hard. "Adrian, listen to me. Until we figure out what the hell's going on, we have to assume Hall isn't going to take this lying down. We've seen what he and his money are capable of. We need answers, and the best place to get them is from her. I need you to sit this one out and let these folks bring her in."

Like lightning, Adrian's hand disappeared behind his back, then returned a second later with his gun. He swept it across the room once before resting his aim on Schultz.

"I'm going to say this one time," he said. "If anyone goes looking for Janine, I'll shoot them."

Ruby walked over to him, ignoring the gun.

"I'll help you find her," she said, offering a warm smile that did little to melt the coldness she saw in his eyes. "We'll track her together and get our answers. I promise."

She gently rested her hand on his outstretched arm. He looked at it for a moment, then shrugged it away.

"No," he said firmly. "This is something I need to do on my own."

She shook her head. "No, it isn't. You're not alone. You have me."

"Ruby, listen to me. If it is her... if it really is Janine, I... I left her for dead, lying beside the body of... of our daughter. Back in Wyoming, she looked at me like she'd never seen me before. I need to know why. And if she does remember me, I need to make it right with her. I love you, but I have to do this on my own."

Her eyes glistened with emotion. She went to hold his arm again but hesitated, then decided against it. She simply nodded, blinked away the tears, and walked back over to the rest of the team. She stared at the floor as her heart broke.

Julie stepped forward. "Look, Adrian, we lost our boss to this war. If Jay holds the key to maybe preventing another one... I'm sorry, but we have to find her."

Adrian snapped his aim to her. His finger slid inside the trigger guard.

"Was I not clear a moment ago? Anyone goes looking for her, I'll kill you."

Roach lunged for him. He grabbed Adrian's wrist and forced his aim down to the floor.

"This... isn't... the answer," he said as they wrestled for control of the weapon.

Adrian dropped his shoulder and fell forward, letting his body's dead weight crash into Roach. The sudden impact knocked Roach off-balance, forcing him to relinquish his grip of Adrian's wrist. As he did, Adrian swung his forearm and elbow into Roach's face, hard enough to send him to the floor but restrained enough so as not to do any real damage. As Roach tumbled away, Adrian stepped back toward the door, gun still raised to the room.

"Boss, please," implored Rayne. "Roach is right. This isn't the way to handle this. Let us help you."

"You want to help?" asked Adrian. "Find a way to get the answers you need without involving my wife."

He opened the door and left without another word.

No one moved except Roach, who slowly got back to his feet and dusted himself down.

Ruby stared at the open door, her eyes uncontrollably misting over once again.

"Should we go after him?" asked Collins.

Link huffed. "I wouldn't..."

"He's right," said Schultz. "Leave him. I've known that man long enough to know when he's best left alone."

"So, what do we do?" asked Rayne.

Schultz looked at him. "You do what I asked you to, son. You find me anyone from Tristar who might know where Hall is, and you bring them to me. Including his wife."

Rayne, Jessie, and Link exchanged glances of uncertainty.

"Is there a problem?" asked Jericho, watching them.

"Yes," said Jessie. "Adrian is to us what Buchanan was to you, okay? He's going through something none of us can understand. He needs us. I don't know about the others, but going after his wife behind his back doesn't feel right to me."

"Same," said Link.

"Yeah," said Rayne. "I can't do that to him."

Schultz sighed. "Look, just because this country is

getting back to normal doesn't mean the world starts revolving around Adrian goddamn Hell again. We'll help him if we can, but Jay worked alongside Brandon Crow for years. If anyone knows where Hall might be and what he's planning, it's her. Right now, she's public enemy number one. Do you hear me? Your loyalty is to this country and this office. That's who you were put together to serve. Not him."

Ruby strode over to the door and pushed it shut hard enough to slam. Then she turned to look at the room in the silence she had created.

"With all due respect, Mr. President, if you go down that road, you will need to declare war on one of the most dangerous men walking this earth. I can promise you, he *will* go to war with everyone in this room if you go after his wife. We all know what he's capable of. Perhaps no one more than you, sir. Everything we've just been through is *nothing* compared to the fire he will rain down upon *anyone* who goes after the mother of his child."

Schultz said nothing.

Everyone in the room looked around at each other, unsure of how to react. Despite all the faith they each had in their own abilities, a small part of them all knew Ruby was right.

"Exactly," she said. "You do whatever you feel you have to, but I want no part of it."

She looked over at her team and smiled. Then she looked directly at Rayne.

"You do what you think is right, Adam," she said. "The team's yours now."

Then she opened the door and walked through it, disappearing as Adrian had done moments earlier.

Jericho stepped toward the desk. "Sir, I hate to admit it, but she has a point. My history with Adrian is well documented, but never once have I called his abilities into question. I agree we need to get to Jay before he does, but like Ruby said, you know him better than us. If this goes wrong... I know what a man will do for his family. Sir, his wrath would be nuclear."

Schultz sighed and sat down heavily in his chair, adjusting his grip on the drip stand. He leaned back and took another deep breath. "Yeah. I know."

Julie moved to Jericho's side. "So, what do you want us to do, sir?"

Schultz looked around the room at the expectant faces staring back at him. The truth was, he had no idea what to do. Half his advisors were still unaccounted for. The military was still in the process of fully reactivating. Borders were reopening, but it would be days before GlobaTech operatives and military troops who were trapped overseas could get home.

There was no rule book for what they faced now. No cliff notes for how to recover after the country had been invaded by a tyrannical corporation.

All he could do was what made sense, regardless of the consequences. And right now, there was only one logical course of action.

He looked at Julie, then at Jericho. "Go get her."

THE END

ACKNOWLEDGMENTS

We made it!

This was easily the longest and most challenging book I've ever written. It was an amazing experience for me to finally tell the story I've been building toward for the last three years.

The Thrillerverse has been an incredible journey for me so far, both personally and creatively, and it's crazy to think it's just getting started!

I wanted to take a moment to thank the people who helped this book come to fruition...

You.

Since 2013, I've been incredibly blessed to accumulate and grow a dedicated and loyal fanbase—first for Adrian Hell, then for the new projects that began on the back of his initial success.

For eight years, you have read the stories I've written, supported me personally and professionally, and consequently become as much a part of my writing career as the characters I've created.

As with every book I publish, it's far from a solo effort.

First, the blood, sweat, and tears I spill on my keyboard are organised and optimised into something coherent by my talented editor, Coral. Everything is then given a makeover by my designer, Daniel—who, frankly, I'm convinced is some kind of wizard!

My awesome review team then let me know if I've hit the mark with it or not (and usually find all the spelling mistakes that slipped through the net!).

Finally, it's released to the world, and you lovely people buy it, which allows me to continue doing what I was born to do for a living. That's honestly the greatest feeling, and I owe it all to you.

Thank you.

EPILOGUE

The television mounted on the wall behind the bar showed live coverage of the presidential address. The barman stood cleaning a glass, watching the woman sitting at the bar, who stared absently at the screen.

"Hard to believe any of that actually happened now, isn't it?" he said.

Jay stared over her glass of whiskey at him.

"Excuse me?" she asked, frowning at the interruption.

He nodded toward the screen. "The president's giving a speech at the anniversary event. Time flies, right?"

Jay grunted and finished her drink in one gulp. She slammed the glass down on the chipped and worn surface of the bar, then pointed to it.

"Just keep them coming," she said. "And don't talk to me."

The barman nodded courteously and walked away to pour another double measure of scotch.

The door swung open, allowing the winter wind to momentarily swirl inside.

Jay glanced over, squinting in the glare of the afternoon sun that shone through the dirty windows. A woman walked in, dressed in a long coat, knee-high boots, and over-sized sunglasses. The woman looked around the near empty bar, then walked over and took a seat beside her. She took her sunglasses off and rested them on the bar.

The barman walked over and placed Jay's drink in front of her, then looked at the new arrival.

"What can I get you, ma'am?" he asked professionally.

"I'll have what she's having," replied the woman.

A few moments later, a glass containing the same double measure of scotch was placed in front of her. She picked it up and twirled the glass in her hand, watching the contents swim around inside.

"You're a hard woman to find," said Ruby.

"Not hard enough, apparently," replied Jay coldly. "What do you want?"

"We need to talk."

"About what?"

Ruby downed her drink and looked her in the eyes. "About the man we love."

A MESSAGE

Dear Reader,

Thank you for purchasing my book. If you enjoyed reading it, it would mean a lot to me if you could spare thirty seconds to leave an honest review. For independent authors like me, one review makes a world of difference!

If you want to get in touch, please visit my website, where you can contact me directly, either via e-mail or social media.

Until next time...

James P. Sumner

JOIN THE MAILING LIST

Why not sign up for James P. Sumner's spam-free news-letter, and stay up-to-date with the latest news, promotions, and new releases?

In exchange for your support, you will receive a **FREE** copy of the prequel novella, *A Hero of War*, which tells the story of a young Adrian, newly recruited to the U.S. Army at the beginning of the Gulf War.

Previously available on Amazon, this title is now exclusive to the author's website. But you have the opportunity to read it for free!

Interested? Simply visit the below link to sign up and claim your free gift!

smarturl.it/jpssignup